The Lame Angel is set in wartime Athens during the Nazi occupation, which produced the infamous Great Hunger "that carried off the starving, first the old people, then the babies." Yet it has for us a contemporary significance. As the eponymous Angel, a private detective savagely maimed at the hands of the New York mafia, says, "It was as if some cruel nursery governess had taken over the running of our lives and was making new rules and new plans." Despite this grim, brilliantly-realized setting, the novel is immense fun with its deadpan introduction of the mysterious Mr Agathos (Greek for "good") who bestows on Angel the ability to fly in order to carry out his subversive missions. This is an off-beat, hugely entertaining novel, beautifully written and bound to surprise.

—Salley Vickers, author of *The Other Side of You,*
Miss Garnet's Angel, and more

THE LAME ANGEL

ALEXIS PANSELINOS

Translated by CAROLINE HARBOURI

RECITAL PUBLISHING
Woodstock, NY 12498
www.recitalpublishing.com

Recital Publishing is an imprint of the online podcast The Strange Recital.
Fiction that questions the nature of reality
www.thestrangerecital.com

Contents

1

Introducing myself

My office is on Gamvetta Street. I got it at a low rent since the previous tenant, a Jewish tailor, had to leave in a hurry, bundling up all his worldly goods as best he could and departing on a ship to Morocco. I met him the day he came to hand over the keys to the landlord, Mr Menagias. He'd tried to haggle at the last minute, hoping to get the value of some bits of furniture which he hadn't had time to sell and was leaving behind deducted from the rent he owed: there was a battered chest of drawers, a little desk with drawers and a standing lamp with a yellowed parchment shade. Menagias wouldn't hear of it: "Get that stuff out of here, you nincompoop, get my premises emptied. Mr Angel" (meaning me) "doesn't have a square inch left for his own things that he'll be bringing over tomorrow." The tailor swore his chest of drawers only needed a lick of polish and it would look really good. It was part of his wife's dowry, they hadn't had room for it at home which was why he'd had it temporarily in his shop. They shouldn't mistreat such a fine piece; "It's genuine walnut, Mr Angel, almost too heavy to lift!"

"Too heavy to lift is it, well I'll soon find someone who'll pick it up and chuck it out of here," replied the landlord coolly, putting his hand out to the tailor once more. "Come along, let's get finished…" I'm perfectly sure Mr Menagias fancied the furniture himself but wanted to get hold of it without paying.

The other man was almost in tears. He turned to me. "It's a sin, Mr Angel—my Sarah's dowry…" He choked, got a dirty handkerchief out of his pocket, blew his nose noisily. "It's a sin…"

"I won't throw your furniture out," I told him, "don't worry. And if I decide to keep it, drop me a line with your address and I'll send you something for it…"

The man brightened up, a smile creasing his face and he grabbed my hand with the hand in which he was still holding the handkerchief. "Angel by name and angel by nature, Mr Angel, sir! Go ahead and keep the furniture—it's all yours! And whenever you can… though I haven't a clue where we'll end up… My brother-in-law Ariko was going to give me ten thousand for it, ten whole thousand! Just give me whatever you see fit! It's a sin! I'll let you have it for five, five thousand to you because you're a good man, an angel! That's not too much, is it?"

"It's far too much. Anyway, it's not walnut, it's only a veneer. I might be able to manage three at some point though I haven't got it right now. Like I said, send me your address."

He looked at me, trying to work out if I was intending to cheat him. But what could he do? Time wasn't on his side. It was the beginning of April '41. The Germans had already entered Salonica, the omens looked ugly, flocks of Jews were arriving from the north like birds driven before the storm, some by one means, some by another, each managing as best he could. In Piraeus people were knifing each other for a place on one of the few foreign packet-boats. The other ships had been commandeered by the Government and, from what we heard, were transporting God only knows what to Crete.

So the tailor departed and I was left with the chest of drawers, the little desk and the lamp, to the chagrin of my landlord; from that day on he considered me "a smooth operator" who'd succeeded in wresting these pieces from his incipient grasp in return for nothing more than a promise. The tailor—whose name I'd noted in an old diary—never did write to me asking for his money.

These three pieces of furniture served me well. The chest of drawers was intended to hold the files that I never acquired, the lamp stood beside my desk and saved me from having to switch on the ceiling light very often, and the desk I put behind the glass partition, in the anteroom, for the secretary I no longer had.

When I first opened my detective agency in an old building at number 44 Panepistimiou Street, on the corner where it joins Harilaou Trikoupi Street, I'd hired Vanda.

That wasn't long after I arrived in Athens and I still had some of the money I'd brought with me. Vanda taught me to drink Turkish coffee which she had a really wonderful way of making. She used to go out and buy it in the Hafteia area, at frequent intervals so that it would always be fresh. The aroma of this coffee invariably reminds me of those early happy and carefree days, when I believed that I was all set to do well. Athens was a virgin market for my profession, so far unexploited. Until I got going properly I'd spend the money I had. I never did get going though.

It was Christmas '37 when the ship docked at Piraeus and disgorged me and my trunk onto the quay of the commercial harbor, for I'd travelled on a freighter under the Argentinian flag. I was now just like the immigrants you'd sometimes see on Ellis Island, back in my own country.

After the U.S. Consulate in Athens—my first port of call—I made my way to a hotel on Ermou Street for a few days. The guys at the Embassy's Information Bureau, alerted by Freddy Lamera and their pals in the FBI, had come up with three different apartments in the center of town for me to choose from. But right from the word go they made it perfectly plain that my profession didn't have any future in this country. Unless I was incredibly lucky, that is. I didn't believe them.

The office was cheap to rent (but then everything was cheap here for someone who earned a half-way decent wage): I took it at once. As for a place to live, I chose the first apartment on the list they'd drawn up for me. It was five easy minutes away from the office. You turned left on the corner of Harilaou Trikoupi and Fidiou then twenty yards further on you came to Georgiou Gennadiou, a narrow little street on your right. Ten more yards and you were there. The apartment had three main rooms, two looking onto the street in front and the bedroom looking onto the yard at the back. The owner, an engineer by the name of Balomenos, was a thug from the Peloponnese who maintained good relations with the cream of society and, if what people said was true, was a personal friend of Lulu, the daughter of the dictator Metaxas. He let me have the apartment without too much haggling because the previous tenants, a couple called Kanellis, had been months behind with the rent, hadn't wanted to hear a word about increasing it, and, as he himself said, had wrecked the place. What he wanted was a professional gentleman and bachelor, like me. What's more, he liked the idea of my job: I'd most probably be a right-wing patriot, not a communist as they were. After relentless pressure on the part of Balomenos, culminating in threats, the Kanellis family (husband and wife both lawyers and a servant-girl from the island of Paros) had taken a smaller apartment on the second floor.

Our apartment block had been built less than ten years earlier; on the other side of the narrow street were some fine old buildings, on the corner an abandoned mansion standing in a garden ("Christomanos' place" as people called it), a little further on the Varvitsiotis house, while on the corner at the top of the street was another little garden surrounding the church of Zoodochos Pigi. Being something of a beginner as regards both the language and the ways of this country, it took me quite a while to realize that this wasn't the name of some saint but meant "the life-giving source"—or anyway something of the sort.

Jobs never did materialize, in spite of the fact that the guys at the Embassy helped as much as they could. I wasn't making any money and my savings were running out fast. The rents for office and apartment and Vanda's salary (not to mention the coffee, which we went through at the speed of light) were eating up my money. So I decided to let the office go. Either because he noticed it or because someone told him that I rarely left the house early in the morning, Balomenos got wind of the fact that I'd begun receiving clients at home. One fine morning he knocked at the door and after asking me for the rent—it was the time of month that it was due—he announced that the sum we'd agreed on was for a residence. If I wanted to use the place as my office too we'd have to discuss new terms. "It causes wear and tear," he said. Or something of the kind.

I'd dismissed Vanda when I let the office go, but all the same at the beginning she'd often come over unofficially "to see how I was getting on" and to tidy up my mess. I resorted to Zisis' café across the street and for a while received clients there; however, a café doesn't really make a very good impression. And the clients who would visit a private detective agency in those days weren't poor wretches but people with money and social standing. People who required both a proper office and a secretary.

The worst was yet to come. It wasn't long in coming. The worst was the war. It may have made it easier for me to find a new office on Gamvetta Street for a very low rent, but it put an end to my last hopes of establishing a clientele and a name for myself. People now had more important things to worry about.

Vanda was Jewish. But either she didn't want to go or she hadn't managed to leave with all the other Jews who were hastily trampling over each other to escape. For something like a year she'd been involved with an officer in the Fascist Youth and seemed to think this would be enough to keep her safe from any trouble.

Her boyfriend was a young man about the same age as her, Nikiforos Velentzas by name, who knew Lieutenant Pylarinos in the Security Police. Pylarinos knew me well: it was he who'd stamped my stay permit and recommended that I acquire a Greek passport as fast as possible if I wanted to open a detective agency. He'd been to America and had contacts in our embassy here. For some reason he liked me. My paperwork was sorted out rapidly and I found myself in possession of a passport and a permit from the Security Police to open my agency. Velentzas was sent to me by Pylarinos. Probably in order to impress me, he was wearing his Falangist uniform—the forage cap with its white braid, a white tie and spats—and had slicked his hair down with ample brilliantine. After questioning me about detectives and America, whether it really was the way the movies showed it, he asked if I needed an assistant. At first I thought he was looking for a position for himself. But in fact he was trying to find a job for his girlfriend. I've no idea what conclusions he came to about me as a result of this visit (certainly he didn't know the most important thing and never would), but he considered that the job was a secure one and the boss a gentleman through and through. He brought Vanda along a few days later.

She was a cheerful and good-hearted kid. She learned the work fast and from the very first week began to help me do nothing. What this means is that I was free to wander around town while she answered the phone and made appointments and so on. The office immediately began to take on a different appearance; a woman's touch was obvious everywhere, and I don't just mean that the place was cleaner. Everything was orderly and in its place. If I'd had work, her salary would have seemed less of a problem to me. When the German attack began, Velentzas disappeared as if the earth had gaped open and swallowed him. A little while later Vanda disappeared too.

In Athens at that time you couldn't practice my profession except in the most demeaning way. The business that most frequently came in my direction was nosing out illicit couples in some hotel room or bachelor pad and, with the help of a photographer—I used Pelopidas Lebesopoulos, who had a ground-floor studio on Gamvetta Street—bundling them up and taking them naked to the nearest police station for a criminal charge of adultery to follow. You needed a heart of stone for this kind of work. But my heart had already grown fairly hard and I did it without a second thought—dragging them off to the station, pale and distressed, stark naked beneath a rough and ready sheet or blanket, trembling and weeping or cursing us and promising the sun and moon if we'd only let them go.

Twice, when the money was good and the social position of the man offering it seemed to promise future favors or protection if the need arose, I did just this. I let the little birds fly and told my clients that the information they'd given me had been wrong. But this happened only twice. A third time, much later, I almost paid very dearly. However, the war got me off the hook then.

I'd been obliged to take the plunge and leave New York, where I'd inherited Freddy Lamera's agency—an old agency with traditions and an established clientele. Freddy was a Greek, born in Astoria, from one of the oldest immigrant families: his parents had been among the first to arrive, at a time when you rarely came across any Greeks in America. My father sent me to work as Freddy's assistant and when he died Freddy had more or less adopted me; being unmarried and without any financial obligations, he left the agency in my hands when he decided to retire.

Not far from Astoria, in Corona, Don Guzman and his lieutenants held power in those days. The "Sicilian," whom the Americans also knew as "Don Gasman," never got on too well with Freddy. However, he'd taken a shine to me—perhaps because I'd helped his consigliere come out clean from a nasty adventure, and I'd done it so swiftly and effectively that everyone was left open-mouthed. Freddy grumbled. "Don't get mixed up with that shit," he kept on saying. But it's a wonderful feeling being high in the esteem of Don Guzman and I wouldn't listen. "He'll become legal," I said. "It won't be long, Jos'll manage it, he's half-way there already. And then just think of the favors we'll get."

Don Guzman never did become legal, nor did I ever see any favors from him. And—fool that I was—in spite of old Freddy's imprecations I got involved with the mafia boss's youngest daughter, Laura. I was rash enough to do what I did without any attempt at concealment. I was secure in the knowledge that the Sicilian had a soft spot for me. The result was that Laurina disappeared overnight—I couldn't even get her on the phone—I destroyed Freddy's old age (the Italian's thugs used to call him La Merda in mockery) and the agency closed down.

One night I heard the sirens of the fire engines. I didn't pay any attention until someone telephoned me. "Your office is on fire," he said. I pulled on a pair of pants and a raincoat over my pajamas and went out into the street. Three blocks further down I could see the glow. I pushed through the police cordon and ran up the stairs. The outer office with the files was burnt to ashes. You couldn't advance a step further—the place had gone up like a torch. The smoke was suffocating and I collapsed unconscious. When I came to, I was on a stretcher with a male nurse bending over me. "You were lucky," he said.

Lucky indeed! A couple of days later, as I was coming back from visiting Lamera, two of the Sicilian's men cornered me in a narrow alley. Beppo, his chief henchman, had always liked me. But what has liking got to do with it? No one quibbles when Don Guzman has given his command. "My orders are to do you some grievous damage, Angey boy," he told me. "Sorry, but you were asking for it."

I don't want to remember that night. Beppo himself severed the tendon of my left leg (this was the Sicilian's favorite punishment—since the early 1930s, when the bastard was at the height of his power, Astoria had become full of men who limped.) However, the worst damage he left to a mute they'd recently brought over from their own country, a numbskull who didn't understand a thing. He did it just as if he were slicing vegetables for dinner...

I was in the University Hospital on Staten Island for two months, in strict isolation. Police Officer Hendry came over twice a week from Astoria to see how I was doing. Instead of pressing me to make a statement about who'd done these things to me (something that in any case everyone knew), the first time he came he told me, "In your place I'd count myself darn lucky to be alive. In your place I'd be thinking very seriously of taking a trip to see my relatives in Greece." When I told him I didn't have any relatives in Greece, he smiled: "In your place I'd find some." Don Guzman or Jos Gasman was sending me a message via Hendry to get out of there fast.

At the beginning I was obstinate. At night I dreamed of finding him and doing to him what he'd done to me. Of cleansing the town of that bastard and his gang. Of being decorated for it at the Town Hall and of being taken on by the Force—with the prospect of becoming its Chief. Old Freddy, who in the meantime had had a heart attack, brought me back to earth. "Hendry was right, you've been lucky. Get out, don't stay here. There's no future for you as long as Guzman's alive. You're finished."

When, about a week before I left, I ran into Beppo in the street, he stopped to have a word with me. He was all smiles, glad to see me alive. "Sicilians," he said with a grimace (he was from Venice, a northerner), "like to hurt you where you hurt them." It was as if he were apologizing. "Why did you sever the tendon in my leg?" I asked. "Jos loves you, buddy," he answered, "so he did it to save your face..." "By making me lame?" I asked. "Exactly," he replied. "The whole world needs to know that the man who dared raise his eyes to the Don's daughter has been punished. That's why he lamed you. The other thing... only you and he know about the other thing. And Lauretta."

This, put briefly, was my story. I could write a whole

separate book about it but it no longer interests me. Other things interest me and it's of these I want to speak. I left my life behind me, the place where I'd grown up, the woman I loved, old Freddy, my mother's and father's graves. I was now making the reverse journey of all the shiploads of immigrants who come to America to seek their fortune. I was returning to Piraeus by steamship, to the land of my origins whose language I thought I knew fairly well (I still used to speak Greek with Freddy in the evenings—he spoke it perfectly as if he'd only just arrived from Greece the other day), a land, however, which I'd only set eyes on once when I was four years old and never since. I was more familiar with Mexico than with Greece. I went to the U.S. consulate, they received me pleasantly, forewarned by Lamera and their contacts at Head Office; they gave my papers to be translated and then were kind enough to talk to the Security Police. The Greek police weren't quite sure what a "private detective" was. One or two high-ranking officers had opened agencies after retiring but—what with the lack of work and what with their advancing age—these had soon closed down. My profession hadn't managed to make a name for itself in the market.

And I was living in limbo. I did a few jobs for some Americans at the embassy, for some elderly English women who lived here. Of my Greek clients during that first period, someone wanted me to follow his daughter and her boyfriend. He put the photographs I gave him into his pocket with an enthusiastic smile, as if I'd just handed him the most valuable gift. He paid me and disappeared. For weeks I used to scan the newspapers in case something about them caught my eye, some drama, some row, but it was a waste of time. Total silence. I ran into them, father and daughter, sitting at Zacharatos' café in Syntagma Square, and they both looked perfectly happy. Just how exactly they'd sorted matters out between them I never did understand.

In the building on Gamvetta Street most of the offices were occupied by lawyers, notaries, some mysterious dealers on the windy side of the law, house agents and jacks of all trades, who gradually faded away as business dried up, electricians, radio repair shops, plumbers and other similar folk. Everyone wondered how I managed to make ends meet and what I lived on. The only person I spoke to much was the photographer, Pelopidas, whom we called Pelos, and his wife Fotini, a slim dark-haired woman with an ample bosom, who kept the shop while her husband was out and about. It was Pelos, enjoying the best of memories of our profitable collaboration, who informed me in April '41 that the tailor's shop was for rent.

2

———

The nephew's aunt

From time to time I used to go into the grand hotels on Syntagma Square and hang around in their lobbies reading the headlines in the New York papers. My eyes were searching for the piece of news I was awaiting—if it happened, then it would certainly make the front page. Only the Gasman's death would make it possible for me to return. It was absurd to be living in the expectation of something like this. But man lives on hope. And clinging to fantasies of this kind certainly wasn't the best thing for me to be doing: you can't settle to work, or live, or meet people, or develop relations or put down roots anywhere when you're constantly focusing on the possibility of packing your bags and going back home.

Nor was my health any better. The climate may have been warmer, the humidity minimal and the springtime air light and fragrant with the orange trees in bloom along the sidewalks. Yet my lameness was worse here.

Lebesopoulos kept suggesting that I get a walking stick; he was sorry to see me walking with a more and more pronounced limp. A detective with a walking stick... highly original. In a profession where you need to be able to pass unobserved, my gait was the first thing someone would notice. If he then encountered me a second time, I might just as well have handed him my calling card. But I didn't get the chance to realize how unsuitable I now was for my work, because work was precisely what I didn't have.

I learned to live on almost nothing. Since I was frightened of spending all my money (and I hadn't even got a return ticket!), I economized, filled my empty stomach with water, chewed on dry crusts of bread and bought vegetables and fruit from the local greengrocer, on the corner of Themistokleous Street, just before closing time when if I hadn't bought whatever was left in his crates he would have been throwing it out. Neither my own mood nor the hot climate made food seem a prime necessity. And luckily ever since I was a child I'd never had much of an appetite. I used to grab a bite of something, standing, and then go out—this was the way I lived. Thus when in '41 the Hunger began it took me quite a while to grasp the difference and I was puzzled at first when I heard people bewailing the situation.

I continually had the sense that I was living in a long, tormenting dream which was taking its time to end and to let me wake up into my own world once more. I'd never travelled further than Richmond, although I'd always wanted to go, for example, to Mexico; I used to buy books and maps and travel guides and hang out with Spanish-speakers, but I'd never had the opportunity or the money to make the trip. Now I looked around me at Athens and Piraeus as if I was watching a movie. Even the language which I'd thought I knew sounded incomprehensible to my ears. Buildings, streets, shop signs were all a series of surprises or riddles that needed to be solved. There were few cars on the roads: all of a sudden I found myself surrounded by models which in our own country lie rusting away in breakers' yards or which you'd see in old films, their handbrake down by the pedals and their horn with its bulb outside the driver's window, creaking past me like vampires come to life, while other models from France or Italy I was seeing for the first time in my life.

Only the streetcars reminded me slightly of pictures I'd seen of San Francisco. The main streets here were lined by low buildings, not more than three stories high; they were of strange archaic design with tiled roofs, statues on their parapets and caryatids supporting the balconies, wooden shutters at the windows to shut out the bright light and heat of summer. In our country, carriages and carts drawn by horses or mules are relegated to outlying neighborhoods or the countryside; here they coexisted with the automobile traffic of the city center, up and down the two-lane avenues linking Syntagma and Omonia and along the roads leading to the capital's country districts, Patissia, the Thon neighborhood, Old Faliron and New Faliron.

The poverty, the shabby clothes people wore and the lack of facilities made an impression on me. Houses had ice-boxes instead of refrigerators, gas stoves were used for cooking, the grocers sold macaroni, rice, sugar, pulses and dried fish loose from sacks. The butchers' shops resembled slaughterhouses. Children's toys were primitive contraptions made of painted wood with wheels nailed to the axles, or else crude dolls and spinning tops; in the poor quarters the children fabricated home-made roller skates out of planks of wood and ball bearings. The streets were full of itinerant hawkers. In our own neighborhood, apart from the fish-seller with his large, round basket sealed with tar and painted bright blue, there was the knife-grinder who used to pass by with his wheel, the tinker who mended the old copper cooking pans from the kitchen, the iceman's handcart, its columns of ice covered with sacking, and a saw and tongs to carry your order into the house, the milkman with his stout glass bottles topped with paper tied with string, or the musical vinegar woman with a small barrel strapped to her back.

When I first arrived I used to wander mainly around the center of town, taken in by its festive atmosphere. The Crown Prince was getting married and the whole city was carnival-like with its floral decorations and arches. The golden carriages, the grooms and coachmen and mounted retinue made you think you were suddenly in the midst of a romantic fairy tale. I liked the king, who was slim and spare, and had a haughty air as he brought his Field Marshal's baton to his cap to salute the crowd. The other official guests followed in limousines, you couldn't make them out. But I liked the king—there weren't any kings in the USA, one way and another he impressed me. And people threw their hats in the air and showered the procession with flowers.

Everywhere you went you saw photographs of the Governor, Metaxas. Sometimes he had a benevolent air, when he was posing as a friendly old uncle, and other times he was distant and grave, when he was posing as the Leader of the Nation. The common people mocked him for the short stature and plump waistline that made him look like a provincial schoolmaster. I soon realized that the king wasn't popular, people blamed him for a whole host of things, the last and worst of which being, as I heard, that he'd saddled them with Metaxas. As well as the king, most people also cursed the English for this. In our own country the English are ancient history; here, they're constantly on the lips of everyone who doesn't like the regime: the English are to blame for everything. Personally I didn't find this at all hard to believe, having read about the American Revolution and the battles between the English and the French in Canada.

But there were people of another kind too.

In Zacharatos', in Zavoritis' and in the Petrograd, well-dressed ladies wearing little hats with veils over their faces, around their wrists the leash of some small dog concealed beneath the table, and gentlemen wearing monocles and wing collars and starched shirts smiled in satisfaction as they lazily enjoyed their tea, their coffee, their cakes or their drink and sent wreaths of smoke to the ceiling as they read *Kathimerini, Estia* or *Eleftheron Vima*, on whose pages were announced in bold headlines the achievements of the government or the goals of the Governor along with photographs of people in the news.

Everyone was always talking politics here, rich and poor, contented and discontented alike. Over there, at home, rich and poor alike go to work in the morning and return home in the evening to have a meal and then tuck up in bed. It's a different world. And I didn't feel the slightest interest in all the things that my fellow-countrymen talked and gesticulated about in the cafés.

I had of course met both types of people. In our own apartment building there were a few of those discontented with the status quo, the Kanellis lawyer couple, for example, and a great many of those satisfied with it—even enthusiastic about it—like Mr Kynigos, their neighbor, or Mr Balomenos on the second floor or Mr Zygadinos, another lawyer, on the ground floor. I'm not sure about Varvitsiotis, a landowner from an old family, who lived opposite. Certainly he was a royalist and anti-Venizelist. And there wasn't any royalist who objected to the 4th of August and Metaxas.

Mimis Papachrysanthou belonged to the first category, those who opposed the current regime. I met him in summer '39 at Karalis' grocery store on Harilaou Trikoupi Street, next door to the St Joseph convent school. This narrow little store was near my home and was convenient whenever I realized at the last minute that I'd run out of something and needed to get it at once. It wasn't for everyday shopping or to be visited very frequently. Only Balomenos, Mr Kynigos and maybe Varvitsiotis from across the road bought their groceries there regularly. Other people were in the habit of saying, "He's got good stuff, but you pay its weight in gold." The shopkeeper himself was a perfect gentleman, always dressed in a suit with a watch-chain over his waistcoat, a bowler hat and a cane. If you saw him leaving his store when it closed at midday and making his way home to where he lived on a side street off Skoufa Street, the last thing that would have crossed your mind was that he was a grocer. In any case, he himself never touched his merchandise, he had assistants for that, he simply sat at the cash register and chatted with his customers. The law courts were just across the road on Panepistimiou Street and all around were lawyers' and notaries' offices—their purses were fat enough.

Papachrysanthou had attracted my attention one noon when I'd gone in to buy something and found him arguing with Karalis about some affair of high politics—as usual, the English were mixed up in the conversation.

Karalis had his own beliefs, but he was a polite and soft-spoken man who never got into arguments. Papachrysanthou had had enough, however, and was delivering a tirade: the policy of "keeping equal distances," he was saying, was a cover for Metaxas' pro-German sentiments and the king had his donkey tethered at both ends—he himself was a creature of the English, Metaxas was a creature of the Germans—and the country, said Mimis, would pay twice over, because we are small and weak and poor and an insignificant quantity.

Karalis disagreed with this. "Greece," he said, "has never been an insignificant quantity. It may be poor but it is honest, and in any case it is already on the path to modernization and economic recovery as a result of the measures the government is taking."

Mimis, although he was setting eyes on me for the first time, turned to me and asked my opinion. Maybe my appearance and my age made him think that I too belonged among the ranks of the disaffected.

I didn't belong there, though. My own discontent was due to my exile in this country, to the fact that I'd been forced to emigrate here. And I wasn't accustomed to laying the blame for my situation on any government. So was it Metaxas' fault or the king's fault that all the people here seemed to be poor and wretched and shouted and gesticulated and tried to rob or cheat each other? Anyone who worked, I believed at heart, could earn money and live comfortably, could shop every day at Karalis' and enjoy his expensive goods.

Since my spirits were low, I always tried to avoid getting into conversation with people I didn't know. I murmured something vague—that the regime frequently organized parades and spectacular events. At this period they were preparing a public performance on Lykabettos of some play, or some spectacle anyway—schoolchildren to play the walk-on parts, dressed in tunics with wreaths on their heads and shields, actors from Athens' best-known theaters, directors and costume designers, workmen transforming the quarries on the hill to serve as the walls of the city of Troy, and newspapers listing the donations in money and material made by banks and manufacturers, while the mayor Kotzias and his workforce were opening a road up to the quarry so that the audience, and especially the cars of the VIPs, could have easy access. The populace, as ever, was seething in outrage.

Papachrysanthou was highly amused by my comment on the planned spectacle; Mr Karalis said not a word but simply counted out my change. As I left, I heard Mimis calling me to stop a moment so he could speak to me.

"Do you know," he told me, "that some young relatives of mine haven't been to school for a whole month because of this fiesta? Every single day they're dragged off up to Lykabettos to practice and rehearse and any thought of reading or schoolwork has gone clean out of their heads. The way things are, their teachers have resigned themselves to it. And their parents, who aren't supporters of the regime, have simply swallowed their objections helplessly instead of withdrawing the kids from this rubbish, because they're afraid of being hauled off to the Security Police. Not that the Security Police had any need of Penthesilea to have them listed in their black books… my cousin, the children's father, is a long-standing trade unionist…"

"What Penthesilea?" I asked, not having understood.

"The play, of course! That sick piece of work they're

going to perform. Penthesilea… you know… the warrior Amazon who was killed by Achilles…"

My expression showed that I didn't know much about any of these people and Mimis burst out laughing. All the same, he was convinced I'd been being ironical when I'd said that Metaxas organized fine parades, and he liked me. The very next morning we ran into one another again outside my house. He bade me good morning cheerfully and said that we were neighbors, he himself lived a few blocks further up on Zoodochou Pigis Street. He offered to buy me a coffee and I accepted with pleasure, for I wasn't making enough to be able to spend money on extras like that. And there, over the coffee that we ordered, sitting among all the strange birds that frequent the Petrograd, we became friends.

He was tall, stooping, probably something over forty years old, with a wandering eye and a purple birthmark at the top of his nose, just under the eye that squinted slightly; he had a mania for Greek mythology and was in the habit of giving everyone nicknames deriving from it (he baptized me Hephaistos). He had formerly been a customs officer in Piraeus but had now opened an accountant's office where he kept the books for various Athenian shopkeepers and tradesmen. It was through Papachrysanthou that I met my single female client—all the others were men. When he first heard what my profession was, he eyed me with distrust. However, the rest of my story, my forced removal to this country and my financial difficulties, apparently persuaded him that I was some kind of political refugee! Thus—in the spring of '40—he referred a woman to me who was the friend or relative of some captain in Piraeus whom Mimis had known since the days he worked at the port. She needed someone to undertake a job of a confidential nature.

And so it happened that one afternoon, wearing my smartest clothes, I rang the bell bearing the name "Stathis" at a grand apartment building on Dimokritou Street. The door was opened by a maid, as pock-marked and ugly as sin, who told me to wait in the drawing room. It was an apartment the likes of which I'd never entered before, neither here nor at home. At the end of the room there was an alcove with concealed lighting, before which stood two carved columns of the most translucent pink marble, there was a large oil painting depicting a hunting scene and a *chaise-longue* covered with embroidered cushions. On the little low tables were scattered an assortment of decorative objects, the most insignificant of which would have fetched enough for me to live on for six months. The parquet consisted of an inlaid pattern of dark and lighter-colored wood. You felt almost ashamed to step on it.

In one corner, on a little oval table in front of a lamp with a silk shade, I saw a photograph of the king in an embossed silver frame. I couldn't resist the temptation of bending to look at it more closely. Behind the glass I could make out a handwritten dedication "to the Honorable Madame Sitsa Stathis, Colonel of the Fascist Youth."

After a little while the lady of the house appeared, accompanied by a tall middle-aged gentleman to whom

I was not introduced. She herself must have been fifty or thereabouts, she wore her hair dressed high above her forehead in two separate strands and her deep décolleté was adorned with lace as fine as crêpe. She gestured me to sit down on one of the chairs and seated herself on a sofa beside her companion.

Mrs Stathis spoke a lot in a style that I'd never come across before. I don't know if it was the accent of her island origins or if it was the *katharévousa*[1] she used (something rare in everyday conversation even among the highest class of people). She touched my proffered hand with the tips of her fingers, addressed me with the phrase "I have the pleasure"—an expression I hadn't ever heard before—and continued in the same vein, saying "this need hardly be stated" which meant "without a doubt," "this is a matter of delight to me" which meant "all right, that's fine," and "he is an ill-raised person" which meant "spoiled."

She was speaking of her nephew, Pepe (Pericles) Demarias by name, her sister's son. His parents had obliged her, almost extorted her, into making him her heir, but for some time she had considered him *unworthy*. She had made a will in his favor, compelled to do so for reasons which did not concern me, but the young man (who was already twenty-eight years old), having completed his studies at the Polytechnic School, was spending astronomical sums of money amassing a

---

1. *Katharévousa*: an artificial, literary, "pure" form of the Greek language created in the 19th century, as opposed to the spoken demotic Greek.

collection of legal and illegal antiquities from official or unofficial excavations. Pepe Demarias had recently ceased visiting her to pay his respects, although he lived in the same building; his aunt owned one floor and his parents another, while the remaining apartments all belonged to her and she received rent from them. His behavior towards her was "absolutely appalling"—"I shall do you the favor of avoiding all mention of the details," she said, meaning that she preferred to spare me them—and she herself had "the strongest possible suspicions" that her nephew was abandoning himself to unspeakable pleasures and mixing with people from "evil circles" What she wanted me to do was to come up with adequate evidence of his vices so that she could change her will and cut him out of his inheritance.

She needed tangible proof, documents, photographs, names, addresses, dates, witnesses. Could I undertake such a confidential job? She had had "the very best of references concerning me from the part of Mr Doukas"—he must have been the man who had spoken to Mimis about the lady and her problems.

I made two grave errors one after the other: I said yes and I neglected to discuss my fee. Such was my desire to take on a case like this. That same evening I received a telephone call from my client at the office: the young man in question maintained a bachelor apartment in the Dexameni area and was spending more and more of his time there. She gave me the address and telephone number. I made a little reconnaissance tour to spy out the lie of the land, I looked at the name on the doorbell ("Per. Demarias") and investigated possible sources of information: the milk shop on the corner, the bakery and the kiosk where the street opened into the square.

In the early evenings Pepe frequented a bar in his own neighborhood. The drinks were expensive here, the customers didn't seem to have anything odd about them, the atmosphere was in no way suspect. I saw him there two days in a row. He drank in moderation, once he had a brandy and the second time Turkish coffee and a sweet. On his own. At about eight in the evening he paid his bill and left, wandered aimlessly around Kolonaki Square, stopped and chatted once or twice with acquaintances, some of them his own age and some older, who looked like family friends or neighbors.

The third day I had more interesting information from Mrs Stathis: there was going to be a birthday party for one of Demarias' friends at a restaurant, with a lot of guests. You couldn't help wondering how she managed to find out about her nephew's movements in such detail. Probably from her sister, his mother. I got myself ready and arranged with a taxi driver to drive me that evening, "wherever I wanted to go," as I told him. He was an old man, grey-haired, with an apron tied around his belly to prevent the steering wheel of his old Ford rubbing on his clothes.

I had already gathered various bits of information about

the nephew from the gossips of the neighborhood, yet nothing incriminating. Nevertheless, I noticed a sort of suppressed smirk as the kiosk man and the bakery woman spoke of Demarias to me. Nothing bad emerged from their words, but the smirk seemed to be implying something. By the evening I was on the right track. There might or might not be a basis for his aunt's suspicions. The company that evening was largely male though two or three women were present who certainly didn't belong to any "evil circles," yet there was something odd about them all the same. The cars—two in all, with my old taxi making a third—went down Vasilissis Sofias Avenue, turned at the Grande Bretagne, and took Amalias Avenue.

Near the Faliron Delta, a little further up, opposite the Hippodrome, there was a taverna bearing the name of some island with little lanterns glowing in the entrance. Entering in the wake of the nephew's party, I saw a large, fully-set table where some other friends were waiting for them.

On the raised stage was an orchestra and two singers, a man in a tuxedo and a woman in an evening dress with artificial roses sewn along the sash. The dance floor was still empty. The lighting was dim. I sat at a table near theirs and ordered wine and hors d'oeuvres. The prices were unbelievable, my pocket empty. My expenses had been beginning to mount up over the last few days and I hadn't been paid any retainer. I'd have to be as economical as possible. Yet not to such an extent as to attract the restaurant's attention.

The laughter and giggles, the conversation and the teasing didn't have anything about them to suggest the "evil circle" into which Pepe Demarias was supposed to be plunging without restraint. The jokes were the usual trivial ones you'd expect from people of their age, all things you'd heard before. The few women in the company had seated themselves together at the bottom end of the table.

After a while my hors d'oeuvres arrived, after a while the place began to fill up and the singer who was doubling as master of ceremonies told one or two jokes to which no one seemed to pay any attention then went on to sing a few Italian songs and waltzes. The Hawaiian guitars moaned in nostalgic glissando, the piano trilled curlicues, the violin hankered after its gypsy origins and the maracas whispered the rhythm. I would have enjoyed myself more if I hadn't had to keep my ears strained to listen to the conversation at the next table.

Late in the evening, when the place was thick with smoke and couples were dancing on the dance floor, I observed some movement at Demarias' table. A small man wearing a suit, with round, wire-framed glasses, was changing places with a broad back that had until now been obscuring my view of the orchestra and sitting down next to the subject of my investigation. They said something, each lit the other's cigarette, then the small man leaned sideways as if he wanted to say something private to Pepe and rested his head on his shoulder. Maybe he was feeling dizzy from the wine. Maybe not. The confidences did not continue but the head stayed on Pepe's shoulder and a voice which sounded more feminine than that of the women in the company sighed and said most distinctly, "Ach, how I suffer… how I su-u-uffer…."

He might have been suffering for a thousand and one reasons: as a result of the flat notes of the singer with the artificial roses on her sash, let's say, or the dangerous dizziness brought on by the wine that came "from our own vineyards at Vilia" or the sad words of the song that was being sung just at that moment:

Night drives you out of your mind
Looking at the stars
I cannot sleep.
Only this will I remember… Adios!
No more guitars, no more banjos,
The ending of a wonderful romance… Adios!

But the sadness or the indisposition of the small man seemed to last forever. He continued to rest his head on Pepe's shoulder and to sigh "Ach, how I suffer…" and by now it was perfectly clear that he was suffering from the sickness one might have imagined and that his cure depended on the rapidity with which the group of friends would decide to pay their bill and go their separate ways, enabling him to have recourse to his physician. Who wasn't necessarily the subject of my investigation—it could be that he was someone else, not present, whose absence made the song about the end of a wonderful romance most apposite. I knew where Demarias lived. Now what I had to discover was where the man who was suffering lived.

3

The aunt's nephew

The aunt's nephew had a broad face with high cheek-bones, fine, slightly slanting eyes and a curious expression. You wouldn't have called him a handsome man, yet there was something distinctive about him—his gaze often seemed to be focused somewhere else, on some unknown, mysterious place. In spite of his bulk and his broad shoulders, his voice was soft and he never raised it like the other people in the company. His movements had a grace and courtesy to them. His friend—the man who was suffering without the guitars and banjos—was made in a different mold altogether: he was small and slight and looked somehow wrong in his dark suit, like a child wearing grown-up clothes. He spoke in a tender, almost womanish, voice and his laughter (for he did laugh, even while suffering) was high-pitched. But then he remembered that he was suffering and was silent once more. It was this man who was my quarry.

I told my taxi driver not to lose sight of the car into which he'd got with some of the other members of the party (Demarias had got into another car) and we followed them as far as Heyden Street, just before Victoria Square, where I saw my man get out. I leaped from the taxi and hurried to catch up with him before he rang the bell so that I could see the name on it, but I wasn't in time. As he pushed the front door open I slipped into the hall behind him. My eye had taken in some of the names on the brass plates outside. The name "Angeletos" struck me as familiar—though I didn't know from where. Up three steps and we were on the landing by the wooden elevator cage.

As I stood there waiting, I could hear him breathing rapidly. He must have been nervous about something. He stood back to let me pass.

"Which floor do you want?" he asked politely.

"The top floor. Mr Angeletos the surgeon is on the third floor, isn't he?"

"No, the second," he corrected me.

He pressed the button for the first floor and when he got out I followed.

"But this isn't the second floor," he said with some surprise.

"Silly of me... absent-minded! Never mind, I'll walk up."

I walked up the stairs watching him through the banisters as he stood outside his door. *Gotcha!* I said to myself, for in my own mind I always used the language I'd learned as a child. I've got you, pal, you who suffer. Just you wait and see how many more reasons for suffering are going to come your way. When he closed the door (from within a woman's voice was scolding him for returning so late), I came back downstairs as stealthily as a cat and looked at the name on the plate. The apartment belonged to Dr Eleftherios Koutsaftis, whose son, etc., etc.

From there on my work was easy. Demarias and Thrasos (that's what he was called) Koutsaftis made no attempt at secrecy. It was enough that their meetings took place in Victoria Square, far from the eyes of the family, of Aunt Sitsa and of all the Kolonaki acquaintances. It wasn't possible to take any photographs: they always met in the evening and after dark you need a flash bulb. This is all very well if you're catching illicit couples in the act in some hotel room, but if you're following someone and collecting material of the kind the nephew's aunt wanted, then a flash won't do at all.

However, one day they made two morning walks, one in the Zappeion Gardens and one to the Acropolis. My little Kodak worked wonders as I played the tourist (American, why not?) taking pictures of the antiquities. They weren't very revealing poses: I snapped them standing by the parapet of the Acropolis, Pepe with one foot on the low wall and his hand on the other man's shoulder. They might have been two good friends admiring the view from up there.

But I caught them a little later in Anafiotika, the old quarter beneath the Acropolis, where their second long walk ended. Here I had better luck. As I rounded a corner I almost tripped over them. The lane leading uphill consisted of a flight of steps. I turned and took the next lane, walking normally like a simple passer-by.

Then I stopped, got my camera ready, calculated the distance and in a single movement darted out from behind the vine that grew on the corner and took my last snapshot of the day. Demarias was leaning forward propping himself against the wall with both arms. The Sufferer had his back against the same wall. A moment later and they'd have been embracing one another. This was the best picture in the series.

I had the photographs developed that same afternoon in Pelopidas Lebesopoulos' studio and shoved them into an envelope. It had taken me nearly two months, but I'd got the material the aunt wanted: bills for private boxes at nightclubs, bills from disreputable hotels, other photographs, lots of them, the names of one or two well-disposed individuals who wouldn't say no to putting their hand on the Bible and swearing something for a reasonable sum. If, that is, the matter ever reached a court of law.

All that remained was for me to visit the apartment on Dimokritou Street and be paid my fee plus my expenses, which were not inconsiderable. I had the forethought to telephone first. She was abrupt and sharp, as if my telephone call had been an impertinence that annoyed her.

"I need an *exposé*," she said coldly.

"I beg your pardon?"

"A… a memorandum is required, a report, mentioning everything you have observed, places, dates, people… every single thing of interest. Clearly written and with your signature."

"Fine," I stammered, "as you wish, I'll draw it up."

But I had urgent need of money—the taxis, the night-clubs, the bars, the long walks, quite apart from buying the films and developing the photos: all this had cost money. Madame Sitsa owed it to me and I had to eat. I called her again.

"Forgive me for bothering you once more," I began. "I'll prepare the report you have requested. However, you should give me something against my expenses… I've been out of pocket for days…"

"Against expenses? Certainly not," she cut me off. "Don't even think of such a thing. When you have finished the work we shall discuss your fee. No earlier…"

"Excuse me!" I protested. "When I have finished we'll *discuss* my fee? This is not how business is transacted, Mrs Stathis. I didn't raise the matter at the start, you are a respectable lady, there wasn't any reason… but I always receive something against expenses, this is what I'm asking for… from the very first day I should have…"

"Listen to me, Mr Sotiriou," she snarled, in a new voice just like a hyena. "It's the way I said. You will bring me the evidence and we shall *discuss* your fee. Till then, you can forget about it."

And she put down the phone. I almost had a heart

attack. I went out and walked aimlessly around the streets. That night I didn't sleep a wink.

When I next met Mimis I told him about this client and her behavior. He seemed upset. "I'd hoped you'd make a bit of money, Hephaistos," he said. "But instead you've got into a mess." And he shrugged his shoulders. "What can you expect from a fascist lady colonel? They're all bastards. And they behave as if they owned the world. Do you know what she is?"

"I know something about her…"

"Well, what d'you expect then?"

The conversation didn't lead anywhere. Mimis felt as upset and awkward as I did. He told me to be patient and to finish the job quickly so that I could go and get paid.

I drew up the report I'd been asked for and when I'd written it I felt disgusted with myself. It wasn't Pepe or Koutsaftis who disgusted me. It wasn't the sickness from which they both suffered. I don't know what it was. You do certain things without thinking because you have to. It could be that I liked those two, it could be that I disliked Aunt Sitsa as much as Pepe did, it could be that I saw no reason to persecute two boys who weren't doing an ounce of harm to anybody and only sought to live their lives privately. It was also the whole business of "the Honorable Madame Sitsa," the photograph of the king and its dedication—and the way she'd spoken to me. You didn't need to be very clever to realize that if and when I got paid, all she'd throw me would be a few crumbs. It was a question whether I'd even cover my expenses.

With a heavy heart, limping abominably, I made my way to Dimokritou Street one afternoon. I was carrying a dossier containing the whole file, the photographs, the evidence and that famous report signed bold and clear. Outside the aunt's building I stopped to set my clothes and my nerves in order. I needed to regain the impassiveness I used to have with clients.

Just as I put my hand out to ring the bell, I heard a familiar voice behind me saying, "Don't bother, I've got a key."

I turned round. It was Pepe. He smiled politely at me, he had his key ready to open the door, then suddenly paused.

"Do I know you?" he asked. (He certainly must have spotted me somewhere.)

I don't really know why I did it. Maybe because he spoke to me politely in his low voice. I stopped him before he got into the elevator and said, "I was on my way to see your aunt, she entrusted a job to me. Would you care to step outside for a moment?"

He raised his arched eyebrows and a trace of nervousness made his mouth tremble faintly.

"It concerns you, that's why I suggested it."

"Fire away," he said, when we were outside on Dimokritou Street once more.

"Here, take these, I'm giving them to you. I spent almost two months gathering the evidence she wanted in order to cut you out of her will, as she said. I haven't had a single drachma for any of it, I was foolish enough not to ask for a retainer to cover my expenses, I've had to fork out from my own pocket. But I know quite well that Mrs Stathis isn't going to pay me a thing without arguments and haggling… and even then it's a question whether my expenses will be covered. Well, too bad. I'm glad we met before I went upstairs… Take the file, burn it, do what you like with it… I'm through with this business."

He had suddenly become bright pink and drops of sweat were springing from the pores on his face. He was struggling to find something to say and not managing.

"What's more, to tell you the truth this work revolts me… I don't know… in my own country I could do it but here it's impossible, it doesn't suit me… I'll probably throw up the investigation agency and go and become a waiter in a restaurant."

"Is that what you do?" he managed to get out. "Are you a detective then?"

"Yes. Listen," (I'd suddenly had an idea), "unless it's necessary, your aunt doesn't need to know I've given the file to you. Better for her to think that all this time I've been doing nothing and that she's got off lightly from a swindler than for her to learn…"

He had begun to leaf through the contents of the file, impatiently crumpling the sheets of paper, the photographs and all the rest of it. "Understood," he murmured. "Understood. Yes. I mean no, I shan't tell her… she won't learn of it…"

It was as if he'd untensed now, as if he'd become slightly smaller as he leaned against the wall and relaxed.

"To whom do I owe this favor?" he asked, his eyes aslant again as usual.

I introduced myself. Demarias put out his hand and shook mine with a grip that almost broke it.

"I'll see what I can do for you, Mr Sotiriou," he said, "so that all your efforts won't have been wasted. Provided, naturally, that I continue to have the means..." (he smiled). "Thank you once again."

The days began to acquire a breathless sense of haste. There was always something new to think about: people were now talking openly of war. Metaxas' supporters went on claiming that everything was fine, that the government was taking care of the place, Greece was a neutral country and friends with everyone. By July the newspapers were writing that the Italians had bombed our ships and were maintaining they'd mistaken them for English ships. I liked the idea of neutrality. America was neutral too. All these people might be perfectly right not to like Metaxas, yet they were wrong to blame him for trying to stay out of the hostilities. Things didn't turn out well though. In August the Tinos episode took place.

An Indian summer had set in at the beginning of October. During that time I preferred not to leave the house at all: I didn't have any work, I couldn't be bothered to get dressed, I didn't have any money to spend, and anyway when you're hungry sleep is more nourishing than aimless walks.

As if all this wasn't bad enough, one afternoon the doorbell rang and a man from the Security Police asked me to accompany him. He didn't do me the favor of telling me why—maybe he himself didn't know—but at any rate he didn't look too bad and his manner wasn't too brusque. I noticed that instead of going to Bouboulinas Street we were heading for Elpidos Street, where the Special Security Headquarters were. As far as I knew, these boys' business was with communists and unpatriotic elements of society—what did I have to do with them? The secret agent took me into an office full of files and said something to the policeman behind the counter, whereupon this man picked up the telephone and dialed a two-digit number. Then he winked at us ("OK") and the first man took my arm again and led me upstairs.

I probably oughtn't to have been too surprised that as well as the fat Commander in civilian clothes with a shiny bald patch on his head I also saw Mrs Stathis' elderly companion sitting in an armchair in front of the desk, the man she hadn't considered it necessary to introduce me to that afternoon on Dimokritou Street. It seems that the lady colonel had found out; either Pepe hadn't taken care to keep his mouth shut or he hadn't been able to. That's the end of my permit, I thought. And I didn't give a damn. What use was the permit to me anyway? It was hardly as if it brought in any clients.

The Commander lashed into me: didn't I know that I was only working thanks to the tolerance of the security services, thanks to my references "from abroad," effectively working illegally in fact, since the legislative framework covering the setting up of private detective agencies was rudimentary if not non-existent? He had been informed that I'd undertaken a case of a delicate nature for a distinguished lady belonging to the highest echelons of society and that instead of carrying it through swiftly and honorably I had sold out to the man I was supposed to be following. How much had I been paid? How much had he given me to commit this dreadful act? Did I know that my client was a personal friend of the Palace and the Governor? Prison was awaiting me with its doors wide open, I only had to choose which one—he'd take care that I received very special treatment. Acronafplia, Ich-Kalé, Averof, Parapigmata… He listed a few more prisons. If my client decided to sue me for dereliction of duty and fraud, he himself would personally make sure that I'd spend the entire time before my trial in the cells and the whole of the rest of my sentence in the deepest dungeon. I'm putting it this way because I don't feel like spelling out his vocabulary or describing his manner.

The other man said nothing. He had got the Commander to do the roaring and threatening while he watched my reactions to what both of them (probably both of them) knew to be a pack of lies. I answered calmly and carefully. I had done nothing of what they were accusing me. I hadn't managed to find the evidence my client wanted. And after a while I'd simply given up the search since I hadn't been paid any retainer to cover my expenses. These expenses had been large and my fruitless surveillance had lasted about two months—Mrs Stathis had refused to pay me a single drachma until I brought her the evidence.

I crossed my arms over my chest and every time the other man stopped foaming at the mouth and expected an answer I replied in a monotone, "That is the truth, as she herself very well knows. I have nothing else to say. If I'd received any money from anyone, then I would hardly have been living so miserably recently, having spent the last drachma I possessed on this business."

The Commander didn't appear at all impressed by my coolness. He pretended to consider my answer impertinent, rang all the bells on his desk in a fury and gave orders for me to be locked up in the cells straight away. I didn't need to ask why. For a long time I'd been hearing stories about the Special Security Forces and about how they held sway as a government above the government. Now I was seeing it with my own eyes. They had no legal right to hold me, they just wanted to scare me. Yet on the other hand a foolish thought passed from my stomach to my brain: At least I'll get something to eat tonight. This didn't happen, however.

I was kept on Elpidos Street for two days. By the end of the second day I was beginning to hallucinate. Time stops flowing when, twenty-four hours a day, you are expecting at every moment to be set free: dawn turns into morning, morning turns into noon, noon into afternoon, afternoon into evening. When finally they let me go I realized that the order must have been given earlier: without anything new having occurred, the night duty officer suddenly came and unlocked my cell at eight o'clock and told me to get the hell out of there. By then I'd heard and seen a lot. Stories about torture chambers and interrogations beyond all imagining used to go round. But to be there locked in a cell right next door to the room with that table with the straps is an experience which until fairly recently, forty or more years later, continued to make me jump up from my sleep trembling and drenched in sweat.

When war was declared on the 28th of the month I was in bed with a fever. Since no one came to visit me, the radio was broken and the voices from outside reached my room indistinctly, I only retain a vague impression of those days. My sleep was disturbed by nightmares. I didn't have the strength even to get to the office. I wasn't thinking any more. Yet a series of conclusions seemed to be circulating through my veins, each one blacker than the other. I was a total failure. I was someone who went on acting as if he were alive when he wasn't. When I finally decided in despair to telephone Pepe Demarias and ask for help, there was no answer. On the fifth day a woman answered and told me he was out of Athens, then put down the phone before I could get another word in edgeways. At least I had his gratitude—God, what a fool. On Elpidos Street I'd hoped they would give me food.

Now, with the winds of war blowing over me, I was hoping that in the midst of all the calamity and destruction Mrs Stathis, if she still remembered me, would forget me once and for all.

4

—

My nightmare comes alive

If anyone had told me in the past that I'd find myself in the midst of a war in Europe I would have laughed. In the streets the men on their way to join the army were singing as they went past in their trucks, people were waving flags and shouting slogans. Everyone of my own age was leaving: Lebesopoulos left his photographer's studio and his Fotini and was one of the first to be called up. A lot of the other people who had stores or offices on Gamvetta Street were called up too. But the recruiting board sent Pelos back because apparently he had flat feet and asthma. He wouldn't give up, though, didn't return to the shop at once but instead scurried around trying to find some way of getting them to take him. Fotini said nothing, simply followed developments. When finally all his efforts to put on khaki failed, her relief was as great as it was silent.

To people who weren't aware that I still had foreign nationality, my lame leg seemed a pity twice over: first simply as a handicap—such a young man to be limping —and second because it deprived me of the chance to go off and fight the "macaronis." The daily subject of conversation on the stairs and balconies of our apartment building was Mr Kynigos' son, as well as the younger brother of the lawyer Mr Kanellis on the second floor, both of whom had left for the borders.

I only listened with half an ear to the news about operations in Europe and barely glanced at the newspaper headlines recounting each day's developments. I went the rounds of lawyers' offices leaving my card, I struggled using every means I could think of to acquire a few clients. From the moment I first set foot in Greece I viewed anything that happened in Europe solely in terms of my hopes of returning to New York as soon as possible —nothing else interested me. No matter that special issues were constantly being published, that the newspaper vendors hurried along the main streets shouting out the news. Instead of shuddering at the division of Poland between Germany and the Soviet Union, instead of agonizing at Churchill's promise of "blood, toil, tears and sweat," instead of being outraged by General Pétain's call on the French to forget their old enmity for the Germans and henceforth to love them equally fanatically, I was spending my savings with scrupulous care, a drachma at a time, keeping on telephoning on the off-chance of finding Pepe at home and banging my head against the wall that I hadn't, right then at the beginning, asked for a retainer for the Stathis case; the only thing that outraged me was the lady colonel's atrocious behavior when I dared to speak to her of money. If only Freddy had been here: I would have asked him who it was who'd said, "years teach us what days don't even begin to suspect."

It seemed utterly improbable that this poor and distant country would ever enter the war. But the very day I said this to myself, the "Elli" was torpedoed off Tinos and the cauldron began to boil over. Even then I still didn't share everyone else's certainty about the inevitable outcome. So the whole world was going to join in the war, was it? Hence America as well? Why, for what reason? This seemed even less likely than Greece entering the war. But by the end of the month we were at war here too.

It was as if the valve had blown off a pressure cooker and the scalding steam was bursting forth, carrying with it the government of Metaxas, who resembled a tightrope walker seconds before he loses his balance and plunges into the void. Mimis explained to me how people felt that in their outbursts of rage and mockery towards a dictator like Mussolini they were also expressing their antipathy for the regime here and for the Governor. And that as they hurried off to fight the Italians on the border they were at the same time taking up arms against the dictatorship which the palace and the English (yes, the English again!) had imposed on them. I could understand part of this reasoning, though another part remained a mystery to me and years were to pass before I understood it. I was still a foreigner here, it wasn't easy.

People used to meet on street corners and discuss the

news arriving from the front, the victories the army was winning, the disorderly retreat of the Gloriosi. In barely a fortnight from the start of the war, the army had entered Albania and bombarded Korytsa; everyone was expecting that by the end of November the Italians would be forced to swim back to their own country. It was a triumph, people were delirious with enthusiasm. The theaters put on revues that had the whole audience roaring with laughter at the Duce as a *foustanella*-clad Greek soldier threw him into the sea; they took Italian songs and replaced the words with Greek ones mocking the vainglorious bravado of the invader. All those who supported the regime were in low spirits, frightened and shaken—all those who opposed it were, on the contrary, having fun.

At the turn of the year, at the beginning of '41, Metaxas died and a new Prime Minister, some banker, took over. Ships carrying English soldiers docked in Piraeus. From one day to the next the "Tommies" suddenly became likable, people showered them with flowers and began to use English words interspersed with their Greek, which sounded utterly ridiculous. The Special Security Forces had forgotten all about me, as had the lady colonel Mrs Stathis—and so too, it seemed, had Pepe, whose gratitude didn't reach the point of trying to seek me out to give me some money as he'd promised.

The Germans were swiftly descending from the north to rectify Mussolini's mistakes. Belgrade was bombed in April. At the same time Piraeus was also bombed, sinking a great many English ships that had been carrying part of the Sixth Division of the Australian forces arriving from Cyrenaica, including the "Clan Fraser" with two hundred and fifty tons of explosives in her holds: the resulting explosion blew up every single building on the waterfront, leaving chunks of metal embedded in walls, trees and the asphalt of the roads. Before they started the bombardment, the German planes had dropped mines by parachute across the entrance of the harbor to prevent any ship from slipping out and escaping.

Sirens became part of our lives. Their wailing made your stomach churn and your blood run cold, you had to hurry to an air-raid shelter or close the windows whose panes you'd covered with sheets of blue paper or sticky tape to stop you being injured by fragments of shattered glass. Terrified Jews began to arrive from Salonica in search of ships on which they could embark to escape and save themselves.

Things were going badly now. Fear and outrage had replaced the wild enthusiasm of the earlier victories. The news from the front was that the army was cut off in the Pindos mountains without supplies, and towards the end of April that the SS were in Grevena. People were saying that the palace didn't want us to fight the Germans, General Papadimas, the Chief of Staff, was a known Germanophile and the orders reaching the surrounded forces were that they should refrain from any engagement with the German Army and should surrender their arms. While all this was happening, the Prime Minister, Koryzis, picked up his pistol and committed suicide. Mimis said that this way the regime of the 4th of August was also committing suicide.

By the 27th of the month the country was occupied three times over: the Italians had arrived along with the Germans, while the Bulgarians had also moved south to gnaw the bones they'd had their eyes on for so long. Through the open windows in our building came voices, conversations, telephone calls, footsteps hurrying down the stairs, doorbells ringing. Suddenly everything was quiet. Someone said, "I can see their flag on the Acropolis" and everyone fell silent. The street had emptied. I was afraid to go out so I lay down on my bed.

I drifted into a troubled sleep and began to have disjointed dreams: I was by the river at Woodside outside the house where an Irish girlfriend of mine lived, I was fishing as I waited for her to come out and join me. But instead her father emerged, with his shirt-sleeves rolled up to the elbow. He took a few deep breaths of air on their verandah, then walked slowly over to where I was and sat down beside me. Happy at this unexpected intimacy, I was about to speak to him, to open my heart to him (a guilty heart actually: I liked his daughter but I didn't love her and had no intention of proceeding to regularize our relations officially), but he didn't give me the time to do so. Without getting up he put his hand across my throat and pushed me into the water with my fishing rod. I was beginning to drown, the river was sucking me down into its depths as if I had lead weights on my feet, through its distorting lens I could just make out his red Irish face and his fist raised in joy at his revenge. I leaped out of bed, hurried to the sink to splash water on my face. It wasn't time for sleeping, those were not days for sleeping, and all my dreams were frightening, suffocating and disordered.

After that day I kept on having different versions of that dream. It became the permanent companion of my sleep. In the streets of Athens, however, a different nightmare was unfolding. Unfamiliar figures, unfamiliar voices, unfamiliar signs now filled the streets: people would step aside, would withdraw to the curb or slip into the entrances of apartment buildings as they went by. There were loudspeakers everywhere and orders everywhere, *Verboten, Verboten, Verboten*…. It was as if some cruel nursery governess had taken over the running of our lives and was making new rules and new plans, they were setting up their own order so that they could control this foreign country and its unknown people more easily. Conquerors fear the conquered more than the conquered fear them. And before too long this fear and mutual dislike turned all those prohibitions into barbed wire and machine guns and arrests and executions, so that a passionate and undisguised hostility broke out.

Law-abiding householders like Balomenos and Kynigos shouted in our narrow street that some idiots were putting all our lives in danger: in other words, the people who'd begun to write anti-German and anti-Italian slogans on the walls, the people who came out onto the roofs with megaphones to help the population keep up its morale in the face of the conqueror's tyranny, the people who took down the German flag from the Acropolis—during the very first days of the Occupation—and the authorities gave out that it had been done by culprits unknown who simply wanted to steal the cloth it was made of. The Kanellis couple on the floor above me pronounced in whispers the names of Glezos and Santas. They knew who'd done it—and as they listened to the threats and the versions given out by the Kommandatur their lips took on a bitter twist.

Mimis also lowered his voice. "It's a radio silence, Hephaistos," he told me. "People have got guts, they spit at them in the street and it drives the Germans into a fury. Even the Italians are afraid of them and we just spit at them like that. We despise them, know what I mean? No one here's the least bit impressed by all those goose-stepping human machines going past."

And so the Great Hunger began. It was a reprisal for resistance and sabotage. And above all for our contempt. Food was commandeered for the needs of the occupying forces, it simply disappeared, prices went sky-high and the black market came into being. Bakeries, grocers and greengrocers closed, stores pulled down their shutters and padlocked their doors, the streets were deserted and food became the daily nightmare haunting all of us. When we went out it was like wild beasts in the jungle on the prowl for food. I didn't see Mr Karalis again until after the war: until then it was as if he'd died, his grocery store closed and never re-opened. All around, all you saw was people asking one another about possible sources of food, their eyes dark with hunger. Within the space of a few weeks houses, fields and entire fortunes changed hands for a can of dregs of olive oil from the oil press, for a few okas[2] of weevil-ridden sugar, for a couple of half-rotten herrings which, in order to save gas or methylated spirits, you'd cook on a fire of newspaper.

One icy morning at the beginning of November, I was having the nightmare about drowning again when I was woken by the doorbell. Feeling almost happy that something had interrupted my sleep, I hurried to open the door. Balomenos was standing there, as red-faced as the Irishman in my dream but with a crocodile smile that bared all his teeth.

"Mr Sotiriou, it's time we had a word… I've been patient for two months but things can't go on like this… and these are strange times, it's a good idea to have your money in your pocket where you can count it, you never know what the next day's going to bring…"

I was two months late with the rent and I hadn't even remembered it.

I didn't know where I was going to find the money, I didn't have a clue. All I had was the muddled thoughts in my brain and the cobwebs on the home-made safe in the floor under my chair in the office. Maybe one of my

2. An oka is a unit of weight.

acquaintances might be able to tide me over for a short while, Lebesopoulos, Mimis… someone.

"Yes… of course, tomorrow or the day after I'll bring it to you," I stammered awkwardly.

Balomenos smiled unpleasantly.

"'Tomorrow or the day after' is rather vague. Tell me when exactly you'll be bringing it so that I know. We have *foreigners* here now, apartments in the center of town are in demand…"

"The day after tomorrow without fail."

"The day after tomorrow without fail," he repeated and moved away. "Without fail, right?" he called as he went up the stairs.

I closed the door and went and sat in the front room which was dark as the shutters were pulled down. The thought of a pawnbroker came and went. Money-lenders were doing good business but the pledge required was large and I didn't own anything valuable enough to raise anywhere near the amount I needed.

I got dressed automatically, put on my hat and went out. I still had the rent for the office safely tucked away in the hiding place under my chair. Mr Menagias had two sons at the front and spent all his time trying to get news of them, so he wasn't likely to come asking for it—I could give it to Balomenos in part payment. But in my heart I knew he wouldn't accept it for it didn't even amount to one month's rent for the apartment. All the same, I got this money out of its hiding place and put it in my pocket, after counting it over and over again and calculating how much more I needed, and whether perhaps I could manage if I pawned my pistol, my watch and the painting of two horses that I had at home (a present from Lamera). But it was absurd even to think of it. Only if I'd owned some rich jewel, worth ten or twenty times the amount I owed for the rent, would I have been able to raise the sum required.

The appointed day came and went without me having found any more money. But although I was expecting another visit or a phone call from Balomenos, he failed to appear to ask for his rent. And a few more weeks passed. It wasn't that he'd forgotten, just that he had other business on hand. There was a lot of coming and going of two taxis whose drivers were friends of his, at night footsteps could be heard in the basement and doors being locked and unlocked. It was the coldest time of winter, the worst period of the Great Hunger. Balomenos played "Tiritomba" on his gramophone and sealed his kitchen windows tight so that no one would catch a whiff of the food they were cooking there; every so often, when everyone else was asleep, he'd go down to the locked storerooms in the basement and let someone in through the service door. After which dead silence would reign once more.

Hearing Italian spoken in the streets only put me into a worse state. Everybody else laughed at the Italians and mocked them, but I trembled: I knew how easily their laughter and jokes and claps on the back can turn to knifings, and how lightly they take other people's disasters.

Everyone considers the Italians to be a cheerful and carefree race. But their souls are as hard as steel and they'll destroy you if their least interest is at stake, or even merely on a whim. The peasants from Naples and Sicily who in their villages harvest their vines and graze their goats have corrupted an entire continent, America, and hold it hostage in their webs. I had personal experience of this and thus barely heard the jokes and jests of my fellow-countrymen about this braggart race who now filled Athens.

What my landlord's nocturnal comings and goings in the basement meant I was soon to discover. And then the noises, the hermetically shut kitchen door (which didn't help much since the smell of food wafted from the front room into the stairwell and caused you great distress), "Tiritomba" on the gramophone and the sudden generosity that drew a veil over my debt—the three months owed were about to become four—all came together.

Late one night I had got up to escape the nightmares that came in pursuit of me as soon as I closed my eyes and was having a drink of water from the kitchen faucet when I thought I caught sight of a shadow moving outside. I tiptoed across the room and from the window I could make out the shoulders and familiar-looking head: it was Balomenos, going down the steps leading to the light-well. It had rained heavily that afternoon and outside there was a strong smell of damp and drains. I went out and stood at the top of the stairs. I was trying to make out some light and to hear what was going on. The door of the service entrance squeaked, it was being opened, I heard steps in the basement corridor, two male shadows went past, one heaving a sack and the other a small wooden crate, and went into the storerooms. I waited there, outside my kitchen door, ready to dart back inside. A short while later the three men came out and, whispering something, went back along the corridor towards the service door. I crept half-way down the stairs and bent down to have a look: it was the engineer and two Italians, of whom one must have been an officer and the other a quartermaster or driver.

"Next time you'll pay me in advance for everything," said the Carabiniere in a soft Tuscan accent.

Smothered laughter.

"No skin off my nose," answered Balomenos in Italian. "I sell everything at a higher price than what you let me have it for. Judge for yourself if it's in your interest…"

The rest of the conversation took place behind the half-closed door, on the sidewalk, so I couldn't hear it. But some sudden urge led me to hurry downstairs, in my socks, just as I was. The puddles left by the rain soaked my feet but I advanced hastily into the corridor and saw before me the wide-open door of one of the storerooms. The wooden crate I'd seen them carrying in was lying there; I tried to open it but it was nailed shut and the labels on it were in Italian which I couldn't read in the feeble light shed by the dim yellow bulb. So I grabbed it and ran back to my kitchen clutching it in my arms. I locked the door and switched on the hall light to read the labels. What little Italian I knew told me that my booty was cans of peas supplied to the Italian army.

The next morning I awoke to the shouts of Balomenos in the light-well. The concierge was squeaking in terror and he was braying so that everyone would hear, threatening divine vengeance and hell fire, swearing he'd have the police over and search every single apartment. Many of the tenants had come to their windows and were trying to puzzle out what had happened. The lawyer from upstairs, Kanellis, who was still pajama-clad and tousle-haired, yelled angrily, "Why don't you find the thief first, before you start loosing off accusations left, right and center. Do you imagine everyone here wallows in the same filth as you?"

Scarlet as a lobster and with all his veins standing out, Balomenos answered, "As regards us, Mr Kanellis, we were always law-abiding citizens, we never learned to rob other people of their livelihoods. And who was addressing you anyway? Who was accusing you of anything? Though why would you shout so loud if you didn't know something about it?"

"That's all that was missing, for you to accuse me of breaking into your storeroom. You claim you've been robbed and threaten to call in the police to search us... What's that if not an accusation against everyone in the building? As for us, it's been ten days since we last had a bite to eat, we don't cook food in secret with the windows closed so that the smell won't seep out, like you do. Go back to wherever you get it from, have a look there to see if you can find what's been stolen from you."

The lawyer went back in, banging the shutters on his bedroom window, while everyone else stayed there muttering and asking each other what had happened. I didn't say a word. But his threat about searching all the apartments scared me. Thus I decided to smuggle the wooden crate with the canned peas in it over to my office. Either I'd find a way of selling them and would make enough to cover the rent I owed Balomenos, or I'd be eating peas for two months.

Of course the threat was aimed at frightening the thief into revealing where the crate was. Not even Balomenos would have risked being shown up in the neighborhood as a black marketeer; and certainly the Carabiniere didn't have the slightest desire to be reduced to the ranks or shut up in the punishment block. The peas were quite safe. However, although I'd had the foresight to conceal them in my office, it hadn't occurred to me that Mrs Leni, the concierge, who was responsible for putting all the building's trash out on the sidewalk would be charged with searching through it. Thus at noon one day Balomenos rang my doorbell and came in brandishing the evidence—an empty can of peas (it was only the second one I'd opened).

"Liars and thieves are happy at the beginning, Mr Sotiriou," he said in a threatening tone.

"Someone must have thrown that can into my trash," I responded coolly. "The garbage is out there on the stairs for two nights before Mrs Leni collects it…" (he was watching me with a sly smile, ready to refute my argument). "Now that you're here, though, you might as well search my apartment. If one can was here, then the others can't be far off…"

I stood back to let him pass, and with a smile that was almost friendly he suddenly said, "We could go halves…"

"What?"

"Half and half. Do you know how much those peas sell for on the market? Or any kind of canned food, come to that…"

"I haven't a clue. I wish I did. But go ahead, search, why aren't you searching?"

"We could arrive at an arrangement about the rent," he was insisting. "All right? Three months' rent… OK, might as well count December as well… four months' rent in return for the crate. And three cans thrown in gratis so you'll have something to eat. Look at it from my point of view. If I were alone in this I wouldn't care. The olive oil I get from my own land I do what I like with. But here there's someone else mixed up in the business—and he's not fooling around… you don't know what Italians are like! He's got superiors, he works in the Commissariat… he'll be court-martialed, it isn't funny. You understand? He'll have me bumped off if I expose him."

Was he scared, or was the crafty fellow trying to sound me out?

"Look here. Finding things that have been lost is my job… Maybe I'll find something. If I don't, then you'll have lost your canned peas and I'll have lost four months' rent. Am I putting it correctly?"

"I'll be waiting," he hissed. "For your own good."

I was more frightened than I'd let on. I left the crate with the cans in it outside his door, rang the bell and then made myself scarce. I kept back two or three cans which lasted me for a month and a bit. In the meantime the Red Cross soup kitchen opened in Canningos Square and the less regular soup kitchen of the parish of Zoodochos Pigi. But they didn't provide enough to live on. Gradually I became as skeletal as everyone else and started to look like a ghost. During the Hunger Mimis was better than a brother to me. Not that he himself was doing too well. He'd go for a while without food, starving and making do with what the soup kitchens offered, like me. But sometimes, if he stumbled on something edible, he'd let me know at once. Twice he saved me from certain death. And this because of the friendship and liking he felt for me. I owed him. He maintained his acquaintances in the harbor and now and again managed to get his hands on a morsel of cheese or a drop of olive oil from its warehouses. While everyone else pretended they didn't know you if it was a question of food, Mimis—unmarried, as I was, and without any dependents—would telephone his friends and suggest that we shared anything that was to be found. We'd hurry over on foot to the most out-of-the-way neighborhoods, sometimes for half an oka of spoilt beans from Turkey, sometimes for a half-rotten herring, sometimes for dandelion leaves or other greens, dry and bitter.

It was the harsh winter that carried off the starving, first the old people, then the babies—the rest of us were slightly better able to withstand it. Not everyone though. Lebesopoulos, the photographer, died in April '42. Fotini told me about it one morning when I saw her in the photographer's studio on Gamvetta Street. She didn't have any tears to spare, her dry eyes were sunk deep in their sockets. Struggling with exhaustion, she was putting together in a corner anything she thought might be sold: tripods, cameras, lights, glass bottles of developing solution, unused film. Whatever money she managed to make from these things she would use to go back to her village. You could live better there, you didn't die of hunger. They still had a few hens and goats at her family home, in a village just outside Patras.

Her hand was resting on a cardboard box. "These are for you, to remember me by," she said with a grimace that didn't quite manage to become a smile. "They're from the good old days," she went on, "it was Pelos' idea, to make a little money from them when business dried up with the war." She pushed the box at my chest and cast her restraint to the winds. "Why don't you come to the village too?

You're not looking good. The way you're going, you'll croak. Men are needed there… for the vegetable plots. And for whatever else men are good for…"

I thanked her for her offer. "I don't know anything about vegetable plots, I'd be useless," I told her.

We said goodbye to one another. When I went upstairs to the office and opened her present I found that in the box were a couple of hundred photographs of naked women, faceless. For a moment I thought it must be some kind of archive of the pictures Pelos and I had once upon a time taken of illicit couples. But I was wrong. There were countless different poses, some like this, some like that, all well lit and nicely finished, and all with the same grey background. First I identified the curtain of grey cardboard that I'd just seen in the studio propped against a tripod. Then—although there was no head shown in any of the pictures—I realized that the model was Fotini herself. Whether or not this gift she'd given me had any relation to her proposal that I go and work in the vegetable plot, the fact of the matter was that nothing was left of any of the charms shown in the photographs.

I was overcome by deep sadness. With Lebesopoulos' death and the closing of his studio I had lost two of my three best friends in Athens. Papachrysanthou was the only one left. And he at least, as time went by, was a daily presence in my life. He'd come by to see me, with or without food. And our few successful expeditions to the various neighborhoods of the city kept us alive until the summer of '42. After which, as the weather improved, nature itself helped you to survive. Mimis taught me to eat jujube fruit straight from the tree—if you drank some water at the same time it made you feel full. Like ants, we worked all summer to lay in supplies for the winter ahead. The soup kitchens improved and more of them opened. In a lot of parts of town it was well known that EAM[3] was helping to keep them supplied.

3. The National Liberation Front, main movement of the Greek Resistance during the Axis occupation of Greece.

5

The appearance of the Big Boss

One evening, at the beginning of January '43, I was still in the office after the hour when the curfew began. I had been lost in vain daydreams, time had passed, the streets had become deserted and the lights had gone out. I jumped up from my reverie and prepared to pull down the blinds and hurry home, darting from wall to wall and praying that I wouldn't run into any patrol. I was just putting my hand out to take hold of the strap by the window when I heard someone knocking at the door. There wasn't a soul about at this hour. Who could have climbed three floors in the pitch dark? Who knew that I was in the office? I was frightened as I asked in savage tones who it was.

"Mr Sotiriou?" a voice asked with great politeness.

"Who is it?" I called again.

"You don't know me, Mr Sotiriou. Or rather you know

me… but assuredly you don't remember me. Agathos[4] is my name."

His name didn't mean anything to me; his voice sounded as if it belonged to someone of a certain age and of good family. I unbolted the door, opened it and took a step backwards, ready for any eventuality.

The person who came in looked more or less as I'd imagined him. In the dim light coming from the window I could make out the white hair and stout body of an elderly man. I was left open-mouthed at the sight of him: no plump elderly gentleman with a prominent belly and several spare tires around the waist had been seen in Athens since before the Hunger. This one here looked as if he'd just stepped straight out of a novel.

He walked into the middle of the room, found the armchair I kept for visitors and enthroned himself in front of my desk with a sigh of relief.

"I've climbed a lot of stairs today, Mr Sotiriou," he said, with something like a twinkle in his voice. "But I absolutely had to see you tonight. I'm glad I found you here."

"Mr…"

"Agathos!"

"Mr Agathos, it's late, you understand… I ought to be at home—and so should you."

"You live nearby, do you not?" he offered, as if to reassure me, yet at these words I grew even more worried.

4. Agathos = Good

In spite of his absent-minded appearance, this stranger was well informed.

"Yes, I do live near here. But what about you?"

"My home is far away, my dear sir! Very far away! But at the moment I'm staying… Yes indeed, I am staying at the Palladion Hotel, in other words five minutes away." (He laughed.) "So for me too, you understand, there is no problem…"

"To put it briefly," I interrupted him, "in a nutshell, since you are also living near here, why don't you go back to your hotel, let me go home, and we'll talk about it all at our leisure tomorrow morning. I have an extraordinarily free day tomorrow, you can't imagine how free…"

He laughed, gave a small choking cough, and I heard him draw breath for his next tirade.

"Oh, ho! You realize, my dear sir, that my business is pressing. Extremely so! Otherwise I would have waited till tomorrow… We are law-abiding people, a blackout is a blackout and the curfew…"

"The curfew…"

"I am glad to find us in such agreement, Mr Sotiriou —Sotiriou… I like your name, I must confess… My son, you see…"

"Your son?"

"Was called Sotiris[5]," my visitor said with a lump in his throat.

"I'm so sorry."

---

5. Sotiris, a man's name meaning "Savior"

"Thank you, most kind of you. Mr Sotiriou, I wish to entrust an affair to you."

Lord in Heaven, I said to myself, for if we went on like this we'd be there all night. "If your daughter is fooling around or your wife is deceiving you…"

"My wife! Oh ho ho! What ever gave you that idea, my dear sir? Indeed… I am not married, Mr Sotiriou."

"I beg your pardon," I stammered, "you were just speaking of your son…"

"Quite right… But… you understand—as the man of the world you are—that the state of affairs… is not always…"

"I understand. Well then, Mr Agathos…"

"Panayotis[6]. Panos for short."

"You had a son called Sotiris whom you have lost… And you are not married. Is that correct?"

"Quite correct. Precisely. And your Christian name, if you will allow me?"

"Angel."

"Angel! Wonderful! We shall suit one another very well, you and I, I am quite certain of it, my dear sir. Angel! Perfect, ideal."

"Perfect? Ideal?"

"I'm just having my own little joke—what does it matter? What matters is that there should be perfect trust between us—do you follow me?—perfect trust. And

---

6. Panayotis, a man's name derived from Panayia (=All Holy), the title of the Virgin Mary

familiarity, of course, within the bounds of what is proper for our acquaintance and collaboration."

"Tell me, this affair which you wish me to undertake, is it of a family nature or something else? You will understand, of course, that we are under occupation, our movements are very restricted and the risks vastly increased. I couldn't take on any affair that brought me into confrontation with the Authorities."

"Rest easy. You could well call it of a family nature, hm, hm, hm, in a manner of speaking. At any rate, pray do not be afraid, I am in a position to cover you, come what may. But what will you… In the end… *in the end*… everything leads to the same circle… Do you follow me?"

"I'm not quite sure…"

"What I mean to say is that all our actions, all our movements, in the last analysis revolve around the central questions and values of the world. The triumph of the just over the unjust, of good over evil…"

"I certainly don't understand…"

"You're quite right. I start philosophizing sometimes. It's my age… pay no attention. In any case all these things depend on your own decision to take on this case. And no one is obliging you to do so…"

"I have one abiding criterion as to whether or not I take on something."

"And that brings us to the question of your fee," said my client in a sudden bold move. He did not seem the slightest bit perturbed. "How much do you charge?"

"Please… What is it that *you* want? When we've sorted that out, then we can get to what I charge."

"You are perfectly right. I'll tell you at once…"

He coughed again and cleared his throat.

"It is about a series of actions that I wish you to carry out for me, my dear Mr Sotiris," he said with a sudden familiarity as if he was preparing to ask me a favor. "I am not in a position and I do not consider it pertinent to entrust you with the whole job all at once. So let us begin with the contingencies…"

"The contingencies," I repeated impassively.

"Step by step. Well then, small services…"

"What do you mean, services? I am a professional…"

"Oh ho! Ho, ho! I don't mean unpaid services, let me make myself clear. You will be well paid."

"Are you by chance an olive oil merchant?" I asked.

"I have been, in my time. But no, I am not an olive oil merchant. Perhaps you would like to know if I am intending to pay you in kind?"

"Money today…"

"Is a devalued currency! Not worth the paper it's printed on! No, I have no intention of paying you in Occupation drachmas, dear sir. Quite the contrary. You will be paid in gold."

"In gold!" I cried out in spite of myself, then lowered my voice and repeated with some confusion, "in gold, did you say?"

"Yes indeed, that is what I said."

And putting his hand into his waistcoat pocket he took

something between his thumb and index finger and let it fall from a little height onto the glass surface of my desk.

If you have once heard this sound, then you will never mistake it for anything else. I made a movement and then restrained myself.

"Please!" he said encouragingly.

I put my hand onto my desk and groped till I found the small, round object then drew it towards me. I picked it up and held it towards the window in the hope that the faint light coming from outside would help me see what it was. It was a gold sovereign.

He took advantage of my silence and told me, "As a first stage, I'd like you to get to know someone."

"To get to know someone?"

"To get to know someone. How else to put it? To become friends with him, to spend time with him. He is an exceptional gentleman, an artist, a little strange, it's true, someone whom at all costs I wish to assist... anonymously... Do you take my meaning?"

"More or less. But why must I spend time with him? Could you not perform your act of charity through some common acquaintance?"

"I have no common acquaintance with anyone, Mr Sotiris. And the assistance I desire to offer this person is of a kind which must not awaken any suspicions in him... For him to accept it, it has to come from some close friend of his, and that friend will be you: a friend, an admirer and, if need be, a provider of help..."

"You said I knew you, Mr Agathos. Yet I can't remember ever having met you before. And because of my profession I have an excellent memory—I don't forget faces. Did you ever live in America, perhaps?"

"Ha ha ha!" I heard him laugh in the darkness and I thought I saw two rows of flashing white teeth (false ones, no doubt). "You seem to know more about me than I do about you, my dear sir. Yes, I have spent some time in America…"

An interesting coincidence. To some extent the knowledge that I was dealing with someone who'd spent time in my own country reassured me. Here everyone was nothing but hot air merchants and swindlers—I'd never managed to like them.

"Whereabouts were you? In the Bronx? In Astoria? Where?"

"Here and there, my dear fellow, here and there. What does it matter? It was such a long time ago, I can't even remember how many years ago. Neither Astoria nor the Bronx existed then…"

"Come," I said, "you're not that old…"

"And yet I am, my dear fellow, but let's not discuss that. I know at any rate that before me I have a man in whom I may have complete trust. You have been recommended to me, otherwise I should not have set out to find you. But to come to the financial aspects. This sovereign is a retainer to ensure your goodwill. These ones here" (once again his two fingers slipped into his waistcoat) "are for the beginning of our collaboration and to cover your expenses over the first days. Next Friday there is going to be a performance at the Olympia Theater of the *Pagliacci* and the *Cavalleria Rusticana*. You will put on your best clothes and go. At the box office you will find a ticket in your name. You will meet the man I want you to get to know at the bar in the foyer. He plays double bass in the orchestra. His name is Miltiades—Miltos—Beratis, from Halkida or somewhere thereabouts. Mr Beratis is an important person, even if he doesn't hold an important position. He's also a superb violinist and a virtuoso pianist—but his wretched fate brought him to Greece instead of allowing him to stay in Germany where he studied and where he had already begun to distinguish himself as a composer... Thus you have at least one thing in common with him... is it not so?"

He stopped, waiting for me to comment or protest or ask him how he knew so much about me. But I didn't do him the favor. Four more sovereigns had now been lying forgotten on the desk for some time and I was experiencing a terrible itch to put out my hand and draw them towards me and allow them to join their sister in my pocket.

"He left Germany," said Mr Agathos, "after the Nazis came to power, he belonged to a group of musicians who were persecuted and forced to leave in order to avoid a worse fate. The tribulations we all suffer under the German Occupation are twice as bad for Mr Beratis, for he was already listed in their books as an enemy of National Socialism. Unfortunately it happens that he is ill, probably gravely so. He is endangered by a pulmonary disease...

he is near collapse, the deprivations have exacerbated his condition… He refuses to do what everyone else does to survive. Instead of going out in search of food, he shuts himself up in his room to compose—all his attention is devoted to his work rather than to himself… You will understand what kind of man I am speaking of. Pretend that you are interested in music, in him—use your own judgment as to what is the best way. And don't let him out of your sight."

"But for goodness' sake, how do you know all this? Is this Mr Berketis, Berkatis—whatever he's called—something to you? Is he perhaps another son of yours?"

"Oh ho ho ho! I like you, Mr Sotiris, I like you. You have a certain, what do you call it, style… No, he's not my son… He's not my son, in fact… But he is someone who has a great need of protection."

"You could say the same thing of the whole of Athens," I responded, stubborn because Mr Agathos was not revealing his real reasons.

"Certainly you could. But each person has his own appointed destiny—how does the Attik song go? Do you like Attik? I'm crazy about him—a huge talent… Well then, Mr Sotiris, the same thing applies to our musician, he's a man who mustn't be lost like that, like a starving cur…"

"Why? Isn't there anyone else who could play the double bass at the Olympia?"

"Oh ho, ho, ho, you put it marvelously well, my dear Mr Sotiris…"

"You keep on calling me Sotiris, my first name is Angel."

"A thousand apologies, do forgive me… it's my age. I was confused, my boy. Mr Angel" (correcting himself). "Ah yes, Sotiriou is your surname… It's just that it resembles my son's name…" (A lump in his throat again.) "Excuse me. No, Mr Angel, it isn't a question of who'll play the double bass in the orchestra. It's the fact that the man is a composer and a fine one, the finest that this country has or will have for a long time…"

"And what's that to you?"

"Ah, don't talk like that! I care about my country, my heart bleeds for it, if I can do something I won't hesitate…"

"I understand. There's no need to go on. Or rather, do go on, but about the work you want me to do for you."

"Wonderful. So, then. I've already told you most of it."

"You've told me a lot." I was being ironical. "Except what I want to know. Which is how did you know I'd take it on? You'd even booked a ticket in my name at the theater."

His finger touched the sovereigns and pushed them towards me.

"Mr Sotiriou," he said. "Relations with a professional such as yourself are a delicate affair. On my side, as client, I've taken care to find out to what sort of person I am entrusting the business that I've asked you to undertake. On your side, all you really need to know is what my name is, where I live, whether or not what I've asked of you is within your capabilities—and how you'll be paid. Am I putting it correctly?"

"You're putting it perfectly well. But I should tell you in advance… if I see that your musician is getting me mixed up in dubious situations or if he's involved in anything illegal, if I don't like him or there's anything odd about him—if he's one of those men who suffer… then I won't go on."

"Men who suffer? But of course he's suffering, my dear sir, who isn't suffering these days?"

"I meant something different," I told him, and explained. "Am I making myself clear?"

"Absolutely. Your expenses will be fully covered and your fee—in the same currency—will, if you bring everything that needs to be done to a successful conclusion, be substantial. You cannot imagine how substantial. Not to mention my own gratitude… As far as I can calculate at this point, your fee at the end of this business will be… eighty—No! A hundred. A hundred coins."

"A hundred sovereigns!"

I stood up. A hundred gold sovereigns… could such a thing be possible! Even in his best days Lamera had never made so much money in New York—not even in that case concerning the judge and the under-age girl… A whole fortune and what a fortune! I could not only pay Balomenos the rent owed, I could buy the apartment if I wanted.

"Who are you, Mr Agathos?" I asked, and leaned

forward with my elbows on the desk, trying to make him out.

He didn't answer. He remained silent and motionless in the armchair, I couldn't even hear him breathing. Then, after a little while, I began to distinguish his face in the dark. It was as if some light from somewhere was shining on it—or better, as if the light came from within the man himself. Suddenly I could see him perfectly clearly.

He wasn't anyone that I knew. Yet his face did seem familiar. Where had I seen it and when? The features of this elderly gentleman were somehow known to me, I recognized his expression, his smile, his eyes. Ah yes, those eyes... deep blue... Eyes that you'd never forget once you'd seen them.

But in spite of this, Mr Agathos, as I had to admit, was a complete stranger to me.

6

____

Georgiou Gennadiou Street

That wasn't all. For hardly had we finished coming to an agreement and talking about the practical details when Mr Agathos disappeared. He slipped out without me realizing it and was gone. I didn't hear either his footsteps or the door closing. I got up, and the very next moment the old man had vanished into thin air.

With five gold sovereigns in my pocket everything seemed a lot easier. A visit to Piraeus with Mimis would find us some food—some of those tantalizing things that people who were in a position to pay for them could often find. I locked up the office without delay and went down to the street, groping for each step in the darkness. I had shoved the coins into the waistband of my pants beneath my belt and could feel them pressing against me as I went down the stairs. A whole treasure of my own! As well as the prospect of earning an even larger one, as my client assured me—all I needed to do was follow his instructions.

There are people who are somehow imposing, no doubts about them cross your mind, as soon as you set eyes on them you know you're dealing with someone who is serious and reliable, someone who will behave decently, who will stand by you and support you. The ideal client. The perfect client. Something more too: a sort of employer in reality.

Come to think of it, from the very first moment I'd christened Mr Agathos "the Big Boss" in my mind. That was the impression he'd made on me. His age, his mysterious occupation, the gold he carried on him and his even more mysterious instructions combined to make up a picture of a person who somehow, inexplicably, managed to keep himself at a remove from all the torments and troubles of ordinary people and to spend a fortune on caprices. Unless, that is, there was more to it than met the eye.

Well then, the Big Boss had ordered me to put on my best suit and go to the Olympia Theater. During the interval (or before the performance began?) I had to identify his protégé who was urgently in need of protection and care… God only knows, everyone in Athens was urgently in need of protection and care… It was a mystery to me just how I'd manage to do this. How does one pick out a stranger from an entire audience, and anyway, why should a musician from the orchestra be in the foyer and not backstage? And how would I get into conversation and become friendly with him when I didn't even know what he looked like?

I knew various tricks of the trade, of course. However, it's one thing to be watching someone, concealed in the shadows of night and secrecy, and quite another thing to walk straight up to him and start chatting. It's one thing to be a detective and quite another to be a master of ceremonies. And anyway, what do you talk about to a person who is a musician?

With these and other thoughts in my mind, I left Gamvetta Street and turned towards Fidiou Street. On the corner of Emmanuel Benaki Street I saw a light in Yannakopoulos' pharmacy. No store was allowed to remain open during the blackout, nor at that period were there any emergency pharmacies on duty at night. Old man Yannakopoulos was a freemason, in other words a person intelligent enough to avoid trouble: if his store was open at this hour, then there had to be a reason for it.

As I walked past he was standing in the doorway. At the back of the store I caught sight of Thanasis, his assistant dispenser, who used to give everyone in the neighborhood their injections—in the old days, that is, when the illnesses people suffered from could be cured by injections. The metal grille that folded open and shut concertina-wise was pulled back; the pharmacist, who seemed to be expecting me to pass by, beckoned.

"Ah, Mr Sotiriou!" he greeted me aloud.

He didn't seem frightened—so presumably he wasn't breaking the law. Or had I perhaps failed to notice some new announcement about pharmacies?

"I was expecting you."

Thanasis also nodded to me in greeting. There was a dim light in the background and the shadows of the old glass-fronted cupboards and the phials bearing the names of mysterious drugs faded into the semi-darkness of the high ceiling. On the carved ledge on top of the cupboards a stuffed sparrowhawk crouched threateningly over customers' heads.

"You'd better come inside," said old man Yannakopoulos.

"Are you open, Mr Mitsos?" I asked. "Aren't you afraid?"

"Bah, Thanasis and I have been sorting something out, we got hold of a little sulfamide this afternoon and we've been doing some stock-taking… We're just closing, we're closed."

He didn't seem very sure of what he was saying, I noticed. And his assistant was looking elsewhere.

"The Authorities are very strict about pharmacies," said Yannakopoulos. "They have priority for anything we've got. And what they don't use themselves they sell on the black… I'd like to have a word with you…"

With his hooked nose and the pouches under his eyes, he resembled an owl. I hadn't seen him in the store for a long time. It was his forty-year-old son Ippokratis who held sway there on a regular daily basis. And he didn't look all that hungry either. Maybe it was the sulfamide that nourished him, or perhaps some other potion which Thanasis pounded in the mortar in the dispensary behind the curtain.

"I've got something for you," he murmured in my ear. "Your client requested complete confidentiality."

I took a step backwards.

"*Your client*," he repeated.

And as he said it his hand touched mine as it hung by my side and I realized that he'd slipped a small sachet into my palm. He gave my hand a little squeeze as if warning me to keep it closed and not to let his assistant see.

"Have something to eat before you take it," he now went on in a more professional tone, "for it's a powerful drug. Dissolve it in a glass of water and drink it down in one gulp. Don't hold it in your mouth, it doesn't taste very pleasant. And don't worry if you feel unwell for about half an hour... The results... are guaranteed!"

"What does it... what client?" I stammered, like a schoolboy who hasn't done his homework.

He gave me a penetrating look, with the air of someone who's trying to summon up all his powers of memory in order to avoid saying what shouldn't be said—a name.

"Your client," he repeated in a low voice. "The client you saw tonight."

"Mr Aga..."

"Well done! Off you go now, it's late and the patrol will be passing any minute."

His assistant, silent till then, opened his mouth and said, "Goodbye, Mr Angel. Take care."

I don't let circumstances get me the better of me. Not even

other people's unwillingness to give explanations—the permanent bane of my profession. Yet without knowing how it happened, here I was, standing in the street holding a little paper sachet containing a drug which I hadn't asked for and which, as far as I knew, I didn't need. Behind me the light went off. The pharmacist and his assistant began to close up the store hastily, ready to slip off into the night. How did they know that I'd be passing by, and at such a late hour too, how come they were expecting me? And what if I'd taken a different route, what would the old man have done then? Would he have brought the sachet to me at home?

I walked up Fidiou Street reflecting on all this. In the atmosphere of illegality in which we all lived, I thought that the paper sachet—if it really came from Mr Agathos—would have some address written on it, some telephone number or name or last-minute instruction which he'd forgotten to give me. But all the same, the fact that a third person from the neighborhood was involved in all this made me extremely anxious.

On the corner of Fidiou and Gennadiou Street I caught sight of a shadow dragging itself along the wall outside the Hellenic Conservatoire. I couldn't tell if it was a man or a woman. What was he doing there at this time of night? He raised his foot and seemed about to step up onto the marble steps of the old building, beneath the sign with the lyre and the ancient Greek writing. But his foot remained there in mid-air, as if his joints were finding it hard to execute this normal movement. Then, slowly, the foot descended. And after the foot the whole body followed with a dull, wooden thud, then lay there motionless. He'd fallen onto his back so that in the faint light I was able to get a look at him: he was an old man in rags, with a white beard that pointed skywards as if indicating the direction his soul had taken as it left him. I'd seen a lot of other people coming to an end like this, but never so close to home, never in this neighborhood. I shuddered as if he'd dropped dead in my own hall. If I stood at my window, I'd be able to see him all night long until the cart came to collect him in the morning.

I hurried to the entrance of our building. It was indeed high time to do so, for already I could hear the regular footsteps of the Italian patrol approaching. I unlocked the heavy iron door, pushed it open and limped up to the first floor.

The first thing I did was to take Mr Agathos' sovereigns out of my waistband. Then I made straight for the kitchen, took the lid off the saucepan containing the chickpeas that I'd cooked a few days ago in order to eat them gradually, one spoonful at a time; I now swallowed two spoonfuls as I stood there, keeping them in my mouth for as long as possible to savor them. A sense of optimism had overcome the fear of hunger. Then I soaked a piece of cotton wool in methylated spirits: my nightcap was going to be an infusion of sage. Zisis had gathered it on Mount Hymettos and I'd acquired it in exchange for two boxes of American wax matches. I still had two boxes left.

Before I lit the cotton wool on the marble surface in the

kitchen, I struck a match to have a look at the round coins reposing in my hand. Then I went into the bedroom, opened the drawer where I kept my underclothes and hid the sovereigns inside a folded sock. Now I needed the hot drink in order to relax and to be able to close my eyes without seeing the ghost of the dead man a few feet from my front door—or the extraordinary figure of the Big Boss. The blue flame illuminated the kitchen faintly. The faucet over the sink invariably dripped, the gas stove loomed blackly before me.

I stood there with my eyes half-closed holding the little pot over the cotton wool until I felt the bubbles beginning to rise in the water. I threw in a measure of sage, stirred it and poured it into a glass. And the bits of herb too—you'd drink the hot drink and then you'd chew the bitter leaves and stalks in order to provide something more substantial than the liquid alone. What with the chickpeas, my stomach would have something to get to work on. I pulled the pharmacist's paper from my pocket automatically. I unfolded it and, before the blue flame died down completely, looked to see if there was anything written on it—and what was inside it. It was an ordinary little sachet containing a golden-colored powder. I bent down to smell it. It didn't smell of anything. As if hypnotized, without thinking, I tipped it into my glass of tisane.

It's true, I can't have been quite in my right mind that night: all the unusual things that had happened hadn't made much impression on me, although they certainly should have. It was partly that those days were so nightmarish: everything was muddled up together, body and mind were assaulted by such a deluge of new experiences and new disasters that everything seemed to be unfolding as if in a dream. I was about to swallow a powder which might have been gold dust but which could just as easily have been poison or plaster from the wall.

I threw the crumpled sachet into the sink and, holding the glass in both hands, made my way to the dining room.

I always left the shutters up in this room in order to have some light. I never used it as a dining room. I ate in the kitchen and before getting up would reach over and put my dirty plate and cutlery into the sink, to be washed when there was a pile of them. The dining room, like the living room, was at the front of the house. It served me as both wardrobe and storeroom. In it I kept various things from my old New York house, still packed up just as I'd brought them from America, as well as Lamera's files which I hadn't wanted to leave behind and the files of the few cases I'd undertaken during my years in Athens. I hadn't got over the fear produced by the fire in New York and didn't want to keep papers in the office.

I drank the tisane in small sips although it tasted foul and I gazed across the road to the old Christomanos house on the corner of Fidiou Street, without letting my glance stray to the steps of the Conservatoire where the unknown man had given up the ghost a short while earlier. The old palm trees in the garden of the abandoned mansion slept motionless like strange, disproportionate Corinthian capitals. The fallen-in roofs of the stables that looked onto

Gennadiou Street had once harbored the erotic activities of innumerable cats. Now, however, most of them had starved to death and those that remained—too weak to run—were easily caught and ended up in cooking pots as part of the extraordinarily inventive cuisine that the Hunger had brought to the city.

In the deathly silence of the street I heard a thumping in the apartment upstairs, as if they were moving furniture or something heavy, then the sound of the wooden shutter being lowered at a window. My neighbors, the Kanellis couple, were also awake—perhaps they were having some evening party and wanted to put on the lights in the living room; they often had guests who'd stay until dawn, waiting for the end of the curfew in order to return home. Then there was silence once more.

These two lawyers, Mr and Mrs Kanellis, invariably passed me on the stairs or at the front door without saying a word, as if I were invisible. For them I was an enemy twice over: a policeman (stool pigeon was what they called me) and the tenant of the apartment they'd been obliged to leave under pressure from Balomenos. Mr Pavlos was tall and thin with a receding hairline and round spectacles for short-sightedness. She was smaller, with a round face, and appeared to be the same age as her husband. But in spite of the full thirty years concealed beneath her coat and skirt and her professional lawyer's air, there was something girlish about her. She was one of those women whose charm is only revealed when you look at them a second time. And, something told me, she was probably sexually insatiable: a maenad who'd do honor to any bed. Since she'd never given me any encouragement, not even a formal neighborly "Good morning," I used to stand in silence and let her pass, raising my hat to her. I dare say she privately used to mock the lovelorn stool pigeon who played at chivalry.

The husband's glance, I have to say, was more vitriolic than the wife's. Luckily we didn't often run into each other on the stairs, we kept different hours. He always got up early and left for the law courts; I'd got into the habit of getting up late and leaving for the office even later, in the manner of shopkeepers into whose stores customers never venture. When I came back home at night to go to bed I'd often see their lights and, as I unlocked my door, I'd hear voices and laughter, lively conversations and arguments coming from upstairs. But at other strange hours I also used to hear a low voice rhythmically declaiming verse in the midst of an eerie silence that frightened me and that made the street seem like a scene in some movie which you've started watching in the middle. These were the times when my neighbor read or recited poems to his guests as they sat in silence and listened. Once I'd put my ear to their door and heard a whole poem, but I didn't understand a word of it. I was amazed that so many people apparently had understood it, for the ohs and ahs and bravos were plentiful.

I can remember my impression quite clearly. I say this now, when I've changed so much since those days when I was merely a foolish American, a boy still young, not yet thirty, who hadn't learned very many of life's lessons. Today I can describe the Kanellis' living room and maybe even the poems that they used to recite. Yet out of a sense of honesty I prefer to write more or less as I would have written at that time, if I'd kept notes of my experiences or if I'd been able to do then what I can do now.

Suddenly I felt a sharp pain in my stomach which made me double up, gasp for breath and sit down quickly on the divan against the wall that served as a sofa. My stomach often hurt, but the ache that's due to hunger is of a different kind. This pain was as if a vial of poison had been broken open and released into my entrails. And it didn't stop there. It grew stronger and spread to my legs, my chest, then to my back, until it felt as if my spine were being convulsed to the point of snapping. I couldn't speak or get out a sound—I was gasping like a fish out of water who knows that if this situation continues a few seconds longer he'll die.

"That's it! That's it!" I heard myself cry voicelessly. "It's the sachet of powder—old man Yannakopoulos has poisoned me… Mr Agathos has poisoned me! I knew it, I knew it, yet like a fool I trusted a swindler who came along and filled my head with vapors and my pocket with five gold sovereigns that are quite likely fakes… He said it himself, he said it! I didn't pay as much attention as I should have. He said he'd been in America… Which means he's the Sicilian's creature, it was he who sent him, he learned where I was and sent him, his executioner, to put an end to me…"

Then all of a sudden there was a buzzing in my ears and the pain passed as abruptly as it had started, without leaving any of that weakness or listlessness that you generally feel when you've just been through a crisis of this kind. I got up and tried my legs. They supported me. I took a deep breath. Neither my chest nor my stomach nor my guts hurt at all. Then I had a good look at the glass I was still gripping in my hands (amazing it hadn't broken!) and decided not to drink a single sip more… Old man Yannakopoulos had said that I might feel bad for a short while but that I shouldn't be frightened by it. I hadn't had time to be frightened. I'd been preparing to meet my Maker!

A slight breeze stirred the palm trees in the Christomanos garden. Shadows were moving against the wall opposite. I could hear voices speaking Italian. I turned and could make out the glossy black feathers on the helmets of the patrol in front of the Conservatoire steps. Curiosity won the day. I stood on tiptoe but all I could see was the soldiers.

I opened the balcony door and went out without making a sound. If the corpse was still there (and it must be) it wasn't visible, being hidden by their boots. The Italians were joking, talking among themselves, then addressing the dead man—what a magnificent joke! And one suited to their blustering character. I knew them well: they're nothing but shitbags, the whole pack of them—unless, that is, they come creeping up behind you in the dark with a knife. And now we had them here. I was always seeing them and hearing them all over Athens. Suddenly it seemed intolerable, quite intolerable. I stood on the parapet of the balcony without the slightest fear that they might see me, trying to put my head as far out as possible to see what was going on. What if the man I'd taken for dead was still alive? What if he was now dying slowly under the Macaronis' crude jokes?

And then something happened which for a few seconds I didn't really take in. Still holding the empty glass with the remains of the tisane in it, I found myself floating above the tiled floor of the balcony, then further away from it, directly over the street. I now had the privileged view I'd been seeking. And I could see the dead body and a damp stain spreading over the pavement. Not blood, it was some other bodily fluid which made the Italians hold their noses and yell at the old man who'd died of hunger "*Puzzi, puzzi*" ("you stink, you stink"). Then suddenly I became aware that I was seeing things which wouldn't have been possible from my balcony. I looked down and saw below me not the balcony floor but the dark asphalt of Gennadiou Street. I froze. How had I come to be over the void? Was I falling? No, I was not falling. I hung there like a ghost, like a spirit, like the angel of the Lord watching the sufferings of mortals.

Instantly the thought flashed through my mind that from this incredible position, breaking all the laws of physics, I might not be able to return to the balcony when I wanted to. The terror of this idea paralyzed my hands, the glass slipped from them and shattered with a loud crash on the sidewalk.

The Italians jumped around with lightning speed, their pistols and machine guns at the ready. The solitude and darkness scared them: someone concealed in the shadows of the narrow street had just thrown something. It would only be a moment before they'd look up, scanning the buildings at first-floor and second-floor height, searching for the culprit. This was the height at which I was now hovering motionless.

I contracted my muscles so strongly that my whole body hurt and attempted to dive back onto the balcony. But, as if the air around me had the density of water and was holding me up, all this movement did was to make me rise higher and even higher, like an airplane whose pilot manipulates the flaps on the wings in order to gain height. Three floors up, four floors up, then the attic, then the flat roof. If the Italians raised their eyes to where I'd been a moment earlier they wouldn't see a thing. I saw them, though, tiny-looking from my present altitude, and I listened to their voices. They wouldn't bother to look up to roof level since the upper part of the building was indistinct in the darkness of the night. They turned back to the corpse, gave it a kick, and set off once more on their patrol, clearly preferring the downhill slope of Fidiou Street to the narrow darkness of Gennadiou Street.

7

What effect the sachet had

I'm dreaming, was my first thought. My body had risen weightless into the air, helped by the movements I'd made, like swimming; the cold night air blew chill on my cheeks and ruffled my hair. My heart was beating wildly.

For me, who all these wretched years had been dragging my crippled leg along, it was like a wholly unexpected, magic cure. I'm flying, I thought. Like a bird—like an angel.

The nocturnal sky over Athens was full of stars. The cold that came down from the north was piercing. The city lay still and silent; only the clothes hung out to dry on some washing line flapped as the wind gained strength. To my right, the long and narrow roof of the church of Zoodochos Pigi, with its rusty grey tiles, resembled the spine of some sleeping animal lying in drugged torpor, indifferent to the misery all around and the cold. I could make out the palm trees in its courtyard, planted around a small fountain decorated with shells that symbolized the life-giving source of the church's name. In the bell tower I saw the bells whose undulating rhythm obstinately and methodically sounded the hours, the half-hours and the quarters (you could hear them just as clearly from the office on Gamvetta Street), and called the faithful to services or tolled for some hurried funeral—the latter being more common these days. In the old days, mingled with the bells that rang for vespers, you could hear in the silence the monotone voices from the Byzantine music class at the Conservatoire.

Now, after midnight, everything was quiet. Everything, that is, except the beating of my heart. The patrol had left, Fidiou Street was deserted once more, the body of the old man still lay in its awkward position on the steps.

I had to go back home. I'd left the balcony door open. I didn't have my keys in my pocket, otherwise I would have gone down the back steps in the light-well and let myself in by the kitchen door. If I rang one of the bells, would they let me in or would they be scared? On the ground floor, the service door used to put the garbage out on the sidewalk was locked. Mrs Leni, the concierge, had the only key to it; and she slept in the little ground-floor apartment in the backyard of the next-door building to the west of ours. It was clear what was going to happen: my body knew before my mind and was already getting prepared: I was going to fly again. I would try and it would happen, this was certain.

The drug... ah, yes, the drug which old man

Yannakopoulos had given me, the parting present ordered by the Big Boss… There was a conspiracy somewhere here, a piece of trickery of the first order… but what? I stood on the parapet of the roof and gazed down without fear. I stretched out my arms. The street gaped like the mouth of a well which gets narrower as it goes down, a funnel ready to suck me in. I flapped my arms. At once I felt the great resistance of the air. With my first movements I had lifted off from the parapet, the tips of my toes searching for it. All fear disappeared. I was flying.

I turned in the air so that I was facing the roof, about two or three feet from the wall, my legs stretched out behind me like a bird's tail, I rose a bit higher then let myself lose height again. After which, sure now of my powers, I began to swim down through the air, floor by floor. Most of the wooden shutters were lowered, only in Balomenos' apartment were they up.

When I reached my own apartment I touched down lightly and silently on the balcony. I've got wings! I thought. Even if I hadn't seen anything reflected in the windowpanes of the building, even if I hadn't observed any changes in my body, it was nevertheless certain. I might not be able to see them but I had them.

And there was no doubt whatsoever: the pharmacist's potion was responsible. Old man Yannakopoulos may not have had a clue about it. The Big Boss was clearly a wizard, a fakir, a conjuror, a miracle-worker, a genie—at any rate someone who bore no relation at all to this godforsaken place and these wretched times. I turned on the light in the bedroom. I examined myself carefully, front and back, in the full-length mirror in the wardrobe. There was nothing: no wings, and no tail either. My face looked just the way I'd last seen it when I shaved that morning, my cheeks sunken, dark rings under my eyes, my nose slightly crooked as always, my teeth yellow from lack of cleaning. Some angel!

I pulled out the drawer with my underclothes in it to check that what I remembered of the earlier part of the evening had at least really happened. The wings and the flight to the roof and back might well be fantasies—well, let them be so, hunger gives rise to strange visions. But the sovereigns I needed to hold in my palm again, to feel once more the weight that is so disproportionate to their size and which always makes gold seem alive.

When I'd done this, I sat down in exhaustion on the unmade divan and put my head in my hands. It wasn't the first time I'd sat like this—I'd done the same thing the evening after I returned home to Queens from the hospital on Staten Island. I'd sat on the bed then too, though perched on the edge so as not to make my wound more painful, and I'd reflected. A heavy door had closed on my life so far; it would never open again. I was at the beginning of a passage whose end was unknown to me; everything had to start again from scratch, my role had changed, the goal of my life could no longer be the happiness and fulfillment that every human being knows. I was handicapped, condemned to wander forever on the fringes of normal life, hiding my pain and my loneliness so that no one, neither man nor woman, should ever guess at them, even if their aim was to try to soften them for me.

The only time I'd ever been to an opera was with Freddy. Freddy was a fanatic opera lover; his greatest happiness was the fact that he made enough money to be able to buy tickets to the Opera, which was then on Broadway and 39th Street. So I'd seen a strange scene there which had remained engraved in my memory. At that time I was utterly in love with Lauretta and, like everyone who's in love, wasn't interested in anything that didn't have as its central subject love and sexual happiness. It was a German opera. In one scene a hideous dwarf comes in and starts leaping around on the rocks by a river in which three blonde ladies are bathing—they were not very attractive, wearing pink and blue gossamer drapery on top of flesh-colored bodystockings to make it look as if they were naked. After they natter on and on for hours, sometimes the dwarf and sometimes the fairies, he becomes angry and gives chase to them. They make eyes at him but when he starts to be interested they run off and begin to mock him and swear at him for being a dwarf and ugly. In the end, in fury, he rushes forward and steals a ball made of golden foil that the fairies are guarding as jealously as their maidenhead and—as Freddy explained, who was shivering and bulging-eyed with excitement—the dwarf then renounces and curses love and all its joys. From henceforth, he says, the sole purpose and joy of his life will be power and wealth (the golden foil ball)—*May Love*, he cries, *be accursed!*

Neither the music nor all the running around on the stage had made me shiver bodily the way Freddy was shivering beside me. But, I have to admit, the music the orchestra played when the dwarf pronounced his curse froze me in my place. After that the blah, blah, blah began again and within ten minutes I'd fallen into the sweetest sleep in the world in my comfortable seat.

It was the music played by the orchestra then that was filling my ears again as I sat that night on the edge of my bed in my little apartment in my old neighborhood, with my head in my hands.

Except that while the dwarf seized the golden foil ball and ran off squealing with happiness, I left at night to board a small freighter which had been found with the help of someone who had good contacts in the docks. My possessions were winched aboard, my cabin was just big enough for a bunk on which to lie down, and the journey to Piraeus took an age. And when I was cast up on dry land once more, I found myself face to face with a new place and people whose like I'd never seen before. The only thing I recognized was the language I heard spoken all around me. No familiar faces; no familiar objects.

And now once again I was faced with a new reality, just as unfamiliar but not as despairing. Horror and the fear of the unknown had now been replaced by a lightheadedness and joy similar to that you might feel if you suddenly won the sweepstakes or lottery, or if an inheritance came your way from an unexpected quarter. You hear music again, the sky is full of light, everything seems to be smiling at you in friendship, vouchsafing you a new existence, a Promised Land that is opening its doors wide and inviting you to take your first steps into it.

I could fly, goddamn it, I could fly!

The lame man is no longer lame, or if he is it doesn't matter. I had discovered the angelic destination for which my existence was intended. From now on, nothing would be the same. No misfortune could henceforth touch me. No fear could paralyze me.

I got up, burning with fever. I ran to the kitchen and devoured all the chickpeas left in the saucepan. This was the end of fear, this was the end of hunger and misery. In the morning I would fly—or rather, no, I wouldn't fly; I should only use my new ability in cases of great need or danger. I would go down to Piraeus for supplies, as I'd planned to do. With five sovereigns in your pocket many things become possible. And then I'd come back home, put my supplies away safely and get myself ready like a lord for the first night of *Pagliacci*. The Big Boss could play whatever tune he felt like on his fiddle. I would dance!

8

The first consequences of flying

I must have fallen asleep with my clothes on. I wasn't aware of the moment when I drifted off. It's quite likely that several of the thoughts and feelings that stirred me came to me in my sleep, even though I thought I was still awake. The plus side was that I woke up fairly early, feeling refreshed and in a good mood, without a trace of the anxiety that usually grabbed hold of me as soon as I opened my eyes. You'd have thought I'd slept for a whole year. I got up, shaved and made myself another glass of sage tea for breakfast. I gulped down a few raisins that I kept stowed away in a tin in the kitchen and began to plan out our shopping expedition to Piraeus. Before doing all this, however, I made sure that Mr Agathos' sovereigns were still there.

When I'd got dressed I phoned Mimis. I was quite willing to lend him as much as he needed to buy his share too, always supposing we managed to track down a bit of oil or coffee or sugar, a handful of dried beans—all the things that had disappeared off the face of the earth.

As I was leaving to go and meet Mimis, I had another unexpected encounter. Mrs Kanellis was going down the twisting stairs, wearing a trilby with a narrow brim and carrying a briefcase under her arm. As I'd already set foot on the stairs while she was still at the top of the flight leading to my floor, I stood back chivalrously for her to pass. She looked as if she was in a hurry, no doubt hastening off to some courtroom or to the Public Prosecutor whose office was just down the road from us, on Fidiou Street opposite the German Archaeological Mission. "Good morning, Mrs Marika," I said.

Being in a good mood transforms people. With Agathos' sovereigns in my pocket and the intoxication of my nocturnal flight still pulsing through every single tissue in my body, I risked giving her a wide smile as I raised my hat. To her and her husband a private detective and a policeman were one and the same thing. I didn't particularly mind that they looked away when they met me on the stairs or at the door of no. 2; it was the fact that across her face passed a grimace, no, not quite a grimace but a spasm of something, of deep disgust—this was what upset me. I'd never bothered them and I didn't care whether they were communists or followers of Confucius. I would never have raised a finger to hurt them—even though I saw Marika Kanellis in my dreams almost every night, and specially in summer, when from the wide-open windows at night—and often in the midday siesta hour too—her breathless mewings would reach my ears.

It would seem that my sudden impulse to greet her—in spite of the fact that we'd never until then exchanged the time of day—hadn't gone down well. Was it my manner that was to blame? The happy smile on my face? Whatever it was, she clearly found it offensive. Instead of walking past me as usual, she stopped short and looked me up and down with eyes that flashed icy tongues of fire. "These are times of great happiness for people like you, Mr Sotiriou, aren't they?" she said.

If we leave out her intention of insulting me, this statement might not have had anything personal about it. Yet I, in the enthusiasm born of all that had happened the day before, had wanted for some reason to transmit something of my own good mood to this lovely young woman. Who knows, maybe at bottom I was thinking that I might be able to help this couple who were having a very hard time of it. I felt like a little god. So instead of stopping to consider what she meant by these sharp, stinging words, I took a small step backwards to give her a better view and, with a barely perceptible flapping movement of my shoulders, rose a few inches above the marble floor, smiled broadly and advanced towards her.

What could she have been able to make out in the semi-darkness of the stairs? That I'd taken off and flown before her eyes? What is certain is that anything done by someone we don't like is taken down and used against him. My smile and my movement towards her—albeit imperceptible—were the last straw. Her reaction was lightning quick. She raised her hand and gave me a slap on the face that resounded through the stairwell like a cough in an empty church. Before I could ask what I'd done to deserve it, she turned and ran down the stairs and out of the door. Even today I don't quite understand how it was that her slap, rather than causing me pain or sorrow, felt like the caress I'd been dreaming of all these months. I put my hand to my flaming cheek and touched it as if I were resting my hand on hers.

I had acquired a real relationship with Marika Kanellis, infinitely more substantial than the silent glances (mine guilty, hers full of contempt) that we'd previously been exchanging at the front door or outside on the sidewalk of Gennadiou Street. Look at it this way, when a woman has slapped you it's the same as if she's slept in your bed: she can't pretend anymore that she doesn't know you. In the old days in Astoria, it had happened not once or twice but countless times that the sweetest caresses and the most precious pleasures had been granted after a slap: rather as if this was a final farewell to the hitherto impregnable armor of the haughty Irish girl or the Jewish beauty who you'd thought would never even deign to look at you.

The marks left by her fingers were still showing on my face when I met Papachrysanthou on the corner of Harilaou Trikoupi and Panepistimiou Street. But if he noticed he didn't say anything. In any case, we had our collars raised and our hats pulled down low on our foreheads to protect our faces and ears from the morning chill.

"What on earth's got into you so early in the morning, Hephaistos?" he asked. "Woke up hungry, did you?"

I explained briefly that I'd got a strange client who was paying in advance and generously—suspicious, all right, but in times like this who'd care if it were the devil himself.

The terminus for the gazogen[7] to Piraeus was outside the Eye Hospital. It was still early and the cold was biting. Everyone says that winter was a harsh one. Not quite as bad as '41, but all the same one of the cruelest winters Athens had known. Personally I think we felt the cold more because we were hungry. In another age, the central boulevard would have been bustling with people at this time of day; now it was half past eight, almost nine o'clock, and the place was deserted. The few people who had come out were walking along at a rapid pace, keeping close to the walls of the buildings to avoid the cold wind, bundled up in overcoats and fedoras and caps pulled down low, their collars turned up and their hands plunged deep in their pockets. Mute ghosts who made an appearance as if they were forced to do so, because it was morning, because there was work to be done and obligations: everyone without exception had come out in search of

7. Gazogens, from French gazogène, were buses, which due to the fuel shortage in WWII were modified to run on the gas produced from wood-burning furnaces attached to the vehicles.

food or to undertake some other activity whose end purpose had to do with the same problem.

The old man of last night was no longer on the steps of the Conservatoire. The Municipality was never usually so quick: it must have been the German guard at the Archaeological Mission—the fine building on the corner of Fidiou and Harilaou Trikoupi Street—who'd ordered them to remove him fast in order not offend those who lived in or visited their mansion. However, at the entrance to the Civil Servants' Arcade you could see the feet of all the people who'd spent the night sleeping in its shelter, wrapped in cardboard and old newspapers tied around them with string for warmth. You looked at them and didn't know how many would be able to get up, when the time came, and gather their things together and move off to another spot.

Mimis wanted to know more about my rich client. But no matter how hard I tried, I couldn't convince him that I wasn't hiding something important from him. Listening to myself speak, I could hardly blame him. I knew very little about Mr Agathos. And the amount he'd given me as a retainer was so improbably large that it was perfectly reasonable for Mimis to suspect I was keeping something from him.

"Watch out," he said, "I can see you getting into bad trouble."

What would he say if he knew all the things I hadn't told him: about the old pharmacist's little sachet of powder and my flutterings up and down the outside of our apartment building?

"At any rate, Hephaistos, you're looking remarkably cheerful," he said as we walked along. "Stopped limping, have you?"

"Bah… chance would be a fine thing," I answered, and began walking with a more pronounced limp than before. All the same, it's true—I did feel better.

For without me realizing it, my new skills were helping me walk, like an invisible walking stick. Mimis held back a couple of paces on purpose and watched me.

"You're flying today, my lad," he said. "Seems to me it won't be long before I'll have to christen you Hermes, old pal!"

In the past too there'd been days when I limped less. Cold and damp made my bad leg worse, while warm weather helped it. Today it was bitterly cold yet I wasn't in any pain. Mimis, who knew only a part of my story, felt for me with all his heart. But then Mimis felt for everyone.

9

———

In Piraeus

The gazogen turned onto Panepistimiou Street and puffed uphill towards Syntagma Square. A pale sun had risen above Mount Hymettus, which showed misty-blue and bare above the rooftops. On the tiled roof of the Eye Hospital black crows were preening themselves and casting sideways glances at the asphalt surface of the road in case they spied anything there that would make it worth their while to launch themselves into the air. I looked at these birds and felt a secret happiness: I too… I too could do what they did, could stretch out my arms and fly. This was my secret weapon, the hidden essence of the new existence that had begun for me the night before and had reached its culmination in the morning with Marika Kanellis' slap outside my front door. The studs marking the pedestrian crossings at the street corners shone like pieces of molten gold… and Mr Agathos' sovereigns were warmed by the warmth of my body. How much had

Mimis noticed of all this, I wondered. Certainly he'd seen the change in my gait—and maybe in my whole mood generally.

He leaned over and murmured to me, "I'll never forget what you're doing today, Hephaistos." I muttered that it was nothing, that he himself would have done the same, and went on looking out at the street. A city of ghosts, it seemed to be, who moved around slowly. In front of the Bank of Greece the two Italian guards were wearing black capes against the cold and their cock feathers stirred in the faint breeze. A skeletal dog emerged from Edouardou Lo Street and dragged himself along past the guards. I imagined he'd take a few more steps and then collapse and die.

In the gazogen all the passengers were of necessity mute. The noise of the engine was so loud that no voices could be heard; we were sitting near the boiler, plunged like divers in the depths of a tank into the pandemonium of the pistons that transferred power to the differential. Opposite us a ragged man was opening and closing his mouth in prayers that no one could hear. Some madman, no doubt. But in those days people did behave strangely.

Every so often the gazogen slowed down, creaking and groaning. Some people got off, others got on. In front of the Army Fund building three out of the seven passengers got off. Each time it slowed (it rarely stopped completely) the noise abated for a moment and the voice of the ragged man opposite us became more distinct: "O Lord, save Thy people..."

"Prayers as a weapon against the invaders!" commented Mimis beside me, in a low voice. "By the way, a cousin of mine left yesterday for the mountains…," he added meaningfully.

"Even the prayers of madmen are heard," I said out of the blue, without knowing in the least where this idea came from.

"Yes," mocked Mimis, "the Lord is good."

He used the word *agathos*. I turned and looked at him, blushing like someone whose secret has been dragged out into the open. What an expression for him to use! All of a sudden the image of the Big Boss sprang to mind. Could it possibly be, I wondered, that I'd had the honor? In what way would that other "big boss" have differed, supposing that he was moved to come down and visit someone? And would the consequences of such a visit really have been so very different?

"I seem to think I'm going a bit crazy too," I said out loud to Mimis.

At Syntagma the traffic was denser. In front of us, the trees and decorative shrubs in the huge containers of the garden in the middle of the square; on our right, the red German flags on the King George Hotel where the Kommandatur was situated. A row of carts drawn by donkeys and mangy horses was moving slowly along in front of the monument to the Unknown Soldier—you didn't need much imagination to know what was in them: everyone quickly turned away to face the garden on the other side, the hurrying passers-by, the dim lights of

Zavoritis' café at the bottom of the square and Zacharatos' café on the corner of Stadiou Street, and in the background the rock of the Acropolis.

"Hephaistos," said Papachrysanthou, "I've a feeling we're not going to find anything in Piraeus... not even for the kind of money you've got in your pocket... Don't waste it on rubbish, d'you get me? Know what I mean?"

"We'll find something, I'm sure of it," I replied.

One by one the various districts of Athens passed before our eyes: Amalias Avenue with its old mansions, the Royal Garden, Zappion. In the square in front of the Russian church the Red Cross had set up a soup kitchen beneath a makeshift awning; the line in front of it stretched back until it disappeared around the corner of Filellinon Street. At Hadrian's Gate a truck carrying Italian soldiers had stopped, clouds of steam billowing from its running engine. The driver and another man had opened the hood and were trying to cool the damaged radiator while the soldiers had a cigarette break, laughing and joking with each other.

Syngrou Avenue opened before us. Straight ahead the Saronic Gulf sparkled in the pale sunlight. Small gardens and empty plots came right down to the narrow strip of asphalt, tin chimneys smoked from the little houses in Harokopou, washing was hung out to dry in courtyards and an old woman was hard at work over a wooden washtub resting on two empty gas bottles.

I was drifting in a pleasant daydream in which I was

seeing once again the expression in Marika Kanellis' eyes and feeling my cheek tingle under her sharp slap.

When we got out at the Gounaris Bridge at the top end of the market, the familiar ruins of Piraeus lay before us. From demolished roofs wooden beams and supports stuck out in disorderly tangles, gaping windows opened onto rooms that were no longer there. Closer to the harbor, great chunks of metal protruded from walls, trees and the sidewalk—the remains of the ships that had been bombed in April '41.

The market was closed. All the same, you could make out signs of life behind half-lowered shutters: every so often someone would duck out from under them and emerge, clutching the breast of his overcoat where some package wrapped up in newspaper was secreted. From somewhere came the smell of wood-smoke.

At one of these doorways, an old soap factory, Mimis bent and asked something. A man appeared inside: I could see his dilapidated shoes beneath the shutter. They said whatever it was they had to say and Mimis turned to me.

"Hang on," he told me, "he's going to take us there."

I understood that we were on the track of something and that someone would come with us to show us the way to a place where we'd need an introduction or a password to be admitted.

It was a boy who came out. He can't have been much more than twenty, as pale as whey and with a harelip poorly concealed by a little mustache with its ends trimmed gangster-style. He went on ahead and we followed. We passed the train station and entered the warren of narrow streets full of bodywork repair shops and dealers in sheet metal and corrugated iron. My leg was beginning to hurt again and I lagged behind. Mimis stopped and waited for me to catch up but the boy didn't slow down—he wanted to get this errand over with as fast as possible. We took a right turn. We were in a narrow dead-end lane about fifteen yards long, full of shuttered stores. From one of the doors came the sound of a gramophone. Two male voices were singing a spirited duet with a lively rhythm, about "harems and diamonds." But the record was revolving more and more slowly, the voices were getting deeper, the rhythm faltering. Finally someone lifted the needle and the music stopped.

Our guide pushed open the glass door, covered on the inside with blue paper and sticky tape, and shouted something through it. In the doorway a giant appeared. He was wearing a sailor's cap pushed back above his broad forehead, in the middle of which some old injury had left a deep pit that gaped like a blinded eye. ("Polypheme!" Papachrysanthou murmured at my side.) However, his savage manner soon evaporated. Instead of wasting any time on words, he made a questioning gesture with his huge hands and, on hearing who'd sent us, smiled, revealing a mouth empty of teeth: dimples on his cheeks, a roguish sparkle in his eyes.

"What are you after, lads?"

"You tell us what there is, pal," answered Mimis, and went in first.

This was the way you used to do your shopping in Athens in those days: the shopkeeper didn't ask you what you wanted, you asked him what there was. Everything had its value; if it couldn't be eaten, it might at least be something you could swap for food. This store had once been a butcher's, to judge from the hooks hanging from the wooden walls. It looked as if there hadn't been anything on sale here for months. They kept the delicacies somewhere else.

"Show us the color of your money, bud," said the giant, and Mimis turned to me.

I put my hand in my pocket, took out a sovereign, showed it to him then put it back again. Polypheme seemed to be thinking. A sovereign was worth forty thousand in those days.

"Two okas of oil, half a cheese and one oka of damaged chickpeas," the giant pronounced. "And two cans of jam. That's what there is."

"Cheese?' asked Mimis. "What sort of cheese?"

"From Tyrnavos. Came today, brother-in-law of mine brought it. Three heads. The others have gone already and this one here that's left the priest at St Sophia's asked for. Sell you half if you like."

"Half an oka of oil," I said, "and half of chickpeas. And a can of jam."

"Got any bread?" asked Mimis.

"The Troumba's the place for bread," answered Polypheme. "The whorehouses."

Seeing us look puzzled, he explained without pausing

for breath. "The whores have set their price at a loaf of brown bread or a loaf of white so the Italians turn up loaded with loaves. The girls sell them and buy whatever else they need."

"Fine," said Mimis, "we'll get on over there, won't we, Hephaistos? I'll take a hundred drams of oil and a hundred of cheese. I'll do without the jam, can't be helped…"

"Listen here, my lad," said Polypheme as he opened the meat refrigerator that should have retired long since. "I don't want you sending anyone else along here. The local trade's enough. You only bought stuff 'cos you came from Memas. Got it?"

"Got it," I said.

With our purchases (bottles and cones of newspaper) concealed under our coats and with a fistful of dirty notes bulging in my pocket—the change from the third sovereign which Polypheme had loaded me with—we set off towards the Troumba. Down by the harbor the wind was cutting. The caiques were bobbing up and down, ropes were slapping against masts and the waves were breaking over the quay. Two German warships as well as an Italian one were anchored well out in the deeper water of the harbor, for the wreckage of the bombed ships made it impossible for vessels of any size to come in and moor; over at the other end of the port a freighter was maneuvering alongside the derricks. In front of the church of St Spyridon was another soup kitchen. We jumped into the ramshackle streetcar that came up behind us, hooting and jangling its bell, and got off before St Nicholas—on the corner of Filellinon Street, just opposite Kalapothakis' lumber yard. The guards outside the Port Authority were keeping a careful eye on us from a distance. We turned up our collars and set off down the dirt road leading to the whores' quarter.

You didn't need to look very hard. There were lines outside the brothels: respectable householders were buying their bread. The Italian *pagnotta* was the best you could find anywhere.

"We're too late," I said.

"Don't worry," said Mimis. "We'll go to Stellitsa, she'll fix us up. She'll give us bread, I mean," he added, just in case I'd misunderstood.

We passed Skouze Street and stopped at the second house. A small dark-haired woman, dry as a kipper, enveloped in a coat and an old fur hat, was chasing away the last customers. "I've sold out!" she was yelling. Undaunted, with all the confidence of an old acquaintance, Mimis ran up the steps and put his arm around her waist. She gave him a sour smile and ran her eyes interrogatively over me as I stood there waiting in the street. Mimis signaled me to come in.

The woman closed the door behind us and stood in silence sizing up my friend.

"You've aged, Meems!"

"You've got younger and younger, Stellitsa," he responded. "Having a good time with the macaronis, eh? Monopolising you…"

"What with the hunger, other business is slack," the woman snapped with a dry laugh.

"No Greek's got money to spend these days. We've come for bread, sweetheart, got any you can let us have?"

"Didn't you hear me yelling at the people out there? I've sold out," said Stellitsa.

'Meems' gazed at her without blinking. "What about for us?"

She shrugged. "Who's 'us' when he's at home?"

And she went ahead of us into the room that served as a waiting room for her customers; I don't know why, but it reminded me of a stage-set in some old comedy with its table in the middle and chairs ranged around the walls and its framed pictures and knick-knacks.

"*Me*," said Mimis, behind her.

"Owe you anything do I, Mimis?" And she looked him straight in the eyes.

"No," he said, quietly. "Just from the kindness of your heart…"

"Ha!" Stellitsa laughed harshly. "You crazy old bugger… the kindness of my heart!"

She turned her back on the two of us and disappeared behind a curtain screening off some inner room that had known better days. We heard footsteps on the stairs outside the parlor. A raucous woman's voice called her name. "Stella, we're back, want anything?"

"No," replied the voice we knew.

Then there were more footsteps and a light, girlish voice was singing *"Torn'a Surrientu"* in a perfect Neapolitan accent as she ran upstairs. I turned to Mimis in surprise but he was looking elsewhere.

Then the woman emerged again from behind the curtain and she was holding two loaves. She looked from one of us to the other.

"Who's he?" she asked, thrusting her chin in my direction.

"A brother. He came down here to buy some food and of his goodness brought me with him. He got his hands on a bit of money and wanted to help his friend… he's something better than family."

All of a sudden the face that till now had had a permanent expression of disgust brightened.

"He's dishy," she said casually as if she regarded me simply as a piece of merchandise—the way men talk between themselves about women. "Will you lend me him for a bit?"

"He's not mine to lend," answered Mimis and his face suddenly darkened. "If you fancy him, help yourself."

Stella laughed.

"I like him," she said. "What d'you think, Meems? Nice shoes, nice hat, nice-looking kid. Got a nice fat wallet too, has he?"

A foolish smile rose to my lips. This was the last thing I needed.

"It won't be for money," she said, addressing me directly

this time. "*It'll be for a loaf of bread!* Just like the Italians. You want the bread? You come and get it…"

She had already put one loaf of bread on the table. The other she still had in her hand. As she moved towards the curtain screening the corridor she held it out to me, the way you hold a bone out to a dog when you want it to follow you. I turned and looked at Mimis. He raised his eyebrows and shrugged eloquently. "What can I say? Do as you see fit…"

I could have told her that one loaf was more than enough for us—but we hadn't yet paid for it and there was no way of knowing what she might ask in exchange. The price of a visit to her was well known. Now we were about to learn the price of a loaf of bread.

10

———

The price of chocolate

For reasons that you will very well understand, I prefer to draw a veil over this particular bit of the story. I appeal to the imagination and the pity of anyone reading this book. For even today I can still hear her magpie screeches of laughter. Life hardens people—and I might as well admit that I myself am no angel, in spite of my name. But even the toughest thug on the streets has some tender place that hurts when you squeeze it, that transforms him into a wailing child. Even Stellitsa must have had some weak spot somewhere: once upon a time it might have been Mimis. But if she did have a tender point I couldn't begin to guess where it was. What's for certain is that I earned the loaf of bread not for my worth but for the vast amusement afforded to her by the state in which the Sicilian had left me. Stellitsa, who like most women in her profession lived in the deep desire to castrate every single male in the world, wasn't for a single instant moved to any sympathy or other such feeling; her peals of laughter followed me right onto Filonos Street. Mimis imagined that she was laughing at my lame leg.

"My blood ran cold when I heard her, Hephaistos. The whore! Imagine it! And you just sat there getting an eyeful of her charms without giving her the whack in the face she deserved? Were you scared of her? Mocking a cripple!"

I didn't answer, lost in my own thoughts. As we walked back towards the station I was trying to see whether I still had my miraculous powers. Alas! My body was as heavy as lead. I was limping just as badly as before. Utter despair. The pain in the severed tendon which always tormented me in cold weather had started up again. My eyes filled with tears. As we were walking straight into the north wind I opened them wide to dry them before Mimis, who was continuing to mutter curses against his heartless Stellitsa, should notice.

It seems I'd acquired the angelic powers befitting my name only to lose them again in the room of a cheap whore in the Troumba for a loaf of bread. It was a punishment. My thoughts were miles away from our shopping expedition, from the oil and the chickpeas and the money in my pocket, or from the sharing out of the spoils that we'd have to do when we got back to my apartment on Gennadiou Street. Instead, they were focused with manic concentration, with unquenchable thirst, with the despairing contrition of a fallen angel, on the hope of once more encountering Mr Agathos, the Big Boss.

At about five in the afternoon, as I was on my way out to go to the office, I ran into my lovely lawyer. I longed for the earth to open and swallow me! I felt as if the whole shaming business in Piraeus was written all over my face. I was on the point of chickening out and pretending I hadn't seen her but her gaze held me. She was hurrying as if she wanted to catch me, to say something to me. The crazy hope that she might be going to apologize for her slap that morning made me stop. She caught up with me, panting, the breath steaming faintly from her nostrils like that of a mare after a hard gallop. I raised my hat in embarrassment and pushed open the heavy iron door with its glass panes for her to enter. She ran her eyes over me.

"Have you only just got back?" I stammered awkwardly.

"Mr Sotiriou," she said, nodding towards the hall as if she wanted me to come back in so that she could speak to me. She's feeling sorry about it, that's for certain, I thought and followed her in.

"I've got only one thing to say," she announced, and her eyes darted fire. "You may tell Balomenos what you please about us… just as you did when you pinched our apartment… but I forbid you first to spy on us, and second to speak to us, even to say good morning. I don't want to have anything whatsoever to do with you,"

"But Mrs Marika…" I stuttered. "It isn't like that! I… How could you have thought… What would I tell

Balomenos since I don't know a thing about you! And what on earth gave you the idea that I was spying? On the contrary, my intentions... and actually just a little while ago someone happened to bring me oil from the village, I was wondering if you'd like some... But what happened today? What did I do? Why did you slap me?"

"Do you think I didn't understand?" Mrs Kanellis asked, well and truly furious now. "Do you think I didn't see... that smile on your face when... that movement to... to..."

Her mouth twisted in a spasm of emotion, her words were strangled by the anger that flooded her. Had she really taken my small attempt at showing off as an attack on her? Serves me right, I thought and—such was my despair at my foolishness of the morning as I gazed at her trying to make her understand—my eyes filled with tears. For some unfathomable reason this seemed to make her even angrier. She turned and ran up the stairs, shouting at me never to dare speak to her again or to raise my eyes to look at her. I gritted my teeth and went back out.

When I reached the office I switched on the lights and locked the door. I lifted one of the floorboards, put the last of my sovereigns and most of the banknotes Polypheme had given me into a little tin and shoved it into my hiding place. Then I pulled the small rug under my chair back into place to hide the traces. After that I opened the phone directory to look up the number of the Hotel Palladion where Agathos had said he was staying.

It would be dark before long. The curfew would soon

begin. The line was busy. In the end some old grouch answered. As I'd feared, there was no Mr Agathos staying at the hotel. The man hung up on me without waiting for any further questions. For a moment I was at a loss. Then I thought that I could drop by the hotel. It was on the corner of Benaki and Panepistimiou Street. I'd look around the lobby, maybe browse through a newspaper for a while as if I was waiting for someone, and I'd see him coming in or leaving. If I tipped him, the man at the desk might have some other snippet of information to give me: the familiar routines of my profession. Yet on the other hand the Big Boss frightened me—it didn't seem an easy matter to risk forfeiting his confidence.

While I was making up my mind I opened the window and gazed out absent-mindedly. There were very few people about; only a young girl was standing at the entrance of the building opposite and rubbing one of her thin legs against the other to keep warm. It was beginning to get even icier. I was surprised. She looked as if she wasn't much more than a child. As if she was waiting for her parents to emerge from some office—yet all the lights were out now and the doors had been bolted and barred for the night. If she'd been begging, she would have chosen to stand on a busier street, Patission, for example, or Panepistimiou.

I heard footsteps, that characteristic sound of booted feet, and strained my ears to listen. Wearing a cape and the black beret with the white insignia of the Bersaglieri, an Italian officer came into sight, coming from the direction of Canningos Square. He saw the girl and slowed down. He'll catch her, I thought, and my heart froze. When he was about fifteen feet away from her, the girl said something to him in a low voice. She'd caught his attention, it seemed.

The Bersagliero stopped and spoke to her. I could hear his voice in the quiet street but I couldn't make out his words. He got something out of his pocket. The girl snatched it and crammed it into her mouth—maybe it was a piece of chocolate; and I was almost ready to believe that there might be some good Italians after all. However, as the girl chewed and swallowed, grunting like a hungry little animal, he put his hands under her skirt and pulled her knickers down around her ankles. He pushed her up against the porch of the building, whereupon his cape hid both of them.

My first thought was to grab some heavy object and hurl it at him from the window. But no one has a very good aim from such a height; the most likely result would be that the Italian would take out his pistol and shoot both me and the starving girl. Then I opened the drawer and got out the revolver that Freddy had given me. It was loaded but hadn't been used for years—I didn't even know if it still worked.

In America there's an expression for the way you look at someone you hate: your eyes flash daggers. I don't know whether it was daggers that my eyes were flashing but, without understanding quite how, I found myself in the air outside my office building, swimming downwards like a fish in water. I knew where to go and what to do. Gamvetta Street seemed to be rushing up towards me, the entrance of the building across the road was getting larger, and the two actors in that tragic and appalling scene were no longer miniatures but were regaining their normal size. I was suspended just above the officer's black beret; I gave it one blow with the butt of the revolver, with all my force, right in the center. The crack, as loud as that of a branch breaking, made the girl give a stifled squeal. As she turned around I saw that her mouth was smeared with chocolate and that she was gazing at me wide-eyed.

The Italian was lying motionless on the pavement. All the girl said was "Oh!" Then she gave me a look of utter disgust. He was her benefactor; I was a murderer. For this little creature (was she about twelve? Thirteen maybe?), all that mattered was the chocolate she'd earned and not her sullied innocence. At her age she'd already seen enough to know that a dead Italian—or even an injured one—meant you could lose your life, and not only you but other people too, who weren't to blame either. I grabbed hold of her hand, pulled her into the entrance to our building and unlocked the door. In the office we'd be safe. She turned and cast a last glance at the Bersagliero, then looked at me with hungry eyes.

"Want a fuck, mister?"

"No, little one, I don't do things like that... I'm an angel," I said with a smile, not quite knowing why I'd chosen to answer like this instead of simply reassuring her that from me at least she had nothing to fear. Maybe I wanted to offer her the hope of one last illusion about the world into which she'd been born. "Where do you live?"

"What's that to you? Do you want it or don't you?"

"I don't. Look, I'll give you some money if you promise you'll go straight home to your mother and not do this sort of thing again."

There was doubt in her eyes—perhaps because I was offering something without asking for anything in return—as well as hope and marked impatience. Was I lying to her? Did my promise conceal something unpleasant? I drew from my pocket a bundle of the banknotes the giant Polypheme had given me and gave her the amount that I remembered the hookers had charged in the smart hotels of New York. She stuffed the money into her skirt pocket.

That night I had a dream—something I hadn't had for years if you don't count the nightmares. I dreamed that the little chocolate-eater was knocking on the door of the house on Filonos Street, the light went on, there were footsteps on the stairs and, as the door opened, I saw a smile of happiness and relief light up the face of hard-hearted Stellitsa.

11
——

A night at the opera

I remembered that I'd read something about it in *Proia* recently. People were talking about it. For some reason that wasn't explained, the curfew would not apply in the center of Athens on Friday until midnight. The Italians were in charge of the city, yet the final word on such matters belonged of course to the Germans. The Greek government issued their orders for the day in the ridiculous language that officials invariably use in this country—announcements of this kind in any case never offer explanations. But I knew the reason: it was because of the first night at the Olympia theater. As I walked along Academias Street that evening I noticed that the sidewalks were thronging with our own Greek policemen as well as the foreign soldiers. It was obvious that important officials would be going to the theater. The balcony on the façade of the Ionian School was festooned with German and Italian flags in a brotherly embrace, with more flags decorating the two ends of the high wall surrounding it. There were very few civilians about.

My best suit hung rather loose on me and smelled of mothballs for this was the first time I'd worn it in two years. I wasn't in the least anxious about the evening; I'd been to the opera before (that time with Freddy) and I knew what to expect: warmth, music that sends you to sleep and a comfortable seat in which to nod off—until the applause wakes you at the interval and you go off to the bar to smoke a cigarette and have a drink. A stupid assumption: but since at long last an opera house was functioning in Athens, I imagined that there'd be a bar for the interval and that at this bar drinks would be available. As for the question of what they'd cost, this didn't preoccupy me the slightest bit. As of the day before yesterday I was rich. What's more, I had serious hopes of becoming even richer. I also knew how to behave at the opera: you don't laugh at the stout soprano pretending to be a fairy or at the elderly tenor acting the part of the young and virile hero. You don't clap while they're singing and you don't whistle when the villain is threatening the good characters. Quite how I'd manage to recognize my man I hadn't a clue—but I trusted the Big Boss. He'd convinced me by now that the things he said weren't just hot air. So if he said I'd recognize the man, then no doubt I'd somehow be able to spot him among a whole regiment of double bass players. As simple as that!

Outside the Olympia even more soldiers were stationed. Apart from the Carabinieri and the Greek policemen, there was a platoon of the SD drawn up in the forecourt. Various well-dressed gentlemen and their ladies were arriving on foot from the direction of Kolonaki and Irodou Attikou Street, while two German military cars were parked outside the Lawyers' Union—the place where the Kanellis couple and other lawyers obtained the meager rations they brought home each day for lunch.

I showed my ticket to the skeletal usher in a bow tie who stood at the head of the stairs inside and went into the auditorium. There were more army caps, boots and epaulettes to be seen than suits, tailcoats and evening dresses. The Germans and the Italians are known for their love of music: this is why the curfew had been temporarily suspended. However, my attention was focused on the orchestra pit rather than the audience. I had a good seat, in the fourth row behind three rows of Germans, Italians and a handful of Greeks. It was diabolically cold. When the theater filled up and the doors were closed we'd probably be slightly warmer. Yet the theater didn't look as if it was going to fill up and it was already almost time for the performance to begin.

The musicians started to come into the pit and tune up their instruments. As they came in I looked at them one by one, standing so that I could make out their faces better. But it was a waste of time trying to guess which was my man. My musical knowledge wasn't such that it allowed me to spot him, even though it ought to have been the easiest thing in the world since there was only one double bass in the orchestra. All the same, my client had seemed absolutely sure that I'd manage—if the worst came to the worst, I'd wait until the end and then go and ask someone to point him out to me.

All of a sudden there was a rustling and a sound of seats folding as the audience rose and turned to look up at the boxes. The officers in the front rows stood to attention ramrod straight and saluted the central box. From the Greeks in the audience came a feeble round of applause which soon died away. It wasn't particularly hard to recognize them beneath the tailcoats, the uniforms and the icy stares they directed at both audience and stage. The Prime Minister Tsolakoglou (with a Hitler mustache) and the Vice President Logothetopoulos were sitting there among the conquerors, looking more like prisoners than anything else; beside them the foreign commanders returned the salutes from the audience, the Italian raising his arm with a clenched fist that reminded you of his countrymen's crudest gesture and the German throwing out his own arm in a Heil Hitler. And between these two men sat a stranger in a tailcoat, with a long, narrow head, bald save for the thick grey fringe around it, and a decoration of some sort on the front of his white waistcoat.

"It's the great conductor, Bodo Froberger," a voice beside me whispered.

I turned to thank my neighbor for this piece of information, which actually didn't interest me—and saw Mr Agathos himself sitting beside me. It seems I stared at him in amazement—I don't know why, unless it was because all the things that had happened since our first and only meeting had made him begin to take on the air of an illusion in my mind and I'd invested his person with all the fascination of someone who works miracles. He motioned me to make no comment with his finger to his lips.

"And who's he?" I asked, as all around us the noise grew louder and the lights were beginning to dim.

"The greatest maestro in the world, man," answered Mr Agathos, shocked at my ignorance.

"I thought that was Toscanelli," I said, to show that I knew something about music.

"*Toscanini*" (correcting me) "is the greatest maestro in America. In Europe the greatest is Froberger."

"Well, that's all right by me," I told him, not wanting to annoy him. "Which one is your protégé?"

He put his finger to his lips once more.

The new round of applause was for the Greek conductor who had mounted his rostrum and was bowing right and left with the movements of a ballet dancer. The auditorium was now dark. The spotlights illuminated the red velvet curtain as it stirred in the draught from backstage. The ballerina raised his magic wand and the orchestra struck up into the first notes.

When the clapping died down and the lights went on for the interval I began to get up but Mr Agathos restrained me.

"One moment," he said. "I have a couple of things to say. I shall come into the foyer with you, Mr

Sotiris—Sotiriou!—and I'll point him out to you. I myself, however, shall keep at a distance. At his side you will see someone you know, and in this way you will be sure that you are not mistaken. The person known to you will certainly invite you to join them and thus you will be introduced to our musician. Not a word about me, though. And by the way, I do beg you to exercise a little restraint over your impetuous impulses… Look what happened to you after you'd been shopping in Piraeus!"

"Something told me you'd know all about it," I muttered. "But I may as well inform you that as of yesterday evening my powers have been fully restored to me."

He shrugged his shoulders, as if admitting that there is a whole set of rules governing such matters.

"All the same, it would not be a good idea for you to push your relations with the Kanellis family, and especially with the lady, to the point of… of bankruptcy, so to speak, ho ho… the couple is of interest, you understand, you will see in due course… Be sensible… You have embarked upon a road from which, as you are well aware, you cannot now turn aside. And thus the more faithful you remain to your—how shall I put it?—to your *angelic* nature… (that's it!), the better it will be for all of us."

"I don't understand what the devil the Kanellis couple have got to do with it…"

"Leave the devil out of it, my boy… There are enough of them all around us tonight… Well then, as we said. You get up first and I shall follow you…"

I got up and walked up the aisle towards the exit.

"You are not called Agathos," I hissed at him as we went through the door. "Nor are you staying at the Palladion."

He didn't appear to be paying any attention to me. He was gazing around him and I had the impression that wherever his gaze fell he was recognizing people.

"Why did you tell me lies?"

"Lies, Mr Sotiriou? Me?"

In spite of this protestation, he was still not paying attention to me.

"I told you no lies. From now on you must keep your eyes and ears open, my friend. You must trust your instinct… And you mustn't be afraid. I shall always be just one step in front of you…"

With that he broke off into one of those belly-quivering old man's laughs of his that made him seem to gasp for breath.

"Froberger has come to Athens to conduct an important work, yes," he continued in a murmur, holding me by the sleeve to stop me going up the steps too fast. "He'll be conducting the orchestra of the Athens Opera. He came tonight to hear them—this was one of his stipulations, so that he'd have some idea what kind of musicians he'd be dealing with. And while we're on the subject, ho ho, I'd be extremely interested to know what he thinks of them. Do me a favor, Mr Angel, my boy, if you find out anything about it, let me know…"

"That brings us to something I've been meaning to ask! Where can I find you—if I've got something to tell you—since no one's ever heard of you at the Palladion? Where the devil are you staying? Why the secrecy?"

"The devil again! He's becoming an obsession with you, Mr Angel, my boy! I understand, of course, it's natural for someone like you to pick up the habits of the people around him... I know... but do try," (he stopped in mid-stairs and held me fast), "do try, at least *when I'm with you,* eh?"

"And how I am to find out what what's-his-name, your German bigwig, thinks? He's hardly likely to come and tell me all about his impressions of the performance."

"Don't be in a hurry, my friend. You'll see, we shall all find out... you first, then me..."

"And I'll have expenses," I interrupted, thinking that this might make him pay attention to me.

"I know. I've taken care of it."

"Really? How? Will I find the money at old man Yannakopoulos' store like your magic powder?"

Our eyes met. His blue ones were sparkling with a happy and conspiratorial smile.

"So you liked it!" he said with all the pride of an inventor who's given you a contraption of mechanical wings to try out.

"I drank it at any rate," I broke in sternly, "I don't know why."

"That is the most important thing," he murmured. "*He moves in a mysterious way,* eh? Isn't that what you say?"

"What *we* say?" I was irritated by his habit of acting as if he were the Virgin Mary. "What *we* say, sir? Aren't you a Christian?"

"What? Ah! Ha, ha, ha! Of course I am, Mr Sotiriou!"

"And what does it matter to you what music the German plays with the Greek orchestra? Are you an impresario? Or a composer and you want him to play your own work?"

He stopped again and lowered his voice.

"Ah, care is needed here, my boy. I'm both an impresario and a composer—but that's not the point. It's a question of my interests, which go far beyond all these things… Look here, trust me. What else do you need to see in order to trust me, eh?"

"We don't know one another well enough for me to tell you," I said in a challenging tone, and watched him closely so that not even the smallest contraction of the muscles of his face would escape me.

He seemed not to understand. We had reached the entrance to the foyer and a strong and inviting aroma of fine cigars was reaching my nostrils, which were flaring as wide as possible to enjoy this delicious scent. If they had cigars then they'd have drinks too, I thought to myself.

"Yes, don't worry, they've got everything tonight in honor of their distinguished guests from the National Theater," said the stout old man by my side as if he'd read my thoughts—or maybe without realizing it I'd spoken out loud. "Do you have any money left? No? Here you are, make sure that these…" (he came very close and slipped into my hand a heavy little cylindrical packet wrapped up in newspaper, whose weight bore witness to its contents—it must have contained five or six sovereigns), "reach the pocket of your protégé tonight, for him to buy food… And you yourself will soon have something further for your pains… There we are—that's him over there!"

He jabbed me with his elbow, since his hand was already holding my arm in a vice-like grip, and indicated that I should look straight in front of us.

At the end of the bar with its white marble top stood a thin man with a broad face and round tortoiseshell spectacles wearing a musician's evening dress, two bald tracks making incursions on either side of the strip of dark hair that remained in the center of his head. He was smoking a cheap cigarette with evident disgust and talking to a red-haired woman begowned and bejeweled like the wife or daughter of a black marketeer. I forgot all about Agathos and his lunacies and opened my eyes wide in amazement.

The woman was my long-lost secretary Vanda.

12

——

I take on the duties of a nanny

"Angel!"

This was the first surprise: she'd never called me by my first name before without adding a polite "Mr"—for her I'd always been the boss. But then that was in a different time and place… The present state of affairs resembled the fantastic landscape of a dream. In the general nightmare around us I was meeting Vanda again as if we were two masked revelers encountering one another in the midst of formality and evening dresses, a delirium of scent and a pressing crush of strangers. From a Vanda disguised as a grand lady, the intimacy of this address, which as my little Jewish secretary she had never presumed to adopt, sounded entirely normal.

"Va…"

Her hand with its gold bracelet playfully covered my mouth.

"You don't even remember my name!" she joked. "It's V-i-c-k-y!"

"Well, at least I remembered it began with V!"

A spark flashed briefly in her eyes and died down immediately.

"Let me introduce my friend, Mr Beratis, a wonderful musician who plays in the orchestra. Mr. Sotiriou."

"Angel," I said, giving him my hand.

Out of the corner of my eye I spotted Agathos' white head emerging from behind a group of people as he craned to see how we were getting on at the bar.

"Miltos," the other man said; his handshake was firm.

"It's a small world," I said to Vicky-Vanda. "I'd been looking for you everywhere… and suddenly I run into you at the theater. I didn't know you liked opera."

"I don't especially. It's my husband who does." And she gestured towards a tall, stout, grey-haired man. It didn't take much effort to realize what tribe he belonged to.

"I didn't know you were married either, my dear Mrs Vicky! Congratulations!"

"And what is Mr Sotiriou's profession?"

It was my turn to shut her up.

"I'm a Greek from America," I told him, "and had my fingers in various pies there. Real estate mostly. Here, not a thing. I'm trapped in Athens and can't budge."

The musician looked at me. He seemed about forty, maybe a little more. Unless of course it was his poor health that made him look older than he was. He had eyes so dark they were almost black with an intense, feverish expression in them, and a face you couldn't call handsome with small, tobacco-stained teeth.

"That's a great misfortune," he commented.

"It's terrible. But—one day the war will end!"

"Assuredly it will… The question is whether one will survive it."

"I like opera," I said rashly.

"In general, or some works in particular?"

"In general."

"Well, you didn't miss an opportunity then."

"Angel adores music," Vicky chimed in.

"What are you called now, Vicky, what's your surname?"

"Paltoglou."

"Paltoglou! A most musical name!"

"We have distinguished visitors from Germany tonight," remarked Beratis. "Were you aware of that, Mr Sotiriou?"

The question was natural enough, yet there was something abrupt or faintly ironical in his tone.

"You're speaking of Bodo?" ("Bodo" I remembered; the other name, the surname, was a tongue-twister that I'd need to hear again before venturing to pronounce.)

"Ah, you know him! And—do you esteem him as a musician?"

"What else should I esteem him as?"

He looked at me without speaking. Then, "I knew him in Berlin," he said vaguely.

"Do you esteem him as a musician?"

"As a musician, yes."

"Do you know anything else about him?"

"It's natural that I should, isn't it? After all, I lived there for ten whole years."

"Ah. So then you must have a lot of acquaintances among…" (I gestured around.)

He didn't help me complete my sentence, merely shrugging slightly.

"My acquaintances are in Germany, not here," he said dryly. "Those of them who have survived, that is, and who haven't managed to escape."

"Miltos is *absolutely* my very best friend in all Athens," Vicky piped up as if she was reciting something. "We met him when he came to our house with some *absolutely* wonderful friends of his" (here she turned towards him with an expression that invited him to remember their *absolutely* marvelous first meeting), "and everyone present was left open-mouthed with admiration. The Cultural Attaché said—yes, from the German Embassy—that there wasn't a quartet like it in the whole of Berlin."

"Trio," Beratis corrected.

"Not a trio like it… And ever since then Perry and I have been *such* good friends with him…"

Mr Paltoglou was approaching us like an old acquaintance. He put his hand on his wife's back and turned to greet us.

"Is this another musician, my treasure?" he asked her, examining me closely.

This fifty-year-old man's face bore traces indicating that

his life had been a violent one; his honeyed tones thus somehow struck a false note. His features hung slack and exhausted on his face, with only his large nose sticking out like the snout of a tapir. His character must have been something similar.

She introduced me: "Mr Sotiriou, a businessman and music lover."

"Ah," he said, addressing me. "When Greece acquires a musical life, it will become civilized. And the Germans will help us greatly in this, as I believe."

"If you will excuse me," said Beratis, turning to leave, "I have to be getting back to the orchestra."

"There's no doubt about it," I replied. "That's why Beef-Burger is here tonight."

I knew I was being idiotic but Paltoglou seemed eager to agree.

"Yes indeed! The fools here take everything the wrong way. The poor Germans are doing all they can, yet in return people do nothing but whine "Occupation, Occupation, Occupation!" You only have to look around you, though: the streets are properly signposted, there's some order at long last, murders and thefts have become things of the past... They came here with the very best intentions... And we... The late Metaxas worshipped them, poor fellow! But those half-wit Anglophiles swept him away..."

"Mrs Vicky, Mr Paltoglou, it was a great pleasure," I said, seeing the musician moving away.

I hurried after him. He was already on his way downstairs.

"Wait!" I called.

He turned and looked at me in amazement. It was time I followed my client's advice and trusted my instinct, the inspiration of the moment or what have you.

"I've got something for you," I said quietly.

"For me?"

"From Vanda."

The name slipped out by mistake. But it was effective.

"You know her name?" said Beratis, growing even paler.

"And her... profession... too."

He took a step back, sizing me up carefully. Then he suddenly closed his eyes and staggered as if he'd lost his balance. I caught hold of his arm. His face had taken on a yellowish hue.

"Are you all right?"

"Yes, thanks, it's nothing. I missed the step, that's all."

"She begged me to give you this," I said, continuing the fiction. "She didn't want to give it to you there in front of her black marketeer..."

"So you really have known her a long time then... And are you really an American?"

"Bah," I said, "as much as you're a German."

I'd already put my hand into my pocket, but just at that moment a large group of uniformed Germans and Italians appeared at the top of the stairs.

"I can't right now," he said breathlessly. "Come and find me backstage after the performance."

He turned and hurried off. At the door to the auditorium the skeletal man in the bow tie was ringing a bell to gather his flock back into the fold.

I found the seat beside me empty and Mr Agathos did not reappear, so I couldn't ask him what I should do next with his musician. My solitude and the music made me nod off and I was soon fast asleep. I woke up just before the end. Something dramatic was happening on the stage, a lot of loud voices and fuss. "It's Turiddu's farewell," I heard a woman near me say to her companion. Turiddu was bawling at the top of his voice, the veins in his neck standing out like cords, then he embraced an ugly old woman and ran off behind the scenery. From the audience burst a storm of clapping and whistling and stamping—that's Italians for you.

As the lights came on amidst the first outburst of applause, I got up and made my way out to the corridor that ran around the theater outside the stalls. It was deserted and desperately cold. By now it had warmed up a bit inside the auditorium, but as soon as you came out you remembered once more the icy north wind that was freezing the sidewalks of Academias Street. Beneath a light with a burnt-out bulb I made out a faded sign saying "Stage." I pushed the door open and found myself in the dressing rooms. The orchestra and the singers were still out there making their bows. I sat down in a dark corner and waited.

They weren't long. The sparse audience had satisfied whatever needs had sent them to the theater that evening, the officers had work to do, and the stalls and dress circle emptied rapidly; in any case they'd been barely half-full. The musicians came backstage, the singers started to take off their make-up in the dressing rooms, all around me were voices, chairs scraping on the floor, the sound of instrument cases being fastened, coughs and snatches of brief, impatient conversations. Miltos Beratis came up to me, as pale as he'd been earlier on the stairs. His slightly abrupt manner had disappeared and he spoke in a low voice as if not feeling able to cope with too much talking.

"You didn't have to wait too long."

"No, not long at all," I told him. "Look here, Vanda, Vicky I mean, asked me to give you this money that she owes you. She didn't want to do it in front of her husband, but she knew me well in the old days…"

I got out the roll of coins and put it in his hand. He held it absent-mindedly and stared into the distance.

"She doesn't owe me any money," he said. "I don't understand, Mr Angel. There must be some mistake."

"I don't know. What can I say? I'm telling you what she told me. Why don't you hang on to it and sort it out when you next meet her…"

He closed his eyes, trying to work out when and how this debt might have been contracted. Or was he feeling faint again? The ever-present Mr Agathos had been right about one thing: the man looked dreadfully ill.

He'd changed and was now wearing a pinstriped suit, clearly made for him in more prosperous days—the jacket was double-breasted and the quality of the cloth still showed even though it had worn thin at various critical spots.

I was feeling anxious in case he got it into his head to give the sovereigns back to me… when I noticed that he was looking over my shoulder with an expression of dismay. Voices and footsteps were heard in the corridor outside, the door opened, and here, once more, were the VIPs: the German commandant, two lieutenants, some Greek in civilian clothes towards whom the balletic conductor was constantly bending, and finally the great German conductor, Mr F. himself, a tall, unsmiling figure in immaculate evening dress.

"Gentlemen, gentlemen!" called the conductor, clapping his hands like a first-grade teacher. "The renowned maestro Mr *Frrrobergerrr* has come to meet you and to have a word with you. We are all naturally deeply moved." He turned to the tall German. "Maestro!"

The distinguished visitor opened his lips a fraction and murmured something brief to the officer who was standing beside him with his eyes fixed on his country's destiny. He in turn bent and spoke to the Greek official. The General Director of the Opera cleared his throat and took a step forward.

"Which of the gentlemen present speaks German?" he asked.

The musicians looked at one another in silence.

"The Director is asking if anyone among our colleagues here is able to translate what the maestro wishes to say to us," the Greek conductor told the members of the orchestra.

I sensed the man beside me shrinking into himself as the betraying gaze of some of his fellows fell on him.

"Mr Beratis?" called the conductor, half inviting and half commanding.

Like a sleepwalker, my man stepped forward from the ranks of his fellow-musicians who were dropping with fatigue and shivering in the icy atmosphere. Most of them had dusted off their instruments tonight solely because of the double rations that had been promised them in return for playing at this operatic feast. Some had already sold them for a handful of lentils or a few drops of olive oil. This whole business, which to some extent had originally seemed like a piece of good luck, was now taking another turn that was beginning to worry them. The curfew had been lifted until midnight but every one of them was thinking about how he'd manage to get home in time or where else within walking distance he might find hospitality for the night.

In the general silence the first exchanges between the great foreign conductor and Beratis could be heard. First came one or two questions; the answers to them were brief and impersonal, sometimes only a single word. Then

Mr F. looked up and raised his voice, now addressing the dumb and hungry flock of ragtag musicians.

"The maestro is very glad to meet you," said the interpreter with his eyes closed. "He has had the opportunity to listen to our rendering of these great works belonging to the Italian repertoire..." (a gap while the other man spoke again in his resonant and precise German) "... He gives proper acknowledgment to the musicality and enthusiasm of the orchestra... with which he will be collaborating during the coming days and weeks..." (muttering among the flock) "...with the purpose of recreating that Wagnerian masterpiece the *Rheingold*..." (the muttering grew louder; the Greek conductor and the Director General of the Opera exchanged uneasy glances) "... which he has chosen himself in order to introduce the Greek public... to the musical culture of Germany... He himself has selected the German lyrical artists who will be performing beside our own singers... But he considers that the orchestra... is capable of giving a satisfactory rendering of the symphonic parts of the work... provided, first..." ("*Erstes!*" called Mr F. as if suddenly angry) "... that we engage in a scrupulous study of the music... that we rehearse zealously... and that we obey the suggestions and instructions of the maestro who, it will be realized, bears the sole responsibility of getting us to perform as a symphony orchestra... with absolute discipline and devotion... qualities which our usual repertoire perhaps does not demand of us to quite such a degree as the Wagnerian masterpiece…"

Beratis took a step sideways as if requesting permission to retire, but Mr F. began to speak again, more rapidly now, and indeed made various cyclical gestures with his hand in our direction, then gave a forced bark of laughter which broke off as suddenly as it had begun. The German officers risked a smile too. After which all eyes turned once more to my protégé who, although again on the point of fainting, took a deep breath and recited:

"We are all, *without exception*, invited by the maestro to the house where he is staying tonight… to the German Archaeological Mission… on the corner of Fidiou and Harilaou Trikoupi Street. For the benefit of those of you who may not know it, the maestro is the son and grandson of great archaeologists and worshippers of ancient Greece: his father was Egon Froberger, professor of Archaeology at the University of Munich, a distinguished academic and collaborator with Schliemann. Hence the maestro already has strong links with ancient Greece. We shall proceed there on foot, we shall partake of a light dinner, due to the lateness of the hour, and shall have the opportunity to converse with the maestro on subjects concerning the art which we all serve."

He had barely finished speaking when a loud thud was heard behind us. It was the oboist who had crumpled to the floor.

13

A working meal

No doctor could be found, nor would there have been any point in finding one. The oboist had given up the ghost in front of everyone—or rather, behind everyone—having used the last breaths he was fated to take blowing down his instrument to send the melodies of the Sicilian countryside wafting up to the important visitors in the box and to the tone-deaf ears of the black marketeers like Paltoglou comfortably seated in the stalls. Mr F., most upset by this event, was asking everyone what had happened.

"*Votre Excellence*," the Greek conductor told him, struggling with his imperfect French, "*c'était un vieux… il a expiré…*"

But the German would not be calmed. Among all the startled explanations and confused instructions as to what should be done with the dead man, he turned once more to Beratis and asked him something. The musician replied without hesitation, avoiding meeting his interlocutor's eyes. I was quite certain that what he'd just stated in magnificent, flowing German was that the man had dropped dead from starvation (the expression on Mr F.'s face made it perfectly clear that the answer he'd received was distasteful to him).

I went over to where all the others were bending over their fallen colleague, to see what was going on.

"Pericles! Pericles! Open your eyes… look at me… undo his clothes, someone… press here, give him artificial respiration…"

I helped them carry him to the bench where they usually left their overcoats and their little cases. He seemed to be a man of fairly advanced age, hollow-cheeked, with dark circles under his eyes. His grey hair fell forward over his face—he hadn't had a haircut recently, maybe because he was an artist, or maybe because like everyone else he didn't have a penny to spare for a barber; anyway, long hair keeps your head a bit warmer when it's cold: God knew what he was doing when he left us with hair on our heads, even though he removed it from most parts of our bodies… His mouth was open, revealing two rotten teeth missing their gold crowns. Many people would willingly have exchanged something to chew with for something to chew on, both for themselves and for their families too. Who knows whether this was what he'd done…

Everyone was milling around their dead colleague in distress, swapping snippets of information ("He looked… He'd taken a turn for the worse… He's left an unsuspecting wife at home, she'll be waiting up for him…

Hasn't anyone thought to notify her... What will happen to the body... The German's given orders for him to be buried with full honors... A musician who's died in the course of duty can't just be thrown without ceremony onto the municipal cart...") I knelt down and tried as best I could to revive him, but it was too late. The man had passed away.

The great foreign conductor knelt beside me, although his distress was rapidly giving way to anger—things like this shouldn't happen to him. A struggle appeared to be taking place within his breast between his fear of death, his anger at this transgression against good manners and the confirmation—if it were needed—that something else was going on in Athens and that this was not merely an unfortunate occurrence. When I turned and looked at him he returned my gaze and said something to me in German. I shrugged. He stepped back, turned to the military commander of Athens and began to tell him something at great speed. The other man listened in impassive silence. And when Mr F. had finished he clicked his heels just as if he'd been receiving orders from his commander-in-chief.

"Gentlemen, let us be going!" the Director General of the Opera announced in a loud voice.

Only then did I realize that during all this time no one had stopped to wonder what a stranger like me was doing in their midst. I took Beratis' arm and we followed the group of important guests who were walking ahead of us. But of course there was an explanation for such a lack of surprise. Many of the musicians playing in the orchestra tonight were more usually employed playing in various nightclubs or tavernas and had been hastily recruited at the last minute to make up the requisite numbers for the performance. If the audience had been the usual one, urgent measures of this kind wouldn't have been needed. But the presence of the German maestro had, it seemed, changed things.

The Olympia theater was by now deserted. The main door was still open, policemen, Carabinieri and the SD fatigue party were waiting patiently outside, while at the curb on Academias Street a row of large cars bearing the swastika was drawn up. The shadow of Mount Hymettus loomed in the distance. We walked down the empty street. Most people turned straight onto Harilaou Trikoupi Street, where ahead of us lights were shining from the windows of the Mission. However, I took the musician by the arm and led him along Gennadiou Street so that he could see where I lived.

"We're neighbors then… I'm on Zosimadon Street," he said.

"At least we'll get something to eat tonight," he murmured as we arrived, the last of the party, at our destination.

The Mission was brightly lit up, all the other buildings on the street plunged in darkness. The double doors were opened to reveal a man in a Tattersall-checked suit standing within; we all pushed and jostled in our haste to get in out of the nocturnal cold and found ourselves in a warm reception room. What luxury! A veritable palace existed right next door to me and I hadn't had any idea of it!

The Germans were more at ease now, they relaxed their military stiffness, took off their caps and gloves and capes and greatcoats and left them in the cloakroom. Then the maestro entered the dining room and we followed, Germans and Greeks intermingled, in his wake.

All eyes were fixed on the amazing spectacle before us. I hadn't seen anything like it for months. And I'll never forget the musicians' faces as they staggered like men intoxicated and struggled to restrain themselves from falling on the food set out on the table. It wasn't either fear or embarrassment that held them back. It was the conditions of our captivity, the feeling that when your jailer offers you a meal it is not right or decent to stampede and devour it instantly.

However, once the signal had been given you should have seen us! Everyone surged forwards like a pack of wolves, and me with them, blessing my good fortune and the wisdom of Mr Agathos and the unexpected developments that had begun to take place in my life. A faint trace of revulsion passed over the faces of the German officers watching us, like when you see someone with no table manners wiping his fingers on the tablecloth or cutting his meat with a fork. As for the great conductor, without doubt he was trying to ignore the scene in front of him and focusing his mind on ancient Greek symposia.

He spent most of the time talking to the German director of the Archaeological Mission, to the General

Director of the Opera and to another guest who was introduced to us (or at least to whichever of us had any interest to spare for him) as Professor Franz Doelger, historian and Byzantinist. The German guests showed great respect and awe for these two great professors who were honoring the country by their presence that night.

"You know something?" Beratis whispered to me when the table had been stripped of every last atom of food, "If the Germans realize that you're not a member of the orchestra, they might well execute you as a spy. And if they realize that you're an American born and bred, then you won't even have time to wait for the firing squad."

"Hush, not so loud, for pity's sake," I whispered back, filled with terror that I hadn't even thought of this.

"Mr Beratis," Bodo called just at that very moment from the head of the table.

These were the only words of his that I understood, for all the rest was in German which, like most of the other people there, I don't speak. He'd asked at the beginning if perhaps French was the language better known to his guests—English, he said, "he knew little and liked less." I don't know what the regular members of the orchestra, who were better educated, would have answered to this question but, as I've said, there were few of them present; the General Director had apparently not noticed this fact, or if he had then he preferred to keep quiet about it to save face. When after an eloquent silence and several definite denials it emerged that the musicians spoke no foreign languages, the German gave that unpleasant smile characteristic of people who don't smile very often and, resting his fists on the table, began to address us in German, having appointed the double bass player to translate for us.

Partly due to my own good memory, partly due to subsequent conversations with my protégé about the events of that evening, and partly due to the hindsight you acquire after adventures of this kind, I am able to remember more or less what he said to us after the *light meal* in the dining room of the German Archaeological Mission.

It was his deep belief, he began, that war was a *great evil*, but also *the father of all things*, and the present war—although he himself was not a politician to be able to judge—seemed to presage as clearly as could be the birth of a new world. Personally, he hoped that out of all the horror and blood a new *Golden Age* would emerge. He also hoped that his Fatherland would impose a true New Order in Europe, by force if it could not be achieved by gentler means, which would abolish social injustices and would make all peoples—or at any rate all those who accepted the terms of the European spirit and the powerful values that the New Germany represented—equal participants in a new political and social reality. The Greek civilization, he declared, was the greatest ever to have appeared on the earth before the German civilization, which indeed was a continuation of it. This fact had been demonstrated by German philosophers, from Goethe, whom he (Mr F.) numbered among the philosophers,

Kant, Hegel, Feuerbach to Nietzsche and Professor Heidegger—who honored him with his friendship; for these philosophers continued the classical dialectic on the subject of *material* versus *spirit*, the *good* versus the *bad*, the *fitting* versus the *unfitting*. It was also demonstrated in German art, whose works were always modeled on classical Greek art, and even by the German language, which possesses all the characteristics, in both syntax and grammar, of ancient Greek. Moreover, he himself, as an artist, had made up his mind to place his reputation and his influence at the service of this New Order in the field of culture, the natural link, that is to say, connecting the old and the new. Greece, as he himself dreamed, as indeed did other important figures in Germany such as the Professor sitting here with us, would once more become the center of the civilized world. And the great German musical tradition would once more meet in this country the source from which it sprang, namely ancient Greek tragedy. Professor Doelger (he indicated the bearded gentleman at his side whom he had introduced to us earlier), the greatest living Byzantinist in the world, had with the cooperation of the Luftwaffe begun to take aerial photographs in order to map the archaeological sites of Northern Greece, leaving his French and English colleagues far behind. In Thessaloniki the Director of the Italian Institute, working in collaboration with the Director of the German School in Athens, would be organizing events notable for their variety, extent and grandeur, which would emphasize the unity and close relationship of our civilizations. And the maestro himself, whom the world did the honor of considering a valid interpreter of the Wagnerian oeuvre, had come here in order to put on a performance of the *Rheingold*, with the contribution of famous German singers who were already preparing to travel to Athens, in order to help lay the foundations of communication between these two peoples. The members of the orchestra as well as any of their colleagues who chanced not to be present tonight should be sure that they would benefit from exceptionally favorable treatment on the part of the German and Italian forces, provided that they were the instruments with which he himself would attempt to forge these new bonds.

The great challenge to the *gentlemen musicians*, continued the maestro, looking one by one at the clarinetists, the violinists and the trumpeters from the nightclubs, who were digesting in silence the Lucullan banquet they'd just gulped down, was that they were called upon to play a crucial role in this reconciliation of the peoples and civilizations of Europe. Tonight's performance—if they would permit him to speak not only with the license granted to an elderly man but also with the frankness of a fellow-musician—was UNACCEPT-ABLE by the standards required for a work such as the *Rheingold*. It was natural that the generally unfavorable living conditions should have had a negative effect on the musicians' performance. But he had the word of the Military Commander and of the Italian Administrative

Commander that *this matter* would be promptly sorted out.

The details regarding the timetable of their collaboration would be announced by the management of the Opera (a polite bow in the direction of the General Director). He himself was leaving in the morning to accompany Professor Doelger to Mount Athos which he had never before visited; and by the time he returned the musicians in the orchestra would already have studied their parts and would have begun rehearsals under his assistant, Mr Forster, who was on his way to Athens.

"Gentlemen," Bodo ended in formal tones, "I expect from you that you will give of your best to this mission in which you have the honor to participate."

And he stood up and raised his glass, while we looked at him in stunned silence. He drained it and, with the air of a man who has completed a performance, began once more to speak German with his fellow-countrymen, occasionally interspersing his conversation with a laugh like the crowing of a cock. His long, melancholy face looked as if it were unused to such mirth and went its own way, giving rise to a lack of coordination between his features. His long, curved teeth could be seen every so often when he opened his mouth wide as he tried with his tongue to dislodge some morsel of food that was stuck between them. Was he perhaps making fun of the ragtag assortment of hungry musicians who didn't know ancient Greek and couldn't keep time in even a "simple" Italian opera? Beratis, who understood what he was saying, didn't tell me—and I didn't get a chance to ask.

I don't think that during the whole of the rest of the time we sat there, drugged by the warmth and the good food, the great conductor addressed another word to us. Only to my protégé did he say something at one point, then remained gazing at him, waiting for an answer: I don't know whether or not he received one.

When at last we found ourselves outside on the street once more the cold was unbearable. Miltos was shivering and staggering as we walked, leaning close against one another in order to offer one side less to the north wind. As he lived on Zosimadon Street, a narrow alley off Zoodochou Pigis after Academias Street, we turned onto Gennadiou Street together. Outside my front door I stopped. I'd prepared a little speech aimed at ensuring that our next meeting would take place very soon, but in the end it wasn't necessary. He looked up at the building, then at me, as if asking me whether I really lived here. After which he tottered and leaned heavily on my arm to save himself from falling. His eyes were glittering in the darkness and his breath came in rapid pants.

"Come up and stay here tonight," I said. "There's plenty of room. I can't see you making it back to your own place."

The Big Boss would have been very pleased with me. I reacted spontaneously, I risked it, I trusted my instinct

—just as he'd advised me to do. I unlocked the heavy iron door and pushed it open. So cold was it outside that the hall almost seemed to be heated. I helped him up the stairs and led him into my apartment.

14

Confidences

The apartment was icy but at least we were out of the wind. The place smelled of damp, of weeks' worth of dust and of human mustiness, just like all homes that don't have a woman to look after them—a bachelor home. I lit a piece of cotton wool soaked in methylated spirits and made a cup of sage tea so that he could warm up a bit and recover. Perhaps it was the sudden food on an empty stomach that had brought on his indisposition. In any case, in my capacity of host I had to offer something to the man who was going to be staying here tonight. I showed him the divan in the dining room and brought him some blankets.

Whether because he was feeling ill or because he was feeling upset, he didn't drink the tea immediately. He held the cup between his palms for warmth, sat leaning back against the wall behind the divan and remained silent, gazing at the opposite wall on which I'd hung the picture of the two horses running on a plain—Freddy's present to me when I left for Greece. I'd hung it there and forgotten about it, never even noticing its presence.

"It's a large apartment," was his only comment.

I began to chat rather awkwardly about Balomenos and the neighbors and about my apartment in New York which was as tiny as could be. He turned to face me.

"You're a strange fellow, American," he said. "What you did tonight could have cost you very dear… pushing in among us, unknown and uninvited, and going to the German Mission like that… You remind me of a friend of mine in Halkida. He was just the same, Tasos he was called, Tasos Markopoulos. He was quite fearless, even when very small he used to do the most incredible things you could imagine…"

"Does he still live there?" I asked, enjoying this new familiarity suddenly flowing between us.

"No. People like that don't live very long," Beratis answered with a wry smile. "When I left for Berlin in '25 he'd already left Greece. I got a letter from him in '31—he'd joined the Foreign Legion and had somehow got hold of my address and wrote to me. He sounded happy, it was a long letter telling me all about exploits that would be worthy of a book. We were provincial boys, don't forget—my own departure to study in Germany was a major event for the whole village. But he left without a word to anyone, he just disappeared all of a sudden and no one knew where he'd gone… You're like Tasos, it seems to me, just as bold… But of course you weren't the only person there tonight who didn't know anyone else, we were a motley lot—half the people there don't normally play at the theater with us, the General Director dredged them up from somewhere when he heard that Bodo wanted to hear what sort of sound the orchestra produced, as he put it. Not that it did much good…"

The fact that he used the German's first name seemed to imply a degree of familiarity. Had they really known each other so well in Berlin? And if so, then why was the other man so cold and distant with Beratis? I'd find out. In the meantime, all we could talk about was this man Tasos, unknown to me, whose foolhardiness so resembled mine.

"It's a bad thing to die young," I said—not very proud of this phrase.

"It's a bad thing to die," he responded.

I realized that he was speaking of himself.

"I think I've already died once," I said, "some years ago."

"In America?"

"Yes, in America."

It was that night in New York, after I came out of hospital. I was sitting on the bed and listening to the groans that kept escaping me, saying to myself, Who is this man? And why is he crying, since everything's over now and nothing matters anymore? I was outside my own body, at a distance from my own self.

I didn't tell him any of this, yet he seemed to believe me, for he looked at me with undisguised sympathy for the first time and nodded.

"Are you ill, Beratis?" I asked.

"Yes," he said. "It's a joke, isn't it?"

He was a mysterious man—an artist. They're always saying this sort of thing, leaving you simply staring at them, they don't even bother to explain, they assume these are things that everyone understands.

"No one gets ill in times like these," he said. "Getting ill is a privilege of peace. These days what finishes you off is either hunger or a bullet, being ill into the bargain is a trifle excessive. I'm ill, yes. But that's probably not what I'll die of."

I was silent, waiting for more. If he told me what he expected to die of, then I'd be in a better position to carry out my mission. However, he said nothing else and fixed his gaze once more on the two horses. I didn't want to press him. Lonely people like him seek someone to open their heart to, to speak of the things that torment them—but the listener has to be worthy: their pain is the only treasure they possess.

Without speaking, he took a flattened cigarette from the pack, drew a lighter from his pocket, struck the flint once or twice and then inhaled the smoke with pleasure and the sort of concentration you see on the faces of opium addicts. Then he indicated the tip of the cigarette, glowing large and red—it was stale and was burning rapidly.

"This is what's killing me," he said with a laugh. "Or that's what the doctors say anyway, but what do doctors know about it?"

Agathos had told me: the man was slowly dying, he'd

said, from a chest disease. If you'd seen one or two other people in this condition, the signs were obvious: the color, the feverish eyes, the nervous movements.

"We're all going to die," I said. "But we don't know what from—the hunger and the bullets are outside us, maybe we'll escape them. But the thing that kills us from the inside never tells us its name."

"You say well, American," my musician commented with his twisted smile.

"Don't call me 'American'," I said. "Some other friends used to, but they stopped when America entered the war. It's dangerous."

"You don't look as if danger bothered you too much!"

"Well, I don't go looking for it…"

"You're right," he said. "You might just as well be calling me 'German'." And after a brief pause added, "You don't become German just because you've lived there a few years…"

This idea seemed to sadden him.

"But, look here, you must have contacts. Why don't you use them? The maestro seems to like you, you know each other, you can speak their language, you're a musician… Why don't you ask him to help you a bit?"

"I have asked him! I've asked him twice, what do you think!" He shook his head and his gaze left the horses and turned to me in the semi-darkness. "That's the problem," he added through clenched teeth. "Both times he told me that the Kommandatur would take care of everyone in the theater. That's what he said."

"I thought you had a closer relationship with him," I commented.

"A closer one certainly. A better one, no. Only in my early days in Berlin. Later, when the Nazis came to power, things changed and many friends changed too. People who used to invite you to their houses—and Germans don't invite you to their houses easily, like we do here—suddenly began to pretend they didn't know you. The things that in the old Germany made you someone special, the fact that you're a progressive musician, that you're a Jew, that you're a revolutionary, turned into stigmas. And even people who didn't condemn you wholesale were still afraid to be exposed as your friends. I managed to collect all three stigmas."

"What, are you Jewish?"

"No, myself I'm not. But my girlfriend was. Half-Jewish. We lived together. And as well as that I was a foreigner, not a native-born German, a southerner, dark-skinned—a suspect color. Early in '36 two of my professors left for good, going into voluntary exile before they got shut up in the ghetto, Jews both of them, German Jews. As for Bodo… at the beginning he reacted quite strongly to all this. He had great influence, a world reputation—not a recent one either, an old one, dating back to the '20s… A big matter for the Germans. He represented the very best they had: a genuine Aryan, an aristocrat—the son and grandson of distinguished academics, a famous musician—there isn't anything they have greater respect for over there… His first public clashes with the Nazis made them freeze. They didn't dare raise a hand against him. They were waiting for an opportunity to get hold of him… and finally they managed it through music itself…"

I scratched my head. I'd heard about quite a lot of this before, everyone had: about persecutions and ghettos for the Jews, about racial purity and so on. But how you set a trap for someone using music, this was what I really wanted to know.

"Bodo belongs to the old German culture," my companion explained. "His gods are Beethoven and Wagner. He himself composes music of their kind more or less" (a slight contemptuous lift of the lip here). "He's the only person who plays it, too. But when it comes to *his gods* he's an outstanding interpreter. When you hear their works conducted by him, you understand why they're so significant and unique… And a great interpreter is important in any art. But new creation, new art is something utterly different. Someone like Froberger would need a new kind of sensitivity and a new kind of knowledge to distinguish the diamonds from the dross… And Bodo is trapped in his worship of the past. He doesn't realize how much his gods were looking forward to the future when they composed the works that he and his kind preserve in golden reliquaries…"

I cleared my throat. "I'm trying to understand," I said. "Certainly I'm familiar with all the words you're using, but…"

"Their meaning escapes you, American, eh?" His laugh choked into a violent fit of coughing. "It's simple. In the old days, before the Nazis, Bodo and his traditionalists always used to call us and our teachers crazy clowns, madmen, lunatics, things like that. But when the Nazis came to power, from one day to the next we became *traitors, bad Germans* (those of us who were German), *degenerates*, a threat to the New Civilization. Do you understand what I'm saying? A new, lower race had come into existence that needed to be gotten rid of—us!"

"I read about those things in America. Whenever someone prominent arrived from Europe, they'd put him on the radio and he'd talk about all that… To tell the truth, I got sick of listening to them, especially with the funny English they spoke. Europe seemed an awfully long way away…" (I laughed awkwardly). "It never crossed my mind…"

"Yes. Bodo lives in a world of his own these days, he keeps clear of all the everyday business of war. It's well known too that he intervened on behalf of quite a few people when Goebbels took their passports away, he threw all his weight into helping them. But naturally he doesn't want to risk his own neck. The Nazis will tolerate him up to a point—he knows that. They're gangsters, people without any trace of a soul… You don't play games with those bastards. When you stop giving them what they want—and a representative of the old German culture is something they want very much indeed—they'll pack you straight off to the camps along with everyone else. Or if you're lucky they'll allow the Swiss to offer you nationality. But Bodo doesn't want to leave Germany.

He knows it's only there that he's a god—all right, a demigod—and that nowhere else in the world is there any place for a German musician who doesn't play any other repertoire. As for America… his greatest rival is in America and isn't at all likely to let him set foot on that continent…"

"That's odd," I said. "I'd no idea musicians were such mafiosi. Toscanini's a nice guy though, if your Bodo went to America he'd be glad."

"You don't know what you're talking about," laughed Beratis. "Never mind. Anyway, Bodo pays the price. He plays his part, he says what he's always been saying and effectively fights against anything new, any progressive ideas, any revolution in music. And when I say 'fights', I mean it! The last time a work of mine was played, in '36, in the auditorium of a small movie theater, I saw him sitting in the back row. Since he was my professor, I went up to greet him. 'I came,' he told me, 'to see whether they were right or wrong.' 'I don't understand,' I said, 'right or wrong about what?' 'About putting your name on the list of undesirables,' he answered, without looking at me. 'Did they ask your opinion?' He raised his eyebrows and said with that slight stammer he affects, 'Do you really think they'd do something like that without consulting me?' I froze. Just a few weeks earlier he'd seen me with Hannah, my German Jewish girlfriend, at a party. The Nazis knew all about her but as her father still had some influence and her Jewish mother had died long since, they looked the other way. She and I had just moved into a larger apartment, I'd borrowed money everywhere… Undesirable! That meant I'd have to leave Germany once and for all within a week… 'And what did you tell them?' I asked. 'That you are the very worst of all, Beratis, that's what I told them and that's what I believe. Goodbye!' And he turned on his heel and left."

His eyes were shut, as if he was seeing all the things he was telling me about pass before him in a waking dream.

"Tonight, as soon as he saw me in the theater he said, 'I'm glad to see you here, Beratis, you are in your own country and doing the best work possible instead of violating our art…' Those were his very first words to me. 'Whatever you say, Maestro,' I answered. Then he told me to translate accurately and began his speech. When Pericles died before his eyes, he asked, 'What happened to the oboe? A wretched end even for such a wretched musician…' 'He died of starvation, Maestro,' I replied, 'like half Athens.' He didn't seem to like this one bit. He turned at once to the German commandant, 'The people here are under-nourished. The musicians who will be playing for me need to have enough strength to blow, scrape or strike their instruments as much as I require.' In other words, when I've had what I want from them you can throw them to the dogs if you so wish. That's the great artist for you. So what d'you think, American, should I go one more time and ask him to throw me some scraps from his table?"

All of a sudden we heard shots from Academias Street. Miltos jumped up and was about to open the balcony door. I restrained him. The shots were near, it was dangerous, at night the patrols weren't a joke, they used their machine guns, hand grenades even.

"Someone with a bullhorn," I said.

"I know," he replied. "There's often someone with one on my own street, I wake up and listen to him. They're kids, most of them. Kids are foolhardy…" (his wry smile again) "like…"

"Like Tasos Markopoulos."

"And you."

We ventured cautiously onto the balcony and looked up the road, to where after the junction with Academias Street it turned into Zoodochou Pigis Street. My friend Mimis Papachrysanthou lived there and would surely also be awake now and listening.

"American," said Beratis, once we'd gone back inside, locking the balcony door behind us. "Better not tell me the truth about yourself if you're an English or an American spy. I'm not a brave man—if they caught me I'd spew out everything I knew or didn't know at the first slap… I'm not made of very stern stuff, I wish I were."

"I'm not a spy," I told him.

"What's wrong with your leg?" he asked, as if this had something to do with it.

"I was lamed," I answered, somewhat foolishly.

"I can see that. What I was asking was how."

"It's not my favorite topic of conversation."

"That means it happened recently."

"Fairly recently."

I opened a drawer, took out an old packet of Chesterfields and gave it to him.

He looked at it, he sniffed it. His eyebrows rose in an arch of admiration.

"You certainly must be a spy," he declared and lit one greedily.

"No, I had them left over… I brought them with me when I came but didn't smoke them. I'd given up for a while. Now I have one occasionally to supplement a meal. My leg dates from America. I had enemies there… they caught me and severed the tendon. I was cobbled together again in a hospital but it left me with a limp, sometimes worse than it is now, sometimes a bit better, it depends on the weather…"

"I see… So you had enemies. What sort of enemies does a man who deals in real estate have? Some client you cheated?"

"No, but as you may have heard, the underworld is involved in every kind of business there…"

"Ah! Gangsters!" he exclaimed and his eyes shone. "Just like in the movies."

"Something like that, yes."

"Didn't you go to the police?"

I laughed. Beratis blushed.

"I'm not as familiar with America as you are, American. It wouldn't have helped, would it? The gangs are omnipotent."

"I was mixed up with a woman," I said. "Without knowing she was involved with people of that kind…"

I could see his eyes in the darkness shining like burning coals. Suddenly my story seemed to interest him a lot, he was waiting to hear more. It was an opportunity for me to repay his confidences about music and his life in Berlin. This is how friendships are built, it is secrets that serve as the mortar that binds them.

"I understand," he murmured, "revenge."

I blew smoke towards the ceiling. My cigarette seemed to have a bitter taste of hay. The tobacco had expired during its long stay in my drawer. But it was something. The dizziness it induced helped us to speak more freely.

"I'm involved with a woman too," said Beratis.

I hadn't had time to reflect on how I'd tell him about Lauretta, and here he was getting ready for a new outburst of confessions. I kept silent and waited.

"She lives very near you. Here. In your own building," he said. "You know her."

"Ah," I said. "Is she perhaps Balomenos' daughter? Or Mrs Kynigos?"

He shook his head. She was neither of these women.

"She's someone I love and admire, someone who inspires me to write music and who makes me feel ashamed that I'm not more actively involved in the Resistance… She's a goddess!"

"Mrs Marika Kanellis," I said, hardly believing my ears.

"Yes," said Beratis.

"But she…" I began without quite knowing what I wanted to say. "Involved with her or in love with her?"

"Isn't it the same?"

"We have to distinguish things. I'm in love with her too" (I laughed) "but I'm not involved with her."

"Involved with her," he insisted.

I stubbed out my cigarette and stood up. I needed to find some excuse to leave the room, even for just a moment, if I was to maintain my cool and not let him see how upset I felt.

15

More confidences

"If you were having an affair I would have expected it to be with Vanda, Mrs Paltoglou I mean," I told him when I returned to the dining room. "All that admiration for you… all that money…"

"Are you joking? I scarcely know Vicky. I've no idea why she sent me that money tonight. I mean to ask her. No, I haven't got anything going with her. I'd feel easier if I did. Marika keeps me in a state of constant agony… They're having a bad time, she and her husband. The only food they have is what they get from the Lawyers' Union soup kitchen, they're penniless… They're not earning anything. They don't have work and even if they did they wouldn't get paid for it… after all, who's got money to spare for lawyers these days? And they're both in the Resistance. One fine day they might be caught and executed," he said, his voice suddenly louder as if he couldn't resist putting his worst nightmare into words.

"So you've visited this building before?" I asked.

"I've come here, yes. When Pavlos is out... I come and see her... I'm telling you because you'll understand... I don't find it easy. He's a friend, I've a lot of respect for him, he's a fine, cultivated person, one of the best there is. And I'm forced to play the wretched part of the common friend, I feel so ashamed, I tremble for fear he might realize what's going on... and what would happen then... it would kill him, it would break him, I know how sensitive he is. And he loves her in his own way... It's true they quarrel, they have arguments. She writes poems that Pavlos doesn't think much of, he criticizes them and hurts her feelings. Then she gets her own back by mocking his political views. She calls him a 'mild revolutionary'."

His voice trembled. It was so quiet now that I could barely hear him.

"She's told him she's suffering from... something gynecological... an inflammation of the ovaries... her doctor has supposedly ordered her to abstain for the time being... you understand what I mean... So that she's not obliged to... She doesn't like lying, she's a straightforward person, Marika, she doesn't stoop so low... And she's so tender, so sweet..."

"Tender? Sweet?" I burst out laughing, I couldn't help it.

"Why are you laughing?"

"I don't know—simply that my experiences of her have been rather different. But after all, why not? I'm one thing, just a tenant living in the same building, and you're another thing… and her husband…"

"You don't like her…"

Even in the semi-darkness I could see that his pale cheeks had flushed. He was regretting having confided in a potential enemy, in a man he didn't know. He was afraid he'd acted rashly in revealing his feelings.

"I told you what I feel for her," I responded. "I didn't tell you what she feels for me."

"I thought you were joking… Are you really in love with her? Not that it would be at all odd…"

"Let's not overdo it. Being in love is a serious state of affairs, it requires a different sort of relationship from the one I have with her… all I do is see her coming in and out, going up and down the stairs, I run into her at the front door, I raise my hat to her politely…"

"The courteous American."

"Courteous, schmourteous. She doesn't want to set eyes on me. And—to tell you something you'll find hard to believe—in the last three days she's slapped me twice" (I was exaggerating slightly).

"Come on!" Beratis was as discomfited as if I'd been a small child beginning to recount imaginary adventures. "Marika slap you? Why should she?"

"Because she loathes me, that's why."

"But what's she got against you?"

"She knows I'm… Or rather, she knows I'm not… left-wing like they are… She thinks I'm an informer… She believes I slandered them to Balomenos, the owner, and that's why he turned them out of this apartment and gave it to me..."

"I've heard something about that business," Beratis said. "That's to say... when they moved out of here Pavlos told me some fascist in the building had pinched their apartment. But as for slaps, Angel, where did that idea come from?"

"From the same place the slaps came from. Your beloved's little hand has been imprinted on my cheek since the day before yesterday. I looked at her impertinently, she said, and in any case she'd very much prefer it if I didn't even say as much as 'Good morning' to her..."

"Oh, I don't know..." he said, clearly unhappy and embarrassed at these sudden revelations.

"Listen," I told him, "I don't bear her a grudge. I like her, I forgive her for everything, as you always do when you like someone... Don't for a moment imagine that I hold it against her... anything but."

He seemed all of a sudden to have fallen into a deep melancholy. For some time he didn't speak. And when he opened his mouth again it was to say that he was heavy with fatigue and that it might be a good idea if we went to bed—tomorrow was going to be a tiring day for him and full of worries.

"Look here, Miltos," I said. "Mrs Paltoglou's money... What are you intending to use it for?"

"I'm not intending to use it. I'm intending to give it back to her."

Absolute. Impregnable. Unbending.

"That's folly, pure and simple," I commented. "You need food. What's more, I'm going down to Piraeus with a friend of mine tomorrow to try and find some. He knows various people there, we went a few days ago… Now that you've got some money in your pocket you'd do much better to use it… Vanda didn't go without in order to give it to you, and anyway the fact that she did give it means she wants you to have it for some reason… Why are you ruling out the possibility that she might simply admire you, like she says? And her husband's one of those people making money these days… I don't know quite how exactly, but he's making it, that's for sure. Some people always do."

"It's the same people making it now who were making it before," Beratis said. "That doesn't change, no matter what happens."

"Now you're talking! So why the nonsense about giving it back and other crazy ideas? Just think—with all that money you could even help the Kanellis couple…"

That did the trick! I'd said the magic word. He was silent, sitting in his corner on the divan. It was obvious that he was now going to think seriously about keeping the unexpected wealth that had dropped into his hands. And maybe he'd come down to Piraeus with us to find food.

"You know something, Angel?" he said, just as I was going out of the room to leave him to sleep. "I'm thinking it was my good luck that made you cross my path tonight…"

"I'll tell you something too… I'm very glad we met… because I'd heard about you from someone… someone you probably don't know but who knows about you… and he told me *that man must stay alive to complete his work*… I dare say he's an admirer or an acquaintance of yours, I don't know what exactly, but he kept on telling me about you… He must have meant your music, I suppose."

"Who was he?" Beratis was suddenly interested.

"Look, it's late. I've got to go out on a job early tomorrow morning. You can stay here as long as you like. I won't be back till late."

Our eyes met in the half-dark of the room.

"While you're here you could even see Mrs Kanellis, it's an opportunity… And since no one knows you're here at my place you're not in any danger—either you or her."

"You may be called Angel but you're one hell of a smooth operator, American," said Beratis and smiled—for the first time that evening.

It wasn't true that I had a job to do that morning. I'd said it on purpose in the hope that the musician would stay on in my apartment a bit longer and would try to meet his sweetheart. He would have had to have a will of steel to resist the unexpected proximity. I hadn't yet had time to reflect much on what I'd learned about the two of them, yet all the same my instinct told me this is how it would be. Later, when I was alone again and in a cooler frame of mind, I was able to sit down and think things through and draw something like a little diagram. Lamera had taught me to draw diagrams to get my thoughts in order: names, dates, people, characteristics, facts and events. If you use this method you can unravel a tangled skein much more easily. To be mixed up with the wife of someone you admire and respect, as Beratis did Kanellis… it was a tough situation. And now from one moment to the next he was suddenly equipped with three aces that gave him a strong hand: money, a trusty friend (me), and even a refuge—my apartment which I'd put at his disposal. Unwell, in love, uncertain and confused as he was, he'd be bound to make use of all three at once.

I wandered aimlessly through the streets. I stuck the usual bit of paper on the glass pane of my office door saying "Back soon" for the benefit of all the clients who would never come asking for me and set off on a long walk around the town. I'd recently got into the habit of doing this as I was dragging my leg less—in fact my gait was almost normal. Everyone walked everywhere these days; public transport, where it existed, was sporadic and the surest and quickest way of getting around was "the biped streetcar," as we used to call it.

The sun was shining, people had come out and for a brief space the misery didn't show so much; there were moments when everything seemed like it used to be as the light caressed the asphalt and the studs at the crossings glittered.

As I walked I was trying to think. I hadn't begun to

like the man yet. All my old professional instincts told me this wasn't necessary; for me, the musician was simply an unhoped for source of income. The Big Boss was counting on my help and there wasn't anything in the least mean about the payment he'd promised. Here, however, arose a second crucial question: all my old professional instincts also told me that fees like this often have trouble with the law concealed behind them; and these days the law wore helmets and boots and spoke in a barbaric language—trouble with it might well prove fatal. What was Agathos hiding from me? Impossible to tell. If my protégé had been anything else, I would have imagined that… But a musician?

I stopped on the corner of Korai Street and gazed at the roofs of Academias and Panepistimiou Street, with Lykabettos behind them, bare now as all the little trees had long since been chopped down for firewood and cooking fuel. All of a sudden Marika had come alive and was haunting me: that face, that body which I watched walking along Georgiou Gennadiou Street in her mannish suit and trilby, with the soft locks of hair falling on her shoulders, that glance which fell on me like lightning, accusing me of being what I was (a man looking at her) and what without any evidence she believed me to be (her enemy)—this creature, the thought of whom was gripping me more and more often, without me believing that I was in love with her, had turned into something new.

What, though? It was the fact that I knew about her and Beratis. The forty-year-old musician with his straight nose and square jaw and yellow teeth, with the incipient bald patch, the haughty air of the artist concealing a stern view of all the people around him—he was the man whom Marika met secretly, with whom she had that private intimacy which no one else sees, he was the man who held her in his arms and heard her cries of pleasure… Everything was different now. Marika had changed: from being a distant and unattainable ideal she had become a mistress.

Her guilty secret had unexpectedly added an arrow to my quiver. What an odd thought! I wasn't about to go to war with her. Not now and not ever. Yet, now that I knew, I felt stronger in relation to her. I was the friend and protector of her lover, no longer the cop or the stool pigeon. I was a respectable professional who lived in the same building. A man with feelings, someone worthy of anyone's respect.

That love affair… I was thinking… that great, secret love affair… how long might it have been going on for? How recent or long-standing was it? Hard to say. I didn't doubt that Mrs Kanellis was possessed of the ardent temperament suggested by the fire in her glance, by the secret swaying of her body as she walked, as if beneath her skirt lay hidden the guilty secrets of all women everywhere, both beautiful and ugly: those caresses, those kisses that no one must know of, that no one dares speak of even though everyone knows of their existence, those impatient steps hurrying to the privacy that lies behind a closed door.

As a lover Beratis saw things one way; my own experience told me something different. I'm referring to that curious matter of her supposed illness, the inflammation of the ovaries, which according to him had been devised for her husband's consumption.

The moans from the open window that frequently disturbed my light sleep indicated that her husband had nothing to complain of: he had his regular share of her caresses. *These* caresses were her husband's: the tall, thin lawyer claimed them and took them as he had every marital right to do. Yet no violence seemed to be involved, her favors weren't apparently granted in a spirit of servility or indifference. Marika Kanellis, it was perfectly clear, enjoyed it wherever she found it. And found it wherever she sought it.

As I turned from Korai Street onto Stadiou Street and wandered aimlessly towards Syntagma, the image in my memory was vivid.

In the darkness of my blacked-out apartment, I had gone along the narrow corridor into the kitchen. I didn't quite know where I was going yet my footsteps were steady. In the half-dark I could make out the gas cooker, the handles on the glass jars once containing sugar, coffee, rice, dried beans—past glories!—arrayed each in its place in the wooden cupboard by the stove: all that remained in the cupboard now were boxes of matches, sage wrapped up in blue macaroni paper, string, corks from empty bottles and some tins of old dried-up shoe polish which had impregnated the whole cupboard with its smell. Above the marble sink the narrow barred window shed a dim glow into the dark kitchen, that faint light that reaches the lower floors from the light-well, just enough to enable you to find your way out onto the metal staircase that leads up to the flat roof.

As I stepped onto these stairs a smell of mold from the storerooms below reached my nostrils. It was January, the halcyon days were approaching, there was a lightness in the atmosphere which you could sense. It brought the scents alive from the old abandoned gardens on Gennadiou Street, as well as the heavier smells from kitchens and basements.

Iron bars separated our light-well from the back of the Public Prosecutor's offices, an old three-story building. I don't know whether they ever took care of its façade, giving onto Fidiou Street, but at the back the plaster was beginning to crumble; you often heard the thud as lumps of it fell to the ground. The tall, frosted glass windows of its stairwell were broken in places, leaving convenient entrances for all the rats that gnawed away at the files in the archives. In the mornings you could see the hurrying silhouettes of people going up and down these stairs.

I went up to the second floor. Every floor has a balcony wide enough for housewives to hang out their laundry, if they can't be bothered to go up to the flat roof, that is, or have washing they don't want to hang out in public view.

The kitchen door opens onto this balcony, and so does one of the bedroom windows.

I'd never been on their balcony before. Once, though, as I came down from the roof, at a turn of the stairs my eye had chanced to catch sight of their double bed and the wardrobe opposite it through the window they'd opened to air the room. But when the hot weather began and they left the shutters open or loosely pulled to, then I could hear the sounds that came to me from above. Often they'd make me dream that I was climbing the stairs, was standing hidden outside the room and watching. And sleep would come to me in an erotic delirium; as the hunger grew more savage, this grew more savage too.

I could hear her voice quite clearly. She was talking to her husband in what sounded as if it was the end of a conversation begun some time before. Silence fell. In my disturbance I was glued to the wall, trying to melt into it so as not to be noticed either by the people I was spying on or by any of the tenants from the floor above who might chance to come out suddenly.

From where I was standing I could see a narrow strip of the bedroom through the gap in the shutters. As my eyes grew accustomed to the dim light, I made out the wardrobe with its mirror shining in the dark.

Then there was a sound. At the beginning I didn't understand what it was. After a moment I distinguished their voices, it was as if they were singing together, yet they weren't singing. Nor were they speaking. They were murmuring and whispering to one another. The sheets rustled. Then there was a louder cry, hers. His answer came as if from deep within a cave, his voice altered, inarticulate. I made to approach but something creaked beneath my foot and I froze in immobility. Luckily only I had heard it. I breathed again. I couldn't stand in front of the gap in the shutters for my shadow would have been projected onto the grey plaster of their walls. I could only creep closer and watch the dim reflections in the wardrobe mirror. Only the voices that accompanied the movements bore witness to the identity of a back or a neck, of the hair or the gently moving legs.

After a little while their voices became more distinct, like those I used to hear from my own bedroom, quite clear now, and her breathing too, and all the quiet sighs that never reached the floor below. Her husband said something. And in the voice of a young girl she replied: "I'm going to have a baby. I shall blossom, I can feel it, *a child will blossom…*"

I would have liked it if a woman spoke to me like that, I reflected. All Laurina could say at moments like these (and ah, how few they were in truth) was, "Come to me, come," or "Come on, honey, give it to me, give it to me," which always made me wonder if what she wanted was for me to get it over with at long last or to go on panting on top of her while I waited for her. With Marika it was as if she was singing or writing a poem—lucky Pavlos Kanellis, I thought, as I fell asleep at six in the morning.

An inflammation of the ovaries? Well, maybe. But probably from overheating.

I looked at my reflection in the shop windows of Stadiou Street and wondered: am I not taller and more elegant, better dressed still in spite of my threadbare suit, am I not more handsome, with my thick hair parted in the center, am I not a better choice as lover than Beratis? And yet she didn't look twice at me, he pleased her and I didn't. Could she somehow have guessed all the things she didn't know about me? That even if she'd wanted me, if I'd wanted her, I could never have been her lover? Did she see some mark upon me that set me apart from everyone else? Who knows? Women have a kind of intuition, they understand things.

High in the sky scattered clouds were moving south by the time I decided to go home. For some reason I'd wanted it to rain, the city seemed sullied with a black dust that had settled over the asphalt and the sidewalks, as if thrown up by the wheels of all the military vehicles. Rain would have cleaned up this black filth, washing it into the drains. And when the sun came out again, it would have shone over a freshly washed Athens.

16

___

And revelations

I could hear voices in my apartment. I picked out hers first, then his quieter tones. My heart leapt in my chest! The miracle had happened, Marika Kanellis had come to visit me—albeit while I was out. For a moment I thought it might be fun to catch her, uninvited, in the home of the man she'd slapped. What should I do? Quick, quick, think. Be sensible. If I put my key in the lock and opened the door I'd certainly have to face an uncomfortable situation, from her maybe more insults, from Beratis a moody silence. If I simply left… well, if I left, then things would take a different direction. I wouldn't put them in an awkward position, I decided, I'd wait.

I went back down, turned onto Academias Street, walked around the block and then along Harilaou Trikoupi Street. There were lights in some of the upper windows of the German Archaeological Mission. The guard could have been made of granite. Further down, between the Mission and the Conservatoire, was a little café that served the surrounding offices and shops. I went in and telephoned my own number. No one answered —but this didn't necessarily mean my visitors had left. Then I had a better idea: I dialed the Kanellis number and hung up when I heard Marika's voice.

Beratis had left too. My apartment was once more empty. Yet it seemed different, and not only because I'd had a guest to stay the night before. A trace of her scent hung in the air. And I was pleased with myself for not having turned my key in the lock a little earlier.

The musician telephoned me that afternoon. First he wanted to know why I'd been so late back, then he thanked me for my hospitality the previous night. He was speaking hurriedly, his voice sounded hoarse, and somewhere in the background a radio was playing a Stella Greca song. He didn't have a telephone of his own, he was phoning from outside, probably from some café. I told him we ought to go down to Piraeus as soon as possible, whereupon he asked me when and what he should do.

"I'll have to find my friend first, the man I told you about," I told him. "Come over to my place tomorrow morning, can you?"

"I can," he said.

The following morning he rang my bell at nine o'clock. I hadn't had any further news from Papachrysanthou but was hoping to find him at some point during the day and stir him into making the expedition. He could stay here, I told the musician, I had to go out on some errands but I'd be back before two.

"But what would I do here?" he asked, slightly puzzled.

"If you've nothing better to do outside, you'll find something to occupy you here," I told him. "If you have, then go."

I saw that he was hesitating. Then he took a cigarette from his pocket and began to smoke nervously.

"Listen," he said, "I missed you yesterday."

I sat down.

"I saw Marika," he added, and fell silent.

This statement had a final tone to it, as if implying "That's all." I was supposed to fill in the rest for myself —and I was perfectly ready to do so out loud, as between men, but Beratis started off again.

"She told me something I didn't know." He smiled suddenly and there was a strange expression in his eyes.

"Maestro, you seem to have a way with the chicks... You've got one taking care you don't die of hunger and another slipping you into her house when her husband's away... Maybe you ought to give me a few lessons on the double bass, you might help me manage something..."

"She's not a *chick*..."

"I meant Vanda," I amended.

"Listen," he continued, "yesterday I phoned her from here and she came... She came to tell me something..."

"Well she'd hardly come to my place for any other reason."

" She says that you're… that you're a police *informer*," said Beratis, blushing up to his ears.

"Yes, I know, she's said the same thing to me, it's a tune I'm familiar with," I answered.

"She says you're a private detective!" he said, looking straight at me. "That you've got an investigation bureau just around the corner on Gamvetta Street."

It was time to get some things straightened out, I couldn't go on acting the Greek-American realtor much longer.

"I have to do something to earn a living," I said, with an off-hand air. "I'd got a license in New York, I had the papers with me… so I opened a bureau."

He couldn't take his eyes off me. Could a musician and a private detective be friends?

"I'm not particularly proud of it, dragging adulterous couples off to the police station, taking photographs of them in bed… But there hasn't been any work to speak of for some time, I only keep the office on because I'd paid the rent in advance. It doesn't make me an informer."

He looked down guiltily. The lawyer must have argued the case for the prosecution convincingly.

"All right," he said. "But why did you lie to me… why did you say you were in the real estate business?"

"What d'you expect, buddy? We're like undertakers —everyone's pleased to see us when they need our services but no one wants to keep company with us."

"Maybe I ought to have paid more attention," said Beratis. "All that money out of the blue, the mysterious admirer who wants to save me from dying before my time, Vanda Paltoglou… You spin wonderful fairy tales, Angel. How about giving me the truth now?"

"What truth? Are you really interested in the truth?" I responded. "I don't think so. People don't recognize the truth when it's staring them in the face. And everyone's looking for the truth. Well, the only truth these days, my friend, is the fact that with that money you can buy food in Piraeus. The truth is Vanda who's interested in your well-being. And is able to help you. She knows you're proud and pig-headed. That's why she got me to do it."

Beratis got up and paced up and down the room, as if he had pins and needles or wanted to wake up from a dream.

"If I spoke to her I'd find out," he said hoarsely. A blush had spread over his face and he looked angry, embarrassed and ashamed. "But it isn't easy to see her… or to talk to her… what with that bastard she's got mixed up with. And I don't want that black marketeer's money!"

"I understand," I told him, "I quite agree. But the bread you'll be eating if we go down to Piraeus will be genuine Italian bread bought at the whorehouses in the Troumba."

"Is that all the answer you're going to give me?" he asked. "We're supposed to be friends, I trusted you with my secrets."

"I don't know what else you want me to say. If you've any reason to suspect me, do what you think best. I trusted you too, I trusted you with my own home, yesterday night and this morning…"

I said this on purpose in order to bring the conversation

back to where it had started. To Marika Kanellis' visit to my apartment 'to tell him something'.

He got up again and stood at the window.

"She's pregnant," he said. "Isn't that wonderful?"

"Indeed it is, since she's a married woman," I said neutrally.

'I told you about that," he said in irritation.

"About the inflammation?"

"Yes."

"And the *abstention*?"

"Yes… She went to see her doctor yesterday, without telling Pavlos, for the tests…"

He looked at me as if he expected me to share his happiness.

"And how does she see it?"

"What do you mean?"

"Is she happy too?"

There was a jaunty glint in his eye that hadn't been present when he'd enthused poetically about his beloved's pregnancy; now we were going to talk man to man.

"Yes, she is… There's no doubt about it."

A groan escaped me. He looked at me in surprise: didn't I believe it, or didn't I approve of this state of affairs?

"Well, but," said I, "now that she's pregnant, mightn't it be a good idea if she *stopped* the abstention?"

His face fell.

"Why?" His teeth were clenched, ready to attack me. He ran his hand over his forehead; fine drops of sweat had sprung out on it in spite of the cold.

"Because if she's pregnant, isn't she going to have to tell her husband sooner or later? It's all very well keeping quiet about a conception, but you can hardly keep quiet about a pregnancy…"

A cloud passed across his face. In the full flush of his enthusiasm he obviously hadn't sat down and worked out one or two basic things.

"She'll have to," he conceded.

He sat down again. He was plunged in thought, twisting his fingers together.

"Take things one by one. Right now what we have to do is go and find some food, that's the first and most important thing. You've got to eat and get your strength up."

"Yes," he said.

"The next thing is to see what to do about this business. Listen, this apartment's at your disposal, you don't have to hang around waiting for her husband to go out. Come here whenever you want, I'm out in the mornings, in the afternoons, often in the evenings too, you can come and see her, you'll have a bit more peace and quiet to think about what you'll both do."

He nodded, then put out his hand and gripped mine.

"You're OK," he said. "But she won't come here, she doesn't want to."

I shrugged. "There are lots of things we don't want to do… and a great many of them we end up doing anyway because there isn't any alternative, don't you think?"

Our conversation ended there. I got up and left him on

his own while I went to the office—or at least that's what I told him. In actuality I went to meet Papachrysanthou to arrange our second expedition to Piraeus.

At midday Mimis was often to be found at the Picadilly, on Panepistimiou Street. This large café's claim to fame was its coffee, for which you paid a fortune but which was in fact roasted chickpeas; however, it smelled like coffee and was the closest substitute. Maybe the atmosphere in the café also helped the illusion. Mimis used to drop in at noon for conversation with some of his old acquaintances. Various other ghosts played *prefa* or poker, there was an old lame billiards table in the corner that no one ever bothered with. You rarely came across any foreigners there. The Germans and Italians who walked down Panepistimiou Street from the Kommandatur in Syntagma preferred Orfanides' or the restaurant in Koloktroni Square, the Kentrikon, which had everything, even meat, although it wasn't a place you could go because of the high prices and because the Germans took up all the tables.

I spotted him sitting by the window. His wandering eye was looking in my direction but he didn't see me. I waved to attract his attention. He gestured to me to come in. The man sitting beside him was putting on his coat and preparing to go home.

"Hephaistos, what are you doing here?"

"I was looking for you," I said.

I sat down opposite him without taking off my coat. The empty hall reverberated strangely, sounds were muted: glasses on the marble table tops, the dull slap of cards on the baize, a flint trying repeatedly to produce a spark, the murmurs of the customers. There was almost nothing to serve—and no one was in a hurry to order what little was available because of the prices. What you saw was a pantomime of a café rather than a truly functioning café in the heart of the city.

Mimis was doubtful. Another trip to Piraeus? Why, have you already eaten what you bought last time? When he heard that it was for the benefit of a friend he grew even cooler about it.

"Look here, Hephaistos," he said, "we need those people, it won't do to push your luck with them for the sake of every Tom, Dick and Harry. All right, you feel sorry for him, but it's the survival of the fittest here. If the whole world gets to know of that little waterhole then that's it, curtains. You won't even find a piece of moldy lemon peel next time you're wanting something. What the hell do you think Polypheme is, the horn of plenty? Besides, he said so himself: don't bring any more customers. He only sold something to us in the first place because we came recommended by a friend."

I couldn't tell him that it was my business to look after the musician, nor that if sovereigns were exploding all around me like bullets from the Germans' stukas, it was because of him. It wasn't that I didn't trust Mimis, but there are rules in this business and if you break them you end up a loser.

"Anyway, no ship's arrived at Piraeus for quite a while," he added. "Some contacts of mine promised to send me word if there was any smoke on the horizon but I haven't heard a peep out of them since. The most you'll find is some more of Stellitsa's bread And you know the way there yourself—there isn't any need for me to come with you."

The mauve birthmark above his nose seemed drained of color.

"What's the matter?"

"Nothing. What should be the matter?"

He was a poor liar. I drummed my fingers on the marble table top as I waited for him to go on.

"I'm not well, I can hardly stay on my feet," he said, gazing out at Korai Street. "Look, on Tuesday I went down there… to Piraeus" (explaining), "and I thought I'd go by for the odd loaf… That crazy bitch cornered me and started to say, well, she's got a mouth on her, you heard her… oh, the rotten whore she's become—do a whore's job and you get a whore's heart."

"You talk as if there was some old business as well," I commented.

"Would it surprise you if there were?" he interrupted me sternly. "If you'd seen Stellitsa a few years ago, when she first went on the game, though she hadn't quite turned pro then… In those days I still had some idea of marrying her, Hephaistos… God saved me…God damned me maybe, don't know which… D'you get me? Know what I mean?"

"Not easily," I answered. "You talk in riddles and hints. We're good friends but you always seem to forget we're not old friends—how long do you think you've known me for?"

I'd noticed he had a habit of doing this, he used to talk as if I'd known him forever, since he was a child.

"Maybe it's my fault too," he said, shaking his head. "Maybe I was responsible for what happened to her, I don't say I wasn't. But what did we know in those days, Hephaistos, when we were twenty or thirty even, we were only kids, no matter that we swaggered like men. Thought we knew it all, life, women, people in general… d'you get me? A load of gammon. OK, it was my fault but her mind had already turned to her little whatsit and the whole of Piraeus had tales to tell of how Stella did it *this* way and Stella did it *that* way—just you try and imagine appearing in public as her fiancé. These days everyone's always trying to find someone to blame for his miseries and woes. For one person it's the rottenness of society that's to blame, for another it's Venizelos, or the king, and for another it's old Mimis Papachrysanthou… well, that's the case here, d'you get me? The lady went professional—and whose fault was it? Mine because I jilted her. You'd think all fiancées left in the lurch when the man couldn't marry them because he was trying to get a few pence together, to make a life, know what I mean, you'd think they all set up in business in the Troumba. Well, no, Madam Stella, all the same, no!"

He stopped speaking and bowed his head. I'd picked up something from all these disjointed phrases, there'd been something between them, something had been apparent that day we went to the whorehouse together, but just how much it had cost him I hadn't realized.

"If I went down to the harbor for something," he said, changing the subject, "it would be for a drop or two of retsina from the Maniatika quarter, from Fondas' place, where we went... yes, that I might do. Or a spot of rotgut to befuddle me so I could stop thinking. I wish the Germans would catch me in one of their roadblocks, Hephaistos, and shoot me as a hostage. Then maybe someone else more useful for the struggle would survive instead. And I'd be able to stop thinking... That old fellow up there in the sky put a whole lot of trouble in our skulls when he made us able to remember and think... A curse... She's got a little girl..." (he was continuing to rave, jumping from one subject to another), "she's got a little girl, you heard her that day we were there, singing on the stairs—the little girl, I mean, she must be about thirteen now, God knows who sowed that seed—she has her there and she's bringing her up in the whorehouse, sends her to school, the kid sits and does her arithmetic and her scripture homework while in the next room her mother is... Let them go to hell, Hephaistos... That's why I say the Almighty planted a great curse in our brains... Know why I say it? I'll tell you. And you'll see what the human mind's capable of. All right, that old business which she holds against me isn't any surprise, I've heard it all before... And when she opens her mouth, forget it, not even the deepest river would wash you clean. She grabs me on the doorstep before I've even got in. And she says all in one go, listen, she says, do you know what I'm going to do with the kid? So I wait to hear what she'll say… They all want their kids to be something, that's why they're supposedly sacrificing themselves and saving money so that their children—those that have got them—can make something of themselves, so they can rise out of the muck, d'you get me? And what does that damn bitch say? A whore, she says, that's what my kid's going to be, and I'm already sending her to work on the streets, the Italians have a thing about little girls, it's time she learned what's what and where the day's wages come from… And she says it as if she didn't give a damn… and she looks at me, she looks at me with such an expression, Hephaistos, I can't tell you… And I got up and left—I didn't even ask for bread or anything. I went home and I washed to get that brothel stink off me… And I kept thinking, why was she saying it all to me, I mean why was she saying it *like that*, d'you get me? In that way! As if it was anything to me what Stella does with her brat, whether she's putting her on the streets or saving money to send her to the Polytechnic to become an engineer… Know what I mean, Hephaistos?"

I was silent. But he said nothing else and I didn't ask, I didn't seek explanations. His distress and his sadness were already bad enough, I didn't like to see him in that state, it didn't suit him—he'd always been all smiles and cheerfulness, even in the worst moments. Suddenly he seemed to have aged, as if twenty years had passed over him in one fell swoop.

So I listened to what he had to say and when he'd finished I asked him again if he'd take us to Piraeus. He realized he was wasting his breath trying to dissuade me. In any case, if it hadn't been for me and the money I'd lent him out of what Agathos paid me, Papachrysanthou wouldn't have been seeing Piraeus or Tyrnavos cheese or olive oil or anything, not in a million years. When did I want to go? The day after tomorrow, I said. Because I thought it would be a good idea to let a full day pass first so that I'd have time to arrange it with the musician, in case he might have other things to sort out.

17

The saving grace of love

It was the times that were like that—don't go thinking the worst of us. While death was hovering over the city, his twin brother love was running through its cold and empty streets. The more the ghost with the sickle could be heard reaping his harvest next door or across the road, the more women gave themselves up to love to maintain their hold on life. Young women, old women, the married, the unmarried, schoolgirls and shop assistants—all of them had the same curious look in their eyes, all were suffering not just from hunger but from that great flame which burns in body and soul and urges survival. As their faces grew thinner, so their eyes seemed to grow larger and larger. Their enquiring gaze would fix on you as they waited for your proposition or hastened to make their own. The dark street corner, the lonely garden or broken-bulbed lamp post, the alcove beneath a flight of steps, the ill-lit corridor in an empty building: all served equally well.

That very morning within the space of a couple of hours I'd had to refuse the propositions of two separate women, both of whom I was speaking to for the first time. One was the little island girl who worked as a servant for the Kanellis couple. I'd gone to the bedroom window to shake out my blanket, on which ash from my cigarette had fallen just before I fell asleep, and saw her leaning against the railings of their balcony where I'd been concealed a few days ago as I spied on her mistress's loves. She was a girl of about eighteen or nineteen, slightly broad in the beam, with thick dark eyebrows arching over her laughing eyes. Her employers, both husband and wife, gave her a lot of trouble; whenever one or other of them was at home you'd hear a constant shouting and scolding. Occasionally I used to hear her crying too. Left-wing ideas and the abolition of class distinctions are all very well, but servants need to know their place.

She said good morning then told me she was alone up there, as if I'd asked. So? The faucet over the sink was dripping, could I perhaps come and tighten it with the pliers, she didn't have enough strength in her arm. I'd never even said hello to the girl before. We used to pass one another occasionally at the front door, that was all. But as a bachelor I must have attracted her attention. It could be that all the things she'd heard her employers saying about me had raised me in her estimation, for after all everyone assesses what he hears about other people his own way.

When I'd finished the job, which didn't require any

particular strength, I handed the pliers back to her and was preparing to return downstairs. She made a face: was I going to leave without having a coffee? What sort of coffee was she talking about? Proper coffee? Konstantina knew all the secrets of the household, no matter how well Mrs Marika hid things. She didn't know if it was real coffee or roasted carob beans but it certainly smelled good when Mr Pavlos made it. I told her that her employers couldn't stand me and wouldn't like me being in their house while they were out. Yes, she was aware that they couldn't stand me, they were always talking about me, but Konstantina "knew what I was like" and didn't believe a word of it. I was a gentleman, I wore a hat which I raised to all the women I encountered on the stairs, to her too—even if she was only *service*. I'd done the favor she'd asked of me and she was going to treat me to a coffee—what was wrong with that?

It didn't seem a bad idea to cast an eye around their apartment. I'd never been into it before, it was unknown territory to me except for the small slice of the bedroom that I'd seen from the balcony and the part of the hall that came into view when the door was left ajar as friends and clients came and went. I sat down on the kitchen chair and waited.

An amusing performance followed. The coffee, she said, was hidden on the highest shelf in the cupboard in a battered old metal jar which they couldn't make up their minds to throw away but which they didn't want getting in the way. Konstantina put a low, three-legged stool in front of the cupboard and stepped onto it. She stood on tiptoe and reached up as far as she could. In a trembling voice she begged me to come and help her. Heights made her giddy and, what with the way she was stretching up to reach for the tin, she was afraid she'd lose her balance. She wanted me to hold on to her. Not for me to stand on the stool and get the coffee, no, that wouldn't be right—simply for me to hold her a bit. I put my hands on her waist. Ah, yes, that was better. Only a bit further down would be even better, she still felt afraid. I moved my hands down. Just a bit lower, she said. My hands went lower. A tiny bit further. Yes, that was fine (my hands were now on her two buttocks), but a little bit harder, if I could grip her more firmly… yes, that was lovely, she wasn't afraid now, but I mustn't let go, I mustn't *play any tricks* on her and let go, I must hold on tight so she wouldn't fall—it made her so dizzy, she'd always been like this ever since she was a child: when her father and mother wanted to get rid of her for a bit (here Konstantina gave a meaningful chuckle lest I miss the point) and there wasn't any work they could send her off to do, they'd lift her into the big fig tree and leave her there as long as they liked, secure in the knowledge that she'd have to stay there until someone went to get her down.

But the search for the coffee couldn't be drawn out any longer. She had to admit that it wasn't where she'd thought. When I let go of her she turned around and jumped off the stool without the slightest trace of fear or dizziness. The coffee was found in an ordinary tin in the cupboard and Konstantina started making it. She'd liked me holding her, she said, she hadn't been at all afraid while my hands were on her, she'd liked it a lot. I seemed to be a strong man, even if I was thin. Mr Pavlos, she began… then stopped and—changing the subject—went on… Mr Pavlos didn't even know how to loosen a screw, he always called his wife who was good with her hands, or Konstantina herself. The coffee boiled over and spilled onto the marble counter. She didn't care, however, except that I wouldn't get my coffee. By now she was almost rubbing against me. She took my hands and put them back where they'd been while she was on the stool. Her eyes were shining, her voice in its lowest register. Her employers would be late back, they'd gone to a funeral at the Zografos cemetery.

"Shall we go inside?" she whispered, nodding towards the servant's room. As in my own apartment, it was at the front of the building and the shutter on its narrow window was rolled down and pushed out a little.

"Listen," I told her. "I like you, you're a very pretty girl. But I haven't got time now, I have to go out. I was on the point of leaving for the office when you called me."

"Some other time then," she said, without losing her smile.

She let me out by the kitchen door. As I began to go down the stairs she laughed and raised her skirt right up to her face—giving me a view for free. Or perhaps showing me what I'd missed.

The second such encounter took place at the office. I was tidying the drawers in the roll-top desk when the door opened without a knock and a head appeared in the gap. It belonged to a tall woman, unknown to me, wearing black, aged about thirty or thirty-five, who looked as if she'd been widowed recently. She asked me if I'd hear her out for a moment. The only striking thing about her was her blue eyes—something rare in a brunette. As not a soul had set foot in the office since the day—or rather the night—the Big Boss appeared, I imagined that fortune was smiling on me. I sat down behind my desk and told her I was at her service. She remained standing. I realized she wasn't a client; on the contrary, she was trying to make a client of me. She probably had something she wanted to sell. And as I sat there, expecting her to ask if I wanted to buy a plot of land she owned in Faliron (just as if I was someone who'd bought all the offices in the building a few days earlier), the woman unbuttoned her blouse, pulled down the right side of her bra and got out a breast whose dark pink nipple still kept some of its youthful roundness.

"How much will you give for it?"

She had a serious air, like someone who reserves the right to decide whether he will or will not sell his goods to a customer.

"Do they go singly or as a pair?" I asked without thinking—something had got into me just then.

She smiled for the first time, believing she'd found the person she was looking for. Without an instant's hesitation she bared the other breast and prepared to pull up her skirt.

"Gently does it, sweetheart!" I intervened. "Don't be in a hurry, it's never a good idea to show off all your wares at once, it makes the buyer lose interest. But I may as well be honest with you, I'm not in a position to buy."

"You? You're a professional, you've got your own office, you're well-dressed, a handsome man… Why aren't you in a position to buy? Don't you have any money to spare?"

"I do have a bit of money to spare," I replied. "But money doesn't buy anything that's of any use these days, by which I mean anything edible—and your delicacies are certainly worth a lot. Don't you have anything cheaper to sell?"

"What do you mean, cheaper?" said the dark-haired woman, and sat down at last in the customers' armchair, buttoning up her blouse again. "You've got nice furniture… Why don't you lock the door to stop anyone coming in?"

"Listen… when I say that I'm not in a position, I mean I'm not in a position. You'd better believe me."

"You married?"

"I'm unmarried. But it's not that."

"Are you one of that sort?" she asked, frowning suspiciously.

"Not that either. It's as I said: I'm not in a position to buy."

"Ha!" she laughed. "Are you a eunuch, maybe?"

I laughed too. How could I not? And since the truth is

always what people find hardest to believe, I nodded and smiled at her, showing all my teeth.

"That's exactly what I am. You've got it in one."

For some reason this answer seemed to be the worst I could have chosen. The woman stood up angrily and, having bathed me in a wash of insults which I'd prefer not to repeat, gave me to understand that a man may not want it or he may not have the money to pay for it but there's no call to insult an honest girl who needs to put something in her mouth if she's not to die from starvation.

Maybe it was Konstantina's fault, whom I'd left waiting for me to visit her tiny room some other day and time, maybe it was the blurred image of that naked back I'd seen reflected in the wardrobe mirror at dawn a few days ago, which never stopped haunting me—at any rate, I got up and went over to her. I put out my hand towards her right breast, the one she'd bared first, without touching it, then into my pocket.

Without wasting time she went and locked the door. She raised her skirt and bent forwards over the desk, asking if I wanted to take her knickers off myself or if I preferred her to do it.

"Come here, come here," I said. "I don't want any dramas, I can't take any more today."

I sat in the clients' armchair and pulled her onto my knee. Then I told her to get her breast out again, which she did willingly. Perhaps she thought I simply wanted a bit of foreplay on the armchair first and would soon get down to the nitty-gritty. But I closed my eyes and took her nipple in my mouth and dreamed: I dreamed first of Lauretta who always loved me sucking her tits and then, as my mind ranged further and further backwards, of another breast, a breast with a different feel and taste, associated with my earliest, darkest, most persistent memories. The brunette with the blue eyes had begun to moan as the minutes passed and I continued like this, one of my arms around her shoulder, the other hand holding the arm of the chair. Aroused by this persistent nuzzling that wasn't apparently going to lead to anything else, she was now trying to satisfy on her own the desires which—one may imagine—buyers in a greater hurry to enjoy her hidden charms would not have continued long enough even to awaken before the transaction was over, the money in her pocket or handbag, and the men wanting to get rid of her as fast as possible.

I can't say I did it as a favor to her. Deep inside me was something that found satisfaction in this sucking. And from my own point of view I considered the money I put in her hand well spent. She stared at the amount wide-eyed (how rapidly I'd reverted to my New York habits, putting my hand into my pocket and getting out a wad of notes without bothering to count them—Mr Agathos had made me rich again!) and asked me whether I'd like her to come back the following morning. I told her to come back whenever she felt like it, but not that week.

Before stowing the banknotes into her bag she glanced at me, and her eyes seemed to have lost their hardness and their air of impenetrability.

"You'll surely have something good coming to you," she said, revealing two rows of fine teeth (only one of them protruded a tiny bit, the one beside the canine).

"You think so?" I said. "Well—let's see what you do with those dirty old notes."

A lot of people used to say in those days that female flesh had become a currency. My own opinion is that love is a balm to the soul; and if it so happened that the sacrifice of female chastity was accompanied by some more substantial reward, like corn-bread, for example, or Italian *pagnotta*, a salted herring, a few drams of oil, sugar or raisins or a biscuit—well, so much the better. Cigarettes or chocolate, the greatest luxuries, fetched the highest price of all, the most unsullied innocence.

In this atmosphere where death had lost its mystery and had become the close familiar of our everyday lives, the whole city gave itself up to love with a hopeless and unquenchable thirst that grew in strength as death spread its wings wider. Marika Kanellis had no need to go searching in the streets. She had a husband who seemed to worship her. And Beratis stricken to the heart. And her days—and presumably her nights—were full.

18

—

An aerial vision

Beratis was silent as we went down with Papachrysanthou that afternoon to his old Piraeus haunts. He'd shaken Mimis' hand and from then on hadn't opened his mouth. He was looking straight ahead, his neck huddled into the collar of his overcoat. He had a spent match between his teeth which he was tormenting.

However, having not addressed a word to him while we were making our way to Piraeus, as we approached its market area the musician began chatting to Papachrysanthou in a fit of talkativeness that appeared unstoppable. A strange outburst of warmth: it was as if he'd reflected, "Well, after all, this fellow's doing us a favor by taking us to people he knows where we might find some food—it isn't really right to put on a sour face and not exchange the odd word with him." And the two of them seemed to be getting along all right: Mimis was speaking of old acquaintances in Halkida, of various mysterious business trips he'd made there before the war, and they launched into a conversation about places and people rather like the kind old brothers in arms have. How about this, then, and what about that? And So-and-So said this, and Such-and-Such did that—chuckling and nudging one another at these reminiscences. All of a sudden I was seeing another side of my protégé, the working-class boy side, usually concealed behind the stiff collars and black ties that he wore. But then of course all of us wear the clothes and the air that go with our job.

Polypheme had nothing but disappointment to offer this time. He hadn't got a thing. Neither a drop of oil nor a morsel of cheese rind nor a single dry bean. He smiled as always, with the same sweet smile that made dimples in his scarred face; as for food, though, zilch—nor did he know where any was to be found. The talk of a ship from Turkey with a cargo of beans and rice had turned out to be mere rumor. And this sort of rumor was only confirmed as fact when the wide boys of the port went down and hung around outside the closed stores (knowing in advance who'd be getting how much of the cargo, which warehouses they'd be storing it in, and what prices they'd be demanding on the black market). But this time the wide boys hadn't put in an appearance. It was doubtful whether we'd find any bread at the Troumba. People who'd just come from there were saying there wasn't a crumb. Such was the information Polypheme gave us.

"Things are getting tight, pals," he said. "Fritz has commandeered all the vegetables in the whole Mediterranean, supposedly for his army. As if those bastards ate vegetables! They're only doing it to make us go hungry…"

"So what do we do?" asked Papachrysanthou.

"When did you last buy something? Eaten it already, have you?"

The giant could remember when we'd been there and what we'd bought. We explained that this time we'd come so that the friend who was with us could buy something.

"Should have brought him last time."

We looked at one another in silence.

"There's an outside chance," said the giant after a moment. "It'll take a bit of walking though. It's up there, in the Maniatika. I'll be going anyway, I've arranged to meet some pals… If you want to come along and take your chance…"

Papachrysanthou looked at me and I looked at the musician.

"But you'll miss the bread—if there is any."

"No," said Beratis, "we'd better try and find bread."

"I'm not going," said Mimis. "You go, Hephaistos, you run along to Stella, she might let you have something… you haven't got any past history with her… she just might. I'm not going there again."

"Tell me where to find you," I said.

"When you reach St Sophia, ask for Salta's dive," instructed Polypheme. "That's where we'll be. And even if he doesn't have anything to eat, at least you'll be able to wet your whistle with some good, strong retsina. And we'll be singing some of the old songs, the best ones…"

Papachrysanthou seemed worried and anxious.

"It's a long way to the Troumba and back, then from here to the Maniatika. How'll you manage, Hephaistos?"

"Don't worry about me," I told him. "You get on your way and I'll meet you both there, with bread or without. And don't you worry either, Maestro, I'll find you something to put in your stomach."

Things had gone badly wrong. If the worst came to the worst, I'd give him some of my own supplies and tell him I'd managed to find them somewhere—and as for me, I'd think what to do. I still had something left to eat at home: even if I'd been a complete idiot I'd have coped somehow.

I came out of the old butcher's shop and took the road towards the harbor. There were no streetcars at that hour of the day; last time we'd been luckier. The road seemed endless. Instead of going along the waterfront I preferred to turn onto Philonos Street behind the church of the Holy Trinity. That way I was sheltered from the wind that was howling through the gaps.

We are curious creatures. You never know what it is that's guiding your steps, what it is that your soul really desires and what it recoils from; for most of us these things have somehow got confused. Normally, the idea of encountering Stellitsa again in her lair would have made me shudder. I'd never felt so humiliated as I did that day in her room, when she looked at me with an expression on her face that flayed me alive. And laughed all the while. But Mimis' story had shed a different light on her: the unknown prostitute, casually encountered, had now turned into a central figure in his life who tormented him and distressed him more than he wanted to show. And curiosity, all mixed up with my need to see her again and to repair the lamentable picture she must have of me from my previous visit, spurred me on as much as the need to find bread for my protégé.

At a turn in the road I caught sight of the ramshackle roofs of the Troumba, the muddy puddles which it was wiser not to put your foot into blindly, the crazy, ragged wisps of smoke that emerged from the tin chimneys sticking through the broken panes in the windows, and the heaps of rubble from bombed houses that every so often blocked the way.

For a brief moment I struggled to remember which was her door. In the end I knocked on the one that looked most likely. The fact that the street was deserted gave me a feeling that I wouldn't be finding any *pagnotta* today—the last time we came there'd been a line outside.

The door opened and in front of me stood an unknown middle-aged woman. She was about to slam the door in my face, announcing that *the lady was not receiving yet*—a curious expression which might almost have been taken from some novel; however, when she heard that I'd been sent by Mimis, she narrowed her eyes and stepped back.

"Stellaaaa!" she shouted, letting the *lady* know she had a visitor.

I recognized her voice: she was the woman we'd heard on the stairs last time, shouting "We're back!" Of the young girl there was no sign.

Stella appeared at the top of the stairs, wearing a quilted dressing-gown with a tear on one side that exposed the cotton stuffing.

"Bah!" she said as soon as she caught sight of me—for she recognized me at first glance. I must have made an indelible impression on her. "What's up, kid? Your juices on the boil again?"

"I've come in the hopes of buying something," I hastened to explain (as if this were necessary).

"There isn't any bread," she said in a tone as abrupt and commanding as if she were telling me to unbutton my pants. "At night... after I've finished with the punters... you might find some then." A laugh like a hiccup accompanied these words. "Or tomorrow, first thing in the morning. Before all the decent householders turn up."

"Thanks," I said and made for the door.

"Wait!"

I stopped and turned round.

"Did *he* send you?"

"Mimis? Yes."

She went away and returned with a loaf of bread wrapped in a sheet of newspaper.

"Tell him to go to hell," she snarled and thrust the packet straight at my stomach like a lance, like a broomstick, like the *weapon for close combat*, as Mimis called it.

"I was about to tell him the other day to do something... for *us*... but he..."

The corners of her mouth were drawn down in a

grimace that made her face seem a mask. Then immediately she gave a harsh laugh like the spark struck from a flint.

"He buggered off to Athens, the bastard… and now he comes to buy his bread here, see? Only to buy his bread. He knows quite well why he comes here. He doesn't go to any other whorehouse. He knows… He says, Stella'll give me some. See? He's got his donkey nicely tethered but he won't even hear of giving it some hay… He acts like he's St Mary, like he doesn't know a thing. Go on, what are you standing there for like a half-wit? Scram!"

Before I could say a word she'd slammed the door. I could hear the bolt being shot home and the key turning twice in the lock.

As I was walking along the dirt road an Italian patrol appeared around the corner by the lumber yard. Something warned me that I must avoid an encounter with them at all costs—the way animals scent danger in the air. I had a guilty conscience, for memories of the business with the Bersagliero and the little girl were fresh in my mind. And the precious burden that I carried tucked under my arm—the bread for Beratis—had to be safely delivered to him as soon as possible.

One of the Italians shouted at me. I couldn't make out the words, but I understood that he was ordering me to halt. The distance between us was now not much more than fifty yards. I wasn't doing anything illegal, or not tonight anyway. I was coming out of a house and carrying a loaf of bread. And the curfew hadn't begun. All the same… as the distance between me and the soldiers grew even less, my fear grew even greater.

Suddenly I decided to run. It had something to do with my memories—all my nightmares always had Italians in them. The shouts behind me grew louder and hoarser. A metallic click: someone was unslinging his machine gun from his shoulder, was raising it, was aiming in my direction. "I've got to reach the Maniatika as fast as possible!" was the sole thought in my head. And all at once, like a bird, I flapped my arms and kicked up my feet behind me. I heard the Italians uttering blasphemies, but this time their voices were full of terror at the completely unexpected sight of some poor wretch who, instead of taking to his heels in an attempt to avoid having his papers inspected… was flying! He was flying vertically upwards, over the roofs, over the trees, disappearing from sight. Not one of them fired a single shot: the last words I heard were "*Santa Madonna madre!*"

As I rose up into the air and turned towards the Lemonadika quarter, I could make out the dome of St Sophia in the distance. Below me lay a landscape of unbelievable beauty. The sun was getting lower in the west, the town and the harbor resembled a miniature painting. Slanting rays gilded the empty, ruined expanse with iridescent colors. You only have to rise a little bit into the air to see the larger picture, the one you can't even conceive of when you're down there in the streets and squares and alleys. When you're flying, you can see where you're going better, you can see further, you don't get lost in the labyrinthine streets that make your pedestrian life so hard. Down there, you have to pay attention to the corner where you turn, the street you take. You have to ask people for directions. Up in the sky, you can see at once how much more you know about the world and how little you need directions and such like. Thus, secure in the tranquil knowledge that I'd reach my destination, having forgotten the patrol and the metallic click of weapons being readied to fire at me, leaving behind the genuine terror that they'd provoked in me, I was able to imagine a scene.

Mrs Kanellis was before me in my mind's eye, in their bedroom on Georgiou Gennadiou Street. The shutters of the window looking onto the light-well were closed, the window shut and the room without light. But the balcony door on the other side was open and a little light shone in from the back yard. A humble tree, one of the kind that grows by itself without anyone planting it, adorns the backyard of our building. She is alone, sitting on the bed. Beside her is a basket full of balls of wool and needles. She's wearing a thimble and spread on her knees is a cardigan belonging to her husband, with a hole at the elbow. She's darning it. And as her needle works backwards and forwards through the worn spot, joining its fraying edges with wool of the same color, there is a smile on her face. Her mind is wandering far. Sometimes her face is lit up, sometimes it darkens. She watches her hands at work on the cardigan, the wool she's using and her thimble; and she remembers her grandmother's hands performing the same task in that distant village with the plane trees and the running water, which is now part of Turkey. (It is a great mystery how she always manages to have the clothes that need mending ready so fast, and so perfectly darned that you can't see where the worn spot was.) The old woman's skill must have been magically transmitted to this girl here, with her fresh cheeks and red lips. She herself doesn't bother to try to remember when she'd acquired this gift. But gifts are brought by fairies. It is they who guide her fingers as she draws on paper or on cloth. It is they who guide her words, so that they form a rhythm as they take shape on the paper, so that they sing. She raises her eyes and looks at the tree, on whose branches the leaf-buds are swelling in preparation for the new leaves of the spring that is already in the air. Through its branches she can see the roof of the Olympia theater. The young woman gazes at the roof of the opera house—an ordinary tiled roof. She never goes to the opera, knows nothing about music, is ignorant of all that her lover does there when he is not with her, and thus the building does not remind her of him.

Without her realizing it, her thoughts turn to the future. This future is not hers alone. It is the future. It is things that she will not see—or will not see in their entirety. Something connected to her, yet which does not solely or absolutely concern her. It begins from her yet moves into the distance, far beyond the cycle of her own life.

She sees an island, a solitary star in the crowded, star-lit sea of night. The sense of the relation she will acquire to her distant star fills her with joy and makes her skin prickle. Something has happened, something has existed, something has occurred. The day before yesterday her husband had taken her in his arms once more after a bitter scene, of the kind that is happening more and more often between them. And, wearied by the stresses of the times and the daily fear of death, she feels a greater and greater longing for life. She abandons herself to his caresses like a child to the caresses of someone who has just beaten him cruelly and unjustly. Her gratitude causes everything else to be forgotten—as if before her did not quite clearly stretch the dark road, the road with no return, which leads one person far from the other. And she smiles in happiness. In her mind are confused the images of her irritable husband, of her calm father, and of her lover the musician, who just last night, when her husband was sleeping at the house of some relatives where he had gone by himself to a party, had crept secretly into the house and had taken her in his arms, giving her the paradise of a different kind of intimacy that she had dreamed of since girlhood. And these images of her husband, her lover and her father fade and are all three melded into another image, as yet uncreated and unformed, but which she knows will be her son, the child she will bear soon and, like another Virgin Mary, will delight in for a short while and then mourn for years. The tears of pleasure and of grief are equally sweet.

All of a sudden I realized that I was losing height. In spite of the cold, my forehead was bathed in an icy sweat. I'm falling! And, yes, I was falling. It was the awakening from a dream in which I was flying. Except that in my dream I had flown but now I was waking and falling in reality. A few yards in front of me were the electricity wires, resembling thick, black washing lines looped between one wooden post and another; and a little further off the tall brick chimney of a defunct factory. With the course I was following—unless I crashed to the ground earlier—I was going to smash into it. My powers were failing, just as one's legs fail one sometimes, except in this case it was more my shoulders than my legs for they were the part that worked hardest when I was flying.

I didn't have any choice but to land as fast as possible while I still had some impetus and a little strength left. I straightened my legs so as not to land in a crumpled, broken heap and was ready to start running—like I'd seen parachutists do on the newsreels—as soon as I touched the ground. I avoided the electricity wires, skimming just below them with a feeling of unutterable relief, and set my course towards the narrow alley lying alongside the factory's stone wall.

I hit the ground clumsily, hurting my knees so much that I cried aloud. And while I was doing the running needed in order to brake, I twisted my ankle. But I didn't smash myself up—I landed, praise be to God. Like a parachutist. As my legs were now in a dreadful state, I attempted to see if I could take off into the air again; flying seemed easier than walking. However, I didn't have the power to do so. It was as if I'd never flown at all, as if I was still trying in my sleep to do something you can only do in dreams. Nothing. Nothing at all. I'd have to walk. To search for the way. To ask directions to Salta's place—or was it Saltsa's, I'd forgotten both the name and the instructions about how to get there. St Sophia. But where was St Sophia? From above I'd seen it perfectly clearly and had set a course for it. But now I might as well have been blind, the streets were deserted, I hadn't a clue which was north and which was east.

When I'd limped to the corner of the alley I caught sight of its dome behind the roofs. I'd navigated well up to here. I was beginning to remember.

In my mind I was struggling to find the words I'd say to my two friends when we met again at the dive where they were awaiting me, and what I'd tell them about all that I'd seen. Everything was strangely intertwined. Maybe later on I'd get some idea of how and why they were intertwined like this. For the moment I couldn't find any explanation.

19

______

The noxious consequences of wine

Salta's dive was a hovel with a corrugated iron roof. Its windows were two holes looking onto the lane, each at a different height, covered with fine mesh screens and curtains made out of old work overalls. The beaten earth floor was as hard as cement, while the three tables sloped at such an angle that all the small copper wine jars amassed on them appeared likely at any moment to slide to the ground. A charcoal brazier in the middle of the room gave off a faint heat; the chimney pipe above it was attached to the ceiling by loops of wire and passed low over the heads of the company.

I had to knock several times before anyone came to let me in. In any case, the latch didn't seem to secure the door half as firmly as the way it was jammed into its warped frame. The sound of voices and singing bore witness to the fact that none of the customers cared a jot that the curfew hour was fast approaching. In places like this, as well as in more elegant ones, all those who'd made up their minds to have a good time were preparing either to remain safely secluded till morning, if they lived far away, or else to slip home later like shadows, dodging from wall to wall.

Over the shoulder of the man who opened the door to me I spotted the anxious faces of Polypheme and Mimis. Beratis, reclining on the floor and lost in the wreaths of smoke from the hookah on which he was taking long, slow puffs, didn't even notice me.

"How're you doing, lad?" I called to Papachrysanthou.

"Having fun," he called back in slurred tones. "We didn't find any food. We're having a drink instead. He's got first-class retsina, Hephaistos! Come and have a drop."

My mind was still full of my flight, of the strange vision I'd had of Marika Kanellis, dreaming as she did her mending; I wanted to describe it to the musician and get him to tell me things about her. About where she came from, for example, about her parents, her talents, if she liked the cinema or reading or swimming: I needed to know whether or not my vision bore any relation to the real Marika.

When I learned that even at the Maniatika they hadn't succeeded in finding anything for my protégé to buy, I became impatient for us to leave—I wanted to get back to Athens, not to be wandering around the streets at this time of day. But I realized almost at once that it wasn't so simple. The curfew would start before we were more than half-way; there weren't any streetcars or gazogens at this hour and it was a long trudge.

"Have some carobs," said Polypheme, indicating a dented tin plate balancing on the largest of its protuberances.

I took one. "Mmm," I said. It tasted heavenly.

He pushed an empty but not unused glass in front of me and filled it with the transparent yellow wine which scented the whole room.

"Alcohol turns to sugar and sugar's nourishing," he pronounced, his cheeks creasing as he winked at me.

Already a stupor was rising to my head. It wasn't the wine, although I'd downed two glasses in quick succession in order to warm up and to put something in my stomach. It was rather that everything seemed to be happening in a dream; such a short time ago, I was thinking, I would have been in the bar on 30th Street, in the company of all the usual layabouts who'd take up position there from early afternoon—the gamblers, the drunkards, the down and outs, the slaves to the bottle, filling the air with their words of wisdom and later the floor with their vomit, if, that is, their neighbor or Jimmy the barman hadn't managed to steer them to the men's room in time. Here it was different: fun was something people had as a company, nodding to one another, talking and drinking together instead of each one sitting in isolation and knocking back his drinks alone. And the tipsiness that overtook us before long was also something shared: it made you forget your worries.

"I'm in love," the musician declared all of a sudden.

"Me too," I said.

"But I have to keep it really secret," he continued.

"So do I," I told him. "No one must know."

"I'm the only person who can understand you," he said through clenched teeth.

"You're the only person who must never find out anything about it," I answered.

"Why? What d'you think I am? A sober prig? Some kind of moralist? A professor of divinity? A churchwarden?"

"You're a *client*."

"Your client? Me? Since when? You selling something or what?"

"Not exactly a client. Someone else is the client. You're a… you're…"

Luckily I stopped there. I wasn't that tipsy yet.

And at that moment the singers started up again with the song that had met with the greatest acclaim that evening; my musician seemed to emerge from his clouds of smoke and intoxication and joined in, his full voice coming from deep in his chest, glancing at me with a smile (for I knew…)

Golden palaces / diamond harems
I'll build for you / and look into your eyes.
You're like an angel / seated on your throne
It makes me dizzy to look at you / my little married girl…
You shall have whatever you want / my little married girl

You'll lack for nothing / you'll live in happiness…

"What's up? Our friend having an affair with a married woman, is he?" asked Mimis sympathetically, ever ready to feel for his fellow-humans.

"He isn't having an affair but he likes her," I said.

"One thing I know," interrupted the musician, who had heard us despite all the singing and clapping. "Mark this, Angel, and remind me of it one day… If I succeed in anything in my life… it will be because of that woman's love… that inspiration…"

He stopped as if he'd run out of breath. Mimis was gazing into the distance. The tavern-keeper slammed our new half-measures of wine on the table. It was an easy matter to lose the thread of your thoughts in the midst of all the singing, the shouts, the invocations of the blind God, the unjust God, the cruel and heartless God who had created us and then abandoned us to our fate here below, in the sterile desert of this world.

Whoever is born a lover of hashish / doesn't know what to do
He drinks and becomes a drunkard / False world
To ease his pain…
Without hashish the world / is not worth living in
Youth's there to be enjoyed / ah, world!
Before its eyes are closed…

"Ah, what a bitch life is! Ah, what a bastard world! Ah, the bitterness and pain!"

The guitar and the two bouzoukis sang. Mouths were open as wide as they'd go, throats swelled and voices rose—hoarse, out of tune, cheerful and full of feeling.

"Is this the sort of music you write, Maestro?" I asked, leaning close so that he'd hear.

"Bah!" he replied with deliberate contempt. "These are *popular* songs. Me, I've studied!…"

You couldn't tell immediately whether he despised these songs or whether he envied them. And although I tried to get him to say more, he wouldn't. He put his hand over my mouth and gestured that I should listen to the music. At one point, between songs, one of the bouzouki players left his instrument on the ground. Beratis picked it up and tried to play it. He didn't have any difficulty: the instrument instantly gave out its sound with the notes he wanted. But his attempts to improvise a taksim like the one he'd just heard were fruitless. Thus for the rest of the evening he remained glued to the bouzouki player's side, watching the man's tricks and effects through half-closed eyes.

The singing continued till morning. As the sun rose we set off homeward.

The cold was biting. The street was still in shadow for the sun reached it from Harilaou Trikoupi Street and Gennadiou didn't receive any light till later. The narrow streets formed corridors through which the north wind blew, drying out the damp on the balconies of Zoodochou Pigis, Ippokratous and Themistokleous Streets; this was an area of small houses, abandoned gardens, empty plots and sickly ailanthus trees that sprouted wherever they found a patch of soil.

Weary from the all-night session, my stomach burning from the mixture of carobs and wine, my head muzzy from the hookah and alcohol fumes, I went to bed even though the day had already dawned. The worst thing was that I knew I wouldn't manage to get much sleep. And in fact I got up at my usual time, bleary-eyed, and washed in cold water at the sink, leaving my face wet in the hope that the water would soothe its redness.

When I went into the front room, I found Mr Agathos enthroned there, with a dog on a leash sitting on its hindquarters and watching me. The old man ran his eyes over me from head to toe as I stood there dripping and scowling. "Mr Angel, my boy," he said, "you do look a mess."

"What's the matter? Have I got egg on my lapel or something?" I asked. The last time I'd seen an egg had been about eight months ago.

"What an amusing Americanism! Did you find some eggs?"

"I made do with carobs and retsina. What do you say to that?"

"What I say," declared Mr Agathos, getting up, "is that you've been exposing yourself to danger quite needlessly… and, even worse, you've been exposing other people too. What ever got into you to go down to Piraeus, Mr Angel? What on earth did you think you were doing in that low-life den?"

"Well, basically we went for food," I told him. "Bread and anything else we might chance on…"

"Had you heard that a ship had arrived?"

"No. But when I went down there a few days ago with a friend of mine we managed to find food even though no ship had come in. Let's start at the beginning, though—how did you get in?"

"We found the door ajar. And since we heard you snoring away, we sat down quietly and waited for you to wake."

The crafty old man! I couldn't disprove it: in my befuddled state it wasn't impossible I'd left the door open.

I took a look at the dog. He was a mongrel, a cross between a German Shepherd and a hunting dog, pitch-black with a narrow white patch on his chest like a tie. Well-nourished too—a wonder he hadn't been caught and eaten; obviously his master must guard him like the apple of his eye and always keep him on the leash. Where could he have left him on the other occasions we'd met? At the hotel? As if he understood that I was thinking of him, the dog bared his teeth and growled at me.

I put out my finger to him.

"He's not mine," said Agathos. "He belonged to a wise old man who died and left him to me to take care of. He's getting on in years. Don't be frightened, he isn't fierce. He's more frightened of you…"

"I see that everyone around here seems to know what I'm thinking, I'm the only one who's left in ignorance of all the things I want to know… May I ask who told you about Piraeus and the rest of it?"

"The rest of it indeed! Mr Angel, my boy," said Agathos in his deep and slightly asthmatic voice, "when we want to find food we don't go looking for it in the city. We go where food is available, far away, in the countryside. In the provinces if need be. Things aren't quite so bad in the provinces as they are in Athens, you must know that."

"Come on! The situation was desperate. I gave your man whatever I could out of my own resources so he wouldn't drop dead on the spot. The fellow we'd been to before in Piraeus is OK, I thought he'd help us out again… And anyway, how does one get to the country or the provinces? What kind of transport are you suggesting?"

"Ah, now you're really disappointing me, Mr Angel, my boy, you truly are disappointing me… What kind of transport! How can you possibly ask? You of all people? I can't believe you're serious."

That damned old man had a way of turning the tables on me. I blushed to the roots of my hair and looked at him like a thief who's been caught dipping his hand into someone else's pocket.

"You mean…" I stammered.

He nodded and spread his arms wide.

"Yes," I admitted, "I wasn't thinking straight, it was

a mistake to involve other people in my shopping expedition. On my own—and if I'd thought about it the way you're suggesting—I could have gone to Marousi or the Mesogeia plain… into the country—I would've had better success. Then none of us would have had to take any risks, the way things are now the streets are dangerous. And all for one loaf of bread."

"Don't think only in terms of the country around Athens, dear boy. The provinces are safer and you can find things more easily. Basic necessities, I mean of course, not luxuries. But the basics, yes, they're certainly to be found. I'm talking about Thebes, about Livadia. Further north is even better… You can do it. You could go there and back in a day."

He bent and whispered confidentially in my ear—although the only creature that could have overheard us was the dog: "Between you and me, I've heard of some very fine dried beans in Kiourka. But I imagine you may need some more *fuel*."

He put five more sovereigns on my table. It was the first time I was in no hurry to pocket them. He wasn't wrong. I hadn't managed to organize things systematically or to follow a careful and precise plan.

"Never mind," he said, sitting down again. "I'm sure you'll manage. But I'm worried about you, I may as well tell you that straight out. I have to say that you worry me, my friend. There's something gnawing at you, something on your mind, something holding you back, in a manner of speaking, from what we might call the hallowed virtue of single-mindedness… Ha, Ha, Ha! Hallowed, yes. I've not the slightest desire to pry into your personal affairs, my boy, but all the same your mind is constantly occupied with—how shall I put it—matters that have no bearing on your profession, on your *vocation* I should perhaps say. I don't know… I don't wish to be more specific. Your feelings are of course sacred and to be respected. But are you not allowing yourself to be consumed by vain hopes? There's one thing I must tell you, Mr Angel, my boy: *a state of affairs* of this sort drains our strength and causes our abilities to wither, so to speak… As you have seen for yourself. When someone is devoted to a purpose, body and soul, he needs to remain fit if he is to… let's call it to rise high, to float in the air. Widows and married women and servant-girls are not for you. You know that. You're aware that up to a certain point you are able to respond, ahem, ahem, to the demands of the situation… Yet always to the detriment of your other abilities… If you don't devote yourself to the job I've entrusted to you…" (he broke off with a grimace).

He didn't seem to be threatening, it was more as if he was trying to explain things I couldn't understand.

"There are things…" I began, in a last attempt to worm something out of him, "things I can't always control. And what's more, Mr Agathos my friend" (I was imitating his own benevolent style—the jolly old uncle from the village), "my job's made more difficult by the fact that your protégé is mixed up with a woman who… who interests me too, if you know what I mean, I can't always put it out of mind—even though I've no more right to think of her than he does, since she's married and her husband is a good, fine man… it's a great misfortune for us all to be in such a tangle."

His face was clouded, he was gazing into the distance, deep in thought.

"Sotiris, my friend. Mr Angel" (he corrected himself). "I know, you are quite right. I don't want to burden your mind with complex ideas. But to put it simply, there are laws more powerful than either you or me, laws that are strict and stern. They say that the sinner will be punished. And the man who interests us is a sinner, as you very well know. We can't leave this fact out of the reckoning. Yet we may choose for the time being to ignore one aspect of him in order to save another: his music is more important than him, this is often the way it is with artists. In any case, they punish themselves… If you continue to look at the woman as you do now, there'll come a point when you and the man you're supposed to be looking after will become rivals. I am aware that your interest in her is theoretical… on the mental level, so to speak, rather than grossly material. You know how the two of them are ensnared in the web of mutual magic, excited by their illicit love. And then in the midst of all this there's a pregnancy, she is going to bring a child into the world… for which I feel responsible… I won't say more, it isn't the proper time—after all, how could I explain it to you?"

The dog gave a short, stifled bark that sounded like a laugh. Agathos turned and looked at it but said nothing. I waited. I've heard a lot of stories in my time but this one sounded the tallest of all…

"Mr Angel," continued the Big Boss as he stood up. "Our relation must be one of total confidence or nothing. Do you have blind faith in me? If you do not, then I shall have to look around for someone else. You certainly possess advantages hard to find elsewhere—but the world's a big place, something would no doubt turn up. I don't want to trouble you further now, let us thus agree on something. You may, if you wish, plunge into the mire when your… nature, let's put it that way, requires it. But not with the woman lawyer! Is that understood?"

"I wasn't aware you'd charged me with living my life in any particular way," I said. "I thought that what you'd charged me with was a case concerning another man."

"It does concern another man. You—and please don't get me wrong—you, my dear boy, interest me because you are suitable for this mission. If I'd wanted you to find a treasure on the peaks of Mt Olympus, you would have been an experienced mountaineer who'd be training on the slopes of Lykabettos. If I'd wanted you to retrieve a chest from the depths of the Bay of Faliron, then you would have been a diver or a former sponge-fisherman and you would be practicing underwater in the cistern of Dexameni at Kolonaki—that sort of thing. Your job, however, is to keep our musician alive through the Hunger…"

"I see. I suppose I'd better start going to the

Conservatoire to learn to play the double bass then," I said, nodding towards Fidiou Street.

He smiled, paying no attention to my words.

"Your obligation is to care about him, not to envy him, to cushion him against all the tribulations and perils—that's your first duty. Your second is to maintain your ability to fly and not lose it because your mind is constantly preoccupied with some woman. What kind of Angel are you, for goodness sake? I chose you for that..."

"You should have chosen a eunuch then," I burst out without thinking. "Someone who'd foresworn love forever."

The Big Boss raised his eyes to my face. "But isn't that just what I did?" he asked in genuine puzzlement.

20

——

A meal and its aftermath

I kept on being woken by the same dream: the image of the empty city after the terrible explosion at Omonia, a week after our night of wine and song at the Maniatika. In my dream I was standing on Stadiou Street and looking at the block where the Excelsior cinema was, as well as Rizos' café and Bernitsas' pastry shop. In the middle of the road stood an abandoned streetcar, its green wooden carriage scored with gouge marks. The Germans had used iron bars and wire netting to set up a road-block in order to check people's papers. On the sidewalks, the lampposts with their electric bulbs on twisting arms; above me, the glass canopies of stores on their metal brackets; beyond me, the low three-story buildings of Omonia, their windows left open by all the curious folk who'd managed to look out to see where the explosion was, now gaping empty.

On the wireless the Kommandant was foaming at the

mouth and howling threats. The name of EAM was more and more frequently on people's lips. The authorities knew that this organization was growing daily and that people of all political persuasions were joining it—not just those belonging to the Left, in other words, but the other side too, who until now had preferred to keep quiet and wait patiently for the nightmare to end. In the provinces and in the mountains, the organization had formed military brigades; in the cities it used clandestine radio broadcasts, sabotage and messages written on walls. A rumor was going around that a special Artists' branch of EAM had been set up.

One Wednesday, about two weeks after the explosion at Omonia, Mimis went to share a meal at his cousin Theofrastos Moltsas' house, on Zaïmi Street in the Exarhia quarter. Moltsas was the railway employee whose two children had taken part in the performance of "Penthesilea" before the war. He'd succeeded in getting hold of a cockerel, there would be food for the whole extended family that inhabited the apartment: they lived communally—whichever member managed to find any food would bring it to be shared by all. The few drops of olive oil on the wild greens, for example, must have been Mimis' contribution, part of the booty from our earlier visit to Piraeus. In other homes different habits prevailed, each member fending for himself and often stealing his relatives' meager food. Mimis took me with him, "so you can meet them"—but also, as he said, so that I could get a meal; he felt under an obligation to me because I'd helped him out with food not long before. The entire family was there: two old ladies, the grandmother and her sister, whom they called "Aunt Clio" and "Aunt Myrto," the two children Pavlos and Pavlina, and a strange woman with dark circles under her eyes whom everyone referred to as "the widow"—she wasn't a relative but was fed by the Moltsas family. Moltsas was a pleasant, talkative man who showed two rows of regular, brilliantly white teeth when he smiled, all of them false, on their red gutta-percha plate. His wife looked askance at me, unhappy at the intrusion of a stranger into their family meal, and made a lot of fuss of Cousin Mimis, or Mimakos as she called him.

Two evenings later, on the Friday, Mimis telephoned me in tears. The Germans had taken Moltsas on Thursday morning, after a denunciation concerning the terrible explosion at Omonia, and had executed him, along with some others, at dawn that very day at Goudi. "At least he died with a full stomach, poor fellow," my friend said between sobs. He would henceforth have to be responsible for his cousin's family, he added.

A susurrant whisper crept through the streets as if Death were whistling in pleasure at his recent harvest. People glided like shadows, heads emerged hastily from windows and then were rapidly withdrawn, shutters remained pulled down even when the sky was dull. I'd arranged to meet Papachrysanthou early in the morning on the corner of Ippokratous Street, outside the Iris cinema, in order to go with him to find his cousin's body at the morgue on Massalias Street. Mimis had now taken over as head of the family and his new authority was commencing with one of its more unpleasant privileges. He was late. His complexion had a greenish tinge to it and his teeth were chattering; he kept rubbing his hands together to warm them—you knew, though, that it was fear he was suffering from more than the cold.

At the beginning of Asklipiou Street he pointed out to me a low, two-story house behind a stone wall. By the gate an old cartwheel was leaning against the wall.

"I'm thinking of taking it to burn in the stove," he told me, "but I don't know who'll help me roll it home."

We turned onto Solonos Street and a few steps further on arrived at the morgue, a long, low building with barred windows giving onto a courtyard. At one side was a chapel—for purposes you could easily guess at. "Oh God, oh God," my companion kept muttering, rubbing his hands more than ever. He was trembling from head to foot. A policeman at the door made a mute questioning gesture with his hands to ask us what we wanted. Papachrysanthou found the courage to open his mouth wide and emit enough sound for his voice to reach the ears beneath the broad-brimmed cap. He said he was looking for a cousin of his who'd been executed, then went on to explain that there was no one else in the family who could come, they were all women and children, so he'd had to undertake this duty. The policeman wasn't interested in the details. He motioned us to enter.

Instantly it was as if there wasn't enough air: the smell that greeted you barely allowed you to breathe. Faintness, nausea and terror gripped our stomachs as we searched in the dimly lit corridor for a door with a sign on it that would admit us as fast as possible to where we needed to go. The doors bore nothing but numbers. Only the very last door at the end of the corridor had an enamel sign on it saying "Office." I knocked and opened it. A man bundled up in overcoat, scarf and hat was sitting before a piece of furniture that must have been the office desk; he didn't even bother to look up from his newspaper.

"We're looking for someone who was executed," I said.

"Who's looking?" he asked in an abrupt and hostile tone.

"His cousin."

"Identity card. Papers. Name."

"Papachrysanthou Dimitrios," Mimis introduced himself, and got his identity card out of his wallet.

"When was he executed?"

"Yesterday. At dawn."

The man reached out with his right hand to a pile of papers and thumbed through them. On the left-hand corner of each sheet a capital letter was marked in black ink. He took the sheets he'd picked out and went through them.

"I don't have any Papachrysanthou executed," he declared, casting a look in our direction full of spite and annoyance.

"Not Papachrysanthou… Moltsas! Moltsas is the dead man's name. Moltsas Theofrastos… *I'm* Papachrysanthou."

"Moltsas? Vault IIIA. He's the only executed M we have today."

He reached for my friend's identity card and noted something in black ink on a piece of paper with the dead man's name on it that he'd taken from a pile of such papers.

"Have you brought a means of transport? How are you going to take him?"

"What? Transport?" Mimis looked around in despair. It hadn't even crossed his mind that he'd be taking delivery of his cousin's body then and there.

"Er, we haven't got transport. I came to see him, to see him first… and when we've done that and everything's in order I'll go at once and get some means…"

The man pressed an electric button on the desk's wooden surface, whereupon after a moment dragging footsteps were heard in the corridor. The door opened and a head looked in.

"Show him Moltsas Theofrastos in IIIA," the man in the office said. "Make sure he's *in order*," he added with a sneer, "because otherwise the gentlemen won't be taking him."

"Get fucked!" Mimis muttered through clenched teeth as we went out into the corridor.

The office man followed us into IIIA with a bundle of papers. He stood back and let my friend go first to identify his relative. Privileges carry with them obligations. The trolleys were pushed back to the wall, each right up against the next, to save space. And on the floor, on brown paper and old newspapers, lay all the host of bodies for which no trolleys were available; they would have looked like store-window dummies were it not for the fact that their repulsive color, their terrible faces and the stink that took your breath away reminded you that you were standing before one of the gates of hell.

There was barely enough space for the number of dead bodies brought in every day by cart, hand-cart or motorcycle. If no one came to claim them within two days, they were piled high on carts—as many as the broken-winded horses and donkeys could manage—covered with tarpaulins tied down so that the wind wouldn't lift them, and borne through the streets to one or other of the city's cemeteries. It was one of these processions that Mimis and I had seen outside the Old Palace on the day we first went down to Piraeus.

"*What! Not him?*" I heard the office man exclaim, in a voice that cut like a whip.

Mimis was standing as far from the dead man as he could, but the man's angry response to his whispered doubts now made him bend closer. "It's not him! Oh Christ! Oh God!" he repeated in a louder voice. He made room for me to approach so that I could look too. The feet I saw, the trodden-down heels of the man's shoes, his socks sagging around his ankles, didn't help. I went nearer. There wasn't any doubt about it—it was Moltsas. His false teeth were missing though, that bright red plate with its regular, brilliant white teeth; someone must have stolen it, or it had fallen out, or he'd swallowed it. "It's him, Mimis, can't you see?" I told him, nudging him with my elbow. "It's him, minus his teeth."

He hid his face in his hands and nodded.

"*Recognized*," wrote the man from the office on his papers, and was the first to leave that pit.

"You see to the formalities and I'll go and find a barrow," I told my friend.

21

An invitation

I hadn't seen Beratis for days. The great conductor had
returned from his tour of Northern Greece and the
preparations for the opera performance were in full swing,
with the result that my protégé was constantly busy with
rehearsals. It was amazing that with death stalking the
streets the law courts and the tax departments were still
functioning, the few stores that didn't have anything to
sell to people who didn't have any money to buy were
still open. And theaters had performances daily. The only
difference was that the time at which they started had been
moved forward to early afternoon, both because of the
cold and to avoid the curfews that every so often were
imposed. The theaters put on new plays, people thronged
to see them. Tickets cost astronomical sums in debased
drachmas. The best seats, though, were secured in return
for food; as a result, the box offices tended to resemble
grocers' storerooms. Evening parties went on till morning.

People gathered together in order to feel stronger in the midst of all the danger.

My only visitor was Beratis. Nevertheless, when he arrived I got up and left. We both knew why he came—and it certainly wasn't to see me. From his second visit we established that I'd be out for about two hours, after which I'd dial my own number: if no one picked up the telephone it meant I could come back home. I'd find the apartment empty again, everything tidy and a faint lingering smell of cigarette smoke. Silence everywhere. Darkness. And bitter cold.

These obligatory expulsions from my own home gave me an opportunity to go and purchase dried beans and the odd bottle of milk at Kiourka, potatoes and spring greens at Marathon or olive oil at Keratea. The musician's supplies were increasing steadily. I'd fly with my pockets full of potatoes—occasionally, if I made an awkward movement or if my overcoat billowed dangerously in the wind, I'd drop a few. With each new trip I was acquiring a different, hitherto unimagined, picture of the country. Outside Athens it was as if the Occupation didn't exist. Birds filled the air, trees swayed in the breeze, I could hear the gurgle of running water beneath me as I flew over the spring at Kefalari or the watercourses at Marathon. Small streams flowed down from Mt Pendeli to the outlying hamlets. Even today these images often come back to my mind, like a collection of old photographs of a lost land. I sometimes flick through antiquated encyclopedias or albums of the epoch, and get the impression that I'm back in reality once more after having slept for a hundred years. None of the songs of that decade are ever heard on the radio now: they're outdated and anyway very few of the listeners who once knew them are left. Twenty years ago you could still sometimes hear what they called "light Greek songs" or "old Greek songs." Now no one knows them or asks for them. But in those days, through floorboards and walls and closed doors, you'd hear people singing them during the long evenings as an antidote to fear.

One afternoon something occurred that I'd always been afraid of. No one answered when I phoned to check that the place was empty. However, it was simply that this time Beratis hadn't got to the telephone in time; as soon as I unlocked the door and went in I realized they were still there. The air smelled different, her scent instantly hit me and my blood froze. What would happen? He was standing at the end of the passage, and behind him Marika Kanellis; pretending I hadn't seen them, I made straight for the kitchen to unload my supplies. I was giving her time to open the door and slip out onto the stairs. Yet when I turned around she was still there, as if she'd been waiting for me.

"Good evening," said Marika Kanellis coldly.

"What a surprise! How are you?" I responded.

"I see that you and Miltos are good friends, I didn't know you were so close."

"Angel finds food for me," Beratis explained with a

slightly guilty air—I got the impression that he was telling her this for the first time.

"I imagine he knows the appropriate people," she commented nastily.

"Outside Athens," I told her. "If you went to your relatives in your native village you'd probably find something."

"My husband and I are both refugees from Asia Minor," said Marika. "We don't have any village or relatives here."

"You've got lots of friends, though, I hear their voices every night. Couldn't they help you find some food?"

"Ah, so you hear us, do you?" she asked, as if this were the only thing that mattered. "Really? Well then, come up and join us tonight, we're having some friends over. Though I may as well tell you that most of them belong to the Left. I dare say you knew that anyway. We're having a dinner party, everyone will be bringing his own contribution. Miltos has promised to bring some oil. A royal feast. Would you like to come?"

"I could bring some chickpea soup," I offered. "I've got half a saucepan of it left."

She was already at the door. "We'll be expecting you," she said.

"I'll be there without fail."

The door closed and the musician wiped the sweat from his brow.

"Why d'you suppose she invited me?" I asked him.

"She'd told me she was thinking of it. It seems... it seems she's rather changed her opinion of you." Then, after a brief pause, "She knows you go out on purpose and leave me here."

"I've brought some milk," I told him. "I bet it's a long time since you last saw fresh milk."

Every time I brought him food, Beratis insisted on paying me for it. I was obliged to invent ridiculous prices, vastly lower than what I actually gave to the shepherds at Kiourka or the farmers at Marathon who demanded almost as much as the black marketeers.

At eight o'clock that evening I took my saucepan of chickpea soup and rang their doorbell. Pavlos Kanellis opened the door. He stared at me with amazement from behind his round spectacles, then his glance wandered from my unfamiliar figure to the saucepan and he smiled faintly.

"Ah, it's you…"

"Your wife invited me," I explained.

"Yes indeed, come in."

He stepped back and closed the door after me.

"It's chickpea soup," I told him as I handed him my offering. "Maybe a little dull though, I'm not much of a cook."

He took it slightly awkwardly and passed it to Konstantina who had materialized behind him; she smiled at me silently and then returned to her kingdom. It seemed I was the first guest to arrive. Mr Kanellis ushered me into the front room. To the left and right stood two heavy desks with drawers made out of some dark wood, there was a bookcase on one wall overflowing with books and two small tables covered with old newspapers. On one of the desks was a shrouded typewriter, on the free wall space various framed paintings. Two leather armchairs in front of the window. The telephone on a roll-top desk stuffed with files.

It was an odd place, not like any home I'd seen before. The furniture didn't match—all of it was old, like things from houses they'd inhabited in other lives which had been brought here to continue to give service. Some pieces looked as if they'd come from a more opulent home: an oak settee, for example, with two tall-backed matching chairs, too large for the hall into which they were crammed. (This hall served as a waiting room when the drawing room was being used as an office and as a dining room when the office had reverted to being a living room.) They were covered in a dark varnish, the uprights of the chair backs and the arms of the settee had carved angles and ended in knobs, while the seats were shaped into circular hollows to receive cushions now non-existent.

The paintings gave a note of luxury to the apartment. They were the work of two artists, one of whom reminded me of pictures I'd once seen in a color magazine in Sol's house (a friend in New York who had hopes of becoming a writer)—objects that were all angles and triangles as if the artist had been trying to do some hasty, rough and ready geometry or was a child who hadn't yet learned how to draw. The other artist was more normal: landscapes lit by a sun—brown instead of white or golden—but as full of melancholy and sadness as the dreams of someone who's contemplating suicide. There were also two paintings of a more usual variety, one showing a mountain landscape and the other people dancing in what looked like a Hungarian inn. The women's skirts billowed as they twirled and the men wore round hats on their heads and were watching their womenfolk sternly, on their brows imprinted all the cares of the hunt or the field: the dance might have been an obligation to be jolly but no amusement had yet reached these men's faces.

"Rika tells me that you're friends with Miltos," the lawyer said, in an attempt to break the ice.

"Rika?"

"My wife."

"Ah yes, Mrs Marika!"

He smiled.

"She told me you were finding food for him and looking after him and…"

"When I can, yes," I answered. "I've had some good luck, managed to find something once or twice. You take it when you find it these days."

Once more a twisted smile appeared on his face. I was chewing on this pet name that I was hearing for the first time and not quite managing to swallow it. The musician always called her "Marika." This is what I knew her as too. "Rika" sounded like a husband's prerogative.

"We've never spoken, have we?" Mr Kanellis continued,

sitting down behind his desk and putting his chin in his hands.

My turn to smile. "And here I am in your house all of a sudden for a dinner party."

"Rika's been singing your praises. She says you're very decent. Miltos will be here tonight as well, he'll be bringing some olive oil. And I gather we'll even be having a dessert."

He was clearly feeling embarrassed, and so was I. It was obvious that I didn't belong here.

"Look, it was very nice of you to invite me but I don't want to be in the way. Your friends will be coming, I don't know them, they don't know me, maybe it might be better if I didn't stay… the last thing I want to do is spoil your party."

"Come on, what an idea! Stay, do stay, Mr Sotiriou. In any case, there'll be so many people here that it really won't matter. It's a shame we've been living in the same building so long without… getting to know one another better. Is it true that you're a Greek American?"

"Yes, I am indeed. I was born in New York, my parents had emigrated to America very young, I was educated there."

"And how on earth did you end up here, at a time like this…? I don't think you've been in Athens long, have you?"

"Not long, no. I was waiting for the chance to go back but then the war broke out… and there's no way for me to leave now that America's joined in."

"Thank heavens it has! The Russians alone aren't enough to defeat the Axis. The whole world has joined the war now, it really is a world war, unlike the first. We are living through unbelievable events, Mr Sotiriou."

"Angel," I said, "my name is Angel."

He smiled. "Yes of course. And I'm Pavlos."

At that moment Mrs Kanellis entered the room. She was all smiles, gave me her hand for what I think was certainly the first time, and asked her husband something about their guests.

"I can see that apart from all your other qualities you're a wonderful cook," she told me. "I tasted a bit. Shall we add some water, do you think, to make it slightly more liquid?"

"Yes, by all means, the chickpeas have absorbed all the water, it'll be better with a bit more, it'll make the soup go further."

"Fine. Stavritsa says she's going to bring a raisin pudding," she told her husband in doubting tones. "D'you suppose it's true?"

He shrugged. "Your guess is as good as mine. Stavritsa has a talent for sweets, I dare say it'll be something special since she says so. She's a friend of ours," he added for my benefit, "Mrs Siniosoglou, born in Constantinople and an excellent cook. She cooks better than she writes, but unfortunately she insists on writing and rarely cooks."

"Pavlos," she reprimanded, "you shouldn't, Mr Angel doesn't know these people."

"All the more reason to speak freely, if he did know

them I wouldn't have said it," he teased. "So what say you, Angel" (getting up), "can you help us achieve the miracle of the loaves and fishes tonight with your chickpeas? Don't stand on ceremony, go on into the kitchen and tell the slavey how much water to add—if it needs any salt, that's something we've got plenty of…"

It was a chance not only to escape the awkwardness of those first few moments but also to say the "Good evening" that I owed to the *slavey*. I must admit that this word rang very unpleasantly in my ears: he might have called her by her proper name, I thought, after all the poor little creature lives in his house. I thus left the couple alone to comment on me in privacy and went into the kitchen.

"Oh, Mr Angel," said the girl when she saw me, "welcome, I didn't greet you before so the mistress wouldn't…you know… How come you're here tonight?"

"Your employers decided I'm not a police informer after all and invited me. What are my chickpeas like, are they too dry?"

"Well, they could do with some more liquid, that's a fact," said Konstantina, uncovering the saucepan on the gas ring.

After giving her my opinion as to the quantity of water that should be added, I returned to the front room. Other guests had arrived. Mr and Mrs Siniosoglou, somewhat older than their hosts: Mr *Tatsis* (Takis, I suppose), tall and stooping and bony, and Mrs Stavritsa, dressed in black, her square décolleté covered with lace, her high cheekbones well rouged, a strong whiff of rose-scented powder accompanying her every movement. On the little table with the telephone directories stood a shallow pan covered with a checked tea-towel prettily fastened all round: this, I assumed, was the pudding. They inclined their heads as Kanellis introduced us and gave the lawyer a faintly questioning look.

"Our neighbor," he explained. "A fine young man, a friend of Miltos."

"Are they from the same town?" asked Mrs Stavritsa.

"What? Oh, I see, no, I'm a Greek from America," I stammered.

"From America!" she cried and clapped her hands. "Good heavens! And how did you come to be here, young man?"

"I was thinking of it when I got up this morning, Tatsis," Kanellis went on, continuing the conversation he'd already begun with the tall gentleman. "I was dreaming of trees, it was spring, the leaves were a pinkish light green, fresh and newly opened, and I thought to myself that I was back in the land of my birth. I was wondering whether our destiny brought us into this world to live through all these things we're now experiencing, all this savagery and inhumanity, this debasement of man as we knew him... if we could have guessed when we were adolescents what our eyes would see, what we'd live through... And I woke up weeping."

The two ladies remained silent for a moment out of respect for the lawyer's confession, then continued their own conversation. For people who were starving, harassed and persecuted, their mood seemed remarkably good. Just at that moment Beratis arrived. He made an informal greeting to everyone present and gave me a friendly nod. The lady of the house relieved him of the small lemonade bottle in which he'd brought the precious olive oil and took it into the kitchen for the *slavey* to take charge of.

Two more couples came in. One, Mr and Mrs Derventzis, Achilleas and Clio, who were about the same age as Mr and Mrs Kanellis, immediately began to argue with the lawyer about the role Russia would play after the war. The other couple consisted of Mrs Agni, an elderly lady of aristocratic bearing with her hair drawn up on her head in a chignon that resembled a crown, and her son, a pale man with lips as thick and pronounced as an African's, who in his dark suit made me think of a dead man walking: Rodolfos was his name, if I caught it right. They shook hands with me, heard the same rigmarole about me being a Greek American without paying any particular attention to it, and immediately started chatting with the others.

Rodolfos began telling them of his troupe of actors and of a theater that seemed to be his. Well anyway, some troupe of actors and some theater. He described the stage sets that had to be constructed, the costumes that had to be made and a whole host of other details which meant nothing to me.

Last of all and somewhat late, two more guests arrived, out of breath from hurrying—for just as they came in the sirens started wailing to mark the beginning of the curfew. The first of the two was a certain Mr Bukovic (yes, exactly: my eyes grew wide when I heard his name, for it sounded so resoundingly East European that I was terrified the door would be smashed open any minute now and the Gestapo arrive to arrest him—and us along with him. However, Mr Bukovic spoke better Greek than me and seemed to be an educated and respected man, not in the least afraid, hence presumably not in the least guilty of involvement in any plot against the Occupying Authorities—though here actually I was probably wrong— and utterly sure of himself and his presence among us).

The second person… Well, of the second person all I could see at first was his back, muffled from his neck to the turn-ups of his pants in a long black coat, or cloak rather, with its hood thrown back like that of a Franciscan monk and a broad-brimmed old-fashioned black hat on his head below which his white hair stuck out untidily. The Kanellis couple and Konstantina hastened to the hall to greet him. Beneath his cloak I noticed he had a black dog on a leash which Konstantina took off to the kitchen. Everyone was enthusiastically repeating his name: he was Mr Kornelios Something-or-Other.

The pale young man with the thick lips, Rodolfos, addressed him as "Master"—so presumably the newcomer had something to do with the theater and the troupe of actors. Neither his name nor his surname meant anything to me. The deep blue eyes beneath the thatch of white hair greeted everyone in the room, smiling benevolently at the presence of all his friends. I stared at him as if seeing a ghost. Was it possible I could be so mistaken?

Last of all his gaze fell on me.

"And this gentleman?" he asked politely in his deep, asthmatic voice.

"Mr Sotiriou," our hostess told him, "a neighbor and a friend… recently acquired."

"A Greek from America," I added of my own accord.

"Fancy that!" said Mr Kornelios Something-or-Other in admiring tones, then promptly withdrew his attention from me and sat down in the deep leather armchair that until now had been Pavlos Kanellis' preserve.

"Do you know Mr Kornelios Something-or-Other?" Mrs Stavritsa asked me without bothering to lower her voice in the general hubbub.

"I seem to have heard of him somewhere," I answered.

"Our greatest tragic actor!" she exclaimed, raising her eyes towards the heavens. "His Lear! His Oedipus!"

She was nodding her head in admiration, thrilled by the festive atmosphere given to the evening by his presence, after which she turned to Marika Kanellis and called something to her about the dessert, which it would be better to put in the kitchen "for the time being."

I made use of the opportunity and stood up. "I'll take it," I told my hostess, who responded to my chivalry with a friendly nod.

Konstantina was hard at work in the kitchen. Three large pans were standing on the marble table-top, each wrapped in a different kind of paper—the guests' offerings.

Beneath the table, his leash tied to one of its legs, lay the black dog, tranquil and obedient, who apparently got on well with the little island girl. However, as soon as he realized that someone else had come into the kitchen he got up and growled.

"Quiet, Azor," ordered Konstantina, without raising her head from her work.

"Do you know the gentleman who just came in?" I asked her.

"Mr Kornelios? Of course I do! He's a friend of theirs," she replied.

So that's it, is it. A friend of theirs. And not Panayotis but Kornelios. And Kornelios Something, not Agathos.

"What does he do?"

"He's an actor, silly! Haven't you ever heard of Kornelios Something?" said Konstantina, turning around from the sink and staring at me as if I'd just landed from the moon. "*The actor... Kornelios Something...*" (trying in vain to stir my memory).

But what memories could I, a Greek from America, have of someone who must have been famous long before I was born on the other side of the world?

"Yes, right, of course," I accepted.

"Why d'you ask? Don't you believe it's him?"

"Hmm."

"Do you know what Mr Kornelios brought this evening?"

"No."

"Stewed hare!" the girl said triumphantly and pointed

with the knife she was holding at one of the pans. "Just think! Stewed hare! What a man Mr Kornelios is! Incredible…"

"Yes, incredible. Where'd he get it? Does he go hunting maybe?"

"He has his methods, that's what he says, I've heard him. He doesn't come here often but when he does he always brings something special… and he never tells where he got it. Or at least I've never heard him tell. Eh, he's a wonderful man, isn't he, there must be so many people who know him…"

"All right, Konstantina, don't you worry about that. Want any help?"

"From you?" she laughed. "If I need help I'll call the mistress… or Mrs Stavritsa… they're housewives… what would I be doing with you?"

The dog watched me with his clouded eyes as I left the kitchen and growled once more. There are some dogs that, once they've taken a dislike to you, remain hostile: nothing you can do will make them friendly. In the Kanellis couple's office the noise of the party was getting louder.

22

—

A party

It is hard to imagine a more motley group of people than the guests at that party. Achilleas and Clio Derventzis were the offspring of wealthy families, people who'd gone to university, who spoke foreign languages, whose clothes would have cost in pre-war prices as much as the whole wardrobe of both the Kanellis couple put together. Yet, as in young animals, so too in young humans these differences in origin are not so very obvious: youth itself masks them beneath freshness of face and agility of body. The common interests and ideas that the two couples shared made them seem more similar than they actually were. Old age shows up our backgrounds pitilessly—perhaps because as we grow older we gradually return to the point we started from.

Both Derventzises were having a fierce and noisy argument with Pavlos about the war, about Hitler, the Russians and the English—they were particularly vehement about the English and Metaxas. Where exactly they differed I couldn't make out. It was one of those disagreements where the participants in fact basically agree with one another, yet each wants the others to see things his way and believes his own arguments to be best.

The Siniosoglous were wearing old-fashioned clothes. They appeared to have known better days. Yet they maintained their dignity of a bygone age and avoided discussing politics. Mrs Stavritsa made a face when she heard the king described as the pawn of the English, not because she didn't think he was, but because she couldn't believe the English were bad—on the contrary! What would they prefer then? The boorish Russians who aren't even Europeans and have no real culture? The muzhiks? But Greece has never had muzhiks, has never had any relations with Russia, which anyway has always been totally uninterested in us, unlike the English who are our friends. She listened to the conversation, but when Derventzis and Kanellis vied with each other for strong words to describe the perfidy of the English, she looked away.

The armchairs and chairs were scattered around the living room among all the other bits of furniture and we were sitting in a random jumble: Beratis was between the Derventzises and the Kanellises, with Pavlos leaning over him to quarrel with Achilleas, while Marika was talking to Mr Siniosoglou and Kornelios Something. My chair was between young Rodolfos Something-Else, who sat in silence with his eyes half-closed, and Mr Bukovic, who was talking to the young man's mother, Mrs Agni, about translations of Ibsen.

Before long Konstantina appeared in the doorway. Mrs Kanellis got up at once and signaled Stavritsa Sinioglou to help her lay the table. Since no one was talking to me, I might just as well not have been in the room. Thus I got up and went out. In the hall a large folding table had been set up with a white tablecloth on it, chairs had been brought from the bedroom and the kitchen, and the women were carrying in cutlery and plates. An expanding plate-rest was placed in the middle for some hot dish to rest on and a basket of bread made its appearance—one slice for each guest. Its color was slightly dubious but no one paid attention to details like this. I'd eaten bread made from the bristles of besoms before and I recognized it. The wonder was that they'd managed to find it at all.

"We are starting with chickpea soup," our hostess announced with a formal air.

Everyone clapped.

"Made and offered by Mr Sotiriou here."

The chickpea soup, which Konstantina had watered down and to which she'd added some of Beratis' oil, was a great success. However, it was the main dish, the hare, that brought the house down. It had been months since any of us had tasted meat and the dish which the servant girl was putting down on the plate-rest promised an unforgettable meal. Only half the animal was in front of us, perhaps even less: a back leg, a front leg and a bit of its side. This rare and wonderful delicacy had obviously left its other half on some other table, in some other time and place. Mrs Kanellis cut it into small pieces and placed one on each of the plates held out to her. Some people got a bad deal, others were favored, but in neither case was this deliberate. There was no time to pick and choose; everyone took what he was given and immediately began to chew: this tasty morsel had dried out as a result of the several re-heatings it had undergone. It was in any case largely skin and bone with little meat on it, especially the thigh which had been divided into three portions, but those of us who didn't have anything much to chew on sucked the skin and savored its forgotten flavor. Any gaps were filled by the wild greens which the Derventzises had brought, boiled and bitter as poison, with a few drops of oil on them.

"A meal like this should have had some wine to accompany it," said Derventzis.

"Indeed it should," agreed Mrs Stavritsa.

"You can find wine, the charcoal seller on Themistokleous Street has some," said young Rodolfos Something-Else.

"I don't drink," declared Pavlos Kanellis abruptly.

Which meant that since our host didn't drink, he hadn't bothered to find any wine for his dinner party—anyone who wanted some could have brought his own.

I was sitting opposite Marika and Beratis. Between them sat Kanellis: a man ignorant of what three other people at the table knew (four if the great tragic actor was who I thought he was), yet now that I saw him close up he somehow was the most interesting person present. Not because he was our host. Beside him, I don't know why, the illicit lovers seemed an inferior breed. Maybe guilt corrupts people's faces. I'd noticed before that the species of the human animal which is governed by passion seems to belong to a different class from the rest, always in some way crouching, ready to lunge forwards or to flee.

Pavlos Kanellis wasn't at all of this kind, his soul was weighed down by nothing except questions of politics, about which he tended to get carried away. To Mrs Siniosoglou he replied that the English are certainly European and more civilized than the Russians, but they are a nation of shopkeepers, their political conscience being guided more by budgets than by the ideals of democracy. In support of his views he quoted some lines of verse:

Trust not for freedom to the Franks –
They have a king who buys and sells.

To Rodolfos Something-Else he said that Myrsine was a better actress than Eleni (both these people were completely unknown to me) and would be much better in the part of Electra now that Eleni was ill. The young theatrical manager was extremely worried about the changes in the cast; he himself preferred Eleni as an actress to Myrsine but avoided saying so.

To Achilleas Derventzis, who was taunting him with being an amateur revolutionary, he replied that only amateurs can be revolutionaries, professionals become ministers and send the police to beat up demonstrating workers.

He didn't pay any special attention to Beratis. Their friendship was of the kind that doesn't need to be continually expressed but is lasting, steady, unshakable and taken for granted. The musician behaved as a member of the family and Kanellis treated him as such. The three of them must have shared their political beliefs and the two men shared their love for the same woman. All the same, the idea that Beratis kept his most precious secret hidden from his bosom friend distressed and scared me. What would happen if one day the truth were to come out?

Marika was not still or silent for a single moment. She was the youngest and prettiest of the women present and appeared to be enjoying, as if by right, the position of leader; she tossed her wavy locks of hair and put forward her own opinions, often different from those of her husband. Her conversation made frequent reference to the position of woman in society; once the war was over, Greek women would certainly acquire the right to vote and to stand for election, indeed why not one day to head a government. Although none of the men in the company was able to resist the temptation to tease her with one of the jokes about suffragettes then in circulation, all agreed in the end that she was certainly correct and that it was right and proper and to be expected that these things would one day come to pass. I watched in amazement as she supported her ideas by reciting poetry, with an enthusiasm and a theatricality that made her husband raise his eyebrows in barely perceptible disapproval. This behavior of hers reminded me of the mating dance of insects of some kind, which I'd seen in a documentary. It was all done for the benefit of the two males yoked to her chariot—for the two of them only: not for me, the third.

To my surprise, her behavior, her reciting, her shining eyes, her voice raised above other peoples' and, nearer at hand, her sharp orders to the servant, made her seem more distant from me than I would have imagined possible. When Beratis had revealed their guilty secret to me, she'd seemed closer, more accessible, a woman who could have been my lover since she was someone else's. Now, in her own home, in the company of her own close friends, I was seeing her again as a creature who could never have had anything to do with me. This cruel goddess with her well-kept secret, this wife who received her lover, her husband's friend, at her party, this harsh and unapproachable presence who had for so long been making me feel ashamed of what I was because she held such a mistaken view of me, who'd despised me and slapped me, and then from one moment to the next invited me to her home when I caught her more or less in the act with her lover in my apartment—now she was once more far off on the opposite bank, had once more become as hostile and alien to me as she'd been when we used to pass each other in silence on the stairs or on the sidewalk of Gennadiou Street.

And of the two men in her life, it was Kanellis who

didn't take his eyes off her for a moment, while Beratis always seemed to be looking in a different direction or talking to someone else, like a guilty man going out of his way to avoid the scene of his crime.

The evening would have continued as it had begun, with the loud voices, arguments and even quarrels that were apparently part of the normal fabric of their evenings together. It would have continued as it began if the devil hadn't suddenly spurred me to go up to the great tragic actor and tell him a few of the things on my mind. This was the first discordant note in the midst of all the passionate arguments exploding like Easter fireworks about translations of Ibsen (I wished I knew who he was), or if Eleni was better than Polyxeni or Myrsine-Whatsit, or whether the English and Metaxas had been worse than the Germans and Italians who were currently killing people in the streets. The second discordant note that evening wasn't my fault but simply our bad luck. However, let's get back to the first.

When there wasn't a crumb left on the table, the plates looked clean enough to be put away in the cupboard without being washed and our backs were aching from the awkward chairs we'd been sitting on, the friends started drifting one by one back to the front room in order to continue their conversations in greater comfort. Marika Kanellis had got Mr Kornelios on his own and was thanking him for the wonderful hare. It was my chance. For in front of a third party the old man would be on the defensive.

"So we meet again, Mr *Kornelios!*" I hissed.

"Do we indeed, my boy?" he asked, casting a rapid glance around. "I don't think so. But then again, who knows? It may be so."

"As well as being an olive oil merchant, you've been an actor, then?"

"Look here, there is a time for everything," he murmured. "Don't try to spoil the evening for everyone…"

"…Mr Angel, my boy," I completed.

"Mr Angel, my boy," he said with a small, sharp laugh.

"What are you saying to him?" Mrs Kanellis asked nervously.

It was bad enough for me to be so audacious as to speak to one of her guests. But to speak in that manner—and to the great Mr Something!

"Who's an olive oil merchant?"

"This gentleman," I told her.

"It's just a little joke we have, Rika, my dear," said the old man in saccharine tones. "Angel and I have known each other a long time, on a professional basis at first, which subsequently evolved into a greater familiarity and friendship…"

"You've known each other a long time?" she asked, as if asking whether I could fly.

"Why not? The gentleman is well-travelled, he's been to America—it was there we met, was it not?"

"Yes, yes, yes," said Mr Kornelios.

"In America? *You?* When?"

Mrs Rika was not distinguished for her tact, it didn't

occur to her to pretend she hadn't understood or to accept what people said without subjecting them to a grilling of this kind. Had he or had he not ever been to America, this was what she wanted to know.

"It was years ago," he told her tranquilly. "You and I didn't know each other in those days…" (he smiled at her).

"Oh, I see! I must say, I wouldn't have expected you to have been there," said Marika Kanellis. She blushed and prepared to move off.

"Don't leave us, my dear friend," the old actor begged.

"I have to go and serve the dessert. Didn't you know? Stavritsa's made us a pudding!"

"A pudding? You don't say!"

He pretended to be amazed although he must have heard it mentioned at least twenty times, since the existence of this famous pudding was announced to every guest that evening as soon as he crossed the threshold. But Marika used the excuse to slip away and the old man was now alone with me.

"You owe me some explanations," I told him.

"Why do you think that?"

"It won't take more than a minute. You set me to look after Beratis since supposedly you didn't know him and wanted to help him without appearing… And now I find you eating at the same table with him, with the Kanellises, with Marika… calling yourself Mr Kornelios Something, the great actor… That's why!"

"Listen to me, my friend. There are some things which we may never understand, yet we continue living just as well—dare I say it—as if we did understand them… Better even maybe… Keep your doubts for another occasion or, better still, keep them to yourself forever. Tonight is an opportunity for me to provide you with the money you'll need for your expenses, don't get me wrong… I had to come, did I not?"

"My expenses are large. The villagers are skinning me alive…"

"Whatever you need."

I'd hardly taken more than a couple of spoonfuls of Mrs Stavritsa's raisin pudding made with biscuits soaked in sugar syrup, when from the kitchen came fierce barking. As if someone had stepped on the dog's tail. Konstantina put her head around the door and her eyes searched for the old actor.

"He won't sit still," she told him hesitantly, "he's lunging at me…"

Conversations were broken off as everyone began asking, "What's up? What's the matter with the dog?" Mr Kornelios Something wove his way between their legs and went towards the kitchen. I followed. I had no intention of letting him use this pretext to escape. That black beast would be calmed with a couple of pats on the head and would retire beneath the table once more—whereupon its master would be once more at my disposition. I wasn't going to let him off the hook.

In the kitchen the dog was barking and foaming at the mouth. His master's voice did succeed in calming him slightly but he continued straining at the leash attaching him to the table leg and no one else dared approach.

"What is it, then, what is it you want?" I heard the old man say. "What's got into you?…Who? What?"

These last two questions were very strange. It was almost as if he could understand the language of the dog's howls and whimpers. Was he hungry? Did he need to be let out? No, it was something else.

"What do you want? What's up?"

I was on the point of bursting out laughing. But just then he realized he had an audience and motioned me to leave the room: "Don't stay here, strangers upset him."

I retreated a couple of steps and waited outside the open door with my ears pricked up to listen. What I heard were murmurs and fond whispers and caresses interspersed with the dog's growling—it sounded like a conversation. After a while the dog was quiet and his master emerged from the kitchen.

"You're still here?"

"Yes, I stayed in case you needed any help," I said.

"Go out and take a look from the balcony," he told me hurriedly.

I didn't understand.

"Go out onto the balcony," he said again. "Have a look along the street, I've a feeling… I think Azor got wind of something… there may be an unpleasant surprise in store for us… have a good look, Mr Angel, my boy. If need be… take to the air and hover a bit to see as far as you can… look for cars, military ones I mean… What are you waiting for? Go on now, quick!"

I went out onto the narrow balcony in front of the servant's room which looked onto Gennadiou Street. Outside our door two Volkswagens were parked with red and black flags on their wings. German soldiers with machine guns stood on the sidewalk while others, with an officer, were trying to read the names on the doorbells with a flashlight. I didn't need to hover. Or to fly either. There would only just be time to warn the party.

"Quick, turn off the lights! Everybody quiet! The Germans are here!"

Someone's hand found the mains switch and all the lights went out, we were plunged into darkness, suddenly you could have heard a pin drop in the living room. Only a small moan—"Jesus Christ and Holy Virgin"—escaped Mrs Stavritsa. Some of the guests tiptoed into the back room. Whispers. Is the staircase safe? The service entrance? The roof? Don't open the door! And if they ring the bell pretend no one's here! They don't break down doors, this sort of thing's happened before…. Sssh… sssh…

I heard the voice of Kornelios Something beside me murmur, "Mr Angel…"

"Down the back stairs from the kitchen and into my flat!" I hissed to him.

"Don't bother about me. Take the musician down-stairs… and Mr Kanellis."

"Oh yeah? Is Kanellis part of our agreement?"

In the darkness he gripped my arm. "You do choose your moments! Take them both, they're the ones who are in danger."

The pitch darkness made things difficult, forced one to move more slowly.

"If you can find them for me," I said. "I can't see the nose on my face."

He glided over the chairs and little tables like a nocturnal bird. I heard his voice in the hall, low yet distinct.

"Mr Beratis… Pavlos… Mr Angel's looking for you… I don't know… he was here a moment ago, in the office… Mr Sotiriou, where are you?"

"Here, I'm here."

I made sure I'd got hold of both the two men I was meant to smuggle out, one with each hand, and pulled them closer to me.

"Through the kitchen, to my apartment, downstairs…"

Even down here we could hear the sound of the doorbell ringing. I didn't put on any lights.

"It's the same as your apartment, you can find your way into the other room," I whispered.

"I know, we used to live here before you," Pavlos Kanellis reminded me.

We lay low in the front room. From the stairs came the voices of the Germans.

"They got in!" said the musician in terror.

"Balomenos must have let them in at the street door,"

the lawyer noted with bitter contempt. "Now they'll break our own door down."

The Germans were climbing the stairs without any attempt to take anyone by surprise, their boots clattering on the marble steps, their voices loud.

"What are they saying?" I asked Beratis, "Can you hear what they're saying?"

"I can't make it out," he said, his ear glued to my front door.

The voices and the footsteps were on the second floor now, they were ringing the Kanellis' bell again, they were banging on the door. The whole building was as silent as the grave, as if no one but the two lawyers lived here: everyone else must have been cowering in terror. In the past, lights would have gone on, doors would have opened, people would have come out onto the stairs to see what was happening. Now silence only.

I wished I were upstairs to see how Mr Kornelios would handle the Germans: he, like me, had no reason to be particularly afraid. Yet fear is catching. It's like when children play hide-and-seek and the other child suddenly becomes an object of terror—he's the enemy in pursuit, you run fast not to be caught and hide where he can't find you. Now, as we listened and tried to translate sounds into images in order to understand what was going on in the upstairs apartment, I was trembling just as much as the others. They hadn't opened the door, the Germans were beating on it harder, crashing the stocks of their weapons on it, wood and metal on wood. Guns! Guns that any moment now would be in the Kanellis' apartment. I felt Pavlos shudder beside me.

"They'll kill them," he said.

"No they won't, why should they kill them?"

German words again, louder this time, barked commands ringing out in the stairwell.

"I'll go and give myself up," said Pavlos. "If they get me, they'll leave the others alone."

He moved away from the door towards the back of the apartment.

"Rika!" He'd recognized his wife's voice. It seems they'd opened the door at last—much better, I thought to myself, because otherwise, if the soldiers had had to smash it, things might have taken a much more savage turn. But I couldn't let Pavlos commit such a folly.

"No, I'll go," I told him. "Nobody knows me, I'm not in any danger from the Germans. I'll go and see what's happening. You two stay here and don't make a sound."

Without giving the matter another thought, back I went up the outside stairs and slipped into the Kanellis kitchen. I was greeted by a whine—Mr Kornelios' dog was still tied to the table leg. No one else was there: Konstantina, it seemed, had joined the guests in the front room.

Yes, they'd opened the door and they'd turned on the lights, no one had said a thing, the Germans had come in with their machine guns at the ready and a blond officer was addressing Mrs Kanellis. Everyone else was sitting rigid, frozen with fear. No one had been killed and no one had been arrested; it was a good thing I'd come back up and very lucky that the other two hadn't come with me.

"My husband isn't here, he's gone to visit relatives in Piraeus," Marika was saying, and a Greek in a mackintosh and a cap pushed rakishly back was translating for the German officer.

"He says 'Where's he gone?' Where?" he translated.

"To Piraeus, I told you. He was going to stay there tonight, his old aunt is ill."

The officer's eyes scanned the room and came to rest on me as I emerged from the kitchen door.

"Who's this man? Where were you? Come here!"

I approached.

"I was in the toilet," I said.

"*Kanellis?*" asked the officer, motioning me with his pistol to come closer.

"Not Kanellis, Sotiriou," I told him.

I got out my identity card and gave it to the Greek in the cap, who looked at it and then at me, from top to toe. Mr Kornelios raised his head, questioning me with his eyes. I nodded in reassurance.

"Where do you live?" asked the man in the cap.

"Gamvetta Street," I answered instantly. I didn't want them to know there was another apartment in the building where the two fugitives might be concealed.

"Telephone him," the officer ordered Mrs Kanellis, "your husband."

"They haven't got a telephone, they're poor people, refugees."

This was translated.

"What has the man done? Why do you want him?" we were all amazed to hear our tragic actor ask in German. "Why do they want him? What's he done?" he repeated in Greek to the man in the cap. He was standing there in front of the armed men with an innocent smile on his face and appeared to be genuinely curious. "I can assure you that he's a respectable person, a lawyer and intellectual, a peace-loving man."

Hardly had he finished this statement when the officer stepped forward and grabbed him by the lapels of his jacket. He spoke with such vehemence that Mr Kornelios had to raise his hand to his face to wipe off the spit. This gesture, it seemed, enraged the noble knight of the Wehrmacht even further: he raised his own gloved hand and smashed it down on the old man's face. A collective groan escaped the guests. Mr Kornelios Something staggered backwards and fell to the floor. Hasty hands helped him up. His smile had not left his lips. With unruffled calm, he addressed the officer once more in perfect German: it must have been either his faultless accent and vocabulary or whatever it was he said that left the other man speechless.

After a formal check of our identity cards the soldiers departed. As they went downstairs the man in the cap advised us to turn out all the lights and go to bed. "You were lucky tonight," he hissed as the door closed behind him.

"But what did you say to him? What did you say?" everyone asked as they crowded around the old actor.

He wiped the sweat from his brow with an Olympian gesture and smiled again, his blue eyes darting sparks.

"What I said to him isn't of any importance," he told us. "What's important is what he said as he left."

"What did he say?" asked Marika.

"That they'd be back."

23

The Sock

In New York, as I've said, I used to know a young writer
called Sol. He lived in the same neighborhood as me, a
couple of houses further along, and worked downtown as
a clerk in the office of a lawyer cum notary. We used to
meet at the basketball court of the parish of St Stephen or
else at Jimmy's bar. Well, he told me that he used to write
his stories not with a pen but on an old typewriter. He
preferred it because it enabled him to use the blind, touch-
type system which he himself had refined into the *perfectly
blind* system. What was his trick? He'd cover his whole
head, right down to his chin, with a large knitted sock,
the kind children are given to put out on Christmas Eve
for Santa Claus to fill. This sock enveloped him in total
blind darkness so he couldn't see what he was typing on
the paper. Thus he could be sure that he was writing with
complete spontaneity, just as it came to him. He rarely
corrected his mistakes, only when his fingers had let him

down on the keys or when he needed to rewrite some phrase that had come out the wrong way round. I thought he must be a bit crazy if he really did this. But then I'd never seen him writing, either with a sock or without, so maybe he was only pulling my leg.

He'd read some of his stories to me: they were good, they seemed real even though they were made up out of his imagination. What with leaving in such a hurry, I never did find out what became of him, whether he ever found a publisher for his spontaneous writings or gained the money and recognition he always dreamed of. Yet recently, as I sit and write my own story, I've been trying to use a method rather like his. I don't mean that I put a sock over my head of course, but I leave my pencil free to write by itself with my eyes half-closed—anyway, without glasses I can't see a thing these days. I can't make out the words or the letters clearly, everything is faint and misty. The "sock" helps, it seems to me, it liberates you from being enslaved by these marks on the paper which have nothing of real life in them; if you stare at them long enough, the words become just a series of units—accents and periods and exclamation marks and apostrophes. They look like skeletons washed up on the sand, belonging to animals that once had skin and life and blood coursing through their veins. There comes a point when you have to look at what you've written, you can't avoid it; but as long as you write with your eyes half-closed (or even shut tight, like Sol) you can escape the sight of those bare bones, you can live longer with the essence of the phrase, with the truth of the image before you have turned it into words, just as you see it in your mind.

So far I've been speaking of myself as if I'd written it all down at the time, as if I'd kept a diary; I speak like someone who doesn't yet know all the secrets in the story. A simple detective, solving the case step by step. That's what I was. And that's what I have to remain now until the story has become clear and things have been put into their proper place. If they ever are, that is.

Once the Germans had gone, Mr Kornelios Something and I went down the kitchen stairs to tell Pavlos and Miltos that they could come back. They were lying low in the front room. Kanellis was concentrating on listening to all the sounds, the door opening and closing, the footsteps and the harsh voices of the Germans on the stairs as they left. The musician had half-closed his eyes as if dreaming and his bitten fingernails were drumming on the arm of the chair with his foot keeping the same rhythm—impossible to know what tune he was singing in his mind. Maybe the song he'd liked so much in the Maniatika in Piraeus, the one about the singer's love for a married woman. Maybe something from the opera they were rehearsing at the Olympia; or maybe one of his own compositions.

Standing behind the great tragic actor I spotted the uncertain shape of Marika, who'd also come down to see what had happened to the fugitives, her husband and her lover. Her gaze wandered from the one to the other and there was a smile in her words: "It's all right, you can come up now. They've gone."

But the good mood of a little while ago had evaporated now, the guests were frightened and anxious, withdrawing into their own thoughts; they thus remained more or less in silence until the sun rose and then slipped hastily away like guilty shadows.

Two days later, early in the morning, a timid knock on my closed bedroom shutter made me leap up in alarm. The silence and the windless calm left my mind still enveloped in the mists of sleep. The knock came again, more insistent now. Like a coded message… I opened the glass pane and listened.

"Mr Angel!"

It was Konstantina. I opened the shutter too. Crouching to avoid being seen, she put her head inside the window so that no one would hear her from the light-well.

"It's the Security Police! They've come for Mr Pavlos again," she said breathlessly.

I hadn't seen the Kanellis couple since the day before yesterday. If I'd supposed anything, it was that Pavlos would have taken care to be offered temporary hospitality in someone else's house. They'd said they were going to come back and they had. Today it wasn't the Germans but the Security Police—however, in either case the end would be the same. I asked the girl where the lawyer was right now.

"He's hiding in the basement. But they're not leaving… they say they're going to wait for him. The mistress is upstairs with them… She's told them he went to the law courts…"

I opened the front door and stood and listened by the stairs. I couldn't hear a thing. All doors were shut and a deathly silence reigned. But from the ground floor the scent of cigarette smoke drifted upwards, a heavy local blend. Someone was keeping a look-out at the foot of the stairs or the entrance, in case the lawyer should spot the ambush as he returned and walk on by. So the entrance was blocked. The service door on the ground floor was always kept locked; Mrs Leni had the key, a tiny little ageless woman devoted body and soul (or so people said) to the landlord. What remained was the flat roof.

The basement stank. It had a passage with six store-rooms opening off it, one for each apartment. However, our contracts didn't specify the use of a storeroom; the only tenant who had this privilege was Mr Kynigos, on the second floor, the Kanellis' neighbor. So he couldn't have got out of here. Had his courage perhaps failed so that he'd gone back upstairs to give himself up? I looked up towards the roof. If anyone had been on the outside stairs I would have spotted him through the open metalwork of the steps.

"Mr Kanellis?"

Something creaked behind me. In the passage stood an

old wooden trunk and a wicker basket for laundry. The lid of the latter moved a bit and I caught sight of his bespectacled face. He hadn't found anywhere else to hide.

"I'll have to stay here as long as those stool pigeons are in my flat."

I pointed upwards.

"The roof?"

"Where else?"

"They went up there first. What if they go back up?"

"We won't be staying there: the roof of the Public Prosecutor's office is next door."

"It's too high, you don't know…"

"Don't be afraid, I do know," I told him and put out my hand to help him get out of the basket.

As stealthily as thieves we crept up to the roof. He took off his shoes and went up the stairs in his socks. I, who had trained myself to walk soundlessly, didn't need to follow suit. At each landing we crouched low, lest anyone should see us from the kitchens, then took the steps two at a time. The flat roof was deserted. Over the roof of the Conservatoire you could see the German flag on the Acropolis and, to the north, the swastikas on the aerials of the Ionian School on Academias Street. We leaned over the parapet to judge the distance between us and the tiled roof of the Public Prosecutor's office. About fifteen feet. A long way for someone to jump without making any noise—a sprained ankle was a near certainty and a broken leg very likely. Yet there was no other way out. The roofs of the next-door buildings were reflected crystal clear in the windows of the Varvitsiotis house. If someone spotted us, they might well tell the look-out stationed downstairs. But the Public Prosecutor's office, on the contrary, lay at the back of our building, the adjoining wall wasn't visible from the street, there were no houses immediately next door to it—and anyway, if anyone spotted us they wouldn't have time to tell the Security Police. For we'd already have found a way out onto Fidiou or Trikoupi Street.

He looked at me and smiled. "This is the second time you've got me away… Why are you helping me?"

"Because I feel like it. Because I'm a good man. Didn't you know?"

He was silent for a moment. Then: "Thank you. But I won't jump. I'll give myself up."

"Don't do it," I told him, "they'll kill you."

He flushed and suddenly his eyes filled with tears of outrage. "What am I supposed to have done, for goodness sake?"

"You know better than me."

He inspected the paving on the flat roof. The awkward position he'd been forced into in the laundry basket had made him stiff; he knelt down.

"Something must be going to happen that we don't know about. Or something has happened—like that explosion at Omonia…"

"Ah yes, the explosion," he said and then was silent. And after a moment: "It's because I've written various articles against the Germans… and against some of their local collaborators while I was at it—that's what it is. I've got nothing to do with explosions or sabotage."

"Tell them that when they catch you. You'll do better to jump, come on…"

He got up. He reckoned the height again. It was time for me to make up my mind.

"I'll jump with you," I told him.

He stared at me, trying to understand. But before he could say a word I clambered up onto the parapet and put out my hand to him.

"Why will you jump?"

"For safety's sake," I said. "Give me your hand."

As he stood beside me I got hold of him around his waist. He made as if to bend.

"Backwards," he said. "I'll hang over the edge and let myself drop. Maybe that way I won't get hurt."

"There's no need. Just hold on to me."

"We'll be killed! Are you crazy?"

It was better not to waste time. If he thought any more about it he'd start resisting and then everything would be more difficult. As I held on to him and he held on to me, I leaned outwards and pulled him with me. For a moment we hovered in the void, then began to drift slowly downwards to the roof. All he managed was a brief groan. He may have thought that he'd already been killed and was now swimming through the air on the way to the Heaven he'd mocked all his life. Then we touched down lightly on the roof tiles. He was trembling all over. He stepped back and looked at me. His whole existence was resisting the question that quivered on his lips, but his eyes were shouting it—who was I, what was I, how did I do that? I motioned him to follow me.

A little while later I put him on a streetcar. He'd go to Ilissia, to the house of the Siniosoglous. He asked me to tell his wife—although this wasn't necessary. He didn't thank me. But as the streetcar moved off, rattling on its rails, he went on gazing at me through the window. I turned onto Gennadiou Street again. Outside the café two guys in fedoras were scanning the two ends of the street. The café owner was standing beside them grinning. Someone was sticking his head out of the Kanellis' window and ordering coffee.

"It's first-rate chickpea coffee!" Zisis warned them, just so they wouldn't make trouble later.

"OK, chickpea it is then, can't be helped," said the security man and closed the window.

At the entrance to our building, the fourth man, the one I hadn't seen but whose cigarette smoke I'd smelled, was lighting another cigarette. What a smoker!

"Where are you going?"

"Home," I said, stopping.

I got out my papers and showed them to him. He may or may not have been able to read, but at any rate the photo was a recent one.

"Beat it."

I shrugged and made my way upstairs. Without delay

I was out of my kitchen door and up the outside stairs to the second floor. I looked through their kitchen window and saw Konstantina sitting hunched with her face in her hands. She might have been half-asleep or she might have been crying. I scratched the windowpane gently. Like a shot she was out on the landing. Her eyes were questioning—her head warningly turned towards the interior of the flat: the security police were still there.

"It's all right," I told her. "He got away."

She opened her mouth. "Oh, Mr Angel," she said in a little voice that had nothing to do with the time or place in which we found ourselves. Suddenly she was alarmed by some sound from within the apartment. A cold, harsh voice was warning Mrs Kanellis: they couldn't hang around there all day waiting for him, they'd be leaving a man at the entrance. The door was slammed as they left. Then silence again.

When the servant returned, Marika was behind her, pale, her lips bitten. She put out a hand to the door frame to steady herself.

"Mr Pavlos is staying at the Siniosoglous… he asked me to tell you."

The servant girl burst into tears. The mistress was holding up better than the slavey.

"Shut up!" she ordered the girl instantly, as if not recognizing Konstantina's right to be more upset than she was herself. Or maybe she was afraid that the servant's tears would carry her away into emotions she was struggling to control. "You got him out of here…" (more statement than question).

"Yes," I said. "Don't be afraid, he's all right, he's safe."

"How?"

"We jumped onto the roof of the Public Prosecutor's office," I told her. "Then we went down the stairs as easy as can be, out onto Fidiou Street, and he caught the streetcar on Trikoupi Street."

"You jumped too?"

"Yes. He wouldn't jump alone, he was scared."

Her eyes narrowed but seemed to be focusing far away, in the direction the fugitive had taken: she seemed angry. Maybe her husband wasn't as much of a hero as she would have liked. Maybe she thought I was lying to her.

She looked up at me. Her mouth was trying to form itself into a smile—and, directed at me, she couldn't manage anything broader or more spontaneous. Her distrust of me was struggling with her relief at the good news I'd brought.

"Thanks," she said through clenched teeth.

"You're welcome. It was nothing."

But just then her knees gave way and she collapsed on the marble-chip floor.

24

———

The musician's room

In the forecourt of the theater a group of German soldiers were standing around, smoking and joking. "Halt!" a harsh voice cried as one of them bore down on me to throw me out. In sign language I explained that I wasn't intending to go into the building, I just wanted to buy a ticket. A meager face with a Hitler mustache was looking out through the glass panes at the entrance. I put my hand in my pocket and went up to him.

"I've got a cousin in the orchestra, Miltos Beratis, do you know him?" I whispered conspiratorially. "Tell him Angel's outside waiting for him. We've got various family troubles these days…"

I glanced at the guards. "What are they doing here?" I asked, nodding at them. "The German maestro's inside," replied the usher. "Everywhere he goes he has an escort. You wait here, I'll go and tell him."

I went back out to the sidewalk and leaned against one

of the marble gateposts. The street was quiet and from time to time bursts of music reached my ears that stopped as suddenly as they began. They sounded like the marches their bands played. When I'd heard this opera in New York with Freddy I'd had a different impression of it.

I heard Beratis' rapid footsteps on the tiles of the corridor. A moment later he was at my side.

"Let's get out of here," he spluttered, like someone coming to the surface after a long, deep dive. "Let's go, I'll tell you in a minute. He almost threw me out of the rehearsal. He's acting like a madman, he's got me in his sights. What he wants is to crush me, to break me."

He was walking fast, dragging me along, his usually pale face now brick red as if he were on the verge of a stroke. All of a sudden he stopped, leaned back against the wall of the Ionian School and tried to get his breath back.

"I'll tell you about it, I'll tell you. Ah, he wants to destroy me, that man. He wants to break me. Wait. What do you think?"

I'd begun to speak but broke off, luckily before he'd realized. For I would have done more harm than good if I'd told him just then about everything that had taken place that morning after he'd left with his double bass, all nice and peaceful, to go off to his rehearsal. However, Beratis' mind was somewhere else, in his own world, in his own nightmare which was very different from that of my neighbors on Gennadiou Street. Even though he hadn't mentioned the man's name you knew perfectly well he was speaking of the great conductor.

"What d'you think? What did you say?"

"Nothing, you tell me. Calm down, though, you'll have a fit or something."

Then suddenly, as if his mind had cleared and he was returning to real life, he asked, "Everything all right over there?"

"Pavlos had to make a get-away." I told him.

"They came again?"

"Yes, this morning."

He gave an inarticulate groan and set off once more at a rapid pace, dragging me along towards Zosimadon Street.

"He got away, he's all right. They'll forget about him. They haven't got time to waste on the likes of us. It's other people they're after, if they catch us then well and good, if they don't catch us they'll go after someone else. The true underground are in hiding, they use false identities and carry out acts of sabotage and send messages to the Allies. Those are the people they really want, not Pavlos. What about Marika? Did they do anything to her?"

"No, they didn't do anything to her. But they've left a plainclothes man at the door just in case Pavlos turns up—she told them he was out at work. But tell me about you, what happened at the theater, why is the German picking on you? Does he really hate you so much ever since Berlin?"

"The man's a lunatic. And I'm a fool, tilting at windmills. I'm doing my utmost to show him that we're good and can measure up to the standard he wants… The great Bodo foams at the mouth and spits right, left and center—did you know he spits at musicians when they don't play the way he wants? It's true, cross my heart! Ftoo! Straight in their faces! And the orchestra can't concentrate, everyone's longing for the break, so they ask him questions—with me interpreting—and get him going on his hobbyhorse analyzing Wagner, time goes by and then he won't let us leave. He makes us stay on to make up lost time. And he calls us a 'gypsy band'. Nothing but trouble is going to come of this performance, everyone's saying so. Some of them were hoping that some good might come of it for us… Now he's so angry that the most likely outcome is that he'll get us all shut up in the Averof prison."

The musician was trembling. And the singers didn't have any better luck than the orchestra. Singing flat! He was irritated by the Italian translation of the libretto they were using, angry at the breaths they took "whenever they felt like it." They were broken-winded, half-dead and useless! Those were the politer epithets he used—there were other, cruder ones. The German singers would be arriving the day after tomorrow, he informed them, and they'd teach them how Wagner ought to be sung.

"He thinks he's dealing with his well-trained, well-paid Berliners. He doesn't want to understand that things are different here, we're a small opera without money, without traditions and without the standards the Germans are used to. And the worst thing is that he doesn't realize we're all struggling, making a huge effort, out of pride and enthusiasm at the honor of being conducted by a musician like him… Broken-winded and half-dead… yes! How could we be otherwise with hunger like this? But I tell you, Angel, and you'd better believe me: I've never heard the orchestra play like they've been playing in our rehearsals with that devil! Everyone is giving of his very best… And he doesn't understand, he imagines he's got the stars of his very own Philharmonic in front of him. What a bastard!"

As he talked we reached his house. I'd never been here before—even though we'd become great friends recently, he'd never invited me. It was a dilapidated small house with a tiled roof and a courtyard and a wrought iron gate. The plaster was falling off, the place hadn't been repaired for years and was decaying into ruin. A wild fig tree growing just inside the tumbledown wall had put out suckers that were thrusting up through the sidewalk. We pushed open the gate which had sunk on its hinges and stuck on the paving stones of the yard and stood in front of the door while he fumbled in his pocket for a blackened key which he shoved into a keyhole which had lost its fittings.

His words seemed somehow ill-assorted with the man I knew. The room in which we now found ourselves was equally ill-assorted. It had a strange smell. I racked my brains to identify what it reminded me of. Then suddenly I got it: it smelled of a Greek village. It might have been due to the damp that had permeated the plaster of the walls and ceiling; or perhaps it was the gas stove in the kitchen; or the plaited twist of dried figs that a year ago they'd sent him from home (home being a village outside Halkida, he'd said), which he willingly offered for me to help myself from. Yes, his room had a *village* smell. A strange environment for conversations like ours!

The smell also didn't fit well with all the photographs from Germany that he had on the walls. One of them showed a group of young men and women arrayed in three rows, the front row sitting and the other two standing, arranged around an old man sitting in the center of the front row with an elderly air and heavy-framed spectacles (without doubt "the professor and his class"); another showed Beratis in a wing collar and black tie beside an ash-blond, well-built man a whole head taller, his hair swept back poetically, wearing a white shirt and a tailcoat, who was shaking his hand as they both smiled into the lens. Smaller photographs showed groups of friends in the countryside, among lush pastures and snowy mountains; they were wearing hiking boots and open-necked shirts and carried walking sticks—I couldn't make out their features in the dim light of his room, but surely Beratis must have been among them. Finally, there was a large, framed diploma adorned with a gold seal and important-looking signatures: the Gothic letters indicated that the unknown language it was written in was German.

Just as incongruous as the smell was the piano with its worn keys; two thick scores were propped up on it, at its feet a violin case, while on the floor were two large piles of music.

Beratis was continuing to speak of Froberger as I went on memorizing the room (a professional tic).

"Today, during one of our breaks, he sat down on the rostrum, called me over and told me: 'Beratis, if I were to go out into the street and order three *Blitzmaedchen* to get up on the stage and sing the parts of the Rhine maidens, they'd not only do it better than these screeching magpies of yours but they'd look a whole lot prettier too. And I'll do it.' 'Why not, Maestro,' I said, 'at least it would mean there'd be three members of the cast that you didn't object to.' He laughed and said, 'Your ladies all look like the witches out of *Macbeth*. How is it possible that in the entire theater there isn't a single good-looking woman? It's just a myth, Greek beauty, Beratis, that's what I've come to realize. Maybe it once existed but it no longer exists now.' I thought he was unwinding a bit and beginning to talk like a human being—everyone fools around and jokes a bit during breaks… So I laughed and said, 'If you went out into the street instead of spending all day buried deep in the theater, you'd see a lot of beautiful women—even though they're suffering from hunger and deprivation.' He lit a cigarette, drew in the smoke and blew it in my face, then said, 'Listen carefully, if you want to get out of my hands alive you'd better introduce me to one of the beauties you mix with. Have you taken that in?' And then he got up and went into his dressing room."

"Maestro or no maestro, he's got his mind on the nitty-gritty," I commented. "How old is Mr F.?"

"I don't know exactly. Old. But he's got a certain

reputation. Not a seducer or anything, I don't mean that, just a bit of this and a bit of that, whatever comes his way. There are rumors of various artistes backstage. Don't ask. He's got a sick personality. But… you heard what he said to me. 'If you want to get out of my hands alive,' he said. And I looked into his eyes as he was saying it. He meant it… I have to get out of here, I have to do something… If I could escape to Halkida…"

His gaze came to rest uncomfortably on the keys of the piano.

"I can't see any other solution," he went on. "We've just got the first night, then one other performance… and then he'll be on his way back to Berlin. If I weren't around just for those days, who'd come looking for me? But on the other hand…who'd be taken back at the Opera after going missing? They'd fire me without a second thought. Tell me," (changing the subject), "have you seen Marika?"

"Yes, of course, I told you. I saw her this morning."

He sat down on the divan and crossed his arms.

"Was she all right?"

"Maestro," I told him, "it seems to me that you're not quite in touch with reality today. I told you how Pavlos escaped this morning and is now in hiding, and how she stayed home with a cop at the door lying in wait for him. Apart from that, yes, she's fine."

He put his head on one side and I watched him, waiting to see what was coming.

"I think I'll just go over and see her," he said finally.

"No. You stay here. You've had enough trouble for one day."

"He wants to crush me, I know it. To humiliate me."

"I don't understand why. He's a famous conductor, you're an unknown musician… You had your differences in Berlin, I realize that—but that was then. Now, though? What's he got against you now? Don't you think you might be exaggerating a tiny bit, Miltos?"

"You don't know him," my friend told me, his eyes flashing with malice. "You don't know him. Bodo is a crusader for German art and music. *Our* works, by which I mean compositions of our school, are what he hates worst, the bane of his life. If he goes along with the Nazis, it's because he believes they'll support his credo."

"Come on, Miltos! If you were talking about territory, about the Sudetenland or Poland, about *lebensraum*, then I might believe you. But music! What's so special about music, for heaven's sake?"

"Wait," he cried, "listen!"

He went and opened the cupboard. He'd converted it into bookshelves, his clothes were all bundled into a corner and the rest of the space was crammed with books and gramophone records in their sleeves. He selected one of these, got a gramophone out from under the bed, put it on the table and wound it up. The record bore a hand-written label with his name on it, for some reason spelled with two 't's. It wasn't a commercially-produced record. It must have been some private recording. He lowered the needle onto it and from the speaker instantly issued a jumbled cacophony. There were moments when I had to cover my ears with my hands.

"Jesus Christ!"

If there were music in hell, then it would be like this. A pianist and a violinist were vying to see who could produce the most appalling discords, just like two naughty children left alone in a room with the instruments. It set your teeth on edge to listen to it. Beratis seemed transported: his eyes were closed, his mouth half-open and his hands clasped as if he couldn't believe in his happiness. Anyone looking at us would have been hard put to say that we were listening to the same music.

"Have mercy on me!"

"Listen. You don't like it, do you? I know. At least you're honest about it, you don't pretend. To appreciate something like this, you have to know about music. This is the new music, the music of our century. It's the music Dr Goebbels calls 'degenerate' and he persecutes its composers and sends them to prison and has them transported to the camps. No art should be treated like that."

He lifted the needle from the record, which continued to turn. He sat down with his knees apart on the bed, forgetting to make room for me or to clear the only chair which was covered with magazines and sheets of music. I remained standing.

"That's what Bodo wants to destroy me for," he said.

"I can well believe it," I assured him with complete

sincerity. "I could sit down at the piano and pretend to play. Would that be music?" I asked doubtfully.

"No, it wouldn't. Because you wouldn't know what rules you'd be breaking."

"We're friends, but we don't always seem to be speaking the same language."

This conversation wasn't very pleasant to him. It showed. His voice became more abrupt again. Over his face had once more descended the veil that had been there during the first hours of our acquaintance, when he was ill and exhausted but also reserved towards a stranger who'd got into conversation with him. However, before too long he recovered and returned to the question that was preoccupying him.

"Listen," he said. "This whole business of Bodo's visit to Athens is going to bring me some misfortune. Some great misfortune. Remember I said so."

25

The outstretched finger

We had hardly finished this conversation when a knocking was heard on the door. We both fell silent instantly.

"Who is it?" called Beratis in terror.

"Excuse me," came a familiar voice.

However improbable it might seem, it was happening. The voice was that of Mr Agathos, his tone the one I'd heard that first evening when he appeared from out of the blue in my office, as unruffled as if he'd simply decided to go for a little walk just as the curfew was beginning.

"It's…" I began, but broke off immediately.

For my client was unlikely to come to the musician's house in the guise of the retired olive oil merchant or any of the other personae he'd served up to me. He'd surely come as the great tragic actor in his cloak and broad-brimmed hat. So what should I do? And what exactly was going on? Was Mr Agathos looking for me, or had Mr Kornelios Something decided to pay a visit to our protégé?

"Who is it?" the musician asked again in a stifled voice.

"Don't be afraid, he's a friend… Don't you recognize his voice?"

When the door was opened, the familiar face was revealed, the white hair, the craftily innocent eyes, and the dog on a leash, wagging its tail. It was my old friend Mr Agathos with his waistcoat straining over his belly, yet somehow different—damn, you could be fooled so easily. He kept changing shape. How could anyone be sure that Mr Kornelios Something was the same man as the one standing here? The musician was looking at him with a puzzled expression: the man's face seemed vaguely familiar yet he hadn't recognized him.

"Mr Beratis?"

"Yes. And who…"

"Ah, Mr Angel, my boy!"

His face lit up as he caught sight of me behind the musician.

"I was looking for you! I do apologize for the indiscretion, but they told me at your office that you might be here with your friend… I needed to see you urgently!"

Beratis stepped aside to leave us room to discuss this urgent matter.

"Your secretary's information was correct," Mr Agathos said again. Then, in a louder voice, "Are you Mr Beratis?"

"I am. And you?"

"Agathos, retired notary. Delighted to meet you."

"It's a pleasure."

For a gentleman of the old school, he told lies with the absolute naturalness of a con man. How'd he cooked up all this? Without waiting to be invited, he stepped over the threshold with the dog behind him on its leash.

"I do hope you're not afraid of him," he said apologetically.

Beratis was looking at the dog but even this didn't seem to help him identify the visitor.

"We'd better go inside a minute, I want to have a private word with Mr Sotiris…"

"Angel."

"Angel, I'm sorry, ha ha ha, I keep forgetting…"

"Would you like me to wait outside?" the musician asked coldly.

"No, for goodness sake… what an idea! I'll just have a quick word with him, you're friends after all, it's nothing confidential. What fine photographs! Were they taken in Germany?"

"How did you know?"

"I recognized the street. That picture was taken in the Nicolai-viertel in Berlin, was it not?"

"Hmm."

"Excuse me, Mr Angel, a couple of words…"

"What secretary? What are you rambling on about?"

"Was I perhaps mistaken? Then she must have been the cleaning woman. I supposed she was your secretary. Never mind. Now, it's about our business…"

"If I'm in the way I can wait outside in the courtyard

for a moment," Beratis said again, annoyed and worried by the stranger's intrusion into his house.

"Don't even think of it! Just one word, Mr Sotiriou."

"I'm listening, I'm all ears."

"Your woman client… the other one… they inform me… there's an entire correspondence concerning her… her arrest is imminent. I had no other way of communicating with you. You've been out since early this morning."

"I had work to do for my *other clients*," I said sarcastically. I didn't know which of the two men I needed to be more cautious about. "And anyway, I haven't any professional obligations to her," I added. "Not to *her*."

"Anyone who has *intentions* automatically has *obligations*," he hissed, lowering his voice. "And in any case the professional obligations which you *have* taken on cover the case… you know which case."

"Then perhaps *other* people who have *other* intentions might be more suitable to give the help needed. Why don't you ask them, now that you've taken the trouble to come all the way over here…"

"Hush… hush…" he interrupted me, with a hasty finger to his lips; and for the first time I saw the finely worked ring that he wore on the index finger of his left hand, set with an oval of lapis lazuli… this must be some new whim of his, I would certainly have noticed if he'd been wearing it before… "Hush, Mr Angel, my boy," he muttered as quietly as he could in the small room. "Do you want to bring about a disaster? If *someone else* hurries off to

help her, he'll be walking straight into the wolf's jaws…
Because I understand the authorities have plans for him
too… plans, not official documents, but discussions are
taking place. About music, about degenerate forms of art
and so on. You take my meaning."

"Yes, a little while ago I got a taste of it."

"Hush, not so loud, not so loud."

"By the way, since when were you a notary?" I sprang
on him.

"Oh, that… But I really was one once, didn't I tell
you? I still have all the files. What can I say, one takes on
responsibilities, it's part of the job… But let's get down to
the main course."

"A good idea," said Beratis, who was sitting by the half-
open window and had caught this phrase.

"A figure of speech!" laughed Agathos.

"Your animal certainly looks well-fed," commented the
musician.

His tone still bore traces of reservation about the
uninvited intruder.

"Don't call him 'animal', it hurts his feelings," said the
old man with his head on one side. "He answers to the
name of Azor."

"It's a wonder he's still alive in times like these. Every
other dog has been eaten," remarked Beratis.

The dog bared his teeth and gave a threatening growl.

"Ssh! Ssh! Silence, Azor. The man was only joking…
He's very sensitive," he explained to us.

"It's the first time I've ever heard anyone say 'Ssh' to a dog," said the musician.

"It's a question of how you train them. I interrupted something, I realize that. Will you permit us, Mr Beratis?"

The Big Boss moved towards the door and made a sign to me that I should follow.

"I can see that it's something urgent."

"Extremely so."

"And I have to be getting back to the theater in an hour's time. We've got another rehearsal scheduled for early afternoon," Beratis said. "If friends of yours are in danger you'd better go at once, don't delay." He gave me a strange look. "Is it anyone I know?" he asked quietly.

"What d'you mean—that you know?"

I was caught unprepared. Mr Agathos stepped in.

"It's someone only Mr Angel can help."

"I'll come along too," the musician announced decisively, and picked up his jacket from the chair.

"No!" (The Big Boss and I spoke as one.)

Had he understood? If he had, then it was the fault of that senile old man who'd turned up uninvited and had whispered supposedly confidential things to me in his great voice that was never turned down lower than a *forte*. Miltos looked as if he had a sudden fever. He almost pushed us out of the door.

"I'll go over to the theater a little early, I haven't time to rest," he muttered.

"Azor," said Mr Agathos.

The dog pricked up its ears and stood by its master.

However, as Beratis took his next step towards the door it growled threateningly and bared its teeth again.

"Your dog," Beratis told him. "Keep hold of it."

"It's not his fault, he took a scunner to you because of what you said about being eaten," Agathos told him. "It would be better if we left first and you followed a few moments later. When he's angry it's hard to hold him back."

The dog barked at Beratis again. The musician gave a little cry. Specks of foam had appeared on the animal's lips as he watched his enemy getting dressed to go out and the low growl continued.

"We're going now, come along, let's go," the old man told his dog in the tone one might use to a recalcitrant child. "Let's go. The gentleman will stay in his house for ten minutes or a quarter of an hour… till we're well away. Come along, Azor."

And the door closed on the startled face of our host. We crossed the courtyard and went out into the street.

"I usually reach out my hand to my protégés," Mr Agathos told me, flourishing the ring on his index finger theatrically. "Today is the first time I've been obliged to do the opposite. The poor fellow was quite ready to accompany us to Gennadiou Street. What a folly! That's love for you, Mr Angel, my friend."

"Are you going to explain all this to me?"

Beside us Azor was trotting along, contented and perfectly well-behaved.

"Have you really not understood yet? The authorities

are enraged by the Artists' Branch of EAM. They're out to arrest the husband of your lady lawyer. He's got his finger in a whole lot of pies, he writes articles for the underground press, he's president of the board of directors of the 'Popular Stage' theater that belongs to our friend Rodolfos, the 'Popular Stage' is putting on O'Neill's *Electra*, which is a banned work so they renamed the playwright Beranger to slip it past the censors. Only someone found out. And as if all that wasn't enough, the day before yesterday the artists and sculptors rejected outright the bust of Hitler carved in wood by the sculptor Nicolas and wouldn't allow it to be exhibited at the Panhellenic Exhibition, on the grounds that it was an *inferior work*. The authorities are thus determined to deal with the artists once and for all, they've decided to round up a few and shoot them to teach the rest a lesson. They've got their great conductor here, they want to show him not only that there aren't any hostile reactions but also that the Greeks are enthusiastic about having the chance to hear a work by Wagner conducted by his most famous interpreter, a distinguished representative of German culture like Froberger. They picked on your Mr Kanellis first. He's a known Leftist, he isn't among the most prominent—the most prominent would be dangerous because of the outcry it would provoke—in other words, he's an excellent choice to set an example to everyone else. Do you want more? The day after tomorrow, Wednesday, they'll be arresting his wife in order to force him to give himself up. You've got time to think what to do and work out a plan to avoid being spotted by the policeman on duty at the entrance to your building."

"I thought your interest was solely in Beratis," I muttered.

All these things were somehow disjointed; my mission, which had been beginning to seem clear and even pleasant, was becoming blurred and vague—dreadful for someone like me who always needed to see where he was putting his feet. Only one thing could I be sure of: that Mr Agathos was in a class apart. And that I didn't know anything whatsoever about him. In desperation I made one more attempt to get him to let down his mask.

"I should remind you that you owe me a few explanations," I said, stopping short in the middle of the road. "If the times weren't so evil, I wouldn't care. But they are... and I can't have dealings, no matter how much you pay me, with a businessman who's lived in America, who having made an appearance as a great tragic actor now tells me he's a retired notary, who knows Berlin well enough to recognize a street from a photograph on the wall, who speaks German so fluently that he can make an SS officer turn tail and flee, who has contacts among the authorities that tell him who's going to be arrested and who isn't..."

I was out of breath from walking; maybe he thought it was from fear. He took on his benevolent air and smiled at me, his brilliant blue eyes shining with good humor. The dog, sitting on its haunches, was watching some birds perched on the electricity wires.

"Do you really think your own biography would sound any more believable than mine, Mr Angel, my boy? When it comes down to it, I'm more than twice your age… Haven't you ever considered how many surprises life holds in store for us? A man may be born in one place and find himself living in another. In the brief space of your own life you've passed from one life into a completely different one, whose existence you'd never suspected. So why should my own odyssey cause you any surprise? Yes, I've been a businessman *in America*" (a smile) "and a notary and a tragic actor—which actually isn't particularly difficult, all it takes is a little chutzpah—and a professor of Philosophy in Berlin—I'll tell you that story another day—and a person whose financial independence enables him to possess the contacts and acquaintances that are so vital *in the times we live in*… Ah, if I'd been a little younger I too might have been involved with the Artists' Branch of EAM (or the notaries' branch, if such an organization exists) and I could have tried to help more directly. As it is, I do what I can to help all those people who are involved—and you must admit, that's something. At any rate I am interested. I must make that clear to you. I cannot remain merely an indifferent spectator. Is there anything so odd in that? Is that so mysterious?"

I couldn't resist one last attack with the ammunition left to me.

"Look," I told him, "getting into trouble with the authorities wasn't part of our agreement—in fact it was specifically excluded. It's one thing for me to look after your protégé and quite another thing to smuggle his girlfriend's husband out of the Security Police's reach. You've got contacts in the SS, right? Well, I've got my own contacts in the Security Police. It was they who did a bit of sleight of hand with various documents in my file relating to my American passport—otherwise I would have been in the Averof prison from day one. Do you really want me to blow all that sky-high now by sheltering fugitives?"

We'd started walking along Academias Street again and were now at the corner of Gennadiou Street, behind the church of the Zoodochos Pigi. The sound of the fountain in its little garden reached our ears. In the narrow street in front of us total silence reigned.

"Every job carries its own risks," Mr Agathos said, with a seriousness that now concealed no joking or irony. "You have undertaken to perform this one. Do it, and you won't be a loser. This much I can assure you, and you must believe me wholeheartedly, without any doubts, here and now as we speak. Otherwise… forget it all."

Well, yes. He had a way of throwing me without the slightest effort. I can't deny it and I can't hide it. And a little tiny voice inside me was telling me that I should do exactly as he said: that I should trust him and believe him without second thoughts, without reservations, and without delay.

26

———

The plot thickens

As I went out the next morning to pay a brief visit to the office, for a moment I was deceived. The thug downstairs on Gennadiou Street had been replaced by another. At the beginning I thought for a few seconds that the siege had been lifted, However, all that had happened was a changing of the guard. The new policeman didn't smoke the shit the first one smoked: to be precise, he didn't smoke at all. He'd moved his look-out post to the doorway of the café, from where he could keep an eye not only on the house but also on the entire street from one end to the other. What this meant was that Kanellis hadn't been at the law courts yesterday, had known that they were coming to arrest him and was in hiding—since he hadn't returned either at midday or in the afternoon or at night. And this in turn meant that if his wife stayed there, it would only be a matter of time before they came for her too—if, that is, the Big Boss's secret sources had given him accurate information.

Instead of going to the office I walked around the block rapidly and went back into the building. The policeman got up from his chair and came over, looking at me suspiciously. I handed him my papers at once, without the slightest trace of fear or guilt. I was playing the colleague: the private detective Mr Sotiriou.

The door from the service stairs to their kitchen was locked. Looking through, I could see the maid's room beyond the kitchen, with its narrow bed and a glimpse of the palm trees in the Christomanos garden visible between the shutters. I knocked and waited.

"Mr Angel!"

The girl let me in. I had to speak to her mistress at once, I told her, it was urgent. I could hear Marika's voice in the office, speaking on the telephone about some case. There was nothing in the least conspiratorial in her tone. She didn't seem frightened. As I came in she knitted her eyebrows in a scowl. She may have stopped loathing me, I thought, but I certainly don't remind her of anything pleasant. I waited for her to finish.

"Mr Pavlos?"

She answered with a gesture.

As rapidly as possible I told her what my client had told me. She asked where this information came from.

"I can't tell you. You'll have to trust me. The cop is still downstairs. They're not going to leave. They want Mr

Pavlos and they'll arrest you to make him give himself up. You've got to get out of here. Now, at once."

"And go where?"

"That's the million dollar question," I said. "But if you hurry up I'll think of something while you're getting ready."

My mind was working feverishly. Yes… that really was the question, and there were other things too which I hadn't thought of. How was I going to get Marika out of the building? She was waiting in silence.

"The same way," I told her, and a broad smile spread over my face which, however, didn't seem to convince her.

"The same way?"

"How we'd get out, that's what I was thinking."

"*The same way*," she repeated, trying to understand.

"The way I took your husband," I explained hastily. "Let's not waste time. We have to go up to the roof."

"The roof! Are we going to jump down onto the Public Prosecutor's roof? Like you did with Pavlos?"

"We can't very well walk out of the front door."

"Are you a patriot, Mr Sotiriou?" Marika Kanellis suddenly asked.

I didn't immediately understand what she meant.

"Are you in the Resistance?" she asked, making herself clearer as she noticed my puzzled expression.

"No."

"But you're a patriot?"

"I haven't ever really thought about it. I suppose I am…

in a way. I help my friends—if you're wondering why I do it…"

"Are you our friend?"

"I'm a friend of Miltos," I answered.

Her cheeks flushed.

"Ah, that's it…" she said.

I don't know if she was finding an answer to her doubts.

"And quite apart from that, I feel a special sympathy for you," I added.

"For *us*?"

"For *you* personally."

"And for Pavlos," she said, but her statement had a question mark at the end.

"If you had a cat, I'd feel sympathy for that as well," I said.

"But Pavlos isn't a cat."

"No, he isn't. Anyway, he's afraid of heights."

She smiled. On the evening of their party I'd noticed that one of her front teeth was slightly chipped on the inner side adjoining the other front tooth. This gave her smile a strange charm; till then I'd rarely seen her smile.

Her expression had changed now. She'd relaxed, was letting herself be persuaded, was losing the reserve she maintained towards opponents in court or strangers on the street. She left me in the office while she disappeared down the passage. When she re-emerged she was wearing a suit, her hair was tied back with a blue ribbon and she had a bag slung over her shoulder.

"So have you thought where?"

"Yes" (this was a lie).

My mind was functioning in two separate parts: one part was thinking of our trip up to the roof and our leap onto the Public Prosecutor's roof; the other was searching hastily for names and addresses, people who owed me favors (I couldn't think of even one), people I could trust (Mr Agathos was out of the question, and anyway he himself wished to stay out of things). To cut it short, Mimis was my first choice in this latter category. I asked Mrs Kanellis' permission and dialed his number.

He picked up the phone on the third ring.

"Are you going to be home?"

"What's up?"

"I just want to know."

"I'll be home till evening. I'll be sleeping at Zaimis Street tonight."

"At the widow's?"

"Cut it out, Hephaistos."

"I've got hold of some broad beans, I was thinking of bringing you some. If you felt like boiling them, we could eat them together."

"Broad beans! You don't say! You're amazing. Where'd you find them? Went to Piraeus, did you?"

"No, someone brought them to me from his village."

Papachrysanthou was doubtful. Broad beans, village— something smelled fishy to him.

"OK, OK," he said, as if wanting to tell me to leave off the fairy tales. "Will you be coming over?"

"In a little while," I answered. "In about half an hour or so... something like that."

Marika listened in silence.

"Where are we going?" she asked as I put down the receiver.

"To a friend. A fine man. Someone I trust." Before she could ask, I added, "I don't know if he's a patriot. I imagine he is."

She laughed. "You're quite right," she said. "Forgive me. I'm abrupt with you, I know. And I don't always tell you my whole thought... that's probably the problem. I trust you. We needn't speak of it again."

We went out of the kitchen to the service stairs in the light-well. Konstantina stood in the doorway wringing her hands in her apron as a prelude to tears.

"Turn the light on in the toilet and lock the door," her mistress instructed. "If any of them come looking for me, tell them I'm in there. Delay them as much as possible."

The girl nodded. We climbed the stairs to the roof. It was a windy day and the shreds of mist in the sky would soon be dispersed. On the washing-line were clothes hung out the previous evening; the billowing sheets concealed us from the buildings across the road. Marika leaned over the parapet and looked down.

"Did you jump from here?"

I nodded. There was fear on her face. Suddenly it was easier for her to believe that I'd pushed Pavlos over the edge to kill him than that we'd both jumped onto the neighboring roof, then gone down the stairs and out into the street. Her expression showed that she regretted her brief moment of trust in me and was now realizing that she was trapped here, alone with me, in my power.

"You promised to obey me," I complained.

"Yes," she whispered, looking down over the parapet and beginning to tremble.

"Don't be afraid. Mr Pavlos and I jumped down and landed on our feet, perfectly fine, without so much as a sprained ankle. But he was holding on to me. And he did *exactly what I said*… Like you, he was certain he wasn't going to get away with his life, either from the police or from the leap. You must simply leave everything to me."

"I got a message from Pavlos today," she said quietly. "A friend phoned."

"You ought to be careful on the phone," I told her.

"We know that," she said sharply. "When you're in the underground movement that's the first thing you learn. All he said was that he'd seen our aunt and that she was in Ilissia and in good health."

"Your *aunt*," I laughed. "Lovely! Whoever was listening will have known without the slightest doubt that you were getting news of your husband."

"So I don't have any reason not to trust you," she continued. "But when I look down my eyes tell me something different."

I climbed onto the parapet and put out my hand to her. "Let's go!"

Just at that moment, from the light-well we heard the voices of Konstantina and a man arguing with her. The little servant was trying to stop him, while he was cursing her, in a low voice for fear the woman on the run would hear them and find another hiding place. Marika's eyes widened, glassy with fear. Now we could hear the footsteps of the policeman running up the stairs.

"Not a second to spare!" I cried and put my arm around her waist.

As she turned to look at me, trying to guess from my face what fate awaited her, the feet reached the top step. The man's cap came into view, and behind him the black, curly hair of Konstantina, tugging at his clothes to hold him back.

All my strength was suddenly concentrated in my shoulders. I gripped her around the waist and kicked off. The head emerging at the top of the stairs had turned within a split second towards the only reasonable place to look: the parapet dividing the roof from that of the next-door building.

And thus, in the very same split second, my body, with Marika Kanellis' body closely clasped to it, had almost automatically chosen the only route left to us.

Instead of the next-door roof, we were heading high into the dull sky.

27

—

The garden

Maybe if it hadn't been during the Occupation, people would have raised their eyes and looked up to the skies more often… but it was and they didn't. The people on the sidewalks were bent, weak and sick. They hurried only when in danger, stopped only to summon up the strength for the next few hundred yards, noticed only what lay in their path as obstacle or threat: a dead body sprawled in a doorway, a patrol, a face watching from a window or from the corner of the street.

If one of these few passers-by had chanced to look up just then, not even very high, he would have seen an incredible sight—most people would have supposed that their time had come, that they were seeing visions, that they'd gone crazy.

Marika kept her eyes tight shut. This wasn't so much from a fear of heights as from the certainty that she was living through a bad dream, and that when she opened her eyes again the reality would be even worse… the cop had arrested her at the entrance… he was dragging her off in handcuffs to the Security Headquarters on Stournara Street… they were locking her in a cell with dozens of other people… and from somewhere she could hear Pavlos screaming as they tortured him.

The wind was blowing her hair back off her face, the morning chill gave her pale cheeks a rosy color, her lips, parted to breathe more easily, revealed her chipped tooth; my heart was beating with its own sorrows, while my mind was trying to fly faster and further than our two clasped bodies to foresee what would happen when we landed.

If I'd been more sensible I would have taken care to land as soon as possible on one of the lonely side-streets off Academias. But I couldn't land: I was holding Marika close against me, her scent enveloped me, her hair caressed my face and her silence brought to mind those other silences of complicity between man and woman.

As we passed above the roof of the Olympia theater, I heard the sound of the orchestra and recognized the song of the river nymphs. I imagined Beratis sweating as he played beneath the screams and snorts of the tall conductor. And my mind flew back to a happier time, when Freddy took me off to Broadway and 39th Street "to hear the Germans."

I avoided the Library and Panepistimiou Street, preferring to fly across Ippokratous Street and from there onto Asklipiou Street. At the corner, by the railings of the Municipal Hospital, I began to descend. The foliage of the trees in the small park shaded the sidewalk; exactly opposite, set back in a courtyard, was that little two-story house. Behind its square window panes the curtains were drawn. By the garden gate was the cartwheel which Mimis and I had noticed the day we went to the morgue. No one had touched it.

Between two old fig trees, their leaves grey with city dust, was a covered well. I touched down lightly, Marika upright beside me. She opened her eyes at once and looked around her, then stumbled, her knees buckling, and leaned against the stone well-head for support.

In my fear I hadn't calculated our landing place very well:—this little garden had seemed an ideal refuge, yet now I could see that the garden gate was secured by a chain and padlock: to get out we'd have to break them somehow or climb over the railings.

Because Freddy always used to say that a good detective shouldn't trust his eyes more than the palms of his hands (by which he meant that appearances are often deceptive and we need direct physical contact with things if we are to assess them correctly), I went over to the gate to have a look at the chain. The padlock was unfastened. I turned to announce this good news to Mrs Kanellis.

She was still leaning against the well with her back to me, shaking out her hair and tying it back again with the blue ribbon. The curtain at the window to the right of the door had been lifted and a pair of eyes was watching the two strange birds who'd just landed in the garden.

"Do you know where you've brought me?"

She used the second person singular. My ears were buzzing with this unexpected mark of familiarity: from the formal "Mr Angel" and "Mr Sotiriou" that she'd always called me till now I had become someone to be addressed in the intimate way, like Kanellis, like Beratis. Thus I barely heard the rest of what she said, an unknown name that sounded a bit like a place name. There were still corners of Athens I didn't know well.

"To the garden of Palamas[8]," she said again.

What's the garden of Palamas? I wondered.

The lifted curtain had fallen back into place. The door opened. In the doorway stood a strange creature, a small, thin old man with a mane of hair as white as his beard, his mustache and the bushy eyebrows over the piercing eyes that had been watching us through the window. His back was bowed and the diminutive weight of his frail body was supported by a cane with a bone handle. He wore checked bedroom slippers, threadbare pajama trousers and a shawl thrown cape-wise over his shoulders. On him all these garments reminded you not of an old people's home but of the robes of a wizard or the costume of some bygone king.

I automatically caught hold of her arm: for what else could I have expected but angry shouts and minatory wavings of that walking stick? We were invaders, strangers, unknown and suspicious interlopers in his territory. But Marika pulled free of the arm with which

8. Kostis Palamas (1859-1943), Greek poet

I was gently propelling her towards the garden gate and approached the verandah steps without fear. I was obliged to follow. If her explanations failed to convince the old man, then some intervention on my part might perhaps mitigate his anger.

"I saw you coming down," he said in a voice that was unexpectedly youthful and light. "I knew that you had come from far off and that your coming was a good sign. Birds rarely visit my garden now, the trees have died, the ground has become rock-hard and the well has dried up—they cannot find anything to drink."

"Master," said Marika, the emotion in her voice audible, "we never plucked up the courage to visit you, my husband and I, though we longed to. I can hardly believe the luck that has brought me to your garden today."

"Your husband?" the old man asked, turning to me, and she hastened to explain.

"No, no…My husband's in hiding. This is a friend."

I prepared to be introduced. Obviously there must have been some sort of acquaintance between them: the man looked like a retired professor—perhaps she'd been one of his pupils at high school, or at some foreign language class maybe. Things looked promising, he might help us, there might be a back door leading onto Ippokratous Street that he'd let us slip out through.

"This spring will be a cruel one," the old man said. "It will carry off many people. What were you doing here?"

"We put in to rest," I improvised, "we saw the well…"

"Had you been flying a long time?"

Ah, thought I, the old man believes in fairytales and miracles. He saw us descending from the sky on his very doorstep and wasn't in the least surprised. Well, better this way… he won't need any explanations.

"I don't know," Marika answered and turned to me. "Were we flying long?"

A smile quivered at the corners of her mouth, part irony since she very well knew how long we'd been flying, part the magical feeling that thrills a child on the Ferris wheel at the fairground.

"Not long," she tried to explain. "Angel carried me up into the air from our house in order to escape the Security Police. My husband is in hiding… He knows all your poems. He calls himself a disciple of yours and says that if our baby's a boy he wants it to be baptised Kostis."

"Kostis! Not Constantine?" laughed the old man. "When are you expecting the happy event?"

"About September, maybe early October, around then…"

"Not till then! October seems to me such a long way off," the old man mused. "Yet it will come… May your Kostis be welcome, my child. One will depart, another will arrive."

"Who will depart?" I asked, trying to keep up.

They seemed to understand one another very well.

"When I was born," he said reflectively—then broke off and was silent as he delved into his memories, "…When I was born, Solomos[9] had been dead for little more than

---

9. Dionysios Solomos (1798-1857), Greek poet

a year. It's something I often thought about later, when I understood that I must follow in his footsteps. He departed, I appeared. And now that I am about to depart… who will appear? Another Kostis perhaps?"

He smiled and with the license permitted to old age rested his hand lightly on her belly, then immediately withdrew it as if ashamed at the gesture.

"It could be, eh? What do you think?"

"I'm certain of it," she told him passionately. "And I'm certain it's going to be a boy."

He put his head on one side and examined her.

"Do you need anything from me?" he asked. "I must go and lie down, I've been in bed for days, it was only today I managed to get up—one would almost think it was on purpose, to see you land in my garden. What a stroke of luck for me!"

"Thank you very much," I said. "We don't need any-thing, we'll be leaving at once."

She came down the steps unwillingly, without taking her eyes off him.

"Just wait till I tell Pavlos, just wait till I tell Pavlos," she was muttering as I led her to the gate. "I've got to tell him at once. He'll never believe me!"

"About your teacher?" I asked.

She stared at me blankly. I was ready to shake the dust of that little garden on Asklipiou Street off my feet fast, but Marika was lingering, taking her time to slip the padlock back on the chain at the garden gate.

"Where to now, Angel?"

Her expression had a savage, heedless joy to it… She was ready to throw herself into any adventure with me, and only God knows the ideas that were beginning to pass through my mind.

"Eressou Street, right at the top of Zoodochou Pigis Street," I answered. "To a friend's house."

The uneven sidewalk was strewn with trash. We crossed Solonos Street rapidly. For safety's sake I walked ahead and Marika followed me. Her black lace-up shoes which from time to time I glimpsed out of the corner of my eye seemed like two small black puppies vying to see which could overtake the other.

"Will you tell me the truth now? I owe you my life, my husband's life. I'll never forget it. So tell me the truth, no matter what it is."

"You seem to be in a mood for conversation," I said. "Which truth do you want?"

"What you are. How come you can fly. Why you're doing all this."

I continued to walk on ahead. I preferred her not to see that I was blushing to the roots of my hair. I couldn't tell her the truth. I didn't even know it myself. Whatever riddles my behavior held for her, all the things that had happened since the night I met Mr Agathos held a great many more for me.

"Don't ask," I told her. "If you don't know of your own accord, then no one's ever likely to tell you the truth. That's something I've learned."

A little further on she caught hold of my hand and stopped me.

"Do you know what the poet says?" she asked breathlessly.

"What poet?"

"The one we just met."

"Bah? A poet, was he? He didn't look like one. I took him for a teacher."

"He is a teacher. He's a teacher of other poets."

A didactic tone: as if she wanted me to know she was speaking of matters of great importance.

"So what does the poet say?"

"*We owe a debt to those who have come, to those who have gone before, to those who will come. The judges who will sit in judgment on us are the unborn, the dead.*"

"I've no idea what it means," I said, "but it sounds good. As if it did mean something."

"What are your relations with Miltos?"

"He's a friend."

"Since when? He's never spoken of you."

"He's spoken to me about you a lot."

She was silent. I didn't turn around but I'm certain the passionate expression she'd had when she spoke of poetry and weighty meanings was gone.

"Which means you're friends," she commented after a moment.

"Just that. I'll tell you something else. It's for his sake I'm helping you. My own feelings about you take second place... anyway, you can't stand me and you don't want anything to do with me, not even to be helped by me, because I'm a stool pigeon."

"Don't be so hard. You ought to know that things are more difficult for us than for other people."

By *us* she clearly meant people belonging to the Left. For all I know this might have been so. But how to explain such violent passion against someone who only ever said "Good morning" to her on the stairs?

We were nearing Mimis' house.

"I'm going to ask you a question now," I said and turned around to face her. "A moment ago you said 'Just wait till I tell Pavlos'—not Miltos, I noticed. Which of them means most to you? I was watching you at your party… your husband has a presence—poetry, politics, theater and so on. And Miltos… at heart Miltos is just a peasant boy. What do you see in him?"

"I'm a peasant too, hadn't you noticed?" she said provocatively.

"Yes, I had noticed."

"Well then?"

"One more reason for Pavlos to be more attractive, I would have thought."

She interrupted. "Listen, I love him, he's my husband. I wouldn't have married him otherwise. But Miltos is in love with me, he's languishing for me, he wants me. And he doesn't consider me a peasant…" (she stopped just in time).

"Like Pavlos does?"

"Pavlos… Pavlos has other interests. Miltos needs me."

And I do too perhaps, I thought to myself silently. Strange woman.

"And another question," I said out loud.

"Go ahead."

"Whose baby is it?"

She stopped short. She looked down at her shoes and then at me, straight in the eyes. A street urchin's smile, the like of which I'd never seen on her face before, sparkled on her lips and in her eyes.

"To tell you the truth," she said, tossing back her hair, "I don't know yet."

I felt full of remorse. Why had I asked? What was it to me? Why should I care a damn whose baby it was? Unexpectedly (or had I expected it without wanting to admit it?) I'd just learned something which maybe—maybe!—my protégé ought to know.

"One thing's for certain," said Marika, suddenly moving forward, taking my arm and setting off along the sidewalk again. "It's mine."

28

——

I hurry hither and thither

Having left my lady lawyer in Mimis' hands, I walked back down Zoodochou Pigis Street as fast as my lame leg would allow. As I passed the corner of Zosimadon Street I thought of going by Miltos' house to see if he was home. However, in the end I decided not to waste time and hurried along towards Academias Street. I turned into Solonos and went down Mavromichali, glancing from a distance at the forecourt of the theater. The soldiers had gone and the doors were shut. The rehearsal must be over. And my musician—had he left?

As soon as I turned the corner by the little garden outside the church I saw that something was going on outside the door of number 2. Apart from the cop who'd been keeping watch, various other guys in fedoras were milling around and the café owner had come out onto his doorstep to gawp. A few paces away I spotted the tiny figure of Mrs Leni, our concierge, and beside her the imposing bulk of Balomenos. Something bad had happened—but I couldn't tell what until I got close enough to see and hear.

As I drew nearer I came within earshot. The circle of snitches parted and two policemen wearing caps came out of the entrance carrying a blanket between them: it sagged, there was something heavy in it. They put it down gently on the sidewalk. I saw that it was Konstantina. Her eyes were shut as if she was asleep. She was still wearing the clothes I'd seen her in that morning. Only the dark stain on the side of her head bore witness to what had happened; her hair was plastered to her temple as if with a blob of tar—but it was dried blood, already darkening.

"Come on, take her away, take her away," Balomenos was shouting. "She's had it, take her away from here."

Mrs Leni was fussing over the girl like a malicious spirit, doing up the buttons of her blouse. It was my last chance to look at that lovely body, growing cold now, her little heart no longer beating.

"Mr Sotiriou," called our landlord, "have you seen either of the Kanellises at all today?"

All eyes were on me.

"No," I said, and knelt down beside Konstantina.

One of her eyes was not quite closed. For a moment I almost wondered—could she be still alive? No one had said she was dead, it was only Balomenos who'd been crying "She's had it" and telling them to take her away. I bent over her. Her half-open eye showed no signs of life. It must simply be that no one had bothered to close it. I put out my hand. I thought she would have liked the idea that I was touching her eyes like that. Except she would have preferred it to be after making love—something I couldn't give her. Much better that she'd never found out.

"She fell," Mrs Leni hissed in my ear. "From the roof straight down to the floor below."

I remembered. I looked up and examined the policemen one by one. One of them had come up the outside stairs with the girl behind him, yelling at him so that we'd hear and hurry to get away, grabbing at him to delay him. But none of the faces looked familiar except that of the smoker who'd been on duty at the entrance earlier.

"Someone must inform her employers," said Balomenos. "Are you quite sure you haven't seen them today?"

"I haven't seen them," I repeated my denial. "I haven't seen them at all today."

"The Kanellis woman jumped onto the roof of the next-door building," someone said.

He was a short, squat man with an unmemorable face, the sort you pass countless times on the street without noticing, the sort it's easy to believe you've seen somewhere before. Could it have been him pursuing us that morning? Who else would know Marika had been on the roof? Unless things that I couldn't imagine had been happening since I bore her off into the air, the man chasing us would be the only person who could know such details. In which case it must have been him who pushed the girl. No doubt about it.

"Who jumped?" I asked foolishly, not addressing any-one in particular.

"They came the day before yesterday to *get* them," sneered Balomenos, "but the little birds got wind of it. The husband's in hiding and the wife cleared off from the roof this morning before they could arrest her. The girl offered resistance and…"

"Resistance! What resistance?" I protested. "That little creature—who did she offer resistance to? These strong lads over here?"

"Why? Got any objections, mister?" the smoker asked in a thuggish tone.

"I can't believe it, such a small girl, what resistance could she offer?"

"She tried to stop them," Balomenos explained. "All right boys, come on, get her out of here, let's get all this over and done with. Someone can stay in the apartment to wait for her employers—they'll be back, where else could they go?"

He couldn't hide his pleasure: the tenants who caused him most nuisance were in trouble with the authorities, and what's more it looked like bad trouble. For him it was pure gain. He'd empty the apartment, supposedly because of the months they owed and hadn't paid, and would rent it to whoever he pleased. These were bad times for letting property. But in the circles in which Balomenos moved such things didn't count: he had the contacts—and was in the best of moods—as long as the Germans continued imposing law and order on the country… He'd find someone… Someone who'd certainly be infinitely preferable to the Kanellis couple.

The thug with the unmemorable face was keeping a distance between him and the blanket. Everyone else was jostling to crowd around it, taking a good look at the little servant without batting an eyelid, just as if she were merely some curious bird caught in the hunters' nets. The other two men helped lift the blanket into the car that was waiting on the corner of Fidiou Street with its engine running. They picked it up and pushed it onto the back seat—it was the blanket from the girl's own narrow little bed. Then the cops got going on their cop business, while Balomenos chatted cheerfully with Zisis about some relative of his in Nafplion, who'd fallen from the castle there and rolled all the way down to the road below without suffering so much as a scratch.

I ran up the stairs, passed the first floor without stopping, reached the second floor. The Kanellis' door was wide open. The telephone in the office was off the hook and was making a bleeping noise. I replaced the receiver. Had they done it on purpose?

The silent apartment seemed to be looking at me the way a patient looks at a new, unknown doctor who enters the ward. The door from the kitchen to the service stairs was open. The girl's room looked as if a whirlwind had swept through it. They'd almost overturned the narrow bed when they pulled the blanket off it to wrap her in, so that it was now blocking the way to the window. In the drawer of a little cupboard by the bed I found a small gold cross on a chain. Without thinking, I shoved it into my pocket.

I became angry then. I closed and bolted the front door. I left by the kitchen, locking the door behind me and went down to my own apartment. An icy chill shivered the length of my spine. I sat for a while in the front room, without going to the window to see what was happening. I put my head in my hands and tried to think. Then I picked up the receiver and dialed Mimis' number.

"The doctor says your cousin should stay put and not go out at all," I told him. "Her condition hasn't improved, on the contrary it's got worse."

"She's as ill as that?" asked Mimis after a brief pause.

"Don't scare her. Her apartment is upside down but I'll take care of it —either I will or someone else will… But she mustn't, she's not in a fit state. She's to stay in bed and take her medicine. Those are the doctor's orders."

"How long for?" asked Papachrysanthou. "The nurse has other patients to look after, she can't stay here forever."

"I'll come over, but the nurse must stay till then."

"OK," he said. "How about you, you all right?"

"I'm fine, the illness isn't catching—though all the same it's best to take care. We'll see."

Now it was the musician's turn. He needed to be told the news before he started trying to find her or doing anything silly.

When I went out, the short, squat cop was still posted

outside Zisis' door. By now I was perfectly sure he'd killed the girl. I looked at him and he looked at me. I don't know what he saw in my eyes but he lowered his own instantly and went inside, calling something to the café owner.

The house on Zosimadon Street looked as if no one was there. I knocked on the door gently in order not to scare Beratis and waited for him to appear. He did so almost at once. He was chewing a dried fig and his eyes widened at the unexpected sight of me. I gave him the news as briefly and undramatically as I could. Without details. I'd had information that they were going to arrest Marika in order to force Kanellis out of hiding: thus I'd smuggled her out of the building just as the cops were moving in. I'd taken her to a friend's house, not far off. About Konstantina I said not a word. This cruel, pointless death might upset him too much, I thought, might make him lose his self-control.

He stopped chewing and gazed at me. "Is this utter disaster?" his eyes were asking. I reassured him. Since she'd managed to avoid arrest, so far so good. We'd let Pavlos know and he'd get in touch with the underground mechanism. Those people would hide them somewhere until they could find out what the Security Police wanted them for, what they were charged with, how great the danger was. Miltos had gone pale and had to sit down on the divan to recover. He made me tell him the story of our escape, he wanted to know the name of the friend who was hiding Marika and his address: what sort of person was Papachrysanthou, how sure was he, could we trust him. Again and again he asked, I lost track of how many times. I wrote down the phone number to make him feel better but warned him to avoid using it—although my friend was not suspect, had never had anything to do with the Security Police, simply minded his own business. All the same, the neighborhood is small, people are curious, the presence of a strange woman would instantly give rise to curiosity, curiosity gives rise to gossip and you never know whose ears it will reach. Papachrysanthou had offered his help the moment I asked for it. But before long he'd have to be getting back to the Moltsas household on Zaimis Street, where he was spending more and more time. And then…

"And then?" asked Beratis.

"And then," I replied, "you may have to give shelter to Mrs Kanellis here for a while."

At this his eyes lit up and he barely managed to restrain himself from falling into my arms. I lay down on the end of the divan to rest, having only just realized how worn out I was from all the day's adventures. I fell asleep—I don't quite know at what point. When I opened my eyes again it was late afternoon. Beratis was sitting at the piano, scribbling notes on the staves he'd drawn in an exercise book. I didn't move so as not to disturb him; after a bit, though, when he put down his pencil, I stood up and tucked my shirt back into my pants.

"What are you writing?"

His tongue explored one of his lower teeth.

"I'm finishing a quartet," he said, putting his work aside

and getting up. "The sort of thing that makes you agree with Dr Goebbels!"

He was joking; yet all at once his face clouded over, his complexion turned grey and a host of worries creased his brow.

"I was working on it while you were asleep. It's too much… much too much. Today was a bad day for me too… And now this business with Marika and Pavlos… I'll have to leave for Halkida. They'll hide me there. I'll find some kind of work. Maybe I could play in restaurants."

He bowed his head and continued: "When I got back to the theater yesterday morning, the German singers had arrived from Berlin. Our maestro" (he said these words quite naturally, without irony, one musician speaking of another) "took them into the foyer. When we stopped for a break he sent for me. He made me sit there while he went on laughing and chatting with them. Just chit-chat, nothing important—he'd put aside the seriousness of German art for the time being. He was recounting all the gossip of Athens and telling them about the monks of Mount Athos: what a crude, ignorant lot they are, what a den of homosexuals, what a pack of lazy good-for-nothings… They use their precious manuscripts to wrap joints of lamb before putting them in the oven to bake, he told the singers, having first taken care to baptize the meat in the font in their church and name it sardine or bream in order not to break their dietary rules, then fall on it and devour it like savages. They've no idea what they've got in their libraries, there are no indexes, no conservation, the papyri and precious bindings are simply left to rot and be eaten by worms. Professor Doelger, who'd been with him, threatened to have them all whipped—and gave the abbots to understand, slightly more politely, that they'd better have indexes and catalogues ready before he returned in three months' time to put some order into the place."

"Well, that doesn't sound too terrible," I remarked. "Yesterday you were scared stiff of Bodo. Has he got over his whim?"

"Are you joking? When the singers left for their hotel and I was alone with him, he lit a cigarette and sat there gazing at me through the wreaths of smoke. And he said, 'Beratis,'—that's what he calls me, German style—'Beratis, I told you yesterday: your conductor is no Alberich and has not foresworn love. There is not a single woman worth looking at in the whole theater. The Rhine Maidens are well past retirement age and as for Freya, she's such a bag of skin and bones that if I were Wotan I'd hand her over to the king of the Nibbelheim along with the gold as fast as possible... I cannot ask favors of this kind from strangers. As an artist you are my equal, you understand me. I find myself in the unpleasant position of entrusting you with the duty of supplying a woman for my evenings—starting tonight. By the bye, before you burst out with whatever folly is on the tip of your tongue, I should tell you that I've promised your head to the Kommandant, who maintains that the Opera is a den of communists. The only communist I know among your rabble is you. Very well, I shall forget it, this I promise, if you will find me a woman—I shall forget not only your communism but also that appalling music you compose. You mentioned all the beauties to be seen in the streets of Athens. I don't circulate in the streets. So find me one'."

Beratis twisted his icy hands and looked at me.

"So what did you say?" I asked.

"I told him to ask the doorman at the Grande Bretagne to find him a woman. There are always dozens of them hanging about around there at night… He was furious. 'I don't consort with prostitutes,' he said. What does he want? The Venus de Milo? But that's not all. The very worst thing is that I didn't just punch him in the face and get up and go. I told him, fool, idiot, coward that I am, I told him I couldn't manage anything tonight but maybe tomorrow… Don't look at me like that, I deserve to be spat on, I know it. If she knew…" (he stopped abruptly). "I've just got time to bundle a few things into a suitcase, close up the house and leave for Halkida. I'll find a way. If I don't find one tonight, then I will tomorrow."

"Listen," I said. "I don't know whether I can manage anything for tonight. But I may be able to find something for your maestro. Leave it to me. I'll think of something."

It's odd, but I had someone in mind right from the start. My next port of call was Papachrysanthou's house.

29

First night flight

Mimis was sweating as if he'd just run a marathon.

"I've got to leave, Hephaistos," he told me with a guilty expression.

The family under his protection on Zaimis Street were clamoring increasingly pressingly for him to visit them.

"The widow doesn't stop phoning, she's beginning to complain… know what I mean? D'you get me?… that she's all on her own with the kids and the old ladies, and they're scared without a man in the house…"

I laughed. "Hey, don't tell me you're stepping into the dead man's shoes in more ways than one?"

He didn't answer, simply looked at me and fidgeted.

"Listen," I told him, "you go to the Moltsas house and leave her here by herself for a little while longer. She'll lie low, she won't poke her nose outside, she'll eat whatever she finds or what I bring her. Don't feel you have to stay here. In fact it's probably better if the house looks completely empty…"

"You're right as always," he said. "But… but, look, she's absolutely, absolutely got to stay inside… She mustn't stir, she mustn't open any windows or doors—d'you get me? Know what I mean? Not a door, not a window, lady…" Mimis repeated, his anxiety turning his smile at her into a plea. "No lights at night, only the alcohol lamp that casts a very low glow, and you take it with you from room to room. Complete darkness! *Without fail…*"

He then pulled his hat down over his eyes and disappeared into the twilight, after first pretending to lock his front door for the benefit of any curious neighbor who might chance to be looking out of the window.

"Where's he off to?" Mrs Kanellis asked. She seemed amused.

"He's adopted his cousin's family, the Germans shot him and Mimis has taken them on, kids, dogs and all."

"Have they really got dogs?"

"A figure of speech."

She got up from the sofa.

"I begged your friend to let me call Pavlos but he was scared… said not a word should be spoken over the phone…"

"He's a bit of an old fusser is Mimis, if we're going to call a spade a spade. Your friends in Ilissia, are they…"

"What?"

"I mean, do they also belong to the Left, the Resistance?"

"No, no. They don't. They're law-abiding citizens, conservatives, especially the old lady… Stavritsa," she corrected herself guiltily ('old lady' isn't an expression befitting a left-wing intellectual), "deeply dyed representatives of the Right! That's why Pavlos went to their house. They're friends, cultivated people. They've got feelings."

"OK, you've convinced me. Call him then and have a word, but be careful, tell Pavlos you're in good hands and he's not to worry. And when you've finished we need to have a word too…"

"Miltos!" she gasped. "What's happened?"

"Nothing's happened, he's fine. But it's to do with him. Make your phone call and then we'll talk."

I turned my back on her and went into the kitchen in the hope of finding something to eat—hunger had begun to prey on me. But before I had time to look Marika followed me into the kitchen. Her conversation with her husband had been of the briefest: maybe she was in a hurry to hear what I had to tell her, or maybe she felt the less they talked on the telephone, the better.

"Tell me," she said.

I found a crust of bread and chewed on it as we returned to the other room. She sat down on the sofa and put her feet up—a favorite habit—pulling her skirt down to cover her knees.

"Miltos is in a difficult position," I began. "The Germans are putting pressure on him."

"What have the Germans got against Miltos? He lived

for years in their country, speaks their language… They ought to consider him almost one of them, a *sympathizer*…"

"Is he in the Artists' EAM?" I asked.

"No, he's not. He's never been mixed up in that sort of thing at all, he only thinks of his work and…"

"Is he a known communist?"

"Miltos is hardly a communist," Marika declared in a tone of something like contempt.

Quite clearly love did not stop her having political differences with him.

"You may not consider him to be one, but the maestro who came to conduct them, Bodo…" I was trying to explain without being sure that I was saying the right thing. "They're putting on an opera… *Bodo*—haven't you ever heard Miltos speak of him? They knew each other in Berlin."

"It's not the first time I've heard his name. Miltos has talked about him."

"Then hasn't he told you that from the very day the man arrived he's been threatening to denounce him to the Kommandatur as a communist? He's been playing cat and mouse with him for days and now he's terrorizing him and starting to blackmail him. Miltos believes he's going to denounce him—the last time they spoke, this very afternoon in fact, the man told him outright that he was going to do it… Unless…"

"Unless what? *Unless what?* Unless he betrays other members of the Resistance?"

"No, nothing like that. Unless he finds a woman for the maestro. Yes, a woman. His order was specific. He doesn't want prostitutes, he doesn't want the kind of girl who goes with Germans in hotels and bars. He wants a beautiful woman, unblemished and pure as the driven snow… And he charged our friend with finding one for him…"

"Ah, the beast! The bastard! The swine!"

"As you say."

I said nothing more and left her to bite her lips for a moment and twist her hands—so upset was she that she was forgetting to cover her knees now. They were beautiful rounded knees, their skin as soft as silk.

"Miltos says the German is determined to humiliate him because of differences they had in the past—something to do with music, if I understood right, but also politics. And believes that this way he'll humiliate him. The point is, the point is… that if he humiliates him, if he succeeds in humiliating him, then he'll leave him alone, he won't denounce him, he'll think 'I've broken his spirit' and he'll let him be. I'm just as sure of this as Miltos is. That's why he said yes. That he'd see about finding, that he'd see about f-f-finding a woman for him. But he hasn't got a clue who to send, he says he doesn't know any women. His end has come, he thinks, there's no hope… The German will hand him over to the Kommandatur, they'll execute him and that will be that. If our lot, the Security Police, get you, at least there's always a chance you might survive. In prison but alive. But if an important German hands you over in person, then, as you well know, you haven't got a hope in hell. Miltos wants to escape to Halkida and lie low there until Bodo has gone back to Germany. If he does, he'll lose his place in the orchestra for certain. What else could I do, seeing him in such a state? I promised to help. I'd see if I could find a woman, I told him, and… I told him… —what else could I have done? And I thought of mentioning it to you, putting it to your judgment… You might have an idea, maybe you know some woman, some friend of yours…"

In one movement she sat upright on the sofa, her back rigid, and looked at me with all the old dislike, distrust and contempt.

"A friend of mine do such a thing, prostitute herself to a German? How little you know us, Mr Sotiriou…" (the second person plural once more—the *close-combat* weapon, as Mimis would have said).

"Mrs Kanellis, I am a simple man… I take life as I find it. Miltos is a friend, almost like a brother to me. I'd do whatever it took to save his life. If I had some woman friend, if I had a sister, if I myself could turn into a woman and go… I'd do it."

She was looking at the floor. She was silent. Thinking. Then she raised her eyes to me.

"You despise me, don't you?" (This time the second person singular—also a weapon.)

I stared at her. Despise her? Me?

"Because I'm a married woman and have a lover… you despise me. Because I'm pregnant and… you despise me. Because you know secrets… you live in the same building… you come to my window at night and… I've seen you, you've come there… you know things that even Miltos doesn't know… And you imagine that because I'm *that kind* of woman I'll go and sleep with that Nazi beast. Is that it?"

"I don't despise you, anything but, anything but!" I bleated beseechingly. "It's because you're a woman who's in love with my best friend, because you want to help him, because you're the sort of woman who'd protect someone who might be the father… that's why I imagined, I conceived, I hoped that maybe, that maybe you might think of a way we could save him from the Gestapo and the firing squad… Other women have sacrificed themselves the same way… Judith killed Holofernes… she went with him—she slept with him and killed him… and Sampson did the same to Delilah… *she* did it to Sampson, I mean… and lots of other women… it wasn't a sin because they were sacrificing themselves for a cause…"

I realized I wasn't getting anywhere and thought it better to shut up. And let her think instead of making her laugh.

"Pavlos is safely in hiding… he's in Ilissia," I murmured after a moment in order to steer her thoughts in the right direction. "What does that tell you?"

She looked at me, trying to make out my expression in the half-light.

"He's all right, he's safe."

"You see? Safe. And he won't be—he won't be coming back for quite a few days, not till he's found out why they wanted to arrest him and what they were planning to do with him once they'd got him…" (I lowered my voice even further). "I myself would be able to take you to the German…"

She swiftly looked away, but her expression was no longer as furious as before.

"And naturally no one would ever find out… I promised Miltos I'd see to it. I'll tell him I found some friend of mine, some client—and that would be that. It's no big deal. One evening, two evenings—the first night of the opera is next week, after which he'll go back to Germany and leave us in peace. And the musicians will be able to start playing 'Yerakina' again… Eh? What do you think? Is my idea really so very terrible?"

"It isn't so very…" she said without looking at me.

I bent to rub my ankle and lower calf, which were beginning to hurt because of the cold.

"I've always thought that you were our evil spirit, Mr Sotiriou," Marika said suddenly in a voice that was now entirely colorless. "Was I wrong?"

"Ah, Mrs Marika! Yes, you were wrong, wrong, wrong. A thousand times wrong. Do you want me to tell you the truth? The whole truth? I'm entangled and there's no way to disentangle myself now. That's the truth. And another truth is that when I started taking care of him I considered it just a job, and it was because of you I began to love him like a brother. How come because of you?

That's yet another truth—so let me tell you it as well... you've told me everything tonight, you haven't tried to hide, so I won't try to hide either. It's because of you since I have certain feelings for you of the kind that are called *secret*—and they made me feel sorry for him and experience through him what I could never have had with you. This is more or less the way things are, and don't ask how or why. Let's call it an abyss that separates you from me (I don't think you'll have any difficulty recognizing that), differences that cannot be wiped out even by love—for I am not your equal, and between people who are not equals love cannot take hold."

"What are you talking about? What's this *equal* that you're on about?" said Marika. "We believe in the equality of all men, Mr Sotiriou."

"You may believe it, but belief isn't enough."

"What do you want? For me to sleep with you to prove that you and I are equals? It wouldn't be too hard—you're a handsome boy, hasn't anyone ever told you that? And love doesn't require much more to establish equality between a man and a woman."

How sweet her voice had become... How she was looking at me. Even as we walked along the street when we came here this morning I had constantly felt her eyes on my back, my buttocks, my neck—which were all set on fire by her glance: her sensuality had been aroused as we flew, as we touched, clasping each other close... she had been aflame too—and anyway, everyone always said I was handsome, both men and women... but let me not listen to her, for my ears are stopped with the wax of the curse, the clay of hopelessness…

"You consider me capable of doing *that* to save my lover," (she said this more as if she were drawing some conclusion from our conversation than as if it were a question).

"Any man would dream of being with you—you are the surest means of saving my friend."

She looked at me with an ironic smile.

"So we'll fly there together, will we? Will you put me down outside the door of his room at the Grande Bretagne, like a gift? And say, *Here you are, Maestro, your wish has been fulfilled, the lover of Beratis, the man you hate so much, is standing at your door ready to sleep with you, so that you keep your promise and do not denounce him?*"

"And he will say, *I always said that communists have the most beautiful women, the most desirable, the ones a man likes to make his own, women who resist and despise the man who mounts them, who seek to be admired and valued and held to be the equals of a man, a creator, an artist…* And the next morning at the rehearsal he'll smile as he looks at the enemy he's vanquished, but he'll keep his word for he will be hoping to have the privilege of sleeping with you again that night, and the next maybe, before he leaves forever."

"And he'll take me into his room, there'll be champagne and caviar on ice, and the bed will be a four-poster with a canopy, and he'll tell me to take off my clothes at once—like a hungry customer visiting a whore."

"No, no. Never. He'll look at you as if you've dropped

from the skies—without knowing that you really have dropped from the skies—and he'll rub his eyes and say: *Madame, if I had ever imagined how you would be, I would never have ordered them to bring me a woman as if she were a basket of oranges, but I would have left the orchestra—which in any case gets worse rather than better with each rehearsal—and I would have gone through the streets searching to discover where you lived, so that I might stand bare-headed, without the cap that covers my bald patch and stops me catching cold, and I would have called on all the spirits to explain to you that my art lies at your feet and that for the sake of your love I would accept any humiliation, so that you might consider me worthy to be your lover even for but one single night...* That's what Bodo will say when he sees you."

"But you're crying... Would Bodo say those words or are you saying them?"

"What does it matter? I or Bodo... in any case a stranger, neither Miltos nor your husband... For one night, or two, say... Three at most..."

She stood over me in fury, flecks of saliva on her lips as she spat her words at me:

"Listen here, little stool pigeon... if you think that I... if you believe that you can tell me what to do because you got me out of the building with those demonic powers of yours... I don't know how and I don't know what you are or what you're after but I never never... go go leave me and if that's what you want then run off to the Gestapo and tell them I'm hiding here so that they can come and get me and put me in front of a firing squad I don't care I don't care at all I don't sully my hands or my soul go away at once get out of here go and I'll take care to let Miltos know what a reptile the person is that he considers a friend and a savior and a brother and where his credulousness has led him and his innocence which makes him think everyone is decent… Do you hear me? Do you hear me? Beat it, go, get out of here, you bastard."

And before I had a chance to rise, as I sat there with her standing over me spitting in fury, she raised her soft little hand again and gave me another resounding slap.

30

———

Second night flight

Paltoglou Ananias

Paltoglou Anastasios

Paltoglou Anna

Paltoglou Eleftherios

Paltoglou Isocrates

Paltoglou-Karakouliambrou Magdalene

Paltoglou Napoleon

etc. etc. etc.

… A whole wardrobe full of Paltoglous[10], how to find the one I want… Oh yes, the address, address… How

10. In Greek *paltó* = overcoat

many of them were in Kolonaki? Not many. Ah, here we are—Periandros: 31 Loukianou Street. Got to be him. I rapidly ran my finger down the column till the Paltoglous ended and the Paltogones, the Paltouzellises and the Paltouzoglous began. I jotted down the number with a pencil so as not to lose it and dialed. There wasn't enough time left to waste any by going around there on the off chance.

Got it in one, bingo, bull's eye as they say at home. Vanda answered the phone.

"I have to see you."

She lowered her voice guiltily.

"What's up?" she hissed at me. "We've got guests tonight, I can't."

I ran my tongue around my mouth in indecision.

"Invite me," I told her with an awkward laugh, "your husband's already met me at the theater, tell him you invited me but forgot to mention it, tell him whatever you like, it's urgent, it concerns our friend…"

"What friend?"

"Miltos. Beratis—surely he hasn't slipped your mind already?"

"Ah. Beratis. Look, it's out of the question. D'you realize who's going to be here tonight? The people I'd have to mix you with? The Minister Gotsamanis, the Italian Cultural Attaché, Papadopoulos, the Director of the Social Security Department, the Director of the National Broadcasting Service, a certain Agathos, a Greek from South Africa, and a dozen other equally distinguished and important people. How would you possibly fit in? How could I even have thought of inviting you along with them? Sorry, I don't mean to be rude, I'm putting it bluntly so you'll get the point. And anyway there's the curfew, how would you be able to come, are you crazy?"

"Mr Agathos, did you say? Agathos, did I hear you right? Well, in that case I'm definitely coming. I'll ring the doorbell and if your maid or your butler doesn't let me in I'll climb in through the window. I have to see you to talk to you about something and I'm on my way now. You invent whatever story you like for Mr Pelerinoglou..."

"Paltoglou, Paltoglou."

"Yes, yes, I remember: Mr Periscope Paltoglou. And if your other guests look askance at me, just pretend you don't notice. What do you want me to be? The Cultural Attaché of the United States?"

"You're out of your mind!"

I hung up. Leaving Marika Kanellis glued to the wall at the back of the room and staring at me as if I were a creature from hell, I opened the door and left.

I stood perfectly still in the shadows for a few moments, taking a careful look around. All the neighbors' windows were tight shut. Then, with my cheek still stinging from her hand, I kicked off and shot straight upwards.

I rose high enough in the air to be safe but not so high that I lost my sense of direction or couldn't make out the streets clearly.

On Loukianou Street I landed on the roof of number 31, let myself into the building by the service door from the roof and walked downstairs, dusting my suit and adjusting the brim of my hat as I went. Their apartment was on the third floor, the only one on that floor—it wouldn't be at all surprising if they really did have a butler. I summoned up all the courage I had left, pressed the white doorbell and took a deep breath. I heard no sounds of anyone approaching the door from the inside, yet it opened and a funny little person stood before me who would have looked like a doorman or a chauffeur if he hadn't been dressed to kill. He looked at me interrogatively.

"Sotiriou," I said, ready to explain that the lady of the house had invited me.

"Half a mo," said the chauffeurette.

Tip-tip-tip went his little heels and lo and behold, there was Mrs Vicky-and-not-Vanda Paltoglou come to receive me in person or to announce that no way was I going to set foot in the sanctum of her drawing room and…

"Come here!" She grabbed me by the arm and hustled me over to the stairs. "I won't be a minute," she called to the doorman.

"Ah, no, my dear Mrs Vicky—you're surely not going to exclude me from such a distinguished gathering… What's wrong with me?"

"I told Perry…"

"Perry-Periandros? I think I'm going to throw up."

"Just stop it!"

She pinched my arm so furiously that in spite of the

layers of jacket, cardigan, shirt and long-sleeved undershirt it must certainly have turned black and blue.

"I'm coming in, I have to see Agathos," I told her.

"I thought there was something you wanted to tell me."

"I've got something to tell you and I've got even more to tell Agathos who involved me in this whole business in the first place. Vanda, you can't imagine what's been happening to me, Beratis is mixed up in it as well and it's all Agathos' fault… And while we're at it, how long have *you* known Agathos? It can't have been a coincidence that he put you by Beratis' side, that night at the Olympia, so I'd recognize him…"

"It's a long story that doesn't concern you," she said. "It was he who introduced me to Paltoglou."

"How very benevolent and philanthropic of him. So that's how you met Paltoglou. Does Agathos do business with him, how come he knew him?"

"From South Africa, what does it matter? Commercial interests, that sort of thing…"

"Hell fire and damnation."

"And how come *you* know Agathos?" (suspiciously).

"He's a client."

"He's your client? Or you're his?"

"You may not be far wrong. Whichever way, the job he employed me for has got me into a really bad mess. And you know what the job is? Looking after Beratis to make sure nothing happens to him before he's *completed his work*… Hear that? Got a clue what it means? Me neither."

"Since you know him, you may as well come in," said Vicky-Vanda. "It makes things easier if there's someone else who knows you. I told Perry… I told Paltoglou… I told him I'd asked you to find some jewelry of mine that went missing."

"So I'm a detective not a Cultural Attaché?"

"Stop it. You'll wreck my life. What about whatever it was you wanted, aren't you going to tell me?"

"It's a rather delicate matter. Have you got time? Because I can't very well just blurt it out without explaining… You wouldn't understand my motives for the proposition I'm going to make."

She had crossed her arms and was waiting.

"I waited and waited for a proposition from you and it never came," she said.

"Well, maybe I can make amends now," I murmured.

In her drawing room the lights were brilliant. On the streets around here neither the curfew nor the blackout seemed to apply, German and Italian cars were parked at the curb, men in uniform stood waiting outside front doors—the Authorities of the country were paying their evening visits.

There was a heavenly smell: the folding doors had just been opened and most of the guests had drifted from the drawing room with its marble fireplace to a buffet that was reminiscent of another era. If I didn't manage anything else, I would at least eat well tonight. I moved over to the table, helped myself to a plate as big as a tray and began to fill it. My eyes flickered rapidly from the dishes of food to all the other people around me who were doing exactly the same thing, except that they were helping themselves slowly and deliberately; on their plates the blue pattern and the gold border around the rim continued to be visible, whereas mine was heaped so full that I had difficulty holding it without putting my thumb in the sauce. I saw Vanda pointing me out to her black marketeer husband whose wide, toothy smile never faltered, not even when his eyes turned steely.

All around me little mustaches, of the kind that resemble small dashes beneath the nostrils which cancel out thoughts before they can reach the lips, were moving up and down as their owners chewed (the fashion certainly existed before Hitler, but for me this type of mustache has forever taken on the name of the dark-haired champion of the blond race), waistcoats were beginning to be unbuttoned and the light from the chandeliers was reflected in glossy pomaded heads. The few ladies in the company had gathered in a little group apart, an invisible henhouse, where they were exchanging idiocies and gazing at everything wide-eyed.

At the end of the room lay another small drawing room in whose doorway I suddenly caught sight of my client's snow-white head: the wealthy Greek from South Africa—not a doubt about it. What kind of game was this devilish old man playing? What frauds was he perpetrating? What risky business was he engaged in in the lonely, chilly, macabre desert that was Athens? What did Beratis and his work or Marika and Pavlos Kanellis have to do with it? How was the little Jewish girl disguised as Mrs Paltoglou involved, and, more to the point, why on earth had I let myself get mixed up in a case which, with each passing day, was taking on new dimensions and showing a glimpse, albeit still a faint one, of the firing squad on the distant horizon.

Extreme hunger is easily sated—my stomach refused to take any more: in five minutes I'd consumed the amount I normally would have eaten in a month. I put down my plate and made my way rapidly towards the little drawing room.

On the way I bumped into Vicky-Vanda's husband who suddenly loomed in front of me like a stone wall.

"Mr?"

"Sotiriou," and I put out my hand, "I haven't had the opportunity till now to greet you."

"Well, you certainly did turn up just at the right moment," he remarked with a touch of the barrow-boy in his tone. "Vicky tells me that…"

"Yes, she's asked me to…"

"To find…"

"Yes, I'm following a good lead… Indeed, I may need her to accompany me—tonight or tomorrow at the latest—to a fence at Thissio—for her to recognize her stuff while I'm posing as a potential buyer… and then I'll deal with the man…" (he was about to interrupt me, with an expression I didn't much like), "but ah, excuse me, I've just spotted another distinguished client of mine. I'd better go and say good evening to him… Mr Agathos…"

"Do you know each other?"

"Indeed we do!"

I laughed so loud and spontaneously that Agathos turned round. He came over to us immediately—he must have been alarmed at my sudden appearance.

"Mr Angel!"

"Mr Panos, what a surprise and what a pleasure!"

"Ahem, I'll leave you to talk," growled Paltoglou, his eyes searching for his Vanda-Vicky.

"What are you doing here, my boy?" asked the old man, instantly putting his back between us and the company and drawing me aside.

"What are you doing here, my dear Mr Panos? Or should I say Mr Kornelios? I'm here in the course of my duties. And you?"

He laughed and his manner altered.

"I am too, I suppose you could say."

"Look, we've got trouble," I said hastily. "I told you right at the beginning that if the affair led to trouble I'd be backing out. Well, it has and I am."

"Are you scared?" he asked.

"Do I look like a fool? Of course I'm scared."

"Do you feel you're in danger?"

"What do you think? They killed the girl almost right in front of my eyes…"

"Not so loud, not so loud," he muttered, taking my arm.

"The Kanellis couple's servant," I added in a quieter voice.

"Many people die, Mr Sotiriou, many people are killed

all around us every day. You see it, I see it. But do *you*, you yourself, feel insecure and in peril of your life? That's what I'm asking."

"Aren't I in peril?"

He put his head on one side and pursed his lips interrogatively.

"Are you not taking your medicine regularly? The medicine your pharmacist recommended?"

"You mean… that I… but what good does it do? Does it make me safe? Remove all dangers from my path?"

"At least it removes you from the path of all dangers… Stop laughing. But you are right, I haven't been consistent in my obligations to you. Here, take this."

He put his hand into his waistcoat pocket and drew out something which he put into my palm. Its weight made me open it to see: five coins.

"And tomorrow night I'll come by your apartment or your office and leave you the same amount again."

"Tomorrow… But today, tonight if at all possible, otherwise tomorrow at the very latest, I have to go to the Grande Bretagne…"

"Don't tell me," he interrupted. "Don't tell me about it, I am not concerned with how you do whatever you have to do… All that matters is that you do it. Keep your methods to yourself: better for both of us, don't you think?"

"Are you so squeamish?"

"We all have our own squeamish places, our weaknesses, our excuses… that's life, that's the way society is…"

"Yes," I said, looking around me. "Very well. Tomorrow I'll expect some more money from you. If we're still alive."

I'm quite sure, although I wasn't looking at him, that he was beginning to smile. The old man would never tell me everything I wanted to know, so there wasn't much point wasting time trying. Now it was the turn of the lady of the house.

Vanda was over in the henhouse with the other women, acting the perfect hostess who looks after her guests. They were all decked out like the Easter bier, just as empty and just as sweetly smelling—the ladies of the gentlemen whose jaws chewed and whose pomaded heads shone on the Persian carpets of the Château Paltoglou. It was easy to get Vanda away from them: I could see that her nerves were stretched to breaking point among all those hens attempting to speak with a French accent.

"God damn that old devil!" I muttered in her ear. "Come on, it's time for us to talk about your jewelry."

"Are you crazy?"

"Isn't that what you told Periscope? And I told him the same: that I might need to take you to Thissio to see the jewelry some fence there has, in case they're the items of your dowry that were stolen."

"You didn't say that!"

"I did say the bit about the fence and Thissio. And I told him that tonight... or tomorrow at the very latest..."

"What is it that you want?"

"Listen to me. Pay attention, you and I have got matters

to discuss, it doesn't matter if we're huddled in a corner. Calm down. Look at me."

She turned her magnificent violet-colored eyes on me, that went so well with her red hair and her translucent skin. Propositions, she said, she'd been waiting for them but they never came… Oh God, what a eunuch, what an idiot…

"What did Agathos say to you about Beratis, tell me. Why did he make you stand next to him at the Olympia that night, do you remember?"

"He told me he needed to help him but didn't want to appear to be doing so."

"And?"

"And what?"

"What did he tell you to do?"

"To talk to him, tell him to take care of himself."

"Ah, indeed!"

"Indeed what? I don't understand, Angel."

"On what grounds were you to talk to him? How did Beratis know you or you him?"

"He was a friend of my brother. My brother was a musician too, a violinist, and they often played together, every week, until Sammy had to leave…"

"Sammy?"

"Yes, why?"

"Nothing. And Miltos, why should you help him? As your brother's friend? What was he to you? D'you want to hear my own theory?"

"You've got a theory?"

"Of course I have, I'm not a fool. Agathos is a secret agent… stop pulling at my hand like that, no one can hear us… and Miltos is too, and he's carrying out some important mission in Athens, all those explosions that have been happening recently, the Resistance is getting organized in Athens too, I don't know the details but anyway something like that. Agathos came to help him set up his network, he wants to get money to him, supplies, maybe a radio so he can communicate with English headquarters in Cairo or with the government in exile, I don't know… something of the sort… this explains all his nonsense about Miltos's *great work* and his desire to protect him so that he can complete it… All right, he may have work that needs to be completed but it's got nothing to do with those screeching quartets of his, I saw him with my own eyes sitting at the piano jotting down music on a sheet of paper, and I'll bet you anything it wasn't music he was writing but a code in the form of musical notes—a musician could easily devise a code like that which could be deciphered later, this explains all the rubbish the old man served up to me to make me do the dirty work while he himself doesn't appear at all, since he moves in circles like tonight's or maybe even higher ones… ha ha ha…this explains his unknown address, the fact that he's able to move around town at night in spite of the curfew, even his dog…"

"What dog?"

"He's got a dog, didn't you know? Azor."

"Half the dogs in Athens are called Azor," said Vanda,

clearly beginning to think I was sick. "Get a grip on yourself, Angel, the man isn't an agent, he's a businessman, he's got a lot of money, Periandros has known him a long time…"

"OK, have it your own way. Personally I couldn't give a damn what Beratis and Agathos are. But listen, whoever he may be, Miltos is in grave danger. A German conductor he crossed swords with in Berlin in the past has told him that he's going to hand him over to the Kommandatur as a communist. And now listen to what comes next: the only way he won't do it is if Beratis finds him a woman, not a whore, not the sort you see in the bar of the Grande Bretagne—a decent woman, pure and unsullied, not a virgin but not a tart either… and Miltos agreed to do it. D'you understand? He has to find a beautiful woman like you to take to the German or else he's had it, you can say goodbye to him. I've already tried three women I know. Only one of them didn't slap my face. Or rather, she did slap me… look, my cheek's still red…"

"Get away from me," hissed Vanda, stepping back. "And speak more quietly!"

"I am speaking quietly. What can I do, you tell me. Do you know anyone who'd be willing? The man's well-known and important, he's here as the guest of the Germans, he'll be conducting a performance next week which he says will go down in history, then he'll be returning to Berlin immediately—so no one would be any the wiser. I need some woman who'll spend one night with him, all right, call it two, who'll be wined and dined, then say goodbye… to save the life of a fellow human. So what should I do, you tell me. We're grown-ups, Vanda, we can understand one another… How about a Jewish girl who'd sacrifice herself like Judith, eh? How about that? It would be an act of resistance, a blow against Nazism, a piece of sabotage… What do you think?… Could you do it yourself? I don't know anyone more beautiful, if I did I'd ask, that's why I'm asking you, and the German isn't just anyone, he's a tall, good-looking man, thin as a rake, mind you, and going bald, but then Periscope doesn't have all that much more in the way of hair…"

She began to laugh, quietly at first, then louder, then so loud that quite a few heads turned in our direction. Mr Agathos started to say something to distract attention from us but it wasn't really necessary, in any case people weren't paying much attention and everyone present was drinking and laughing as if they'd been paid to do so.

"Angel!" she cried in the sweetest of tones, with the air of a lady who's just heard the wittiest joke of her life, then muttered, "Get out of here while you can, you fucking cripple, you cheap pimp," as she smoothed down her red curls.

She almost pushed me to the front door and as I crossed the threshold gave me another violent pinch on exactly the spot already bruised by the first.

Distressed and anxious, seeking to save the situation and avert disaster, Mr Agathos appeared behind her. Stuttering various incomprehensible phrases, he came out onto the landing with me and, once he was sure that the door had been securely closed behind us and that no one could see us, shook his head like someone who's given up all hope.

"Ah, Mr Angel," he said, "I know, you're trying to do your best, I don't say the opposite… but, my boy, the world extends a lot further than your own nose, how can I put it? And while you're wasting time working out whether it's worth getting the dignity of some woman a tiny bit crumpled, or your own dignity, and worrying about what I or he might be, discussions on an altogether different level are taking place at the German Archaeological Mission between Froberger and Professor Doelger, about the future of European culture, about the future of art, about the fight against degenerate forms of expression and their representatives… things far harder to decipher than any spy codes written in Arabic or Morse or ten-point Elzevir or notes on the stave. Do me a favor, my boy, concentrate on our job, have faith in an old man who's seen a lot and knows—the world is larger than the center of Athens. Those people are planning the death of our musician, the death of your friend, the death of his girlfriend and of their child who will have a role to play one day. What are you or I or Vanda or Paltoglou compared to all that? Not a thing. Come, pull yourself together, get going, fly, hurry, wake up, wake up now… it's time…

31

—

Third night flight

"Wake up, Mr Angel, you scared me! Are you all right?"

I had to wake up. I'd fallen asleep in my clothes in the armchair in my office and was shivering like a soul in hell, my teeth chattering. I opened my eyes, my surroundings swam out of the mist and I saw that I was at home. Hunger and strain had got the better of me and I'd keeled over just as I was, in my armchair. I'd been sleeping with my mouth open, and since I hadn't shaved for two days, my hair was tousled and I was icy cold, I must have made a convincing corpse.

Yet how often does it happen that we open our eyes in a dream, how often do we think we've woken and only then start dreaming. She was bending over me and prodding me gently since she didn't quite like to shake me, her expression altered by stress and worry, her eyes beneath those thick dark eyebrows like burning coals trying to penetrate the mists of sleep in my own eyes.

"I'm dreaming."

"No, you're awake," she said. "Are you all right?"

"Me! Are *you* all right?"

"I'm fine, sort of fine," she answered with an attempt at a laugh which seemed to say that she was still hurting all over.

"It was only yesterday noon…"

"Were you there?" she asked, "When they took me away?"

"They took you away wrapped in a blanket and everyone thought you'd had it, I closed one of your eyes myself…"

"I felt you caressing me," she said. "I got hurt because I fell from the roof—that short one in the hat pushed me and I fell, I was trying to catch hold of his legs so that you'd get away…"

I leaped up. So it wasn't a dream! What I thought I'd seen—that had been the nightmare, the misinterpretation… Oh thank heavens… I took her in my arms and laughingly embraced her. The front room was dark, the shutters lowered and pushed slightly outwards as always, so that between their slats you could make out the balconies of the Varvitsiotis house; dead silence reigned in the street. The girl was making little squeaks—the way I was squeezing her must have been painful but she didn't want to pull away from me. She asked after her mistress and Mr Pavlos and was filled with happiness on learning that they were both safe and in hiding.

"I found the kitchen door unlocked and I came in to

find you," she explained in answer to a question I hadn't asked. "The policeman downstairs has gone, I stayed a couple of hours with Mrs Leni, waiting till it was dark, then I came up and rang our doorbell but there was no one there and I was afraid… I started imagining things… that's it, it's over, I said to myself, they've caught them and killed both of them…" (she burst into tears).

"Don't cry like that. Do you want to stay here? I don't know when they'll be back and until they return… I've got money, we'll find food, I've got everything… you can stay if you like."

"You're kind!"

"Where were you hurt?"

She didn't need to tell me. A bandage on her head trapped her hair on one side and made it spring out ridiculously on the other. At least at the First Aid Center they'd washed off the dried blood that had looked like a blotch of tar on her temple.

"I hurt my back too… just here," she said, taking my hand and putting it somewhere below her waist. "Right here. It hurts," she whispered and her voice dissolved into something like a sob.

I let go of her. For a moment she was undecided, looking around her at the apartment; although its layout was almost identical to theirs, nothing was the way they had it.

"If you tell me where you keep your dusters, I'll dust everything in the morning and wash the floor."

"Are you in such a hurry to get to work again? I don't

have enough money to pay a servant. You'd do better to lie down and rest. I'll light the gas so you can have a hot bath."

"I know where it is," she said, jumping up. "Everything's the same, the gas is in the same place—I know where."

"Since you know, go ahead," I told her. "The bathrobe is on the shelf by the bath. You can turn on the light, it doesn't show from outside."

She went off to have a bath and I felt the need to smoke, something I hadn't done for some time as my stomach was almost never in very good condition, with the result that I'd left my cigarettes in a drawer in the dining room. Now I felt like having one. I went and rummaged around, found the packet and took out a cigarette. Half the tobacco fell out when I tapped it on my fingernail. I blew smoke towards the ceiling and looked out of the small window at the Conservatoire with its terracotta balustrade fronting the roof.

The sky was cloudy tonight. Across it swept only the beams of the anti-aircraft searchlights, meeting and parting again like acrobats who run onto the stage from different directions, perform their act, then withdraw. You know what I was thinking. God knows, we're not kids any more... As I'd said (if I'd said it) to Vanda-Vicky... yes, naturally, the idea was well and truly fixed in my mind now; and it wasn't for the sake of Agathos and his sovereigns, or Beratis with his bitten fingernails and his blasted caterwauling quartets, but for my lawyer and her aaah her hmmm and her chipped tooth, the ribbon in her hair and her stinging slap aaaah her slap aaaah AAAAH…

"What's the matter, what is it?"

The girl newly risen from the dead is standing in the doorway, trying to distinguish me in the dim light filtering through the window behind me. She sees nothing but a shadow. Nothing but a vague figure. Mr Angel, the wonderful Mr Angel, me, exhaling smoke towards the ceiling in an apparently grand manner and thinking thoughts of the kind that make me incapable of flying when I think them.

"Nothing, I'm thinking."

She turned to leave. At which point I noticed that she'd wrapped herself in the bathrobe and was holding it closed in front since it lacked both buttons and belt—I'd never been too concerned with the way I looked in my bathrobe, bachelor and useless fool and… oh, forget it, that I was.

"Every cloud has a silver leaning," my father used to say in his strange Greek (living in a foreign country, working eighteen hours a day and my Sarakatsani grandmother must all have had something to do with his odd version of his own language—at any rate not a single one of his fellow-countrymen could understand him: "Be a good fellow and say it in American, Thodoras, we can't make head or tail of your gobbledygook"). He must have known something about it: his life was full of clouds and yet he was always cheerful.

She'll accept yes she'll accept—this was what was filling

me with guilt and remorse, the fact that whatever I asked of her she would do. And be happy into the bargain that it was I who'd asked.

But everyone, absolutely everyone, even she, demands something in return; I knew this, and I knew very well what I'd have to pay in return and I knew very well that I didn't have the wherewithal to pay it—she didn't know, of course, but, as the few remaining old signs in shops had it, please count your change, no error recognized after you have left the cash register (these signs were only in Greek for the Germans don't deign to bother with lowly transactions like we do, nor do they need "Do not spit on the floor" and "Do not lean out of the window" in the Piraeus train or "Leave elevator promptly" in the contraption in the central post office—one side goes up as the other goes down and you jump off when it reaches your floor).

I decided fairly automatically to have a bath. God only knows how long it was since I last got into the bathtub—it hadn't mattered till now, but now it did and I had to have a bath. I waited motionless in my armchair for her to emerge, like an animal lying in wait. I heard her close the door, then her rapid footsteps over the icy marble-chip floor of the hall on her way to the kitchen.

"Where are you going?"

"To the servant's room."

"I use it to store things in, don't go there, what would you do there, go on into the bedroom. And leave the robe in the bathroom, I'm going to have a bath too."

"Shall I get it ready for you?" (willing).

"Get what ready? Don't bother, I can manage, I'm used to it."

I found the light switched on, the bathtub as clean as it was possible for such an old stained bathtub to be, the robe damp but neatly folded on the closed toilet seat. It's not bad having a servant. I soaped myself and reflected. If only I'd wasted less time trying to persuade two self-centered and disdainful women… two women who mightn't have found it so very difficult to accept the commission if it hadn't been me negotiating it. Who might have enjoyed it, each in her own way. One to save her lover and the probable father of her child, and as yet one more act of resistance against the arrogant invader; the other to avenge her people, now scattered to the winds, her family and the masquerade she was obliged to live under the protection of her black marketeer husband… The servant girl was the only one who'd do whatever she did for my sake, for my sake alone, because I asked her to and my wish was enough, because she trusted and admired me and because anything I requested of her couldn't be wrong in my eyes and therefore wasn't in hers either… She was the only one who wouldn't feel the need to act insulted or to start pinching and slapping me to prove how outraged, proud and independent she was. All this girl would ask in exchange would be that I accept her love, so that she'd know that I understood it and that my request had been made because I recognized and valued her love; it would show, if not my love for her, at any rate my appreciation of her love for me. Just imagine—there are still women who fall wildly in love with you, like Lauretta back home, who never asked a thing from me, who never complained that I was seeing other women, because a man has needs and can't spend all his time with one girl, going to the movies or holding hands on the Ferris wheel in the fairground—and when she did give herself to me, she did it so that I wouldn't go with other women any more, so she'd know that I was hers alone and that she'd done whatever a woman can do to be a man's wife even without a wedding, even though she knew Gus would never give his consent because he had other plans, had something grand lined up for her, with the idea at the back of his mind of using such connections to advance himself and his family.

Nor was it necessary for me to sit down and tell this girl the whole saga about Agathos' concern for Beratis who was in danger, and about how Beratis had been obliged—idiotically, in my opinion, out of the sheer terror he felt for Mr F. and his own foolishness—to undertake something he couldn't perform; indeed, if I stopped playing the role Mr Agathos was paying me to play, if I threw it up and abandoned him, where would he turn other than to his lady love, Mrs Kanellis? Or even to Vanda-Vicky who'd been helping him survive… (people find it easy to believe that others are ready to sacrifice themselves for them, that others have fallen prey to the charms and the value which they alone see in themselves). And the outcome, the outcome, to be honest, if you come to think of it, ha ha ha, the outcome with either of these two proud Amazons would have been a hell of a lot more immediate and positive. One thing for me to suggest: quite another thing for Beratis to ask—either from Marika or from Vanda! Am I wrong? Agathos had found a rather ineffective way of helping his Chosen Artist. He'd have done much better to secure the favor of the two women instead of my services. However, like all old men who think they know everything, he'd been confounded by his own secretiveness!

Yes, the little servant girl only needed to know what I wanted her to do. The when and the where. Nothing else. And all because *I was a gentleman who raised my hat to ladies on the stairs, and even to her!*

She lay on the bed opposite and I reclined in the armchair. She asked me to open the front of the robe I was wearing to reveal my chest and my belly—*if I wasn't too cold*—and she herself unbuttoned the dress she'd put on again to sleep in, a whole series of white buttons from throat to mid-calf, and let it fall back to reveal her freshly washed, sweetly smelling body like a gift in its wrappings: her breasts high, her belly flat, her legs, still with a childish down on them, open. The only thing she wore was the little baptismal cross which I'd given back to her. And she told me about the island she came from and about her home, and the whole story of how she'd left when she was twelve and come to Athens to work, and how the employers she first went to had loved her and treated her like their own daughter, and Mr Agesilaos who was a retired headmaster had taught her all the things she'd missed learning on the island, then his wife got ill and was admitted to the Sotiria hospital and never came out—she was a lovely, gentle lady—and after that there wasn't enough money left to pay for a servant (her clothes, her food, her room and a little bit of pocket money each week), so she had to find another job and the headmaster himself found her this one here—Mr Pavlos was handling some case of his and mentioned one day that now that his wife had started working as a lawyer they needed a skivvy for the housework. And right from the very first days—for she wasn't twelve any more but fifteen, then seventeen, and nineteen now, well, call it twenty, her birthday was next month—she'd noticed the tenant on the floor below, who her employers bad-mouthed all day long, calling him a creep and a stool pigeon, she herself wasn't educated enough to be able to see the bad in people but she noticed that he always behaved politely and had a sweet face—even if he was lame, though his limp was kind of attractive too if you thought of it that way—and he seemed like someone who'd seen a lot and suffered a lot in his life, and he was always so polite and...

"And he raised his hat on the stairs..."

"Yes, to all the ladies, and to me too..."

And, quite apart from everything else, she'd studied his face and examined one by one the lines around his mouth which gave him such a nice expression, and his eyes that were kind and so dark they were almost black, and his voice which wasn't rough, it was more like a caress if you thought of it that way, and his double-breasted jackets really suited him, not like Mr Pavlos who'd look like a scarecrow whatever he wore, so clumsily was he made, and who was always peeking up her skirt—never mind the fact that he was an educated man and had a young wife.

I both listened and didn't listen; my mind kept wandering to her mistress. For I am one of those wretched people who belong nowhere, who instead of enjoying the joys of the world that holds them in its embrace are constantly focusing their gaze higher, further, as if happiness and joy might exist somewhere further on, on the other side, far from here, beyond us. Whatever.

32

———

Faust and Helen

"Now that I am no longer afraid to think for myself without texts and theories, I find in all their music, philosophy and poetry, which I studied for so many years, one flaw that mars it—just one single flaw. It's a fatal flaw though. It's the fact that someone like Goethe, someone of such stature, could imagine Faust, that wretched, decrepit old scholastic, marrying (and for love, he says!) our own girl, our own barefoot, dark-browed, straight-nosed, clear-eyed girl, that joy, that breath of beauty and life. I don't understand and never will understand this ill-assorted match-making. Only a German, only someone who has a purely mental apprehension of all the things which here you touch and breathe and see bathed in light, could have conceived it. Only a German would dare imagine that the prize he took possession of (not something he became himself, merely something he took possession of) could ever be the body of Helen of Troy."

These words are written in my musician's notebook—I

still open it occasionally when I feel a wash of nostalgia for those days. He says other things in his notebook too, but all the passages about music are Double-Dutch to me. Maybe I'll show them to someone who knows such things and get him to explain. When you think where I started from, I've managed to learn quite a lot. I have my limits though.

The sock is one way. I'm not disputing this, I've used it. But I saw and learned much more from flying—where are you, Sol, now that I'm able to tell you how much one sees without a sock over one's head? And the things I learned have remained with me despite the fact that I've ceased to fly. I've seen everything from above, and that's not something you forget, even when you're earthbound. So now I can almost see the scene as I would have seen it then, flying above the city: a meager, bent figure, his overcoat buttoned up and a hat on his head, walking up Panepistimiou Street towards Syntagma with a girl on his arm. The curfew has not yet begun, it's still light, the sun is setting over Mount Aigaleo in the west, the two of them are walking rapidly without speaking. Whatever they had to say has already been said. Everything else is communicated via their linked arms, absorbed through their very pores directly into their souls. His face is grey and morose. He no longer feels any happiness that the job he'd undertaken is nearing completion, it is no longer enough that his client will be pleased and will place a pile of gold on the glass-topped desk in his office. He'd like, yes, he'd like, he'd really like to be glad at what he's doing, yet he isn't. He's changed now—and he doesn't want to feel ashamed. Because the girl at his side is not in the least ashamed by what she's about to do, she's happy. From time to time she asks him something, a little anxious but proud that matters of such importance depend on her. *Mr Angel himself…*

"But I'll tell him first that I want something to eat," she says.

"Of course."

. . . .

"Then that I want to have a bath."

"Fine."

. . . .

. . . .

"Will you tell him about me?"

"Of course."

. . . .

"Will you stay?"

. . . .

"No, I can't do that."

. . . .

"And me… for how long?"

. . . .

. . . .

"One or two days. Not more."

. . . .

. . . .

"Will he go away then?"

. . . .

. . . .

. . . .

"He'll go away then."

. . . .

I settled myself in a corner of the bar. I needed a drink, any kind of drink. There was no need to bother about respectability: the people entering and leaving the hotel represented every imaginable permutation of uniformed and un-uniformed thuggishness. I had money in my pocket (I sure did!) and I'd have a drink. I went and sat at a little round table. Behind the grille two employees were talking on the telephone and by the elevators stood a bellboy in a red cap—suddenly I was back in the Plaza Hotel, waiting to meet the consigliere of Don Guzman (may he rot in hell) in order to give him the piece of evidence that would get him out of trouble. At the back of the bar sat a group of officers, their caps on their knees and their tunics buttoned to the throat, laughing and telling jokes in German; they remained watchful all the same, for there were many senior officers about and they didn't want to risk a reprimand. Various little ladies were powdering their noses and then burying them once more in the foreign newspapers they were pretending to read —one poor creature was holding hers upside down.

Lambros Karabinis had opened the door to us—it was a small suite with a vestibule, a hall, a sitting room, two bedrooms and two bathrooms, one small and one large

(Konstantina told me all this). Lambros was a hotel employee who because he spoke German had been detailed to act as valet and spent most of the time there when the maestro was in the hotel.

"Say that we were sent by Mr Beratis, he knows what it's about."

Lambros gave me a broad grin, took Konstantina gently by the arm and led her into the suite.

"Fine fine fine, don't worry, I'm here."

He was showing me out. The girl turned and looked at me. She'd certainly prefer me to be with her during the first minutes of their meeting.

"I'd like to tell him something," I attempted to persuade the valet. "I speak English."

"The maestro doesn't speak English."

"Yes he does. We ate together some nights ago. *He can't stand the language*, but that's another matter."

"Listen, you don't need to tell him anything. I'm here. Don't worry."

I was about to leave when Bodo himself appeared in the hall doorway. He'd seen us huddled together in the vestibule and had come to investigate. His expression was stern. Then, to my amazement, he raised a minatory finger and shook it at me, saying in English, which he certainly mangled more than was necessary, "I know you! I've come across you twice already! Once at the Mascagni and once at the dinner at the Mission—but you haven't come to a single rehearsal. Don't you dare present yourself as a replacement musician tomorrow…"

And, certain that he'd impressed me with his powers of memory, he gave me a brief, malicious smile which at least showed that he wasn't going to take the rebuke any further.

"And what have we here?" he asked in German that I could understand.

His aquiline expression disappeared, to be replaced by another, more withdrawn and sly, as he fixed his eyes on the girl's face.

"What have we here?" he said again, more slowly this time, pushing past the valet and motioning her to approach. Oh, Beratis, pal, I did you an injustice… "Ha ha ha!"

His unpleasant laugh revealed his crooked teeth and made my hair stand up on end. I was on the point of grabbing the girl from his clutches and leaving with her, leaving with her fast and never coming back. Instead, and I really don't know why it seemed to me that I was making a counter-offensive against the incipient effusions in front of me, I said sharply, "She wants to eat. And she wants a bath."

Lambros prodded my chest decisively.

"But yes but yes but yes, I'm here, didn't we say? Don't be afraid. Everything will be carried out perfectly, *trink mein form.*"

Was this something German? The expression was widely heard in those days but I'm not sure what it meant—probably that everything was OK.

The whisky, however, wasn't OK—it didn't taste the

way I remembered. I ordered another one. It was the same. My mouth tasted bitter, a strange feeling gripped my stomach, my eyes were dry. And I hurt all over. I must be ill, I thought. I gave up trying to find the old whisky taste—I never would, for it belonged to another time and another place. Here it was different. All it did was burn my pharynx raw.

Outside the Kentrikon restaurant a row of military Volkswagens was parked. The place was full of the German officers who were in the habit of eating there at the dinner time customary in their own country, that is to say the early evening. On the sidewalk outside stood a line of bent, shadowy figures, shifting from foot to foot in the cold: every so often the kitchen staff emptied the leftovers into two large bins, whereupon the shadows surged forward and caught them in the air. If it was early, they'd devour them on the spot; if it was getting late and they risked being caught in the streets by the curfew, then they'd secrete their treasure somewhere among their garments and hurry off.

I was hungry too but I had some food at home.

And my little Konstantina must already be seated at the table beneath the amazed and impatient eyes of the maestro.

33

———

Thissio

With a heavy heart, with thoughts resembling painful knots in my stomach, I made my way back to Gennadiou Street. The apartment felt emptier than ever before. I'd never felt this way about it in the past: me and my leg and my memories of New York had always seemed to fill it perfectly adequately. I would shut myself up here and dream of my life, both past and future. Today, though, the apartment was not only empty, it was painfully empty. I don't know why I say *painfully*, yet this is the way it felt to me. I wandered from room to room aimlessly, went into the bedroom and looked at my empty bed, went into the bathroom and for a moment seemed to see lying in the bath the body which yesterday had lain naked on my bed before my eyes.

Into my mind then came Beratis' frightened face. How I hated him at that moment! Everything was his fault, he was responsible for what must be happening right now over in Syntagma Square—he and his tuneless quartet, damn their bows to hell. All the same, I didn't pick up the phone and start cursing him; instead I jumped up and hurried out. Zisis was just closing his café.

"What's up, guv?" he asked me in his usual bantering tone. "Forgotten to go shopping for dinner?"

I didn't bother to answer, merely quickening my pace.

Zosimadon Street was deserted. I knocked sharply on the door, expecting to see his face appear as he opened it. Not a sound, though; he was out. I began to leave, biting my lips in annoyance, then turned back, took a scrap of paper, scrawled a few words on it in pencil and pushed it under his door.

Without wasting any more time, I set off for Papachrysanthou's place. If I couldn't vent my anger on the musician, at least I'd find Marika there and I'd tell her that she and her lover could sleep easy—an innocent creature was paying the price for their convictions and I myself had helped set up the whole squalid business. Like the stool pigeon I was, in fact.

I met with a surprise. It was Mimis who opened the door to me.

"Ah, Hephaistos," he said. "Just the lad I wanted."

His words sounded slightly odd. Behind him in the living room I could see the blankets on the two armchairs pushed together that did duty as a sofa, and beneath them his guest fast asleep.

"So early?" I asked, pointing at the sleeping woman.

He nodded and drew me into the little kitchen.

"It's the best cure for hunger," he whispered. "You should have brought something for her to eat. There's not a crumb here—I'm not living here any more, whatever there was I took over to Zaimis Street for the family."

"I don't have anything either, only chickpeas. Goddamn it, it's nothing but one trouble on top of another."

"That's what I wanted to say, Hephaistos, I wanted to ask you about all *this* business," (he gestured towards the woman in the other room). "How long's it going to last—put yourself in my position… It can't go on, you've got to find somewhere else for her, I've got the jitters, d'you get me, know what I mean?"

He came close to whisper in my ear, for the house was small: although, technically speaking, we were in another room, we weren't more than three or four yards from Mrs Marika.

"The widow's a moaner, God only knows, it's nag, nag, nag non-stop for this, that or the other, she's always wanting something. My late cousin spoiled her. At the beginning the railway workers' union let her use his coupons a couple of times, but now they've put an end to it. She's got her own and the kids' coupons, the old ladies don't have any though, so they share whatever rations they get. *A little while ago,* she goes on at me, *you had half a bottle of olive oil, go back to wherever you got it from and say you want more.* And when I ask how the hell she thinks I'm going to pay for it, she goes over to an old chest and gets out some lacy silk knickers left over from her dowry and says *These are worth something…* Does she seriously imagine I can trade her pissy knickers for beans? It's not that I care, mind you, if I had anything I'd give it her, you know me, they're family, I have to take my poor cousin's place. But the fact is I'm broke. So I said to myself, well, I'll just have to grit my teeth and get my ass over there and go and see *them*."

He gave me a meaningful look.

"Go and see who?"

"Those people, who d'you think? …My old pals… the Papathanassis crowd in the Thissio area…"

I scowled—I couldn't remember having heard a thing about them, it was perfectly possible that Mimis was under the illusion just then that we'd known one another for years, or else he was confusing me with someone else who was familiar with all his doings in bygone decades, at a time when I wouldn't even have been able to find Greece on a map.

"What are you talking about, Mimis? You'll drive me out of my wits…"

"Ah yes, you don't know all that stuff… old history, ha ha, I'm getting addled!" He slapped his head with the base of his palm and grinned at me. "I'll have to tell you all about it."

"Never mind, just give me the essence. What are you getting at?"

"If we're to drink the essence we'll have to boil up the bones first. Otherwise you won't understand why I want to tell you what I'm going to tell you. Once upon a time," explained Mimis, "there was a young man who didn't have much in the way of brains. He grew up in a strict family with a father who was an old-fashioned royalist…"

"Cut out the literary bits, can't you, Mimis. Have we got to have the story of your life? At least tell it straight, in the first person and all that."

"OK, though it's a way of passing the time," he agreed. "All I'm trying to say is I wasn't always a republican and the company I used to keep in those days, as is natural, was mostly kids from families like mine. I changed my views, saw the light, know what I mean? When my old man made a mess of things. In '15 a bobbin factory he had went bust and none of his acquaintances would lift a finger to help him. Didn't mean a thing that he'd done them favors, didn't mean a thing that in the good old days they'd had a fair amount of cash out of him—they pretended not to know him. The old man took it hard. And other troubles began as well, for trouble never comes along singly but always drags its relatives in its wake: my mother's extravagances didn't help, nor the family lifestyle which isn't ever easy to cut back on—we ought to have moved house to another neighborhood, ought to have changed our habits, but we didn't do a thing, just continued the same old way. Anyway, it wasn't long before the old man kicked the bucket, I was the oldest child, had to go out and earn my bread, just odd jobs here and there, a drop in the ocean, my education counted for nothing. You always hope you'll get lucky one day. Well, to cut a long story short, there was an old school friend of mine in the neighborhood, Papathanassis, a regular scamp—he always liked me, we'd done things together, played truant, run around, gone whoring, everything you can think of, well, that's not the sort of thing you forget, and Papathanassis had fallen on his feet young, his old man and his brothers knew people in Piraeus and Salamis, they dealt in contraband, made pots of money... He spotted me one day hauling home an old, broken ice-box on a barrow that I'd got from a gypsy and he called out to me, 'Hey, pal, what kind of shit is that?' Well, I wasn't going to have him feeling sorry for me so I acted like everything was fine, I was doing all right, etc, etc, but of course he knew... 'I'll set you up in Piraeus,' he told me, 'managing a warehouse. You game? If you do it you'll get so much per month' (the amount took my breath away—it was real *money* in those days), 'but if they catch you then it's no names no pack drill, I never set eyes on you and you keep mum about us.' I didn't say anything, but I turned it this way and that in my mind, I lay awake several nights in a row, and the following week I went to my boss (I was working at an auto body shop at the time, cutting sheet metal) and I told him, 'You know what? I'm quitting, found myself another job'. He didn't say a word, what could he have said? He paid me a pittance for back-breaking work—anyone else would've walked out ages ago. I gave it out in the neighborhood that I'd found work with a shipping company (handling supplies, I said) and told my mother the same thing. And every day I'd take the train from Thissio down to Piraeus... near the area where we went a while ago, Hephaistos, remember?

The warehouse wasn't far off. It was an old soap-works which Iliaskos' bank had closed down—it got into debt, the bank foreclosed on it, it was shut up and left to rot. The Papathanassis family had secured the area, near St Haralambos, they cleaned up some of its rooms and used it to store contraband. Some of their stuff arrived by ship and was unloaded either surreptitiously or openly—they had bought off various customs officers—some of it came by cart from Elefsis, and some on caiques and barges from Salamis across the water. They handled guns, cigarettes and cigars, furs, salmon and caviar, cloth and spirits and wine—you name it, they dealt in it. It took quite a while cleaning up the soap-works: after all, you can't store furs and caviar in a place that stinks of rancid dregs and caustic potash and tar. We cleaned and we blocked up the holes in the walls and we even fixed up a door that from the outside looked rotten and ready to collapse if you kicked it, but on the inside was as good as armored. We didn't fear a police raid half as much as we feared the other scum from the port—don't go imagining they were organized gangs, they were just groups of shore-bound riff-raff, the sort of underworld the area's full of... So I entered that kingdom as its watchman and protector. And my salary was in accordance with the value of the goods I was guarding. My time there went well. No one squealed on us, there weren't any raids, neither by the police nor by anyone else. But in the meantime I'd met various people in Piraeus and since I was getting increasingly nervous about earning my money illicitly I made up my mind to go legal and went off to learn how to be a customs officer under Mr Paul—God rest his soul—Paul Bakas. I didn't part with my old pal from Thissio in anger though, I simply told him how things were, he understood ('you're not cut out for it') and let me go. When a little while later I heard that they'd been busted, it didn't occur to Haralambis—that's what Papathanassis is called—to think that I might have been the weak link in the chain, and of course I wasn't. His family, his three brothers and his father, are all royalists and right-wingers, in the old days they used to be supporters and party bosses of Kondylis and then of Metaxas. I knew they were armed and doing other kinds of dirty business, beating people up, terrorizing the refugees in their shanties and communists at demonstrations... They put up some candidates at the elections... you know, the usual sort of business... They did a whole lot of things. The family became the terror and scourge of Thissio. And what d'you suppose they are now? They've turned into an entire organization, a proper army!"

"I've heard of them," I said.

Mimis nodded.

"Everyone at Thissio knows them. And I've got a family to feed that I got landed with out of the blue, and there's not a thing I can do about it—they're my responsibility. I'm telling you all this because you've been like a brother to me—that's why you can come with me, we can go together and if I introduce you to Haralambis as a brother of mine you'll be able to buy something too, he'll see you right, I'm sure of it. The thing is... the thing is... *you* might be able to find something to buy somewhere else, but *I'm* on my beam end and haven't got anywhere else to go, so it isn't right or fitting... know what I mean? D'you get me?"

He stopped speaking and bowed his head. I waited. In the end he looked at me with a complaining expression and burst out, "I can't hide the communist woman and at the same time have dealings with Papathanassis... I'm saying this for her sake too. If something happened tomorrow and they caught her, she'd say I'm a police informer... And if he finds out I'm hiding her... if one of them should come around here and get a glimpse of her... I dunno. What d'you think, isn't it too risky?"

"Yes," I said, "it is. We'll have to find somewhere else for her, give me a day or two and I'll fix something. In any case her own lot are looking for places where they can hide. She might even be able to leave tomorrow."

He nodded, feeling calmer now that he'd managed to get out what was bothering him. And actually the idea of a visit to Thissio with him was very timely, the reason being that in my mind the thought that Konstantina would soon return home kept on going around and around, and she'd need to stay with me until her situation was sorted out. And I'd have another mouth to feed. This latter idea was the only sop to the guilt I felt about her...

On the following day, we set off at noon for Thissio.

It was raining with a fine drizzle that you could hardly see but that you could feel penetrating into your skin from everywhere, through your collar and your buttons, drenching and chilling you. As we turned the corner by the Grande Bretagne I was overcome by anxiety and began to limp so badly that my companion stopped to give me his arm. With my head bent and my eyes averted, my gaze fixed on the monument of the Unknown Soldier with the German guards in front of it as motionless as statues made of black stone, I hurried to get out of the square in order to cease having the hotel windows gazing down on my back.

Since the cutting wind was an icy blast as we came out of the square, Mimis proposed that we take a short cut through the narrow alleys behind Filellinon Street. Plaka was gasping in the chill like a patient in fitful sleep. There were few people about, the stores were closed, garbage and decay everywhere. In the better houses you could see lights turned on here and there, for it was as dark as late afternoon, but as we proceeded the houses grew dark and silent, the poor dwellings seemed empty and abandoned. Tiny, slim candles glowed in churches, then our route twisted and climbed; if it hadn't been for the Acropolis looming above, you could easily have lost all sense of direction. Finally we emerged onto Dionysiou Areopagitou Street, walked downhill beneath the northern flank of the Philopappos hill, and were soon in the narrow streets of the Thissio district.

The rain had brought to life the mud in the potholes

once more, you had to walk hugging the walls if you wanted to keep your soles out of the water. On some of the roofs chimney pots were belching smoke. We passed through a small square formed where three lanes met, with a eucalyptus tree in the middle on whose bark carved swastikas obliterated a hammer and sickle. Two hundred yards further on we reached the corner of a street with two-story houses, built more recently. Outside the door of one of them, a group of idlers, about ten in all, were watching us. Mimis made a sign and we slowed our pace.

"Here we are," he hissed. "Gently does it, let me do the talking."

I didn't at first understand why he said this. The idlers were idling, we were going to visit someone, what need was there for any talk with them? Then I realized that they formed an unofficial guard who wouldn't let us pass unless we presented our credentials. This was my friend's business, and he was doing it gravely in a low voice as if applying to the secretary of some Minister for an audience. One of the fellows—they were all young, hard-eyed men—got up and went up the steps to give notice of our presence. It was quite a while before he returned. I'd begun to think that we were going to leave empty-handed when an upstairs window opened and a fairish head looked out.

"E-e-e-e-e-p!"

"E-e-e-e-e-p!" replied Mimis and pushed me towards the steps.

The house smelled damp and there was fresh paint on

the walls. Through open doors you could see various strange types smoking or playing backgammon or cards. Someone was speaking on the telephone. In other rooms women were busy washing the floors or cooking and children's voices could be heard. The walls of a large room were decorated with transfers: idyllic gardens and moonlight over lakes. In one corner, rather like a shrine where icons are hung, I could make out photographs of Himmler, of the king and of Metaxas. In here the Occupation seemed not to exist—everywhere else, the photographs of King George and Metaxas had been removed from stores, public offices and police stations. Here they were still in place—the inhabitants of this house were obviously not afraid of a visit from the authorities. We were in a sort of command post, the seat of some organization, either official or unofficial but certainly not seeking to conceal itself.

Nevertheless it was also a home—and a large one. From some kitchen came the forgotten smell of frying. Mimis gave me a sharp dig in the ribs, smiling proudly like Moses when he led his people into the Promised Land.

On the upper floor we were greeted by a man of about Mimis' age, though better nourished, with sparse fair hair through which you could see his sunburnt, freckled scalp.

"How goes it, Haralambis, old pal?"

"Fighting… You tell me. How are you doing with the hunger?"

"The least said the better," Mimis told him. "This here

is my friend Angel, a private detective, he was born in America but came to live in Greece just before the war."

Papathanassis' expression altered as he ran his eyes over me, as if he was now putting me through a different sieve in order to form an opinion of me.

"Bitch of a life, isn't it?" he said to me.

I don't know why he said it. Maybe because I'd come from America, or maybe because he was aware that business was hardly flourishing for a private detective in Athens. I felt myself obliged to smile.

"Angel is like a brother to me, or better even! The other day when he got his hands on some cash he took me with him down to Piraeus to buy food—how can I put it, the lad's pure gold."

"D'you need anything, Boss?"

A swarthy face was stuck through the doorway and looked into the room. It belonged to a boy of at most seventeen, and either his mother or his father must have been black for there could be no other explanation for his color and his short, tightly-curled hair.

"I do. I need coffee. Three cups. You'll have some, won't you?" he asked us.

It must be rare to see two people answer with such an identical expression of total stupidity. And when the coffee arrived I felt a faintness that I hadn't experienced for ages: it was real coffee, not made of chick-peas but of genuine coffee beans from a coffee tree, properly roasted, crushed and ground and boiled with sugar (if only the lady of the house had put two or three more spoonfuls in!) which filled your nostrils, made your saliva flow and intoxicated you. Anyone hearing us sip it noisily and then groan "Aaaa," and "Aaaaaa" and "Aaaaaaah, dear God" would have imagined that in this cold room orgies of quite another kind were taking place. And when Papathanassis calmly opened a box of English cigars and offered them to us, then we went really crazy. We drank our coffee and smoked in silence, like lifers in prison receiving a visit.

"All right, tell me what you want," said the fair-haired man abruptly.

"Well, you see, Babis," Papachrysanthou explained, now smiling without cease, "it's like this. One of my relatives got into trouble… my cousin, they executed him… and you know me, he left a widow and orphans and a couple of old ladies, I'm the only male left in the family, I've taken them on, what could I do, I could hardly leave them to starve. If it were just me I'd have managed, I wouldn't have come. But when you've got five mouths to feed… I have to find something to put in their bellies, they'll die otherwise, it'd be a crying shame, wouldn't it? That's all there is to it, d'you get me, see what I mean? Five mouths. And me makes six."

"And seven with this handsome lad here?" Papathanassis asked nastily, pointing at me.

"No… what an idea! He's not involved. I told you, Angel's got some money, if there's anything available he'll buy it for himself, it's me who's in a difficult position, a wretched position, I simply don't know where to turn."

"Hmm," growled the other man. "And your late cousin, what was he? A commie?"

"Lord no! Just imagine, poor Theofrastos a commie! No, he was an old Venizelos man, a republican, a supporter of Papanastasiou… he was a patriot and a fine lad. Other people dragged him into it, the railway workers' gang…"

"They're all commies, every man jack of them. And what d'you suppose Papanastasiou was? A communist, that's what he was, without knowing it himself."

"Well, there you are… and from one moment to the next you find yourself in trouble, know what I mean?"

"I get you," said his old schoolmate.

"I can see you're doing pretty well in Thissio—coffee, cigarettes, all sorts of delicacies. I bet you have meat and butter too…"

"Steady on, Mimis pal, leave the meat and butter out of it. What d'you think we are here, the Grande Bretagne? You do find the odd thing, yes, but prices are sky-high, not everyone can afford them, right? You find small quantities. The militia manage better at the Makrygiannis Barracks, but they're a whole organization, not small fry like us… They get it from everyone, both from the Germans and Italians and from the English. That's a proper set-up for you! The Kommandatur sends them something every week from the supply truck. The English send something with one of our men, a Greek, someone you'd never even notice, an old white-haired man like a pensioner, every so often they send them gold sovereigns in a kit-bag. They do indeed. But we're not merchants, we're patriots, we're the only people left who think of our country first and only afterwards of our stomachs. The militia hunt down the commies because they want to show the Kommandatur they're doing something. We hunt 'em down because we don't want any of 'em here when the war ends. There's a difference. Anyhow, this neighborhood's quiet, you won't see any bullhorns or roadblocks or patrols around here, we do the job ourselves a whole lot better than the Germans ever could. What they do is kill at random, like animals. Whereas we know who needs to be got rid of and we get rid of them swift and clean—no roadblocks, no hoods, no firing squads, no fuss and bother… Bang bang in the street and there you are."

He talked as if someone had wound up a clockwork mechanism in him. Mimis' old school friend didn't seem to be a man of many words, in fact he'd probably said to us all in one go more than he usually said in a week—maybe it was for Mimis' sake, having not seen him for such a long time. Something in his tirade seemed to be borrowed from the words of someone else, or perhaps from a printed pamphlet, if such things were in circulation in the city.

"I dunno," said my friend uncertainly. "Maybe that's the way it is… What can I say? At any rate the Germans shot my cousin, and the man was an old syndicalist, a quiet family man who never bothered a soul."

"EAM does the damage and everyone who's simply minding his own business gets into trouble," said

Papathanassis darkly. "Every day the people who pay at the roadblocks are the ordinary folk who get put in front of a firing squad."

Mimis was bright red, shaking his head every so often as if having second thoughts, agreeing with everything instantly and looking the other man in the eyes as he spoke.

"The men down there outside the front door," said I suddenly, "don't look to me much like people who mind their own business and don't want trouble, like decent householders, let's say…"

The fair-haired man looked at me as if all this time he'd forgotten my presence. Then he laughed. "To every job its own apprentices," he said.

I didn't understand him and didn't try to understand right then. Papachrysanthou was staring at me wide-eyed like someone trying to keep his balance on a train rail. I preferred to keep my mouth shut and wait to see how our visit would end. I didn't want to spoil his business for him.

"I'll tell you where to go to find food, a few dried beans, maybe a little oil, I don't know. But if he's got anything, he'll let you have it."

He opened the window and shouted. Within moments the young man with the dark skin was standing in the doorway, a pistol in his hand.

"Put that away," said our host. "You'll take them to Bakopoulos' place—from me, whatever they want."

"Right you are," replied the boy and stood up straight as if coming to attention while receiving his orders.

In the midst of all the embracings and back-slappings of our farewells, briefer though than when we arrived, Papathanassis' voice rang out, hoarse and threatening.

"What d'you think you were doing, pal, coming and play-acting here? I know you inside out, I know your ideas, you've been a leftie and all that rubbish ever since you were a kid! How come now all of a sudden you think everything I say is so fucking marvelous? Don't let me ever see your face again, you hear me? Not unless you've got any useful information for me."

34

Beneath the Acropolis

An even greater surprise was awaiting us at Bakopoulos' place.

The black kid took us without speaking to a building three streets away, placed two fingers in his mouth and whistled as if giving a password. The door was opened and we found ourselves in a little room full of the tools of a shoemaker's trade: leather, glue, cutting tools, nails and lasts. For Bakopoulos was not a grocer but a shoemaker. In the back room, behind a grey calico curtain, sat three men playing cards and smoking—three mouthpieces in a hookah and a rather unusual smell in the atmosphere. Our guide put his mouth to the black marketeer's ear and began to tell him something, while at the same time the man gestured us to enter his sanctum.

Among the three card-players a white head instantly stood out, and a pair of bright blue eyes, and a double chin improbable for the times bulging over a buttoned-up shirt collar, all of them belonging to a man wearing his greatcoat and sprawling on a chair. At his feet a dog watched us, ready to obey his master's commands. And while the other two men had the air of people whose entertainment is being interrupted, the white-haired old man gave me a wry smile showing his regular teeth that looked false and put down his cards on the table in a decisive movement. Papathanassis' words about the English sovereigns sent to the right-wing militia were still ringing in my ears… It was suddenly as if a light had illuminated things… or as if they were plunged into even deeper darkness. So, the great tragic actor!

"You here?" I said, gaping at him.

"You here?" he replied with an unpleasant smile.

"Bah, do you know each other?" exclaimed the shoemaker.

"Indeed we do."

"Hurry up, Pipis" (Pipis was Bakopoulos), "I'm not leaving tonight till I've recouped some of my losses…" said the third man in the company.

The shoemaker removed the cloths that had been thrown over various crates and baskets and showed them to Mimis, who since he hadn't recognized anyone present had his mind entirely on his shopping.

"I see you're in a hurry to spend your fee," said the old man.

"I was not aware that I'd received my fee, this is the first I've heard of it. I've been looking for you," I answered.

"And you have found me. To him that seeks…"

"Not so. It's rare that someone manages to find you," I interrupted.

"It depends…"

"…On where he looks for you—is that it?"

"Precisely, my friend. What are you doing here?"

"How about you? What are you doing here? A few days ago I ran into you in completely different circumstances. I must say…"

"You are easily impressed," he said. "When you reach my age you'll see that human beings have many aspects and lead many lives—and I have friends and acquaintances everywhere, as I have told you."

"So I see. One moment though…"

I left him and went over to Papachrysanthou who was picking out a bag of beans, some dry biscuit and some soap—he was responsible for a family now and was making his purchases accordingly. I contented myself with some broad beans the man had, dry and yellowed with age. I never used to eat broad beans but the time had come when one had to learn to eat everything. I paid Bakopoulos on the spot while Mimis got whatever he wanted free, a gift from his old school friend—this must have been among the things that the kid had whispered in the shoemaker's ear. And the shoemaker simply made a note on a folded piece of paper that he took out of his pocket and then immediately replaced in it.

"Is it the time—and the proper place—for me to tell you about your affairs?" I asked the old man rudely, as he continued to look at me with the same half-smile.

"If you have anything to tell me, then yes," he replied.

"I am not sure that we're in the right place to talk about your protégé…" I said.

My mind was racing at a thousand miles an hour as I tried to understand whether here was where his base was, and he simply went for strolls around the center of town and Kolonaki. Whether he might be Papathanassis' man or Papathanassis his. Whether his grand plans included Papathanassis and his armed thugs. Whether he was laying a trap for Beratis or whether, on the contrary, the nationalists who hung out in Thissio were being used, without their knowledge, in his scheme to save my musician while at the same time their mouths were being stopped by the Allies' sovereigns.

I'd known other people like him in New York. People whom you couldn't easily place in a single category, half outlaw, half police informer, no one thing entirely but a little of everything. Was the Big Boss something similar? And how did he get his hands on the English sovereigns? I was beginning to smell quite a few rats: until then, in the center of the city which I mainly frequented, the reputation of the Thissio area had struck me as exaggerated, as a myth of the kind grown-ups recount to scare children—a sort of bogeyman for anyone who might be thinking of carrying out subversive and illicit acts, which actually was the easiest thing possible in those days since everything was prohibited and the only thing permitted was to obey orders.

Now, seeing Thissio from close up and smelling the

indistinct odor of blood that it gave off, I realized that a couple of streets away from the law-abiding center of Athens, with its established routine order of a city under foreign occupation, its blackouts, its curfews and its hunger, there was an incredible *cour des miracles* with quite another order of its own and with different rhythms, a part of Athens under the rule of home-bred rather than German or Italian occupiers, where people like Papathanassis and the royalist militia in their barracks beneath the Acropolis controlled everything.

To be there, like us, because you had an old school friend from whom you hoped for a favor was one thing; to be there playing cards as if in your own home, with Azor lying at your feet, in the company of a black marketeer of a shoemaker and his colleagues, a mere three blocks from Papathanassis' house and another three blocks from the Makrygiannis Barracks—well, this couldn't be either coincidence or chance.

"I think we have completed our business, you and I," I said coldly. "How much money have you left for me?"

"I have left it in the hands of a trustworthy and respectable person, the pharmacist Yannakopoulos, opposite your office. It's a small and heavy packet…"

"And what does it contain? Another one of your powders?"

"No, the money that I told you I would give you if you brought the work I entrusted to you to a successful conclusion."

"And have I brought it to a successful conclusion?"

"Have you not concluded it?"

I looked at him. The old man was as impenetrable as a brick wall. I could see right through Mimis (and it was a sad sight that day). But with the old man I couldn't.

"Yes, I imagine that I've completed the work. Your protégé is now safe…"

"So I hear," he said, half-closing his eyes. "We shall see."

"I suppose I must believe you, and since there's no likelihood of me ever discovering where you live to ask you to make up the shortfall if the sum of money is not correct, I must trust your word. You have settled my account."

"I have settled your account."

"A hundred?"

"A hundred."

Humans can't let things rest sometimes, can't leave things to fall into place by themselves. Something was irking me: it might have been my reaction to the fact that I'd never before had a client who wasn't in my power or who didn't become so during the course of our association. That was probably it. For, instead of simply pulling myself together and telling Papachrysanthou that it was time for us to be going, I said in a loud voice, "Do your fellow card-players here know that you carry English sovereigns around as casually as if they were raisins?"

Everyone looked up in surprise.

"Ah, my boy, you are trespassing beyond the limits," said the old man, and for the first time I thought I'd managed to make him angry. "You don't know what you're talking about, do you?"

"Don't I?"

He must have made an invisible movement and prodded the dog, for it immediately stood up and bared its teeth. Lightning flashed from the Big Boss's blue eyes.

"Big words won't get you very far, Mr Sotiriou," he shouted in rage. "You have no sense of measure and you have no professional conscience. But we have finished, you and I, and I have no further need of you, you understand. It may be that you will meet with some accident—I wash my hands of you."

And by letting go of the leash which until then he had been holding under the table, it was as if he was ordering the dog to attack me; it was already foaming at the mouth and wild, brought to a fury by the sound of its master's shouts.

Mimis, seeing that things suddenly looked dangerous, grabbed me by the arm with the hand that was not holding his shopping and dragged me with him as he retreated to the door of the shoemaker's shop. Behind us we could hear the frenzied barking of Azor.

When I got home a pleasant surprise awaited me. Konstantina had returned and had set to work, washing the floors of the hall, the passage and the kitchen with whatever she'd found to hand. I caught my breath. Rapid thoughts flashed through my head... calculations... What had happened with Bodo? Had he dismissed her? Had she run away? Or was it that the opening night of the performance was drawing near and the musician needed his mind in its proper place in order to carry his great task to completion? And how come the girl had come straight to my apartment?

"Ah!" (A huge smile, her eyes wide with joy at seeing me.)

"You've come back!"

She nodded, then immediately her smile faded.

"Do you want me to stay?"

"Yes, stay."

She let go of the floor-cloth and leaned on the arm of the armchair. Then covered her face with her hands. She was crying now. Ach, and I who had thought…

"What is it? Come."

Her shoulders shook with sobs.

"What happened, what did they do to you? Did anyone bother you? Did he bother you?"

She nodded again.

"He did bother me, of course he did. But you knew that he'd bother me and now you don't want me here any more, I'm… I've turned into a slut…"

"No, you're the very best girl I know, what are you talking about, I mean it!"

She looked at me distrustfully and then smiled again.

"Do you know what I had to eat there, Mr Angel? You couldn't even begin to imagine. There was absolutely everything and Mr Bodo had whatever I wanted brought to me…"

"That's good."

"I'm still not hungry again! I stuffed myself. Every so often…" (she laughed out loud) "I said to him '*Essen*' and he rang a bell and Loukas came and asked 'What is it you want now?' and Mr Bodo waited and he wasn't angry, he watched me eating and he smiled… he's a good man, even if he did do what he did to me."

"I knew that when I took you there… You have to be on good terms with the Germans, then you're not in danger. And you learned some German. Does '*Essen*' mean food?"

"Yes, it means to eat… And as soon as I said it he rang the bell. And the food was brought upstairs on a covered trolley with little wheels, and you should have seen the silver knives and forks!"

"And he sat and watched you?"

"Yes. He liked to watch me eat. He was quiet. And when I told him that I wanted to leave, to go home, he let me go. He's a kind man."

"Well, he's an artist, a musician…"

"It doesn't matter that I told you, does it?" (I shook my head.) "Only there's one thing I don't understand… most of the time he talked on the telephone and then went straight to sleep. He wanted me to be in his bed all the time and to look at me… just like you… like it was the day before yesterday, after I had a bath…"

"Yes. I imagine that the maestro suffers from the same sickness as me—in his case as a result of age."

I hadn't told my story to Konstantina, I'd only spoken of a sickness and she appeared to understand. Maybe she didn't care."

A little while later she asked me if I had news of Mrs Marika and Mr Pavlos. I told her they were both safe and remembered my promise to Mimis, not yet fulfilled, to move Marika from his house and hide her somewhere else. However, at the moment I still didn't have a clue where I could take Mrs Kanellis to hide.

35

Other unexpected events

Mr Agathos' little package was waiting for me at Yannakopoulos' pharmacy. Thanassis, his assistant dispenser, handed it to me and wished me godspeed as I left. I went straight to my office, counted the coins and stowed them safely away under the floorboard. It was the right amount; he hadn't cheated me. I could now consider myself rich—I could do something with this money, when the war finally ended I could even return to New York, if of course it was safe to do so. After America entered the war in '41 no news from over there ever reached us: I was longing to get my hands on the *Herald*, which often ran articles about the various gangs and their gang warfare. A photograph of Jos in his favorite Italian restaurant riddled with bullets from his rivals' machine guns would for me have been the equivalent of an announcement that the war had ended.

But although this actually was the way things happened,

it was to be years before I learned of it. And by then I was no longer interested in going back to New York. My links to the place were severed when Lamera died, which wasn't long in occurring, while the bonds linking me to Athens were growing ever stronger, as tends to be the case with places and friends with whom you've shared adventures.

While I was gazing out of my office window at the gentle slope of Fidiou Street and at the sparse passers-by, I heard the door opening. I turned around and saw an unknown woman standing there and looking at me. Unknown? No, not really. Because as I took a closer look at her I recognized the tall, black-clad woman who'd once visited me, who'd promised so long ago to come again soon. It was her blue eyes and her snaggle tooth that jogged my memory.

"What are you doing here?"

"I told you I'd be back, I don't forget good friends."

"I don't forget friends either. But I thought you'd have remembered from last time… I can't make use of your services."

She looked at me and shook her head.

"You're not telling the truth, I know that, but you're a decent guy all the same. If only there were more like you."

"I'm not sure about that… But maybe if there were, then we wouldn't have wars like this."

"Help me," she said, and moved extremely close to me. "I beg you to help. They'll get their hands on my house, I need a loan. Don't you know anyone who could lend me twenty-five sovereigns? Fifty's what I really need, but that's a huge sum, I'll have to get it bit by bit. Don't you know anyone? Or do you have any money you could lend me?"

"What d'you imagine I am?" I asked hoarsely.

For was it not a curious coincidence? I'd just hidden away my treasure under the floorboard. Could she have been spying on me from somewhere? Not so very long ago she'd been more than happy to pocket my Occupation drachmas—yet during the time we spent in the shabby armchair she could easily have been casting an eye around the office, noting where the cupboard was, where the shelves were, where the drawers were.

"Must be a pretty big house if you need fifty sovereigns."

"It's a house and a hectare of land in Maroussi," she explained. "We were in difficulties, my mother took out a loan against the house so that we wouldn't die of hunger. Now I'm moving heaven and earth to find the means to pay back the moneylender so he won't take the house."

"I don't want to offend you, but to get fifty sovereigns with the merchandise you've got to offer you'd need twenty tits, not two. And that's putting it mildly."

Suddenly she seemed keyed up, as if my words had excited her. She rubbed up against me and I felt her breath on my neck.

"Listen," she said, "let me take care of you the way I know how, I'll come every day and if within a week I haven't resurrected you from the dead, then my name's not Ismene."

"Ismene… that's a pretty name," I said foolishly.

"Ismene Agathos… You need to know who you're entrusting your treasure to," she murmured. I started and gripped her hands.

"What's that you said? Agathos?"

Her blue eyes glinted as she nodded a friendly assent, her lips parting to reveal her teeth.

"Aren't we friends anymore, Angel?" she asked, as if slightly put out.

"Look here, it's too much, don't you think so? Are you in any way related to Panos Agathos?"

"Never heard of him," she answered with a light laugh.

Her laugh failed to convince me. I took a closer look at her eyes—their color wasn't one you come across very often, in either men or women. A coincidence like this, both the eyes and the name… And her boldness in coming to ask me to lend her sovereigns… Damn it all, I might have long since lost my nose for the job, but this particular business stank to high heaven.

"Got an identity card?" I asked her.

"An identity card?"

"Yes, an identity card. You come asking me for a loan, how am I supposed to know who you are? I've only met you once before and we didn't exactly exchange names and addresses. You're selling me this story about a house and a hectare of land in Maroussi—and just because we once had a grope in an armchair I'm meant to lend you money? And not just money but sovereigns into the bargain?"

"I'll put half of it into your name. We'll go to a notary. You can have half a hectare and half the house. I've got power of attorney to…"

"You're out of your mind."

"My word of honor."

"Are you crazy?"

"No, just desperate, can't you see?" Then, changing tone, "What are you standing there like that for and not making use of me? Tell me lies, take whatever you want from me, cheat me, hit me, throw me out—what sort of a man are you, haven't you got a single bone in your whole body?"

"They're all cracked."

She reached up and unbuttoned her blouse, then pushed me back into the armchair.

"Not for money," she said, "not for anything, just come like last time. Shut your eyes and imagine you're with the woman you wish you were with, imagine you've got her here, ready and willing and begging you for it… come."

I must have closed my eyes as she instructed: it was better that way, easier when my eyes were shut to imagine Konstantina or Marika—or even Lauretta, whose face and smell I was finding it harder and harder to recall.

When the storm abated—mine rapidly and hers more slowly—I realized that the only way of getting rid of her and her strange proposal that I lend her twenty-five sovereigns (or fifty?) would be to lock up the office and leave, each of us going his or her own way. Thus, my thoughts a jumbled disorder, limping abominably again, I prepared to make my way up Fidiou Street, throwing an abrupt goodbye in her direction.

However, Ismene Agathos (who bore no relation whatsoever to my client—she herself had declared this unequivocally) continued to walk along beside me. When I asked where she was heading for, she replied that she was living at the top of Solonos Street at her brother's place. In that case, I said, I'd accompany her to the next corner, then I'd be turning off onto Gennadiou Street. Where did I live? A little further up… (it occurred to me to use Papachrysanthou's house as an alibi).

I was already beginning to make plans, for I could see that it wasn't going to be easy to get her off my back, when we were obliged to stop short and wait on the sidewalk at the corner of Gennadiou Street as a Mercedes with a German number plate swept pass at speed. It was shiny and powerful, the red flag fluttering on its right wing and its polished chrome reflecting the sky; it braked sharply at the corner and the driver turned the wheel hard left to turn onto Fidiou Street.

At the gate of the German Archaeological Mission the guard and various men in civilian clothes came running out ready to open the car doors. A rapid glance was enough to show me, inside the car, that well-known head with its halo of hair around the funny little bald patch and the cold-fish expression belonging to the great Mr F. My heart lurched. I averted my face and was preparing to continue on my way, when the brakes were jammed on and through the rear window Bodo's marrow-like head emerged, calling: "*Kyrie Angelus!*"

Jesus Christ, *Kyrie Angelus* indeed! Where on earth had the old bastard picked that up from? It's true that his memory had astounded me when he'd recalled having spotted me among the members of the orchestra. Assuredly my face wasn't going to escape him—our last meeting had been all too recent. But my name?

I stopped, swallowed hard and thought of pretending not to have heard him, but just at that moment the non-commissioned officer who was driving opened the door and got out, signing me to approach.

The maestro was all smiles.

"How are you?" he asked me in flawless English.

"Very well, and you?"

"I invite you and your companion to lunch, it's sudden, I know, but I feel under some obligation to you… And there are various matters about which I'd like us to talk… If it is not too much trouble, naturally, and if it doesn't disrupt your plans… or the lady's…"

At that point I realized that Ismene Agathos was still standing beside me, listening, her gaze insistently fixed on me.

"I am on my way to lunch with Professor Doelger at Faliron, why not join us? We'd bring you back to town afterwards, naturally. Will you come?"

Although I'd received my fee, I still felt responsible for my musician's fate: it would have been idiotic not to have seized such an opportunity. I was desperately trying to get rid of my black-clad visitor—and what could be a better way than a lunch engagement at Faliron?

I turned to her: "Good afternoon to you," I said.

But Bodo had other plans. Perhaps if he hadn't spotted the woman at my side his invitation would not have been forthcoming. His memories of that exquisite example of Greek beauty whom I'd brought to his hotel were vivid—Konstantina had reported, secretly flattered, how much he'd liked her. And Ismene Agathos, looked at objectively, was also not far from the classical ideal. I was definitely a man who escorted magnificent examples of Greek womanhood; and an outsider always values acquaintances of this kind in the places to which fate has brought him.

"As a matter of fact," I told him, "the lady is not actually with me, she'd simply come to my office and I am accompanying her a short distance—she has to go home."

"Your office? I thought you were a musician," the great conductor remarked sternly.

"Yes, yes, yes, of course I am. But no one can make a living from music these days, I'm obliged to… you understand."

"No, but you will explain it to me," he said. "And the lady? Would she not like to accompany us to Faliron for lunch?" he continued, directing these words towards her and now miming someone traveling for a short while then sitting down to eat.

"*Avec plaisir*," said Ismene at my side, and the maestro's face lit up.

"Ah, *une dame qui parle français*," he said.

It appeared that this language—which unfortunately was just as unknown to me as his own—didn't irk him as much as English. Apart from being the language of civilization, French was also the language of Vichy France.

36
─────

At Faliron

Enthroned in the back seat of the Mercedes, Ismene Agathos in the middle with the maestro and me on either side of her, and Professor Doelger in front beside the driver, we drove down to Faliron more or less in silence. For apart from "*avec plaisir,*" my black-clad Visitor (this is what I'd decided to call her, by analogy with Visiting Nurses) didn't know any French. But this didn't diminish Bodo's enthusiasm, and he was continuing to speak in this language with, as far as I could judge, an excellent accent.

As we were getting out of the car, I found the opportunity to mutter to her hurriedly, "If you play your cards cleverly, you may be able to get your loan."

"Looks like it," replied the Visitor cheerfully. "But if I do get the loan you'll lose me as a client. Would that be in your best interests?"

"I don't have such a great need of clients."

We'd stopped outside a fish taverna by the beach and

the two Germans (the driver was on duty and so didn't have the right to enjoy himself like us) were exclaiming in delight at the fresh sea air. The grand old villas stretched away along the shore behind the narrow dirt road and the lofty trees quietly hummed springtime melodies. The sea was translucent, the sand white and the scattered pebbles glowed like precious gems.

"I had to come to Greece sooner or later," sighed the maestro, "and this was my best opportunity to do so. I worship your country."

We found a table by the window. All around us German officers were lunching in the company of beautiful women: the sound of low-voiced conversation, the chinking of cutlery and glasses, from time to time a woman's laughter.

"Those women are doing well for themselves," Ismene murmured in my ear.

"And those men are doing even better," I replied. "Look, even if you hear odd things, don't get mixed up in my conversation with the German. The danger's great…"

She raised her eyebrows dismissively and turned away. Bodo placed her next to him, with me and Professor Doelger on the other side of the table, while the driver, having instructed the taverna-keeper to serve us at the double, clicked his heels and told his two important passengers that he'd be in the car if they needed him.

"*Kyrie Angelus*," said Bodo again in his bastard Greek, then continued in English. "From what I understand, you must be a reserve player in the orchestra. What instrument do you play?"

I knew instantly that I shouldn't disillusion him, and in any case I had to repair the damage done by my thoughtless reference to 'my office'.

"As the Angel that I am, I play the harp," I answered.

"The harp, eh?"

He didn't show any surprise, in spite of the fact that I knew the harp is always played by women in orchestras.

"I had a male harpist in Berlin too. I don't want women in the orchestra. If they're good-looking they distract my musicians, and if they're not then they bother me!" (He gave a loud laugh.) "So it was you who played that wonderful solo on the night of the Mascagni?"

I hadn't a clue what he was talking about but I nodded my head affirmatively.

"If I'd known I would have asked for you for my performance. Your harpist is half-deaf and has no tempo, she is ruining the finale of the *Rheingold* for me."

"Indeed," I said. "As I told you, I'm a reserve player. And I have another job. My father had a business, a driving school, and I run it now—one has to do something to earn a living, the times are hard."

"You're friends with Miltos Beratis."

This wasn't a question. If one could judge by his memory for faces, the fact that I'd been sitting with my musician throughout the entire evening of that dinner at the Mission certainly can't have escaped his fishy gaze.

"Great friends."

"So what does he tell you?" (His eyes were focused on some German officers who were paying their bill and preparing to leave.)

"What does he tell me?"

"About our work, about the performance we are rehearsing."

"Oh, that! What should he tell me? He's enthusiastic about it."

His gaze now focused sternly on my face. Without him saying anything, I understood that he didn't want random answers and that the subject mattered to him.

"He's enthusiastic," I repeated. "He considers you the greatest musician of the century, didn't you know?"

He didn't reply at once. Then he said wryly, "And I consider him the worst composer of the century. What say you, is there a worse one?"

"Not that I can think of," I told him. "There might be, I suppose. You're better qualified to judge."

"We are speaking freely, we are sitting at table and there is no need to be afraid. If you have an opinion that differs from mine, you may express it."

"I'm not afraid," I declared. "But I don't consider that I'm qualified to judge just because I play an instrument a little."

"Ah yes! You should tell that to your colleagues, both here and in Germany, who consider themselves consummate music critics just because they scrape on a fiddle or blow through a reed with holes in it. Ha ha ha! At long last someone with a bit of sense!"

This latter remark was addressed to Doelger, who murmured some reply as he chewed his food.

In the meanwhile the taverna-keeper had placed before us a veritable treasure of seafood and fish, fried potatoes and real bread and wine—and it was no easy matter to take your attention from this food and listen to what others were saying. The Visitor had plunged into her food and was emitting little moans as she ate, as if making love; her lips glistened with grease. But the maestro had other cares on his mind: food came second.

"I have come to this country on a mission," Bodo declared. "I don't know if you understand me. There is a cultural heritage which I am fighting to preserve in the midst of the war. Many have criticized me for this. Yet some people, who understand, admire me for my struggle. Art is greater than politics, *Kyrie Angelus*. Politicians come and go, art remains. And the art of Germany is the most important art in Europe and in the world, it will remain long after Hitler and his heirs have vanished. I am aware that it is not so very well-known in Greece—even though it arose from your own classical art and from the aesthetics of your great philosophers, even though it is a continuation of them, it is nevertheless unknown and misinterpreted. People consider it grave and somber—but the art of ancient Greece is equally grave and somber. If I hadn't come here to put on the *Rheingold*, who would have? Who would have thrown the bridge of music between our two peoples? What our soldiers are attempting to do with weapons, because they are challenged by the backward-looking Allies who do not want to see Germany ever raise her head again, we artists will achieve in a more stable and lasting manner. Do you understand what I'm saying? Europe will be united one day, by its culture—and its culture will be basically ours and yours. People like your friend Miltos don't understand this at all, they seek to promote an art which places emphasis on dissonance and disorder and subversion. But there is no art that can be made from such materials. Do those who are fighting against us not realize that they are playing the game of Whitehall and the Elysée, the game of the Americans and of European imperialism, of the powers that rule the world, that overthrew Napoleon and resisted the unification of Germany under the Second Reich, and that now resist the Third Reich? Yet this third attempt of theirs is doomed to failure, and they know it. They've even formed an alliance with the Bolsheviks. They may now applaud the surrender of von Paulus to the Soviets, but before too long they'll have to swallow their joy, for the Bolsheviks are something alien and hostile to Europe and its culture. One day Europe will be united under the leadership of Germany, this much is certain. And the English entered the war to prevent the unification of Europe yet one more time—they had no other reason, they acted just as they have always done… And Europe is European culture."

He fell silent as abruptly as he had begun speaking. The light in his eyes went out and he looked down at his plate, on which a half-eaten dorade, its bones laid bare, with the various ruined fragments of potatoes and onions surrounding it gave the impression of a battlefield.

"Sacrifices have to be made, unfortunately, blood has to be shed. Nothing new can be born without the spilling of blood," Bodo went on, while Professor Doelger nodded. "Each of us must play his own role in his own field. Miltos came to Germany and studied music, yet he was a foreigner and it is hard for a foreigner to imbibe a different culture. He understood nothing save that a system exists which must collapse—and he found it easy to join the ranks of those determined to demolish a culture of which he was ignorant. One could perhaps claim that discussion and argument are sufficient for matters of this kind. But we are in the midst of a war and must fight with whatever weapons we possess. Miltos knows I have no love for him… And I don't believe he admires me, as you say he does."

"I know he admires you, for he's told me so," I insisted, made dizzy by all this philosophy and glad at last to hear words I could understand. "I'm perfectly sure of it."

"I dare say it's not impossible," he mused. "Human beings are contradictory creatures—at bottom we often love our worst enemies and on the contrary hate the people we think we love. Well, so be it…"

He didn't seem disposed to continue speaking of his theory of art and a united Europe, and devoted himself to his food like the rest of us.

"But to come to you," he said, finishing his plate and

draining his glass of wine. "How is your driving school doing?"

"Barely surviving," I replied. "Who wants to learn to drive these days, Maestro? There aren't any cars, there isn't any gas, everyone is simply trying to find something to eat."

"Yes, I gather there's a great problem with food supplies for the population."

"I doubt if you realize how great it is."

"I can certainly see how our lovely guest is eating, she has hardly raised her head once from her plate, she's devouring her food like a starving kitten. Tell me, *Kyrie Angelus*, is the young woman to whom you introduced me a few days ago a relative of yours?"

"Yes, she's my cousin."

"And this lady?"

"Another cousin."

Bodo laughed. "Then I must congratulate you on your family, you are handsome representatives of Greek beauty. I'd go as far as to say that the eyes of the lady who is with us today are even more attractive than those of your younger cousin. Is she married?"

"Ah no," I said, "she's a widow, poor girl."

"A widow! My condolences. Did she lose her husband in the war?"

"No," I answered, gaining in boldness since Ismene didn't understand a word of the English we were speaking—nor would I have cared so very much if she had understood. "They caught him in a roadblock and executed him in reprisal for some slogans written on a wall."

"There are times when I fail to understand our soldiers," the great conductor said to Doelger.

"War is war, Bodo," the other replied in English, then went on to add something in their own language which I couldn't understand.

"And is she facing difficulties in life, your poor cousin?"

"Huge difficulties. She came to my office today to ask if I could lend her some money to save her house from being taken from her. But of course I don't have the amount she needs. To be accurate, I haven't got a *sou*."

Bodo rested his elbows on the table and intertwined his fingers, shaking his head all the while as if saying what a pity it was.

"A beautiful woman like that must find it even harder to defend herself," he concluded, eyeing her interrogatively.

Ismene Agathos understood that we were talking about her and looked up from her plate, which she'd seemed to be on the point of licking.

"Very hard indeed. Do you think, Maestro, that you might see your way to doing something for her?"

"If she will allow me, with great pleasure," the conductor replied.

"I think she will have great pleasure in allowing you," I responded promptly. "The maestro is interested in your case," I told her in Greek. "What do you say, are you game for a few visits to the Grande Bretagne?"

We returned to Athens in the early afternoon. Between Bodo and Ismene Agathos a mute understanding had been reached which needed no interpreter. The maestro had taken a liking to me. Perhaps because I'd listened to his lecture on German music and the unification of Europe through culture—it often happens that we take a liking more easily to those to whom we've opened our hearts than to those who've opened their hearts to us. Outside the taverna some skeletal dogs were waiting to fall on the leftovers thrown away: their bones almost jutted through their hides—they'd probably only escaped being eaten since there was no meat on them worth eating. Some equally wretched two-legged creatures were there too: the brotherhood of peoples brought about through music and art probably didn't mean much to them.

My gain would be twofold: I'd be able to reassure Miltos Beratis that Mr F. no longer intended to denounce him to the Kommandatur. And the Visitor might stop visiting me and asking me to lend her her namesake's sovereigns.

37

Dress rehearsal

Marika Kanellis had left Zoodochou Pigis Street of her own accord. When I went over there to see her the following afternoon, Papachrysanthou's flat was empty and silent, as if it had accepted this state of affairs. Its owner was now sleeping at the widow Moltsas' home and its most recent guest had flown the nest; at some point a new tenant would appear and set up house there, in even more reduced circumstances than his predecessors.

Beratis might be able to fill me in on a few more details. Thus I needed to catch him somewhere between the theater and Zosimadon Street.

The north wind had begun to blow more strongly. The weak February sun failed to warm the sidewalks. From time to time various unknown passers-by attracted my attention. It was as if I were two people. One of them was still in New York where nothing ever attracted your attention on the street—everyone would be hurrying about their business and everyone looked more or less the way you'd got used to seeing them. The other self was someone who had awoken in a different place and time, where the appearance of the people all around you was constantly changing in odd ways.

It wasn't only that you saw rich clothes and poor clothes, which in any case was equally true before the war. It wasn't only that people's clothes were threadbare and shabby, as they were in the first year of the Occupation. It was that now the clothes you saw all around you had become part of an unbelievably imaginative stage set: any bits that were lacking or worn out were replaced by home-made improvisations fabricated from ill-assorted materials—cardboard from cigarette packets in shoes, string in place of missing buttons, strips of cloth as a substitute for belts. You'd even hear of lots of people who'd cooked all the leather that they owned. Shoe soup and belts in sauce: new dishes to be served. And a boundless appetite for any kind of novelty.

I'd stopped and was looking at the strange hat worn by a tall hunched man on the opposite pavement with his collar turned up. It had once been an ordinary fedora but the crown had been cut out and replaced by something metal, something that resembled the bottom of a tin plate.

Right behind the man with the anti-aircraft hat I spotted Beratis walking, the holes in his shoes patched with cardboard (his good pair he wore only when he was going to play). I watched him go into a watch store, not much more than a hole in the wall, which appeared to be closed. When he emerged he saw me outside the door. Encounters on the street had taken on a different quality these days: you were glad to see that the other person was still alive and about. It had become an everyday habit to ask when someone spoke of a third person, "Has he died?"

Beratis was shivering with cold so violently that I suggested he come to my place, as being nearer than his.

We ran up the stairs to warm up a bit; as I put my key in the lock, I called to Konstantina.

"What have we got to eat?" I asked.

"What did you bring?"

"This gentleman," and I nodded towards Beratis who was staring at her like a half-wit.

"But isn't this the girl who used to…?"

"Yes, the girl from *upstairs*."

"What's she doing here?"

"Whatever she used to do upstairs when her employers were there."

He sat down in the one good armchair in my living-room.

"Bring something, whatever we've got," I told Konstantina.

Today's menu consisted of five almonds, a dry biscuit with a little jam spread on it and a handful of raisins.

"Marika left," Beratis told me before I asked. "She's gone to some friends of hers in Kolonaki—the sort of house that's unlikely to be searched…" (he winked). "Pavlos has also moved, he's hiding in Koukaki."

"In Koukaki!" I exclaimed. "Right next door to the right-wing militia?"

He looked at me uncertainly.

"I was in the Thissio area recently."

"Bah, don't worry about it. An acquaintance of mine was in hiding for three weeks in the heart of the Thissio area, a mere couple of yards away from the Makrygiannis Barracks. Sometimes the best place to hide is right next door to the hornets' nest."

However, he announced, there was other, more pleasant news. The maestro seemed to have forgotten about him and no longer showed any interest in him. He barely spoke to him. And once, as he stood on the rostrum, he'd even looked at him and given a smile!

"I don't know what happened about that business," my musician said, "but it looks as if it got sorted out in one way or another."

"Of course it got sorted out," I said. "Didn't I say I'd come up with something?"

With Konstantina in the house I didn't feel like telling him the whole truth. In any case, it was hardly necessary. The job had been done, the maestro had clearly been pleased.

"I found him someone," I said vaguely.

He went on staring at me. Who, he insisted on knowing.

"Go on."

"Someone. You don't know her. She came to my office

asking for a loan. It was probably a man she was looking for."

He swallowed the last raisins. His pale face was flushed. He looked me in the eyes, waiting for me to come out with all the things I hadn't said, as if what he'd just heard wasn't adequate.

"Who did you send? Tell me who."

"Someone you don't know. A stranger."

"You're lying," he said abruptly.

"What makes you think so?"

"I just know. You're lying."

It wasn't reasonable, I pointed out, why should I lie to him?

"You told Marika about it," he said softly, so that Konstantina wouldn't hear her name.

"I told her, yes. Shouldn't she have known?"

"You asked *her* to go, you bastard," he blurted out, in a louder voice now.

He was blinking rapidly and his mouth was distorted with anger.

"Is that what she said?" I asked calmly. "And what else did she tell you? That she agreed to go?"

He jumped up.

"You had no right! It was a foul thing to do! You didn't have any right to do it. I didn't ask you... I didn't ask you if you could... you offered to find someone of your own accord. How dare you do that?"

"I didn't ask her to go, are you out of your mind? If she told you that, it's because she can't stand me. She's the last woman on earth I would ever have thought of, even if they'd had you in front of a firing squad."

"So if you didn't ask her, why should she say you did?"

"I don't know. Women say all sorts of things."

"Oh, wonderful, so now we're misogynists, are we? Lovely way of looking at things."

"I never claimed to share your way of looking at things, neither yours nor hers… I've got my own way of looking at things and I say what I think. But even if I had asked her…"

"She would have thought it was my idea, don't you understand? She knows we're friends, she knows you know what there is between us—you don't have to be a genius to work it out. If I hadn't told you to suggest it to her, you would never have dared…"

"She can't have a very high opinion of you, in that case," I said, still keeping my cool. "Sit down. Get a grip on yourself."

He sat down again, trembling, and stared at the toes of his shoes.

"The woman I did suggest it to, only she refused, was Vanda, Vicky, Mrs Paltoglou. She almost scratched my eyes out. I'd hardly be likely to make such a suggestion to your lady lawyer, seeing as how she can't even say 'Good morning' to me without slapping my face."

"So you've said before. I don't believe you."

"It's your right not to believe me. And it's your right to have whatever opinion of me you have."

"She was right in the end when she told me it would

be better not to get mixed up with you, you're twisted, you're not a person one can trust with secrets."

I shrugged. "I took an unknown woman who was looking for that sort of adventure to your maestro. I haven't the slightest doubt that she'll even manage to get some money out of him. Her name is Ismene. If you want, why don't you pronounce that name tomorrow and see how he reacts? But in any case, I assure you, he's not going to bother you, not even to hand you over to the Kommandatur as a communist. That business is over and done with."

"We don't have any more rehearsals. Today's the dress rehearsal. The opening night's on Saturday with a repeat performance on Sunday, then he's leaving, he's going back to Berlin, he says."

I suddenly felt weary and depressed about the whole business, though I didn't know why exactly. It was a job I'd been paid for, a job I'd completed. Whatever happened subsequently was in the hands of the good Lord.

"I don't know," I said again, though I hadn't said it out loud the first time.

He was talking. Perhaps he was beginning to regret what he'd said. However, in the midst of all the weariness I felt, I decided not to let him off lightly.

"All right, I'll tell you the truth," I told him. "I did ask her."

"You asked her what?"

"I asked her to go to the Grande Bretagne herself."

He turned his face away like someone trying to conceal an expression of revulsion.

"And what did she do?"

"She gave me a rougher side of her tongue than ever before. She swore at me. She slapped me again. She lashed out like a lioness in defense of her honor and dignity."

"I like your irony," he said. "I can imagine how she would have reacted."

"That's the difference between us, Beratis," I told him. "I found her reaction…"

I stopped, groping for the right word. In truth, how had I found her reaction?

"I'm all ears," said my musician. "How *did* you find her reaction?"

"To tell you the truth, I felt sorry for you, pal. And I was sorry twice over, because she was incapable of realizing that if she *had* agreed, I wouldn't have let her go. And I wouldn't have. Of that you can be sure."

He waited to hear more—now his expression was agonized rather than sarcastic.

"No?" he said.

"No. And not for your sake… For my own sake I wouldn't have let her go."

He lay back in the armchair and remained motionless, lost in his thoughts.

"Is that why you suggested it to her then?" he asked in the darkness that was enveloping us now that the sun had sunk behind the roof of the Conservatoire.

At last he'd understood. And at last I myself was beginning to understand.

38

A first and a last act

People say that cripples have a different mentality, that for them everything is filtered through their handicap, and that their handicap itself is the measure by which they judge things and people. Everything indicated either that in the end I hadn't managed to move Marika Kanellis or that my attempt to win her sympathy had been doomed from the start. But assuredly the fact that I limped wasn't to blame. I'd realized it now and it didn't bother me: she belonged in a different world from me. Konstantina would have had the same chances, let's say, if she'd happened to fall in love with Pavlos Kanellis.

I didn't have any right to complain. I'd been paid to do something and I'd done it. At least I supposed I'd done it. For I never understood whether the job I'd taken on concerned solely the safety of Beratis. Well, at any rate I'd been paid. So the job must have been done. This is the way it often happens in my trade: you carry things to a certain point and then they say thank you, how much do we owe you, and that's that. You never find out what happened with the photographs you took, with the lady you followed, with the documents you managed to get your hands on and passed over to your client.

My friendship with Miltos, too... It was what in our country we call "collateral damage"—something that can't be avoided. The eggs that have to be broken to make an omelet. Our relationship had come full circle. How could it have been otherwise?

On Saturday evening I got my good suit out of the wardrobe. Konstantina admired me in it and sung my praises, she said it suited me and I looked very handsome in it, just like an angel. If she wanted, I suggested, she too could go out that evening: tonight the curfew had been lifted in the center of town. Maybe she might manage to go to the cinema and see a movie.

"You go out, I'll stay here. I'll be here waiting for you when you come home."

Her calm expression did me good. I left the house and set off for the Olympia theater.

Apart from the military cars that were parked on Academias Street, both outside the theater and on the other side of the road, the sidewalk and the theater forecourt were empty—even though it was almost time for the performance to begin. I showed my invitation at the door (Bodo F. had sent it to my home address by courier) and limped up the stairs to the dress circle to find my seat. The first gong was already sounding, there was a bustling hum as the audience filled the stalls, the lights were dimming.

In the central box sat the new Prime Minister, Mr Rallis, with the usual faces around him—or at any rate, if they weren't the same old people they resembled them. In boxes to the side sat the military administrators, the ambassadors of the Axis countries, some Bulgarian official visitor with raven-black hair and medals on the front of his tail-coat, the Council of Ministers *en masse*, the heads of the public utility corporations, the director of the Opera, never still and sparkling with pride. There were also the people who always go to the Opera: various old ladies with fans, diverse gentlemen of indeterminate gender accompanied by ladies of equally indeterminate gender, all of them resembling vampires who'd emerged from their sarcophagi and would return to them at the end of the performance, to sleep again before the sun rose.

The theater wasn't full, quite a few seats were unoccupied. It could have been the price of the tickets that was to blame. Or it could have been the opera, which wasn't Italian or French or one of the usual operettas. In the front of the stalls I spotted the curly red hair of Vanda-Vicky, with Paltoglou at her side. I thought I could make out Beratis' parting among the musicians in the pit. Then they all sat down and disappeared from sight.

Three final strokes of the gong and the conductor made his appearance. Tall and haughty in his perfectly pressed, glossy tails, with his halo of hair around the bald spot and a row of medals on his breast, he stood, cast an aquiline glance over the audience, bowed stiffly, then turned to his orchestra. I could get up and go, I reflected. It was strangely cold in here. But I preferred to stay until the point I remembered from New York—when the dwarf who steals the fairies' golden ball pronounces a curse on love. That tune the orchestra plays. After that I'd go home.

And then the curtain was rising and there they were, the three ladies, waving their arms in the air and beginning to swim through the cardboard waves and various rocks made out of painted brown paper coated with glue to stiffen them.

I became aware of someone next to me and immediately a familiar voice whispered, "The day after tomorrow in the evening I'm leaving for Berlin with him!"

Out of the corner of my eye I recognized Ismene Agathos. I nodded and smiled: I'd known perfectly well that she'd snaffle the German.

"Congratulations," I said out of the side of my mouth. "But how about your mother and the house with a hectare of land in Maroussi? And the money lender?"

"It'll all be sorted out now I've got the money," she laughed, her snaggle tooth protruding beside her canine tooth. "I'll never be able to thank you enough. You saved me!"

As the music got louder and the fairies sang their fairy songs about fairy business one after the other, we could speak less softly.

"You should thank yourself, I wasn't intending to take you along to Faliron, you insisted on coming."

"It isn't just that."

"Ah. What else is it?"

She motioned me to be quiet. I turned to look at the stage. The dwarf had emerged from behind the rocks. I don't know where they'd unearthed the singer in New York, but he was short and hunchbacked with a twisted leg—perfect for the part; here, my compatriots had a dwarf who was a strapping hulk of a lad, made up with charcoal eyebrows and lines like wrinkles around his mouth, who kept hopping around bent double as if he had lumbago. The fairies giggled at him just as if they were making fun of his poor acting and not at his attempts to grope them.

"You're a decent kid," and she put her hand on my knee. "The war has turned all of us into animals… When it's over, we'll have to forget what we became during it…"

"It hasn't made everyone into an animal," I said.

"It hasn't made you into one. I was speaking of myself. And others. When it's all over… I'll try to repay my debt to you."

I turned and looked at her. She was speaking seriously. But I had no idea what she meant. What debt?

"What debt?"

"One that I know of and that you'll learn of. Now hush."

It was the moment—as if she'd known—when the dwarf (God help him) was getting ready to pronounce his curse. He'd mounted to the highest point of the rock. The fairies were squealing around him, pretending to be afraid, and he was standing firmly with one foot on an invisible plank behind him and the other foot in a careful hollow in the brown-paper rock. Bodo was waving his arms and shaking his head like a clockwork doll, the back of his neck was bright red; the musicians were bending over their instruments as if they were all seething together in the cauldron of hell and struggling powerlessly to unloose the fury which his movements seemed to be demanding.

"Look at him, Jesus Christ, just like a jack-in-the-box," said Ismene beside me, affecting despair. "If only he were half as active in bed…"

And then the king of the underworld stood up to his full height like a fearful scarecrow and some woodwind instruments began playing that tune I like. I heard him bellow out his curse on love, renouncing it forever, may it be accursed, his purpose in life would henceforth be the power given him by the gold which he shook as he laughed and mocked the fairies for their predicament.

He took a sudden step backwards, the plank gave way under his weight, with a cry of genuine agony he plunged down and a loud thud was heard as he landed ten feet below on the boards of the stage. The audience roared with laughter as if a brittle veneer of respect (for the work and for the famous German conductor), which they couldn't genuinely feel, had cracked. This unexpected mishap was more entertaining than anything else they'd seen or heard so far. Bodo turned to face the stalls in fury, and the voices and laughter died down; however, as the orchestra now had to play a tricky bit by themselves, he was obliged to turn his attention back to the musicians. And the audience, like schoolchildren when the teacher isn't looking, began to laugh again. Quite a bit of clapping was heard too.

When I turned to see what Ismene thought of this unexpected ridicule, my black-haired Visitor was no longer in her seat.

As I hurried out of the Olympia theater, my sole thought was to go home and find Konstantina there.

When I opened my eyes the following morning, my gaze instantly focused on the pipes of the radiator which, ice-cold for months now, seemed to support the bedroom ceiling in some magic way, slender though they were and situated in the most unsuitable place for such a task, in the corner of the room. In the past, when the heating used to function on cold days, the two pipes would gurgle and groan and as I fell asleep I liked to think that at the point where they disappeared into the ceiling lived two tiny magicians, one good and the other evil, called Gombe and Lolé. That's what I named them, in the way children give names of their own to things they don't understand—arbitrary names, which nevertheless have meaning and significance to them. For months now, for two whole years in fact, Gombe and Lolé had ceased to make their groans and gurglings and gazed down in melancholy on the cripple who slept each night on the bed below them.

My gaze swam slowly up to the ceiling and I could see my own body lying there below, the bedclothes making a high mountain over my knees and two smaller hillocks over my toes—for I held my feet pointing vertically upwards and occasionally moved them from side to side. My head was still deep in the pillow, my eyes half-closed and my mind wandering in a state somewhere between sleep and waking. This is me, thought the brain that accompanied my gaze floating somewhere near the ceiling. That thing down there. Me. Who else? But it was another unknown me, to whom nothing was as familiar as this bedroom, as the inorganic, sporadic sounds of furniture creaking, while the bright sunlight shone in the backyard where the meager ailanthus tree grew, and a vague hum reached me from far off like the forgotten sound of a living city.

I realized that I was still dreaming, but now I was awake and must get up and open the window. I'd smoked one of the last cigarettes in my packet the night before and the room stank.

As I opened the glass panes I remembered that it was Sunday. Street sounds are always different on Sundays, you're aware of this even when the city remains deathly and frozen on weekdays too. It was almost spring, the tree in the yard had buds from which the new leaves would unfurl, which in summer would cast their shade on my balcony.

Then I heard a strange noise, a distant rumble. Perhaps clouds were gathering in the west, maybe it was raining somewhere and would have started raining in the center of Athens too by the time I'd got up and got ready to go out. If I did go out, that is. For I didn't have any cause to do so, especially not if the weather was about to break. If it had been sunny, I could have taken Konstantina for a walk to Zappion and the National Garden or the Pedion tou Areos park.

While I was shaving with water heated on the stove, the phone rang. It was Mimis.

"Hephaistos," he said, "the earth is shaking out there, can't you hear it?"

"I can hear something but I don't know what it is."

"Get dressed and come out," he told me. "I'll meet you on Academias Street. Everyone's come out into the streets. Palamas has died and everyone's on their way to the cemetery."

That was the name of the poet with the garden at the bottom of Asklipiou Street. I went out onto the dining-room balcony. Gennadiou Street was deserted but there were people on Academias Street. The hum was getting stronger and sounded like the noise of a crowd.

But why did everyone have to come out into the streets? What did it matter that a poet had died? All these people, starving and bloodied, all this flock of terrified animals who lay low at night and emerged in the morning to search for something to eat, this swarm of insects who blew spasmodically hither and thither, these strange creatures with their odd appearance, their torn clothes, their string and cardboard and bags and tin cans, why should they care about the forgotten old man with the dry well in his garden? Mimis had his mind on the Moltsas family day in, day out, on the favor of Papathanassis, on Greek myths and painful longing for Stellitsa. So suddenly he'd heard that some poet had died last night and now he wanted to go running off to the cemetery? Why? Why had Marika called him Master and told him that if she had a boy she'd call him Kostis, which was the old man's name? When I wasn't present in her life, Marika Kanellis and her husband spent most of the time talking about Palamas and other poets with their friends, and quarreled with anyone whose opinion differed from theirs, and all this was part of a world utterly different from mine—for in mine trailing people and getting paid and brutish instincts and lowly revenge were what figured most prominently… Ah, what a world I lived in, and what a world she!

Agathos had charged me with protecting an unknown musician—but he didn't appear to give a damn about Vanda or Stellitsa's daughter, about cousin Moltsas or Thanassis the pharmacist's assistant or me. He never would have employed me to save someone from our side of the tracks. Was it that these other people belonged to a race apart? Were they the salt of the earth? A higher caste with a different life and other values and needs? Even if on the street they looked just the same as me and you, as Zisis the coffee-shop owner, as the Varvitsiotis family or the Balomenoses and the Yannakopouloses and the

Papathanassises of this world? For me, as for anyone else born in America, a poet was nothing more than someone who wrote poems—using language that an ordinary person would find a bit difficult to understand. Here, it seemed that a poet was something else, more closely related to everyday life.

When would I, in whose ears the only poetry that reverberated was that cursing of love, when would I ever get the chance to hear Kanellis reciting Palamas in their front room:

> *And you will hear the redeemer's voice,*
> *you will strip off the garb of sin,*
> *and once more ordered and light*
> *you will move like the grass, like the bird,*
> *like a woman's breast, like the waves,*
> *and no longer having any lower step*
> *on which to fall further*
> *down the stairs of Evil,*
> *for the rising that calls you once more*
> *you will feel growing on you, O joy!*
> *the wings,*
> *your great wings of yore!*

Should I get up and leave as soon as the war was over or should I stay and learn this special language, just as I had come to know the people who spoke it? Nothing could be more difficult, for no one would have the kindness to teach me. I'd have to attempt it on my own. And because I'd have to attempt it on my own I wouldn't need Papachrysanthou's company. It was late, the day was cold, I was hungry: Mimis would have to hurry if he was going to be in time for the funeral service in the church, the only solution was for me to summon up all the powers still left to me and to take off from the roof on Gennadiou Street, flying high enough not to attract attention. I'd go faster and be a lot less tired than if Mimis had to drag me there limping.

I rose up with difficulty to the point where I could still make out streets and directions, flapping my arms and legs hard as I swam through the moist air. The crowd was becoming denser, looking like ants when the farmer's plowshare has sliced into their nest. I'd never before seen so many people gathered together. From one moment to the next, the city had ceased to look like the empty and deserted Athens I knew and instead resembled the busy, bustling version of itself that I'd seen when I first arrived a few years earlier. It was as if the Occupation had ended or had never existed. I'd no idea the place had so many inhabitants. People were coming from the center and from the outlying neighborhoods, the streets were sinking beneath the weight of so many feet, the police and the foreign patrols stood grimly aside, watching the crowds pass as they all made their way in the same direction. Narrow tributaries and streams debouched into the main arteries of the city, squares were seething with ant-like figures, legs walked rapidly, faces resembled those of relics—nothing but eyes!

From where I was, high up in the sky, I could neither weep with them over the body in its simple coffin nor could I draw warmth from the sudden sense of brotherhood that had enveloped the crowd, who for so long now had been hiding in fear, avoiding standing next to strangers or talking to their neighbors or sharing their griefs and hopes. I wouldn't remain up here any more. I wanted to be down there among them, to hear what they were saying and be warmed by their breath—so many people! I was flying above them, suspended high in the moist, cold atmosphere of a February afternoon, alone and alien, unknown, remote and different. Far below me on the ground I began to make out familiar figures for the first time: the Kanellis couple, Mimis, the Derventzis couple and Mr Bukovic, Rodolfos Something-or-other, Beratis. And there were the Sinisioglous… People whom I knew well by sight or by the sound of their voices.

I began to make gentle movements and to descend, to descend, then further—I still had all my powers intact, I could steer in whatever direction I wanted. And thus, without anyone noticing me, I landed and was swallowed up by the crowd.

No one noticed me, no one turned to look at me as I stood there among them. I smelled the smell of the people near me, details suddenly became clear and stifled me, soiled collars, uncut hair, dirty handkerchiefs in people's hands and at their eyes, voices lost in sobs. And from my own clothes a similar smell arose, my own smell, that of my body which had come to life again, my pores which had opened, my skin which had been warmed. And it was warm there, it was the first time I'd felt such warmth in the cold north wind that swept through the cemetery. I pressed against strangers and let them press against me. I heard words with which I was familiar, which I'd heard before, which I'd learned—words no longer belonging to an unknown, strange language that I didn't know, which I stored in my mind so that I could ask someone later what they meant. And these everyday words coming from all around me were like the first words that you speak as a child, round and shining, brand new words, unworn and unused words which have a weight and power and music of their own.

Palamas' funeral. The national anthem suddenly swelling forth like thunder in a storm, causing the birds to fly from the branches where they were nesting as if disturbed by the shots of hunters. I didn't know the words of the national anthem. Among all the sea of people who knew them, I alone fitted those other words to the music as I sang, those words which Pavlos Kanellis had quoted at their party:

> *And you, immortal, divine,*
> *who can achieve whatever you desire,*
> *you, Freedom, on the plain*
> *walk drenched in blood.*

It wasn't only grief for an innocent old man who had died. It was also our desire to anger the Germans as they waited to one side with their wreaths, and the polished officer standing to attention before the coffin beneath the icy silence of the mass, who took care to disappear as soon as possible and was swallowed up in the crowd which showed no fear of him and no respect.

We had set ourselves to demonstrate to Bodo F. and the singers who'd come from Berlin that we didn't give a shit for the *Rheingold*, and that its second performance tonight would not take place, because we couldn't care less for the brotherhood of peoples through art and we weren't the slightest bit interested if the woodwind instruments in our orchestra didn't have such a clear and sparkling tone as theirs.

In all the brilliance of yesterday's evening at the Opera there had been a smell of death. Here in the First Cemetery, where I now stood without my invisible wings, everything had a different redolence to it and the air was fragrant with the springtime that was about to arrive. It was different. Even I could feel it.

I turned and saw them standing near me. Marika, with Pavlos at her side, holding hands tightly and both weeping, and Beratis a little further off among his colleagues from the Opera, his small mouth tight-lipped, pale and shivering, and near him Mr Kornelios Something—yes, he was here too—in the role of the great tragic actor, standing among actors and painters, among poets whose existence I hadn't yet heard of. And in the midst of all these people, warmly protected inside her round belly which would soon start to swell, the child whom the old man had foretold would one day succeed him. Another part of my mission that remained in darkness.

39

———

Final flight

In turbulent times, crippled or lonely people, various madmen who collect shells or stamps, others who spend their lives at the racecourse or in the stands at the stadium, amateur painters who struggle an entire lifetime to succeed in having one of their paintings hung at some exhibition of work by accountants at the Parnassos Hall, or those who traipse from office to office trying to sell the handy potato-peeler they've invented don't make much impression: nobody notices them. However, when a few decades have passed without hunger and executions, without war and bombings, without armies of one-armed or blind men begging at street corners or selling little icons or playing the accordion, then an unmarried former policeman, lame and unsociable, who tells stories that are hard to believe when he's had a few drinks, is someone to be pointed at and about whom comments fly as soon as his back is turned.

What is good, in any case, is to have a clear conscience. To have found your treasure shining in the sun when you returned to your barren field and to have said "Praise the Lord who made it all come out well in the end."

I have had a quiet conscience of this kind as the years rolled by and I have memories to recount to anyone who isn't bored stiff listening to them. What's more, I also had my moment of glory when, during the ceremonial cutting of the New Year cake in a restaurant in the western suburbs, my colleagues awarded me a medal and a commemorative plaque framed and mounted on artificial velvet.

I managed to get a pension too, and indeed a double one: both as the oldest member of a profession that has gradually developed in this country and as a war veteran—as a result of various machinations which I can't be bothered to go into here, it was recognized that I'd been injured and lamed in the Resistance. I'm doing fine.

A year ago, encouraged by the favorable impressions of another pensioner whom I met in my local café, I decided to spend a few days in a small hotel in a village in the eastern part of the island of Paros. The journey seemed interminable because the sea was rough and the captain gave orders to proceed at half-speed in order to avoid too much pitching and rolling. Finally we arrived and disembarked. It was late in the season and holidaymakers who had jobs or children at school had already left. The only visitors remaining on the island were foreigners and Greeks with a private income, to whom the September sun seemed gentler on skins that had become more sensitive or wearied by age.

The bad thing was that the bus for the village had already gone and the next one wasn't till the afternoon. I arrived at the hotel just as the sun was sinking behind the mountains as you looked in the direction of the port. Nikolas, the owner's son who looked after everything, welcomed me and asked whether this was my first visit to the island. When I said it was, he gave me a mass of useful information. The water here was brackish, he said, I shouldn't drink it. The sea was shallow and warm at this time of year, I could choose between the big sandy beach to the north or the small cove right in front of the hotel. You can swim alone there without anyone bothering you. They boy's kindness impressed me, because in other places this sort of service is charged for separately.

I enjoyed myself and soon decided to prolong my vacation for as much as another ten days. The sea was wonderful and the visitors few. There were some foreign girls who lit fires on the beach at night with their friends and played guitars and sang. In the morning peasants would come down to the beach with their donkeys, selling fruit. At midday I'd eat in a little shack by the sea, or at the hotel where Nikolas' mother cooked delicious vegetables in oil and where there was always bread of a kind whose like it is impossible to find in Athens.

In the afternoons I went for walks. Outside the village there were shady streambeds full of aromatic plants and reeds and wild figs. Hedges of reeds separated these places from the vegetable gardens, where you could harvest grapes and tomatoes without anyone stopping you, which you then washed and salted in the sea.

At night I slept soundly since from afternoon onwards the air was cooler and from the cypresses and bushes the trilling of the crickets came like a sea of calm sound. I hadn't felt so well in years. The swimming and the sun were good for my leg; I was barely limping and pain was a thing of the past.

One day a local woman came into the hotel restaurant at lunchtime. She greeted everyone in a bell-like voice, received the formal responses that are customary in these parts, and started chatting with Margarita, Nikolas' mother, who with her eldest daughter was peeling potatoes for the evening. Their conversation was lively, the woman had known the family for a long time, she may even have been related to them, she adored Nikolas and treated him as tenderly as if he'd been her own son, and he in turn kept calling her by the familiar names of Mrs Dina and Dina. Then, when he'd finished his work, the young man sat at one of the empty tables and began cutting the rind off a slice of bright red watermelon. He invited her to come and taste it, whereupon she came and sat at the other side of the table, almost next to me.

"I'm envious, Nikos," I told him. "Give me a slice of watermelon too, it's tantalizing to see it."

The young man laughed and called, "Mother, a slice of watermelon for Mr Angel!"

At this the woman turned and looked at me. She smiled

with a trace of embarrassment and moved her chair back a bit, as one does when one doesn't want to sit with one's back to someone. Nikolas put the watermelon down in front of me. But although the slice was larger than his it wasn't such a good color, being more pink, whereas his was as red as blood.

"What's all this, Nikolas?" I laughed. "It's no joke, mine's not nearly such a wonderful color as yours."

The woman turned and offered me a large piece on a fork. "Here," she said, "the fork is clean, it hasn't been used. Eat it, Mr Angel."

I took the fork, but before I bit into the juicy morsel I looked at her, ready to thank her, there wasn't any need, I was only joking, my own slice was fine. Her voice speaking my name helped me to recognize her, just as her changed appearance—that of a woman aged about sixty who's given birth to children and worked in the fields and chopped wood and milked goats—didn't help.

"Konstantina!"

"Dina," she corrected. "Are you well? Are you strong and fit?"

Her tone was a little bit that of someone asking how come I was still alive.

"Ah, you know each other," said Nikolas, putting a new slice of watermelon on the table, as bright red as his.

"We knew each other in Athens, in the Occupation, the old days," said Dina and leaned towards me. "So the winds brought you here!"

"They made me throw up all my insides before they

brought me. But yes, they brought me and here I am. Fit and strong."

"And as handsome as an angel, that hasn't changed," she said, so boldly that I was confused.

For a moment her eyes shone with their old spark, just like when she used to look at me from the little balcony outside her kitchen. I fell silent as a whirlwind of images swept over me: things that she knew I remembered and couldn't express. She waited for my emotion to subside and then began talking again, now in the guise of Mrs Dina.

How had I happened to come here? How long would I be staying? Did I like the island, everyone liked it. People who come here always weep when they leave, they don't want the dream to end. Had I seen how beautiful the place was? Had I ever seen anywhere else so beautiful?

"I've been here a fortnight already and I can't make up my mind to leave."

"You must come back," she said. "Next year. We're here. The island is always here."

She'd said the same words when she embarked at Piraeus on a caique that was sailing for Naxos. My island is there, waiting for me. There wasn't anything else we could do. The times were going from bad to worse. My money had taken wing and flown. I discovered this the next time I lifted the floorboard in my office on Gamvetta Street. This must have been what the Visitor had meant when she told me that she'd be eternally grateful to me. When and how had she managed it? Did she know that I hid my money there? Had she seen me? Or did she have first-hand information—though I couldn't be sure from where. My survival was now problematic, and even more so with another mouth to feed. Konstantina had lost her job with the Kanellis couple: the earth appeared to have opened and swallowed them. We looked at things from this angle, we looked at things from that angle, and we both reached the same conclusion: she'd have to return to Paros. She didn't want to go as a servant to any other household and it was the only work she knew. If I didn't want her and couldn't keep her, then she'd have to go back to the island. But her island was always there waiting for her. The poor girl cried as she waved her handkerchief at me from the stern of the caique, and I cried too as soon as the distance between us was too great for her to see me crying.

She remembered everything. When we met again the following afternoon, when she came once again to Margarita's hotel to find me, who'd gone there for the same purpose, she suggested I should come to her house and she'd give me coffee and preserved fruit. She was a widow, her two sons were living in Athens where they had businesses of their own—it's a matter of great pride on the island to say you have your own business. She gave me directions as to how to find her house. On coming out of the hotel, which was situated on the village's main square—actually just a broadening of the road—I took the uphill path to the left towards the mountain. The houses ended about a hundred yards further up and immediately above, where the slope leveled out a bit, behind a drystone wall, you could see the roof of her house.

"I've got the best view," she said as she welcomed me. Within the open neck of her blouse I noticed the chain with the little baptismal cross that I remembered.

I turned and looked out at the unforgettable view, the sea stirred by a light northerly wind, and all around the neighboring islands which the clear autumn atmosphere made appear nearer and smaller than you could have imagined possible in the height of summer or in the early morning when the sunlight blinded you. The colors were those that painters envy and despise and that photographers can never manage to reproduce. Colors which you can only see, for language has no words with which to describe them.

Konstantina and I didn't talk much (in the privacy of her house, up on the mountainside, she allowed me to call her by this name) and I realized that she was asking more than she was telling, as if she wanted to verify that this really was the first time I'd been to Paros. When she was sure, she relaxed. Village people seem strange to our eyes, it's hard to know what they are thinking, they imagine things that wouldn't occur to us.

Then, when I got up to leave and she had to go to bring in her goats, she said, "Tomorrow, if you like, I'll take you and show you something."

I was too frightened by her curious silences to dare ask what it was she wanted me to see. I went to bed early and on the following morning I walked to the corner of the road by the hotel and looked straight up the hill to see the roof of her house. The house was there, although nothing but the roof could be seen for the slope hid the rest. At noon I ate again at Margarita's but Konstantina did not turn up. I felt disappointed and went down to the beach, something I rarely did in the afternoon. Then in the evening, as I was having a drink with Nikolas, who'd taken a liking to me, and with various other old men spending the summer here, who irritated me by speaking to me as if I was their contemporary (although I was, and might even have been older than them), Konstantina suddenly came into sight at the back of the kitchen, talking to the cook. I got up and went over to her.

"I waited for you."

"Now's the best time," she told me.

And she motioned me to follow her. I told Nikolas to make a note of what I'd had to eat and he gestured that I needn't worry about it.

We took the dirt road off the main road and continued for sixty to eighty yards. The houses were becoming fewer and all you could see in the half-light were fences, cypress trees and a few gardens surrounding old stone houses whose stucco was crumbling. After eighty yards we turned left and began to walk downhill in the direction of the shore. She slowed down and signaled me to be quieter. The path was dark and uneven, full of stones that projected from the earth as well as low bushes in the middle and at the sides, real ambushes. If you didn't have a flashlight after sundown you needed to know the path well—otherwise you'd be in for some unpleasant surprises. I realized at any rate that she was more concerned about our feet making a noise on the stones than about the potholes and pitfalls. At one point she put out her hand characteristically and went on ahead. The darkness of the path concealed us, but our footsteps would be heard.

At the end of a small verandah, built with island-style arches, smothered in geraniums and climbing plants and jasmine, a woman sat under the light darning socks or embroidering, it was hard to see which from a distance. Konstantina stopped me with her hand and motioned me to look.

"She comes early every summer and leaves late in the autumn. She's on her own now, a withered old lady. I work for her. I do the washing and the cooking. Sometimes I bring her the odd egg," said Konstantina.

I shook my head like a man who knows that people must have a reason for telling him the things they tell, yet I didn't understand why she'd brought me here to show me this old woman. If she supplemented her meager means by working for holidaymakers in the summer, this was more or less what all the local women did, those of them who didn't rent rooms, that is. I didn't understand, or else I was prevented from understanding by the terror that grips you when you reach my age and someone holds up a mirror that overturns all the delusions you harbor about eternal youth.

I was standing before a house which had known better days, with its plants, its flowers, its pots and its ornamented verandah, except that now the shadow of night prevented all the marks of time and resignation from showing.

Konstantina's silence made me look again more carefully. I had seen this scene somewhere before. Somewhere I'd seen those fingers that had now laid their work aside and were absent-mindedly caressing the woman's tired skin in an automatic attempt to smooth it, to give it youth once more; I'd seen them pushing the needle through with the thimble; this woman I had seen before, her mind far away, a smile coming and going on her face, her thoughts leaping into the future then but now turning back to the past—to something which seemed to be linked to her existence but which no longer concerned her directly. Something had happened… something had existed… something had occurred.

I began to shiver as if feverish. I grabbed hold of Konstantina's arm and gripped it hard. She turned in the darkness, beneath the stars which here beyond the village shone so bright and seemed as near as the islands opposite. She smiled. And, treading carefully so as not to make any noise, she drew me away and we took the road back, I to the hotel and she to her house.

I had seen Marika Kanellis the day after the performance. I'd distinguished her among the emotional crowd at the poet's funeral, beside Pavlos who probably thought he was safe in the middle of the throng. And I saw her again on Liberation Day, in Syntagma Square, in the midst of the victory cheers and enthusiasm, in the midst of embraces and declamations, of the flags and palm leaves and flowers that rained down on all sides.

Marika Kanellis and her husband returned to the flat on Gennadiou Street a little while after the Germans left. With them they brought a baby, a boy. When the child turned one year old they moved house and left. After that I lost sight of them. But I'm quite sure the child was Kanellis' and not Miltos'. Whether Marika knew or not doesn't matter. She probably did know, though, as soon as she'd given birth to him and saw him for the first time. The spitting image of his dad, as people say!

I saw her again for the last time at Beratis' funeral, ten years later, when the musician died in the prime of his life and at the peak of "his creative work," as someone who read the funeral oration over his coffin said. She was standing there, pale and dry-eyed, with Pavlos Kanellis, who'd also come, crying inconsolably beside her.

And then…, then I don't know, I used to think I saw her every so often but I could never be sure. I often thought it was her but then it turned out to be merely someone who resembled her. After a certain point I realized that all the women I mistook for her were the age that she had been when I first met her; maybe in fact I did run into her without recognizing her. That's how dreams remain—they never grow old. In all of them we are young—always young.

After a while I ceased to see women who looked like her. I ceased to hear voices that sounded like hers. You would have thought that the sort of people who lived in those days had vanished, along with the women's names that have changed, the skirts that have got narrower or fuller, shorter or longer according to the fashion. And the fashion for the name Marika was apparently over.

After so many years, after so many new generations succeeding their fathers and mothers, so long after the Occupation went to join Asia Minor, and both of them the Balkan Wars, and all of them the Turkish dominion and Byzantium, consigned to the realms of history—after all this time nobody now calls their daughters Marika. Is it not a pity? After so many years when I too had been dead without knowing it, did this middle-aged peasant woman from Paros have to show me an old lady who comes here in the summer and lives alone and solitary in that little house?

And Pavlos? "Ah...," Konstantina made a gesture with her hand, "they divorced a few years after the war. "Mr Pavlos died in 1960, I think, of a heart attack. He'd had problems with his health... ever since the Partisan War" (Konstantina was not a political animal: this was what people on her island called the Civil War, this was what she too called it). And their son, what became of him? Konstantina laughed. "He's fine, he grew up. The old lady adores him and is always telling me stories about him. How grand and successful he is. But when she thinks I'm not looking she cries and cries, as if she'd lost him forever… I don't know, she never says anything against him…" The usual story. There comes a point when all children cross the river and leave the old folk on the other bank, sure that at any time they want they'll be able to come back and find them still there.

Is there a mother who has given birth to a son and not wept because of him?

There's one thing I didn't discover about this child: whether the old poet's prophecy came true, the one he made in the garden that day we landed there. But that's because I've never looked into it.

I left the island with a heaviness in my soul. I think this state continued for a long time, months maybe, until I decided to get to grips with something and to stop dragging myself through life without occupation. So I began to plan a book of reminiscences. At first I thought about writing of my life and adventures in New York. Then later I decided not to write about all that. I'd start straight off from when I arrived in Greece.

On the boat returning from Paros, however, these were nothing more than vague intentions and scattered thoughts, nothing specific. I felt a weight within me and a discomfort caused by this weight which somehow had to be cast out of me. Since I thought that I must be suffering from a bout of angina and needed fresh air, I stood on the deck and watched the island of Paros recede over the horizon.

"Holidays over then?" asked the white-haired gentleman beside me, who also seemed to be returning to Athens from the island, or maybe from Naxos.

"Long since," I joked without turning round.

The wind was strong but warm and pleasant. It drowned voices, so that you had to shout like the sailors in order to be heard.

"You're lucky, my friend."

Very often as I wander through the streets of Athens I happen to notice the faces of people of an age that is called mature, frequently old people, and I feel I've seen them before, exactly the same faces, ten, twenty, thirty or forty years ago. It's as if all the people who were old during the Occupation have continued to live on, unchanged and identical, through the decades that followed. Of course, it's probably their children or grandchildren. It is only I, safe and secure in the sense that I don't change, don't grow old, am not altered—and hence don't make the same impression on anyone chancing to notice me on the street—it is only I who pass through the streets of this city like youth eternal, like an eye unencumbered by corruptible flesh. Yet this old gentleman here, with his protruding stomach, his teeth so regular that they appeared to be false and his deep blue eyes that looked at me with a twinkle, surely I couldn't have been mistaken—I knew him, and indeed well. But if he were still alive he'd have to be over a hundred. Moreover, I now looked a lot older than him, for he'd stayed just as he was when I first met him, unchanged. I saw all this in his eyes as he examined me with some curiosity and perhaps a small dose of sympathy.

"Your holidays are over, mine have not yet begun," he said gravely. "And if you think that you have suffered misfortunes in your life, consider what others might say who have never known what you have known."

"Look here, sir…," I began but he stopped me with a gesture of his hand.

"I know what you're going to say. Nevertheless I insist that I paid your full fee in gold. I can't be bothered to go into details here and tell you, Mr Sotiris my boy, what you would have suffered during the Civil War, at the hands of cut-throats like Papathanassis on the instigation of Mrs Stathis, the lady-colonel, if I hadn't removed your little treasure from its hiding-place in your office. You must be content with my assurance. Good heavens, have I still not gained your trust after all these years?"

I said nothing. I turned and looked once more at the shadows of the mountains fading into all the hues of the west over a sea whose deep blue was the color of his eyes. Whether this diabolical old man was a hallucination or really was standing there beside me, what did it matter? Whether I'd heard him say these words or whether I'd simply thought them myself, didn't it amount to the same thing?

After a silence he said, "I don't know whether you've managed to improve your relations with music at all. If you have, then a record has recently been issued by Deutsche Gramophon which contains amazing recordings dating from the war with Bodo F. and the Berlin Philharmonic and which has been very well received. It seems that when he returned to Germany his interpretations reached such a peak that even the Allies let him go scot-free for his collaboration with the Nazis. Many people say it was his Greek mistress who raised him from the dead. Quite literally."

About the Author

Alexis Panselinos read Law at the University of Athens and worked as a practicing lawyer. His first book, a collection of stories, appeared in 1982 to great acclaim. In 1985 his novel *The Great Procession* won the State Prize. His novel *Zaida or A Camel in the Snow* was nominated for the 1997 European Literary Award. *The Dark Inscriptions* received the Novel Prize from *Diavazo* literary magazine in 2012. His latest novel *Light Greek Songs* won the 2018 Prize of the Athens Academy. His novels have been widely translated into French, German, Italian, Polish and Romanian. He has received the Great Award for Life Achievement from the eminent literary magazine *O Anagnostis (The Reader)*. He lives in Athens, Greece.

About the Translator

Caroline Harbouri, born in London, is the author, under the name Petrie Harbouri, of three novels: *Graffiti* (Bloomsbury, London 1998), *Our Lady of the Serpents* (Bloomsbury, London 1999), and *The Brothers Carburi* (Bloomsbury, London 2001). She is a translator of gardening books from French and novels from Greek. Since 1995 she has been the editor of *The Mediterranean Garden*, a quarterly journal on plants and gardens in mediterranean-climate regions. She lives in Greece.

A Request

If you enjoyed this book, its publishers and author would be grateful if you would post a short (or long) review on the website where you bought the book and/or on Goodreads.com or other book review sites. Thanks for reading!

Please see the next few pages for other offerings from Recital Publishing.

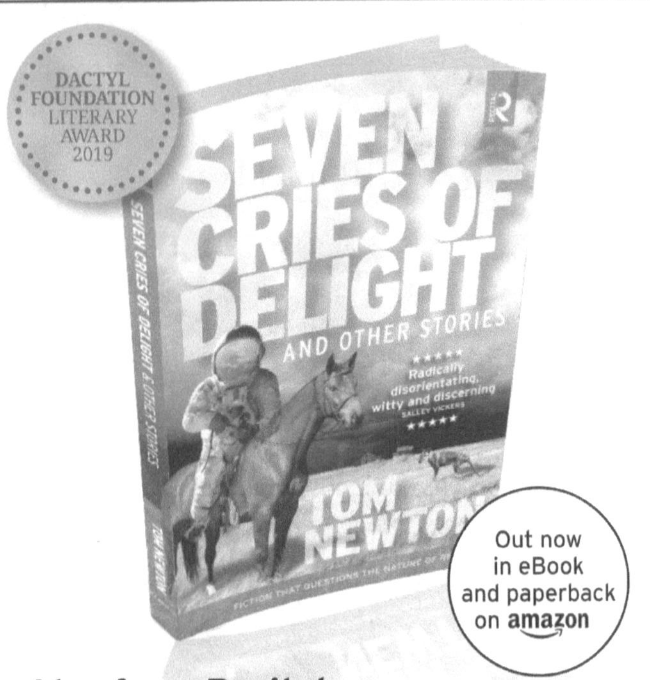
DACTYL
FOUNDATION
LITERARY
AWARD
2019
SEVEN CRIES OF DELIGHT & OTHER STORIES
SEVEN CRIES OF DELIGHT
AND OTHER STORIES
★★★★★
Radically
disorientating,
witty and discerning
SALLEY VICKERS
★★★★★
TOM NEWTON
FICTION THAT QUESTIONS THE NATURE OF
Out now
in eBook
and paperback
on amazon

www.ingramcontent.com/pod-product-compliance
Lightning Source LLC
Chambersburg PA
CBHW031045110726
47900CB00003B/815